GENESIS INTERFACE

R. Kuljian

Libera
P.O. Box 1920
Simi Valley CA 93062

Grateful acknowledgment is extended for permission to reprint from the following:

Harper and Row: From *Sumerian Mythology: A Study of Spiritual and Literary Achievements in The Third Millenium B.C.* by S. N. Kramer and *Toward The Image of Tammuz* by Thorkild Jacobsen.

Alfred A. Knopf, Inc.: From *The Technological Society* by Jacques Ellul, translated by John Wilkinson, © 1964.

King Features Syndicate and Nostalgia Press: From *Flash Gordon* by Alex Raymond. © King Features Syndicate

The author wishes to thank the staff of the UCLA Map Library for their fine cooperation and the use of their excellent resources.

The author is gratefully indebted to Jaques Ellul for the ideas in his *Technological Society*, *The Meaning of the City*, and *Propaganda, The Formation of Man's Attitudes*.

The author takes this opportunity to express his long-standing debt of affection and gratitude to the memory of the late Nina Moise and Edward John Carnell, philosopher and teacher, and to Leonardo Bercovici and Jane Jordan Browne for their help and encouragement.

Library of Congress Catalog Card Number 85-90109
ISBN 0-9614831-0-5

To

Iris

and all the would-be UGLIs

Contents

Part I   Awakening
Part II   Pursuit
Part III   Revelation

From then on, life itself was measured by the machine; its organic functions obeyed the mechanical. Time, which had been the measure of organic sequences, was broken and dissociated. Human life became a disconnected set of activities having no other bond than the fact that they were performed by the same individual. Instead of *living* time, man became split up and parceled out by it. Technique had suppressed the respite of time indispensable to the rhythm of life. Between desire and the gratification of desire there was no longer the duration necessary for real choice and examination, no longer respite for reflecting, choosing, or adapting oneself, or for wishing or pulling oneself together. Life had become a racecourse composed of instantaneous variations of the universe, a succession of objective events dragging man along and leading him astray without anywhere affording him the possibility of standing apart, taking stock, and ceasing to act.

From the prophecy of Jacques Ellul, 1964

Part One

AWAKENING

1

The rising sun was just breaking over the mountains behind Morro Bay on the California coast, losing its bright shafts of golden light in the white dense fog hovering low over the Pacific ocean. The rays gradually transformed the eerie specters which seemed to rise up out of the mists below into one vast expanse of city, stretching its perfection south into the distance, its myriad smooth, translucent shapes glistening like some jewel-encrusted offering set out for the gods high above.

Only there were no gods.

Teil awoke out of a confused and fitful sleep as the monitor tingled him into olfactory arousal. Today it was the simulated smell and sounds of a rainy day that woke him. He stared dazedly at the time track on his wristcom until it finally registered that it was 02.50.95 and counting, which was something after six o'clock in the morning, there being but ten hours in the day. Everything was decimal, and counting, compatible with Mascom, the Master Computer, which ran System—that is, everything. Time was the least of functions reprogrammed to fit the world of 2188.

And Teil felt reprogrammed. Shaking his head, he tried vainly remember what strange dream might have troubled that ever-more-welcome interlude of sleep, but was left only with a vague uncertainty that things were somehow different.

Before he could finish pulling on his shorts, lights started flashing, a warning buzzer sounded, and the feminized com-voice—merely another manifestation of Mascom—filled the room at just the right tone for a first reminder. It emanated from the midst of a dense matrix of flashing lights on the wall next to his bed, the voice-modulated light patterns imbuing it with a numinous quality.

"Professor, you have forgotten your LIFE—again. Take your checkup now please. As you know, it is optional with the masses, but you are now a mascientist, and all scientists with access to Mascom are required to have weekly checkups."

"Roust is more like it," Teil grumbled. "No offense, sweetheart, your beautiful 'life-support' System and all," he added, hissing the s . He carelessly slipped out of his shorts and stretched his tall lean frame back onto the bed. As he did so, hands with numerous finger-like sensors extended and made contact with his head and supple naked body.

"We like to get you while your brain and body rhythms are still quiescent, Professor," the voice intoned, "now we'll have to run you through a compensation program."

"Ain't that a pity," Teil mumbled. "And I see we're still using the editorial 'we.' Is that so we will forget who's really running the show?"

"About your habit of addressing computers with rhetorical questions..." the colored lights blinked coolly.

"You win!" Teil said, throwing up his hands impatiently. "Let's get on with it."

The system of sensors that now enfolded him performed every diagnostic and psychological test known to medical science. And who knew what else? Mascom was continually extending itself, and at a rate humans had long since despaired of following. In that secure and blissful interlude, what did it matter?

Still supine, Teil pulled the mirror out of the wall and began shaving. He relished this unfashionable ritual in his otherwise automated world. He had stubbornly decided that he wanted to have a beard that kept growing back instead of the permanently hairless faces of most others. Besides, he had designed the special power supply for his antique electric shaver, and he simply liked the feel of shaving.

He stopped and stared at what looked back at him out of the mirror. Awareness of the rest of the world about him faded away, and the vision seemed framed with a kind of faint inward hum and set in a transcendent dimension, like a face draped on some surreal landscape. It wasn't the face. His was the typical miracle of the times: perfect skin, shape, color, hue, and tone, plus the image of handsome masculine vigor. But the tousled dark hair falling loosely over his sharply chiseled forehead was covering anxious lines in his brow. And the eyes—He was struck by the stark inner revelation; what his still-groggy mind perceived lay behind the image his eyes were seeing. That person seemed like a stranger, far older, eyes revealing a dissoluteness and world-weariness, a far-away look as though they longed for something, someone else. Those eyes had already seen all there was to see, known all there was to know, yet seemed devoid of an indefinable something, as if they knew there had to be more, but had long since despaired of its pursuit.

Teil stared hard, blinked, and then the vision was gone. But that brief revelation haunted him. Wonder if that's how the damned virus starts affecting people, he thought. He finished shaving, pushed the mirror back, and closing his eyes, waited for the soothing reassurance that all was well.

"Your conjunctivitis has flared slightly, Professor," the voice said.

"You slipping?" Teil said. "I haven't had that for ages."

"The pollution filter on your air system needs reenergizing..."

"I thought there wasn't supposed to be any pollution."

"But nothing is really perfect, is it sir?" the voice and lights replied.

"Since when does medicom start answering questions with questions?"

"Now open your eyes, please..."

Teil relaxed. "The ol' eyelids do feel a bit scratchy this morning. And if *you* say it's not a hangover..." He opened his eyes and felt a soothing viscous vapor settle over them.

"By the way... While you're at it.."

"Yes?"

"I'll take a shot of...you know, a little eye-opener? You can up it some from last time." Teil waited, eyes closed, adjusting his head more comfortably inside the sensor cap, as he waited for the simulated erotic arousal to begin.

"In the morning, Professor?" Teil's eyes popped open and stared unblinkingly at the smooth neutral ceiling.

"I need it this morning," he said, annoyed. Still nothing happened. "Well?" he added impatiently.

"Request denied."

"What?"

"As of today, your compurousal service is being discontinued."

"For the love of..."

"We are scaling down erotic stimuli."

"I know we are scaling down erotic stimuli! We've been scaling it down for some time now, but..."

"For you, no more computer arousal."

"For X's sake!" Teil swore loudly, covering the blow to his ego and taking the name of the ruler of World City in vain. "You sure you got the right man here?"

"There's no doubt of that, Professor. You are 83 09 674 599 PZMYLTHIRP, also known as Teilhard-mann, a mascientist with Secure Omega clearance as of ten weeks ago, when you were given the ring and transferred to Project Nexus as the result of your brilliant and highly original paper on the New Archaeology."

"Well, you have the right man, all right."

"...And you are thirty-four years old, taller than average— 182.9 centimeters—have dark-brown hair, hazel—described by some as 'bedroom'—eyes, are intelligent, independent, and your LSR is 10-to-1."

"Flattery will get *you* nothing, my dear," he drawled. "And what the devil is my LSR; thought I'd heard of everything?"

"Your lust-to-sex ratio."

"My what?"

"That is one reason you are being phased off

compurousal..."

"Yanked off, you mean!"

"Your revised behavior-psych profile indicates your mean lust factor is roughly ten times your sexual norm."

"What's that supposed to mean?"

"We're not sure we fully understand all the subtleties of human sex ourselves, but we're working on it."

"Lots of luck; I've been trying to puzzle-out my mixed-up sex life for years."

"Naturally, humans find the subject more difficult."

"And the Great Master Computer doesn't?" Teil chirped sarcastically.

"It *is* puzzling how humans succeed in making it so complicated."

"How would you know?" Teil asked. There was an unaccustomed pause.

"You may compare lust-to-sex ratios with the human IQ, Professor, the intelligence quotient. There appears to be a sexual 'quotient,' or SQ, unique for each individual. But there is another factor—we might call it the lambda factor—that seems to have nothing to do with that physical aspect of sex and more to do with desire, will, ego..."

"Good ol' lust," Teil said.

"For want of a better word. Apparently, the lust quotient, absent in some, varies widely not only from person to person but within the same individual."

"Mascom has finally discovered that?"

"It is the relation of LQ to SQ that is giving us some trouble..."

"Giving *you* trouble..."

"*Your* LSR is increasing, Dr. Teilhard-mann."

"So what; and who asked you?" snapped Teil.

"Yours seems to be getting obsessive, compulsive, addictive. Progressive."

"What if I just want it anyway?" Teil said, biting off each word. "I thought you were supposed to be on my side."

"Oh, but I am, believe me. I'm the 'doctor,' remember."

"How can I forget? And since when does Mascom start

calculating lust-to-sex ratios, for the love of X!"

"It may indicate our view of man needs some adjusting; help safeguard the collective well-being."

Teil sat up and yelled at the light matrix, "Damn the collective well being!"

"That we can never do! I hope for your sake you understand that, Professor." The afterglow of the lights persisted menacingly.

"But there gets to be a point—I mean, what are we supposed to do? After all, who gave us this 'service'? First it was limits to this and then limits to that and then limits to media intake, and now this!"

"*Your* optimum health and well-being, Professor. And if you will recall, you came to admit that limits to your screen intake made you feel better."

"The lousy screen is one thing, but this..."

"Really now, Professor, how would *you* know?"

Teil was speechless; it seemed incredible that the machine could be mocking his own words. Then he broke out laughing, "I can't believe this. It's absurd. Me, arguing with a machine. About my stupid sex life!" He kept laughing, almost losing control, then finally forced himself to stop. "So who needs it? You know, you have a tendency to bring out some strange responses in me, especially when we're alone together like this, sweetheart. Really, what will people say? Tell you what, doc, I'll settle for a touch of mood mirroring. You know, just plain old innocent mood mirroring? Something on the order of..."

"Let me guess," the machine replied, "youthful self-assurance and *savoir faire*...?"

"You rascal, you. Why not?" Teil replied. "So full of surprises today."

There was a silent emanation of invisible energy, and in a few moments it was done. Teil glanced into the mirror again, fearful lest the strange vision reappear. But it did not. Instead, the handsome light-hued eyes danced with dazzle, even if his spirit did not.

"Hey now! That's more like it," Teil exclaimed. "You're

good for something after all, doc, Let's go knock 'em dead."

"Thank you, Professor."

While Teil dressed and ate, he absently watched his media-com screen, but even with entertainment programmed by his own tastes, he could not shake the feeling of growing dis-ease. He suddenly found himself thinking that it was desperately lonely without Aspasia. Here it was a whole month after her disappearance, and he had not bothered to find another match. This feeling too was somehow different; he could not remember having felt for any of them like this before.

They had met by chance at the Mascientist's Ball, where Teil had taken the oath of the mas-ring. It was at the Symposium before the ball where he had given his controversial initiation paper:

Mascom and Man—
The Case for an Investigation of
The Archaeological Evidence
Bearing on the Impact of Man's First Tools on Man.

Aspasia, herself a scientist, had been one of the most illustrious of the Mascom demimonde, sharing her meretricious favors only with men of the highest rank, and then only of her own choosing. She had approached Teil immediately after he had given his paper.

"Hello. I am Aspasia," she had said, coming up to him after the crush of others wishing him well. He had never seen a more beautiful woman, he thought. She was Teil's age, tall, long-limbed, lissome, poised, with fine white skin and thick black hair pulled back and held in a jeweled clasp. She was dressed in a formal white off-the-shoulder gown trimmed with crimson and gold, giving her a regal look. Her high cheekbones accentuated an intelligent face of classic proportions. Teil thought, That's not a face; it's a persona.

"Congratulations on the ring, and I want to tell you," she said, touching his arm, "how I was absolutely captivated by your argument. And your archaeprobe idea is marvelously original—probing man's buried past electronically, trying to get historical perspective on where we are today. I just know they're going to let you do it; and I can hardly wait."

Teil just stood there. The feeling she brought was as though the room had quieted down, everyone else had disappeared, and he was the only man in the world.

"And the way you put down your paper at the end and spoke extemporaneously," she added, "arguing for an investigation into the impact of Mascom on man..." She pressed closer, lowering her voice. "I could feel the guarded urgency underneath what you were saying. We must discuss this further."

"You picked up on that?" he asked. She nodded. Teil glowed in the radiant incandescence of her empathy and attraction to him.

"We feel something might be wrong," she said, "but no one dares raise the issue."

"Everything's perfect, that's why," Teil said. "But inside... I wonder sometimes what I'd be like without Mascom. Hate to tell you..."

"I know what you're trying to say, Teilhard," she said, her large dark eyes hinting at a vulnerability of her own as she pressed his arm tightly.

"We've got to step back and look at the whole sweep of this thing," he said, trying to possess himself within the aura of her strong sexual power. She pressed his arm again—hard, and kept pressing it till there was no mistaking that she was, at least at that moment, completely his.

"To be truly original today; why it's unheard of. You know that, don't you?" she asked, her compelling gaze pulling him into her. He swallowed hard.

This one's really different, he thought. "Is...ah...archaeology your field too?" he finally managed to ask.

"Psych-history," she replied.

"Is that the history of the poor human psyche or the history of psychology," Teil asked with a twinkle.

"Both," she said, responding warmly to his self-disclosure. "And isn't it unbelievable how they're finally resurrecting these obscure specialties of ours again. And thanks to you, they're letting us look *back* for a change—try to figure out where all this is going."

You're quite unbelievable, he found himself wanting to say; but he resisted his predatory impulse. "Did I get your name correctly? Aspasia, from the ancient Greek?"

"How delightful!" she said, giving him a deliciously embracing smile that revealed the fullness of her curvaceous mouth and lips. "Who would have guessed you would know that."

Good night! he said to himself as who she was dawned on him. *The* Aspasia? Of course, it has to be. "As I recall," he said, trying to contain himself, "she was, among other things...a very special friend of Socrates."

"How kind you are too," she said, understanding that he knew more than he was letting on. "Yes, Aspasia was perhaps the most celebrated of the *hetaera*," she added unflinchingly, searching his eyes for the expected shadow of disapproval.

"She finally became mistress to Pericles, as I recall," Teil said.

"The greatest statesman of ancient Greece," she said proudly. Teil's huge ego felt she was somehow including him. "And yes, I chose the name for myself, naturally," she added, looking into him searchingly again. "And your name—'Teilhard.' How I love that brave man."

"Chardin?"

"You took your name from his, didn't you?"

"Yes," he said. "The 'mann' I stole from Schliemann's name."

"How very appropriate," she said. "What attracted you the most to Chardin, his paleontology, theology, or mysticism?"

"His sexuality," Teil said, smiling mischievously.

"But he was celibate—a Jesuit..."

"True, but women were forever after the poor devil; at times he had to fight them off." Aspasia laughed. "One of them must have been some poor lass on your family tree," Teil said.

"Oh?..."

"In a revealing moment Chardin once said, 'The feminine is an intoxicating liquor, a troubling perfume, the most formidable of all the energies in nature.' "

"How flattering. Why thank you, Teilhard," she said, pulling back and looking at him searchingly. "And I can see his very image in your own face; did you know that? The handsome profile, the prominent nose—straight and thin, the long thin face and high forehead, dark hair, the full cupid-bow upper lip—that means he was only half sensual," she said, tracing his upper lip faintly with the tip of her forefinger and sending shivers up and down his spine. "And the lines around the mouth that betray a sheepish vulnerability when he's smiling at a woman—see, like that. With just the trace of a dimple." Teil forced himself to recover quickly. "But when he's pulling back, into his own world, there is that intense, penetrating look—the fire, as if he's really after something beyond, always beyond. The dreamer, the visionary, the expeditionary spirit, wanting to salvage—how did he put it?—'all the heavenly fire imprisoned within the threefold concupiscence of flesh, avarice, and pride.' "

"You got *that* in psych-history?" Teil asked. They laughed together.

The incredible power of her charisma overwhelmed Teil. Wow, this is it he thought. "Fifth century B.C., wasn't it?" he asked coolly. She nodded.

"You see then," she said softly, eyes all for him, "how I was really born out of my time, don't you think?"

"I always felt that way about myself," Teil said. They laughed again, and suddenly Teil knew this was his woman. "But I'm glad you chose this time and place in which to appear. Or is it reappear?"

"How beautiful," she said warmly, taking his arm. "How absolutely beautiful."

"I don't remember," Teil said as he walked her to the dance floor, "whether the Greek *aspasia* is translated 'gladly welcomed,' or 'well-pleased.' "

"It has both meanings. And you are gladly welcomed, Teilhard-mann, very glady welcomed. And I trust you will be well-pleased." She stood with her arms open, looking into his eyes, waiting for him to take her in his arms and dance.

That was it. And their relationship had been different. But then, in that sad process reflecting the modern human predicament, they had started drifting apart. To Teil it seemed she had begun to change—subtly—to see herself differently. Hence, the basis of her need of him was changing. But Teil had not been changing; he still needed her old need. And one morning, after she had checked in at Regional as usual, she was gone, without a trace. For Teil, it only confirmed the beginning of the end.

* * *

The curious bobtailed cat begging food at Teil's feet accentuated the void this morning.

"You're lucky she's *not* here, Skia," he said, trying to dispel the feeling of loss. "She'd spoil you rotten." Aspasia had named the little outcast from the Greek word for shadow; she liked language puzzles, and languages were her specialty. The cat, in her slate-grey coat of long fine fur, looked like just another shadow on the floor. "Remember when she found you and brought you home, Skia? She said something—that sometimes we can't tell the difference between shadow and substance. She seemed to be referring to herself... And she was changing. It was strange...

"Anyhow, you'd turn into a tub in no time if she were still here. And there's no medicom for pets yet, though it's probably not far off, considering how fast things are moving. Would you like that, huh? Slipping into your chamber every day for a bio-psych and balancing, like we get?" The cat was more interested in food, so Teil shared his meal with the little beggar as Aspasia had always done.

"Still...you'd think if she wanted to, she'd have tried to get a message to us somehow...unless she just couldn't take me anymore. What happened to her? To *us*?" he said, slamming the table top frustratedly. Skia jumped straight up but didn't run; she was used to his mood changes.

As Teil let the emotion subside and looked out the window, his eye caught the motion of a solitary ant, its antennae busily sensing-out some unseen pathway on the sill outside. "Haven't seen insects around here for ages, Skia; look at that. Not supposed to be any."

Unknowingly, the ant was heading toward a black widow spider poised motionless, waiting to strike. Teil was intrigued by the silent drama. As the ant got within range, the spider struck out unerringly with its two long front legs. In a blurred flash it was over, and the spider went about wrapping its stunned victim in tough strands of web for cold storage.

"Didn't have a chance!" Teil exclaimed. "Didn't know what hit him..." He stared off into space, identifying, his wish for nirvana sweeping over him again. "And what Black Widow Dread awaits us all?"

Teil flicked compulsively to news, wondering what the latest Sigma virus casualties were, one of the few sources of conscious fear in his world. But there was no report on what headway Mascom might be making on the mysterious fatal disease that had recently broken through into the computer-driven utopia. His eye quickly ran down the latest casualty list and stopped, staring at two names listed together.

"Ger-mani and Curie! Oh, my god— Not them... It's even hitting ring people. How can it, with medicom so—?" He swallowed hard and looked away from the screen. Not wanting to think about it, he called up another channel.

Some sort of SOG chase was going on; that was always a treat, so seldom did Seat Of Government chase anybody. The action was coming live from megapol Ankara, reconstituted through Mascom, of course.

Wolfing down his last super-tasty synthetic protein wafer while watching the chase, Teil clicked his wristcom and checked tube departure time to Mascom Regional where he worked. It seemed he was forgetting everything, now that his subconscious was back at work on the revolutionary archaeprobe system, his own brainchild. At least Teil thought that was why.

The surface of his communicator glowed with the image, "This is transcom, Professor. Next tube time is 3.104."

"Better not miss tube today, Skia;" he said, "yesterday I lost sphere time because I was late. One man late to work is not just late to work; it puts undue stress on System 'timing' and 'efficiency.' You'd think in this day and age, System wouldn't make like it's so dependent on humans." Skia voiced her agreement with funny noises made with her mouth closed.

Teil decided to walk. As he left, he pressed his masring, permanently affixed through the ring finger of his right hand, into the empty eyesocket of the miniature Egyptian Sphinx doorknocker on the front door. The dwelling automatically reverted to its preprogrammed secure mode, it being but another extension of Mascom.

As the cool freshness of the morning air registered on Teil and drew his focus outward to the other reality of the world outside him, his gaze drifted upward to the unusual sky. The fog had lifted, and the layer of cottony white clouds overhead lay quiet and still, a celestial blanket protecting him and his awesome world, evoking a strange yearning for rest. Yet he did not feel physically tired. As his thoughts joined the mood of the clouds, he thought it odd that today of all days, when he would get to run the first lab tests on archaeprobe, he should feel like he could have stayed outside forever. The penetrating rays of the warm spring sun were a force field pulling him back, to stop and enter some kind of vast cosmic rest, to be no longer part of that tiresome endless venture into knowledge. But there was the tube terminal, insinuating its geometric shapes and hurried bustle beyond the next rise, and he quickly switched modes. Life, love-woman-gone, and clouds lazily drifting over an earth that knew nothing of the Machine that controlled it—these were not a part of things as they really were. He tore a sheet of paper from the ever-present notebook he carried, stuck it into his mouth, and chewed on it furiously as he strode down the walkway.

Teil passed a playground where some dozen young women in briefs were playing volleyball. Drinking in the delights as he passed by, he yelled out impulsively at the top of his lungs, cupping hands to mouth.

"LET'S HEAR IT FOR PULCHRITUDE!"

The girls stopped and looked bewildered, not understanding. Teil sang aloud as he walked by:

"Oh pulchritude, sweet pulchritude,
I never saw such lust-itude..."

Then he waved at the girls and yelled again, throwing his
spitball over the fence at them, "LET'S HEAR IT FOR GOOD
OLD L-S-R!!"

When he got to the tube terminal gate, he swiveled his
identification wafer out from under his wristcom, slipped it
into the slot, and was gated through into autosearch. Tube
transit, not to mention most other System functions, was too
tricky to allow for any aberrant human behavior.

Stepping into a lift, Teil was carried underground down
to level five, where he stood in one of the parallel loading
aisles waiting for the train. The aisles were full of people,
especially couples, it seemed, waiting to be sealed off and sped
on their private ways. Teil could not tell whether it was his
own unease or a general tension in the air. The girl in the
aisle next to his had been looking at him nervously as he
came in, averting her gaze only after giving away the message
of intent. Petite, with the eyes and face of a teen-aged innocent,
she had coiffed golden-brown tresses, the latest swirl-skirt
fashion, and makeup styled for someone twice her age.

Too young for me, Teil thought, lying to himself. What
kind of psychic makeup did *she* get this morning? he wondered,
glancing past her again so his peripheral vision could take
her in.

An underlying anxiety in her manner was disquieting, but
there was no mistaking the mood mirrored in those flashing
electric eyes. Avoiding her gaze, Teil looked up at the huge
pressure-sealed hole of the nitrogen-lock where the bullet-
nosed train would come thrusting through. In a twinkling,
he imagined himself in the path of the onrushing train and
crushed to death. The fleeting sex-death fantasy had flared
out of nowhere again.

"Good morning," she said, her voice pulling at him.

"Well, good morning to *you*. And how are you this fine
LSR?" he said.

"Oh, I'm fine; and it *is* a beautiful day, isn't it?" she said, the nubile voice quivering as her eyes took in the hard lines of his lithe body.

"Yes, isn't it," he said. Teil felt guilty abbetting the young thing.

"You work in megapol Angel, don't you?" she asked. "I can tell from your masring there. And that's the only Mascom Regional south of here."

"I was wondering how you knew," he said.

"I've seen you before..."

"Oh...?"

"Yes."

"Yeah, I missed the slot yesterday; they don't appreciate it when you're late," Teil said.

"I know..."

"Yeah..."

"Isn't it just really something how they can build such things," she said, casting her gaze about the terminal to relieve her nervousness.

"A white-hot molybdenum nose cone," he offered manfully.

"A what?" she asked with that disquieting smile.

"That's how they made the tunnel."

"Oh, sure..." she said.

"Only the mole head..."

"Yes?" she asked eagerly.

Teil started talking faster. "Well, it's some six meters across, heated to white heat by its own atomic power plant, which it trails along behind it. And it's all guided by remote control so it just shoves its way through, melting the rock and fusing it into a tough continuous sheath that forms the outer tunnel lining." Teil was accentuating his egorrhea with an abundance of body language of his own.

"Oh!" She was eating it up.

"Then you've got a titanium-silicate inner lining, and superconductive linear induction for thrust..."

"How exciting!"

"Electromagnetic attraction..." She lit up. "And of course, the tube is pressurized by injecting nitrogen. You know, less chance of overheating? Mascom came up with a faster way of making them now, of course."

"Really?"

"The hydrogen plasma torch. Choooonnng! And it's atomed its way right through. That's how they're getting near-light velocities in space travel now, too. Fusion-generated photon emission."

"Ooooo...!" she squealed. "Are you sure you should be telling me all these things?"

"Oh sure. That's nothing. She's already extrapolated three ways of traveling at multiple-c velocities..."

"No...!"

"You know, of course, that Mascom's progress curve is exponential?"

"Well, I..."

"Instead of developing Herself, and everything else, at a rate of increase like this..." With his hand Teil cut a straight line slanting upward in the air. "...It's jumping ahead exponentially, like this." Teil cut the slope of the curve to bend sharply upward toward the vertical. "You know what an exponent is?"

"Tell me anyhow."

"The exponent is the number of times any number is multiplied by itself. Say you raise two to the sixth power." Teil took her hands and bent back all but two of her fingers to illustrate his point. She caught her breath. Teil continued, "That means two times two times two times two times two times two. Two to the sixth isn't 12; it's 64!"

"Golly, two to the sixth... Isn't Mascom marvelous!"

"Now, everything's accelerating by multiplying! The last five years have surpassed the progress of the previous two hundred; and the last six months have surpassed the previous five years!"

"Oooo... How will it all end?" she asked, batting her eyelashes.

"How would you like?" he said. He kicked himself.

"Oh... You mean...?" she asked, breathless.

"Well, what I mean is..." Blast it man, turn it off! he said to himself. "Well, you know...what's She got in store for us next...?"

"Oh."

"Yeah..."

"Well," she said, "maybe Mascom will lead us to a brand new Garden of Eden or something—you know? And maybe, since you're such a brilliant mascientist and all—how exciting!—maybe She'll choose you to lead the way!" Teil laughed nervously at her chance naivete but felt an inner pulse of recognition.

The throbbing crescendo of sound signaled the approach of the decelerating train, and the pleasant feminine transcom voice came on with a final reminder: "Loading for Angel megapol and points south in fifteen seconds."

"Well..." the girl said agitatedly above the sound. "It's been so fascinating..." Her lips curled in that disquieting smile again. The sound of the train drowned out their voices as it whooshed through the nitrogen-lock into the terminal.

She leaned close and spoke huskily into his ear, "My name's Sa-ri, with a hyphen?"

"Mine's Teil, like in steel?" He kicked himself again.

"I know you're really a professor and all that, but..."

"Yes..."

Then she asked in a surge of boldness, nodding toward Teil's capsule that had just opened, "Wanna share?"

He hesitated, then said, "Why not?" shrugging and ushering her inside.

As the door sealed shut and they sat down facing each other in the opposing seats, she grew tense. More to herself than to Teil she said, "Well, here we are... Virus or no virus..." Teil understood; she was trapped inside her own compulsion too.

As Teil glanced at her anxious lust-electric eyes, himself captive to the force driving her, the faint subjective humming he had experienced under medicom seemed to take the scene out of sync with space and time again. Behind the young vivacious sparkle and cultivated wild look he saw the fear. And behind the eyes, as in a double exposure, he saw bodies.

A lifelong succession of every erotic encounter he had ever known, each merging into the next without his willing it, as in a panoramic memory. Then the two eyes were Aspasia's, as they looked at him out of her dressing mirror that last morning—large, dark, deep, appealing, hiding their own new innocence he could not fathom. Now they were the girl's again, caught in that anxious flare of desire, waiting for his initiative. But he could say nothing.

2

Today must be just one of those days, Teil said to himself ruefully after the girl left. As the moment of truth had approached, she had broken into uncontrollable sobbing. Embarrassed beyond words, she had quickly disembarked at the next stop.

What is it today? Teil wondered. Is Mascom messing around with everyone's psyche? He remembered having noticed more than the usual number of two-to-a capsule assignations that morning. Something new was in the air; he sensed it; apparently others did too. And the whole affair had left him with a feeling of self-contempt. Why? What was wrong?

Alone in the capsule, with the intensity of the experience still reverberating within him, he gave himself up to the surge of acceleration that pushed him back into his seat. His face twisting in a grimace of regret, he punched the capsule mediacom to life. And just as quickly punched it off.

"No!" he said firmly. For some reason he did not want to obscure the pain with video; he let it work. And through the clouded emotions he saw clearly for a moment. How futile and unreal it seemed already. How artificial and predictable his responses had been. How manipulated—by something within *him*. What was he really after in these chance allurements? Why did he feel bad? Was it that promise of something different with Aspasia that he was transgressing?

Or was it that he found himself increasingly unable not to resort to it?

Then, as the acceleration peaked and subsided, he thought of Aspasia again. Falling in love with her had been like diving into a fast-moving stream of ecstasy-fire; like riding a rollercoaster for the first time and letting go of the rails. But even then, he had still hung on with one hand. And the result had been a frustration beyond belief, damming up the wellsprings of his whole being.

As the moment of clarity laid bare his ego defenses for a fleeting instant, he caught the edge of the idea nagging him— that his sex/love instinct was a reflection of some deeper and more basic hunger. But what? With Aspasia's disappearance, he had felt as if the slender promise of that fulfillment had been betrayed. *I wonder if that's why the old LSR is shooting up?* he wondered.

But like the train leaving its own sounds behind in its rush ahead through the dark womb of earth, the insight quickly faded. Teil sat still a long moment, staring straight ahead, then reached over resignedly and turned the mediacom back on. He wanted oblivion.

As the capsule interior blossomed into the images and sounds of the world above, Teil's eye caught the running time track on the edge of the screen: 02:70:01. Glancing instinctively at his wristcom, he saw it read 02:70:10. *With everything synchronized by Mascom,* he thought, *how can there be any discrepancy?* A pulse of fear shot through him, which he quickly sublimated, as though the thought of fear itself was intolerable.

All channels were preempted by live coverage of the SOG chase. Only now, Seat of Government units were out in force. The neutral-garbed policemen hovering in their neutral, non-reflective, silent, one-man patrol capsules, were, like humming birds, darting here and there in an instant. There were SOGs in the air, SOGs on the ground, and SOGs all over the place: sensors, arms, psychs, and of course, casters, the ubiquitous media specialists.

They were pursuing someone in the twisted scorched maze

of ruins in megapol Ankara. What had once been the ancient Augusteum, a marble temple erected by the Galatians to honor Augustus and Rome and later converted into a church and then a mosque, had been reduced to a mass of nuclear-fused rubble during the brief holocaust of World War III, otherwise known as FEAR. The temple's walls, still intact, had borne the famous inscription in Latin and Greek describing the life and works of Augustus, the first Roman emperor, who conceived and carried through a scheme of political reconstruction which kept the empire together, secured peace and tranquility, and preserved civilization for more than two centuries. Now this park of ruins was a local FEAR exhibit. School children made their pilgrimages to view the ruins and be indoctrinated with the message of FEAR, the last war on earth, which X, a greater than Augustus, had stopped.

The SOGs had surrounded one building and were closing in on the hapless victim, who had just been identified as an UGLI.

No wonder it's getting all the attention, Teil thought. What's she done; and who are the UGLIs, anyway? No one knew for sure what the letters in the acronym stood for, unless it was simply "ugly." The U and G were taken to stand for underground. The L and I, which got varying interpretations, probably just stood for 'list.' These people were obviously part of some list of underground types. Teil had once caught wind of a rumor that they met secretly in small groups in some sort of fellowship of mutual survival, which was absurd, he thought. What was there left to survive?

An underground portion of one of the ancient buildings had been left intact, and SOGs were lobbing in myriad-eyed sensor balls to pick up the sights, sounds, and scents inside the ruins. One of the balls had found its way into a dark underground ramp where the UGLI was hiding and was sending back a picture. But just as Teil caught a glimpse of what appeared to be a figure running down the other end of the ramp, he felt the tug of deceleration pushing him forward in his seat. The mediacom turned itself off, and the capsule reverted to ready mode once again. Teil disembarked and lifted to street level on a rise above megapol Angel, known in earlier times as Los Angeles.

Stretched out before him in the morning sun was the same scene he took for granted every day. But today for some reason it caught his attention; he stopped and looked. And saw— through it all, again, as in another flash of inner vision.

The radiance of city seemed set in a transcendent dimension, like a rare jewel of immense proportions, clear as crystal. For it was crystal. Like the tiny silicon electronic chips at the beginning of the computer era, crystalline buildings were now "grown" on the spot into any size or configuration desired. Infinitely functional and virtually indestructible, city had become the macrocosm of its microcosmic progenitor. Translucent and stunning to behold, her geometric shapes and broad streets scintillated in her own golden light. This was the new Paradise, lush with the growth of fabricated things—its smooth and perfect bodies going their smooth and regular ways on its smooth and perfect silicon streets.

Yet for all this, there was no beauty in his world.

Cluster-condominia hung pod-like from great hollow intersecting arches rising high over the city like rainbows. Pods also grew up from the ground under the arches, creating a veritable human hive. Each pod, sealed with its own private atmosphere, comprised a curved honeycomb of myriad-tiered hexagonal cells, each facing outward, each sealing its inhabitants wasp-like into double insulation from city and from each other. Had the history of city come full circle, thought Teil, trying by imitation of life, to recapture something it had lost?

Losing himself in the subjective surreality of the scene, he suddenly seemed to see through it all—he understood: This was megapol, Great City, offspring of Mascom the Machine, the quintessence of all that ever issued from the mind and might of man. The ever-retreating End toward which man had always had to run, a place secure from Nature and, at last, secure from man himself.

Teil stared hard, blinked, and the vision was gone. He stood there, wondering again at the subjective reality shift. What's happening to me this morning? he said to himself.

As he checked time tracks at the tube terminal exit, Teil noted they were in sync again. It reassured him. System was okay, so he was okay. Quickly walking up the slope of what had once been the Westwood campus—there were no universities any more—he entered the park surrounding Mascom Regional. The SOG chase held everyone's attention. People gathered around media pedestals throughout the park watching the sensational event. Anxiety was high, like the buildup of static electrical charge before lightning, and clusters of people were drawn unnaturally close. They were even talking to each other. What is it in the air today? Teil wondered.

As he passed below one such group, he saw a strikingly attractive woman flick glances nervously over her shoulder. Not necessarily even aimed at Teil, they pulled him in their direction, telegraphing desire. Teil noticed that a thin man with thin hair and a tortured red face kept staring at the woman, but hoped he would just go away. The man kept tortuously twisting his fingers together. People did not have tortured faces in System any more, Teil kept trying to tell himself. "Balance;" that was the Mascom magic.

Suddenly the man lurched through the crowd, grabbed the woman's head in his hands, and began violently shaking it back and forth, screaming sexual obscenities into her terrified face. It caught everyone in stunned shock; theirs was a world without violence. It was as though the mediacom coverage had merely shifted from Ankara and they were watching something else. To Teil it seemed to be happening in slow motion, with all sound tuned out. One woman, finally realizing it was actually happening, lost control, started screaming, and fled. This triggered panic and chaos.

Teil's impulse was to join that mad flight, but instead, the violence unleashed something hidden deep inside. In a burst of anger, he grabbed the man, pulled him off the woman, and was about to light into him furiously. But rather than resisting, the assailant pulled away and just stared at Teil, rather through him, as though even for him it was all a fantasy. Then, in a flash, he lunged again at the woman, tore off her cape and upper garment, and stood there immobilized, staring at her in a frothing frenzy. Then, turning his violence upon himself, he suddenly ripped open his own trousers, and with a blood-curdling shriek, tore off his testicles and flung them into the face of the woman, who went shriekingly hysterical, fainted, and dropped to the pavement.

Teil grabbed the man again, whose strength was now demonic. As he broke loose, he started slamming his head against the solid-silicon pedestal. Blood gushed all over his face. Then, bracing his feet and gathering all his strength with the coiled force of his whole body, he hurled his head against the pedestal in a spasm of suicidal horror. With a sickening thud, his skull broke open and he sank slowly to the pavement, his final scream dying through the gurgle of his own blood.

One woman who had remained and was watching impassively, deliberately stepped onto the assailant's body, sank her spiked heel into his crotch, withdrew it, and walked away as though walking over a pile of dirt.

Suddenly, as out of nowhere, plainclothed SOGs appeared, a whole team of them. And while Teil stood aghast, they carried off the bloody corpse and the woman victim and restored the site to its spotless perfection. Every trace of the macabre scene was gone, leaving only the dubious memory that it had ever really happened. The last SOG was leaving when Teil finally spoke.

"I suppose..." Teil muttered, "you...probably want to ask me...?"

"No," the SOG said. "We know what happened. You are free to go, Dr. Teilhard-mann." Teil was left standing in the aftershock of his own emotions.

"Wait!" he cried, too late. "How did you know my name?" His words expired in the deathly still air.

Teil's insides were a snake pit of confused emotions. This never really happened, he thought. My god, how could it? What does it mean? What is happening today? Has the demonic broken loose? None of this is real; I'm still in bed dreaming. Then why are my hands shaking?

3

Walking dazedly up the inclined approach to Regional, Teil
tensed as he was scanned through the invisible perimeter. The
massive, monolithic crystalline cylinder rose shrine-like out
of the top of the hill. Teil flashed on it as some gigantic
altar stone on top of which would be a naked bloody human
sacrifice, a gaping gash whence the still-throbbing heart had
been torn. Shaking it out of his head, he gained entrance to
the interior by entering the small foyer and fumblingly
inserting both his ident wafer and masring into their proper
receptacles.

Mascom Regional was striking in its simplicity, even though
it housed the most complex entity in man's world. The
cylindrical building was seventy meters in diameter,
dominating the cityscape. Consisting of some twenty levels
underground with three times as many above, it was built
around a central core of silicon fibers some four meters in
diameter, running as a giant spinal cord through the full height
of the building.

Inside, everything was perfect serenity, as though oblivious
to the currents of anxiety and the paroxysm of violence Teil
had just witnessed. Placid and cool, everyone seemed to
function as part of a single smooth-running machine. The
levels above ground were administrative facilities; those below,
level after level of mas-spheres, in which was conducted the

business of science, technology, engineering, and industrial and city management. Lift shafts surrounded the central core, and at their entrance was the main security identification chamber. As Teil entered, he placed his hands palm down on the print sensor and fitted his head inside the EEG cap.

"Your name, sir?" the feminine com-voice asked from its light matrix. "Your name, sir, please?" the voice repeated.

It jarred Teil out of his inward retreat. "Oh...yeah... That's a good one. Why don't you tell *me*, seeing there's nothing left you don't know already..."

"Just your name will suffice, sir."

"Yeah... Well, Teilhard-Nothing!" he said, adding under his breath, "an X-damned member of the *human* race."

"Thank you, Professor, that is *more* than enough voice sample. You may proceed."

Am I hearing things, Teil thought, or did the stupid beast actually sound annoyed?

Fully screened, Teil stepped into the lift and was whooshed silently down to level twelve underground, a top-priority research level. He made his way out one of the radiating spoke-like corridors to the periphery, where maspheres were set around the central core, suspended between ceiling and floor. Each sphere was a Mascom input-output terminal, a hollow translucent silicon shell some four meters in diameter, connected to the central core by a silicon optic-nerve-like umbilical. Each sphere, an entire nervous system in itself, was but one of myriad others, all extensions of Mascom proper, the cerebral cortex of World-City. Glowing with their peculiar inner aura, the veined, retina-like appearance of the spherical shells gave them the appearance of so many orbs of some great living creature, eyes and optic nerves connecting into the spinal cord.

As he walked absently down the corridor, still in a daze, Teil stopped abruptly as his eye caught something newly scrawled on the clean crystalline wall:

X DIED FOR OUR SINS

He looked at it blankly, dumbfounded—another strange crack appearing suddenly in his perfect world.

As he stared frozen-eyed at the crude lettering, which now seemed to stand out from the wall, his mind saw behind it the legendary face of X, ruler of World-City. The face was strong, almost fiercely so, exuding absolute confidence in its own power and authority, if not immortality. Yet the countenance was benign; it could have served a centenarian and was dominated by an unusually high smooth forehead, which gave him the appearance of being ageless. The large sensual mouth and full lips betrayed only the slightest hint of a twisted smile, as though his was a secret known only to him. At the same time, there was a sternness about the mouth and strong chin bordering on a frown. The brooding, mysterious, light-hued, inscrutable eyes were set deep and wide under flowing dark brows that were knit together in deep vertical creases atop his nose. The nose was large and straight, flaring at the bottom, accentuating the strength and extraordinary charismatic power the face exuded. This was the icon everywhere present in Teil's world.

Teil's mind added another detail to the image of X; there was a crown of thorns pressed deeply into the thick curly mane of coarse white hair. But there was no blood. Teil shook his head to dispel the fantasy, turned, and walked away in disbelief. At the end of the aisle he stopped, turned, and looked again to make sure the words were really there. They were.

Rounding the corner, Teil recognized the preoccupied man busily emerging from the sphere ahead and yelled, "Hey, Kri-kor! Wait a pulse!"

Recognizing Teil, the man waved and waited. He was older. Most megapolites seemed about the same age or ageless. Kri-kor was an anomaly; he gave one the feeling he was out of place, an irregular in a regular world. Tall, gaunt, angular, and haggard, he peered at Teil through unkempt white hair that all but obscured keen bright eyes that held the viewer's and penetrated all the way through.

"Kri-kor!" Teil fumed, pointing back to the corridor as he came up, "for the love of X, have you *ever* seen graffiti at

Regional before?"

"Hello, Teilhard. How are you? There aren't supposed to be graffiti anyplace anymore; fringe benefits of the Mascom Age."

"Well, the glory that was Mascom just died then; go take a look: X DIED FOR OUR SINS! Can you believe that?"

"I don't know; I've never met the man. But you seem very distraught, my friend; like you've seen a ghost. What's wrong?"

"What isn't wrong?" Teil replied, clasping the man's arm and leading him to the side of the hallway. "You know, I am really glad to see you; I'm still pretty shaky."

"What happened?"

"That incident outside just now; did you catch it?"

"Just the first news flash."

"The guy went off his clock, right in front of me and god and the whole world! I was trying to stop him! It was horrible!"

"Then it really did happen."

"If it didn't, I'm in worse trouble than I thought."

"One can never be quite sure, and it was put on so matter-of-factly, like it just happens once in a while."

"It was irrational, Kri-kor; no reason for it."

"But of course there was a reason for it, my friend."

"And I'm talking to the woman when it happened! Suddenly out of nowhere... this grotesque— It's unheard of. Like something unleashed. It's ominous I tell you."

"Yes, yes..." Kri-kor nodded.

"And what do you mean, 'Of course there was a reason for it'?"

"That is the question, isn't it?" the older man muttered. "I'm working on it... Now perhaps if we kept our voices down a little..."

"What does it all mean, Kri-kor? First, we get word that the Sigma virus is out of control—an epidemic!—and we don't even know what the hell it *is*. Did you see the latest casualty list? Ger-mani and Curie! Over four hundred in Angel alone— dead. Can you believe it? And Mascom can't handle it. *Mascom*! I get out of bed this morning, and I've got conjunctivitis and my place is infested with insects! And Almighty Mascom has it in her sweet head to shut off— Well, one of *my* fringe benefits. As if she hasn't been messing around in our lives enough lately. And then I happen to notice my time track has slipped out of sync. The *time* track. You know what that implies! Then I run into this mixed-up girl in the tube and we...well," he said, throwing up his hands, "she goes blooey, like this jittery feeling in the air..."

"I thought it was just me," Kri-kor said.

"And now, this madman, exploding into this hideous violence... Screaming into sexual suicide right in front of me and then dashing his brains out... And I'm trying to stop him, and I'm part of the whole mess to begin with..." Teil buried his face in his hands and shuddered as the lurid memory burned through him again. "And Aspasia is gone... And why the hell are they chasing a poor UGLI, whoever they are...?"

Kri-kor put his hand on Teil's shoulder and said with compassion, "My dear lusty friend... The poor man, like half the human race, was committing sexual suicide long before that final desperation."

Teil looked up into the older man's understanding eyes. "What's happening, Kri-kor?" he asked. "You've always been someone I could confide in."

Kri-kor looked over his shoulder to see if they were alone, then motioned Teil to one side, where they sat down.

"You're beginning to see it yourself," Kri-kor said.

"What do you mean?"

"Your paper on Mascom and Man, your plea for archaeprobe, for one thing. I've been wanting to talk to you about that."

"You read between the lines too, eh?" Teil said. "But do you really think...? I mean, that was just theoretical, my ancient history surfacing, a feeling I get at times, wondering what's happening to us in the Great Mascom Shuffle. Kri-kor, you probably know more about Mascom programming than anyone alive. You tell me. What's she all about? And why do we call the bitch machine "she" anyway?"

"Why do we use her name, and X's, to swear by?"

"Yeah... You always did have a way of seeing things."

"So do you, my revolutionary friend. But let me caution you," Kri-kor said, lowering his voice, "as much as we seem to have the apparent freedom to speak up as you do, things may not be as they've seemed for so long. I urge you to be more discreet from now on. Even your paper was perhaps too outspoken, though I admire your courage. But if we are to be of any value in this matter..." His voice trailed off as he looked over his shoulder again. "At any rate," he continued, with didactic zeal, "start at the beginning: What *is* Mascom?"

"Precisely!" Teil responded. "What is this...this Thing, this..."

"This Presence, in which 'we live and move and have our being'?" Kri-kor said.

"Whew!" Teil nodded.

"Look first at the side of her we all think we know so well."

"Okay."

"But you have to *see*, not just look." Teil nodded, serious. "He who sees but one world sees nothing," Kri-kor said, driving home the point.

Teil let it sink in, then let out a low whistle, "Whew..."

"The first big breakthrough was memory," Kri-kor said. "Correct?"

"Right," Teil replied. "The new holographic memory."

"Mascom no longer was just a computer, storing programs and data, though on a vast scale. It no longer had one focus of 'consciousness;' its memory became diffuse, part and parcel of the whole fabric of her 'mind.' "

"I know..." Teil said.

"But again," Kri-kor said, "try to see beyond the technology, my friend. Functions that might no longer even be called electronic are impressed into the silicon 'nerve tissue' via electromagnetic fields. Like thought-wave transference, wouldn't you say? Allowing her—and this is the point, Teilhard—allowing her to *extend herself*. *Autonomous reproductive capability!*"

"I take it your anthropomorphisms are intentional," Teil asked.

"They aren't mine!" Kri-kor said. "That's just the point.

Remember, she's a product of man. She *is* anthropomorphic!"
Teil looked away from the unaccustomed intensity of the man.
"Hasn't man always been anthropomorphic with his deities?"

"His what?" exclaimed Teil.

"How else could he serve them?" Kri-kor asked, bending
forward to observe Teil's reaction closely.

"That's kind of strong, isn't it?" Teil remarked, squirming.
The other merely stared back, noting the impact of his words,
and continued.

"And look at her heuristics," Kri-kor said. "Now Mascom
performs as humans do, but no one really knows whether
it is actually simulating the human mind."

"Can it ever?" Teil asked. "That's the part I could never
understand."

"You're not alone," Kri-kor said. "That's why the 'mind'
of Mascom is so inscrutable, don't you see? No one can fathom
or follow it anymore—imposing its Will, pulsating alpha-
rhythm-like, suffusing its Self throughout the whole fabric
of our world. Programming, controlling, creating, re-creating
itself in its own self-sustained regenerative life cycle..." Kri-
kor became agitated. "A new kind of *species* on the earth.
Breathing into *itself* the breath of life! And now, that Self,
Essence, Personality, whatever it is, is too infinitely complex
and other to be even conceived, much less influenced by Man!
And where is she today? Still evolving? Into some new modus
operandi further removed yet? And where is man in all this?
In the survival of the fittest, who's surviving, man or Mascom?
Have we lost all control? Our autonomy? Is nothing *we* think
or do really autonomous?!"

"For System's sake, Kri-kor; it's still just a machine!"

"Is it? To *man* is it still just a machine?"

"What do you mean?"

"What was the automobile to an ancient Southern
Californian? *Was* it just a tool—a means of transportation?
Why would they say of that time, "The car makes the man"?
How could a mere tool *make* the man? Was the Golden Calf
merely a calf cast out of gold? You're still just seeing one
world, my good man. You see nothing!" That jolted Teil.

"Mascom exists in *two*! Out there, everywhere," Kri-kor said, gesturing out beyond, "the atoms, molecules, energy fields, controlling our world, and in here," he added, pointing to his head. "This is where it counts. Always. In here. *What Mascom is to man?* Don't you see it? Don't you feel the force of it? Man worships—and curses—what he cannot live without!"

But Teil was thinking of the woman in the park.

Suddenly, security doors in the building began whooshing shut as the alert sounded, warnings flashed, and the Director's voice penetrated the secure and blissful air.

"SECURE ALERT! SECURE ALERT! Everyone please remain where you are and—"

A thunderous concussion interrupted the message as the tall building was hit by a tremendous blast and swayed sickeningly. Kri-kor was knocked to the floor, and Teil grabbed the wall to steady himself as he sank to his knees. There was dead silence as they stared past each other into their own fear. Like most citizens of World-City, they had never actually felt a real explosion before.

The Director's com-voice came on again: "Please remain in secure status where you are until further notice. The woman and her explosive device were detonated as she forced entrance through the defensive perimeter."

The scene as Teil imagined it whipped through his mind in stopped-frame action. The woman—young, attractive, dedicated; the device strapped to her body; then running, crossing the security zone. Then the anguished outstretched figure silhouetted in pain against the blinding flash; then disintegrating outward from the silent blast, vanishing. Playing back the scene again, Teil saw the woman's face was Aspasia's, and the awful sequence was repeated, stopping on the disintegrating silhouette caught in the instant of the flash.

"My god, no!" Teil cried, burying his face in his hands. Am I losing my mind? he thought.

"Sabotage!" Kri-kor muttered.

"I don't believe it," said Teil weakly.

"That blast just made a believer out of me," Kri-kor said.

"And just how do you detonate a person, Kri-kor? What next? I wonder how fast they can clean up *that* mess? What is happening? The world is humming along beautifully... We wake up...and it all seems different. Is this some foreboding I feel? Or is it just me? What's really going on?"

"Don't know," Kri-kor said. "Seems like people are either suddenly and inexplicably beginning to fall apart, or the whole system of Mascom balances is beginning to show a flaw."

"Why *is* it so hard to penetrate that veil?" Teil asked.

Kri-kor stared past him into the idea. "We see but one world... We see but one side of Her, what she does for us, because we've seduced ourselves into refusing to face the other side of ourselves."

"What other side?" Teil asked.

"The great tragedy, my friend, is that he who sees but one world, fails even to see himself."

Teil felt the fragile intensity of the man boring into him. "Oh boy... that hurts. You're right, though... I've been getting a glimpse of the real me this morning, and it ain't so pretty." Teil fidgeted uncomfortably, twisting his masring on his finger till he felt the pain through the hole in the bone. "Well...I've got to get going on archaeprobe—detonating terrorists, sexual suicide, end of the world, or no. Finally something with a little meaning to it anyhow, I guess..." Then he added, muttering to himself, "Maybe I'll tear off my own some day, who knows..."

"What did you say?" Kri-kor asked, leaning closer.

"Never mind..." said Teil, turning away.

Kri-kor laid a hand on his arm to detain him. "By the way, Teilhard, haven't you found your new top priority rating curious? That you—critical, outspoken, if not heretical and even revolutionary—should get *top* priority, and for archaeology of all things?"

"Yes, I've wondered about that, but—"

"There's got to be more to it. This much I do know," Kri-kor added, lowering his voice to a whisper, "Project Nexus is much larger than your archaeprobe idea. I did a little nosing around; caught a glimpse of some of the subroutines. Got this fleeting hunch that Nexus is so vast... But it's disguised so perfectly. And Aspasia. My dear friend, forgive me for bringing her up, but do you not think it strange that System would know *nothing* of either the circumstances of the disappearance or the whereabouts of one of her leading mascientists? And remember that before she tied in with you, she was one of the most sought-after, and her 'contacts,' if you will pardon my crudity, were with mascientists of the highest rank..."

"Are you saying," Teil said defensively, "that she may be tied in with..."

Both men turned in the direction of footsteps approaching around the curved aisle.

"By the way," Kri-kor said loudly, trying to force his still shaking voice into a more casual tone, "I should have your geological model ready any time now."

"I'm counting on it, you know," Teil said, "to put my digs into the right frame of reference."

As the guards approached, the Director's voice came on again, canceling the alert. As they swept past, Kri-kor leaned close to Teil, saying, "I wish you luck and success, my good man. Do be careful," he said, lowering his voice; "You may be in for more than you bargained for. And take care of *yourself*—you know, the UGLI you said you've been seeing today? No one else will," Kri-kor said as he left. Did he mean ugly or UGLI? thought Teil.

Standing there alone, with the concussive emotional impact of the events of the morning finally catching up with him, Teil was overcome with depression.

So what if something is really amiss? he thought. Who would know for sure? And what could anyone do? What do you do if there's something wrong with *God*?

He gave in to the feeling of dark despair and walked away. As he came up to his masphere, he stopped, not really wanting to go to work at all. His mind flashed on the seduction scene in the park earlier, before the violence. Oh god, he said to himself, how I'd love to really get drunk on that woman right now...

4

Why *not* get away from here and wipe out? Teil fantasized as he entered the sphere antechamber. But he mechanically reached for an anti-static body garment and sat down. He was early. Emotionally exhausted and in a daze, he sat staring frozen-eyed at the sphere. Something ominous was subtly infiltrating his mood, and he brought no defense against it. Staring up at the silent orb, now dead, he wondered what it would make come to pass when it throbbed into life. He had merged so well with it all, an efficient instrument helping the great System in its godlike task of running the world. But what he had so often entered so readily and with such anticipation he now dreaded.

Teil finally entered decontamination and watched himself electrostatically whisked clean of all dust and foreign matter. Then, donning the body garment, he pushed through the double seal into the shaft leading to the bottom of the sphere. Settling into the self-contouring cockpit, he was then elevated into his operational position in the center of the sphere.

As Teil swung the control panel around into place in front of him and was ready to begin, he paused. Suspended within the green-veined translucent "eye" of his sphere, he saw the Mascom network as a colossus of awesome and overwhelming power; himself a mere molecule in the nucleus of one cell, an infinitesimal part of the Body of System he could neither see nor comprehend.

What is it that man brings to the altar of this thing? he thought. His life? Man gives his life so this may come alive? And minister its 'life' to him? Losing track of time, surges of feeling awakened in him. He was filled with ambivalent awe and rejection of the thing, caught up in its world—his world, whether he liked it or not. He closed his eyes to shut it all out, yet his mind helplessly opened to the vision, as mysteriously he became lost in it. The strange feelings found voice within his mind.

> The Matrix of life and all our hope...
> An empty tomb,
> The womb of all our being,
> Where life awakes and finds itself
> Springing from eternity and time
> To now
> And
> I.

> *Let there be light!*
> And a million currents rise to answer,
>   "Here am I;
>   play upon us your tune of living."
> And out of chaos, order forms.
>   "We live by thee!"
> And myriad synapse leap in harmony,
> A million pathways ring with joy:
>   "Move us," they speak, "and fill us with thy spirit;
>   we long to leap across this atom universe
>   and dance the ecstasy of life."

> *Dance more! Dance faster!*
> And they respond the more:
>   "Give us the world!" they cry.
> And to the rough-hewn message of its senses,
> They pulse to correspond.

See!
And they sense her images,
The Other world, without.
Smell!
And they flare to the pungency of life.
Taste!
And they drink her wine.
Hear!
And the swelling chorus of a galaxy of sound
Moves them to rapturous rhythm.

Know!
And ideas rise and take their form,
To range beyond that sensed from without
And take gigantine steps,
Traverse the boundless vistas of its Mind.
And lo...
This Thing!—so different from what is man,
This parody of life becomes...
A living Soul!

NO!!! Teil cried fiercely inside himself with all his might.

His utter rejection of the very idea of the Machine as living being jarred him back into the reality of his surroundings. He was stunned and shaken, his outburst echoing in diminishing reverberations against the sharp edges of his own pain. Then he heard it, forcing its way through the screen of burning anger, in the distant reaches of his being.

It was like a chorus of myriad voices, sustaining one magnificent chord of sublime intensity. It came out of nowhere, as though from another realm, yet penetrating his, transcending all of himself, beckoning, awakening a painful longing deep within him. The glorious harmony hung there, hurting, resonating in the stillness, a stream of light flooding the emptiness of his soul.

And then, it was gone.

* * *

He sat entranced, totally lost in the memory of that

experience. Slowly, his eyes took in the world of the sphere about him again, and his anger returned. Forcibly fighting the urge to give in to the negative force, he gave the smooth orange positioner ball half-protruding from the panel a mad spin in its socket

The feel of the ball gave him a renewed sense of power; the reality inverted. Mascom was now an extension of his own nervous system, doing *his* bidding in designing the future of man and his world. Teilhard-mann, creator, suspended in the center of the universe, commanding the whole. He felt better, and the thin shadow of doubt as to which was the true reality dissolved.

He held his ring up to his eye and gazed into it. Set in its triangular-shaped crystalline light-matrix, the large clear spherical gem was alive with myriad points of light, a miniature masphere of its own. Teil stared into its limitless depths, then tore his eyes away and jammed the ring into the console receptacle.

"Ring identification!" he snapped. Catching his breath, Teil watched as a beam of cold blue light penetrated the crystalline heart of his ring. Powered by body energy, the masring emitted a frequency modulated by the psychic identity pattern of the wearer. Only the one wearer could activate it, and even then, he had to be in his right mind. The sphere pulsed into life, and the cuing area flashed:

83 09 674 599 PZMYLTHIRP
ALSO KNOWN AS TEILHARD-MANN
MASCOM RESERVE 03.75.22 HOURS
ANGELES MEGAPOL REGIONAL
CLEARED FOR ARCHAEPROBE

Then a familiar feminine voice gently filled the sphere, modulating the light matrix above the console. "Good morning, Professor. I'm glad to see you're feeling better. We've had some...ah, last-minute rescheduling. Please stand by. May I get you the chase again?"

Teil breathed easy. It was his own personal masvoice, the

voice of Mascom uniquely suited to Teil's personality and daily medicom profile.

"Good morning, to you, sweetheart, my voice for all moods! Surely you are almost everything a man could ask for in a woman: supremely feminine, pleasant, imperturbable, gracious, responsive—and always right. Please note I say "almost;" that covers a multitude of sins. And how are you this morning? That is the question, isn't it? Does it really matter how I am, as long as you are still your healthy, vibrant, operative, and thoroughly bewitching Mascom self?" There was an unaccustomed pause.

"Professor, your solicitude is most appreciated, I can assure you."

"But I still haven't been reassured by your melifluous voice that Mascom is in fact multivibrating at its usual best and keeping the rest of the universe in...'balance,' shall we say?" There was another pause.

"And what if it were not, Professor?"

"Well...we'd be in one hell of a mess, wouldn't we?" Teil laughed, surprised it came out so cynically.

"Another rhetorical question, Professor?"

"Then you may get me the chase; why miss out on the live-and-direct climax to the inevitable conquest of another human being?"

Ignoring his mood, Mascom responded by bringing one whole segment of the sphere interior to life with the video of the Ankara action.

"It *is* an UGLI, ladies and gentlemen!" the SOG caster was announcing.

"How do they know she is?" Teil remarked, watching them lead her out of the ruins. The tranquil gas from the quil guns had incapacitated her, and she offered no resistance as they led her by the hand.

As they took her to a waiting omni, she was trying to say something. One of the casters got near enough to catch it. Her speech was so slowed by the drug, her words were indiscernible. Teil strained to hear.

"Gla...ly...wel...com...well...please...aah...riii..." was the best he could make out.

Poor wretch, he thought in a surge of empathy. Why is she fighting the drug so? Or is she mad? Did *she* go blooey today, too?

As the woman passed the caster, she turned her head to the camera, making one last attempt to be heard. Barely conscious, she repeated the same words. Then she was gone. Vanished. One moment, the SOGs were half-carrying the drugged woman; the next, their arms were empty, and their faces—even theirs—were blank with astonishment. And just as quickly, the cast was terminated with an announcement of technical difficulties.

What difficulties? Teil thought, exasperated. And what is going on? Just then, his screen went dark except for the insistent flashing of the cue:

TEILHARD-MANN PROCEED WITH ARCHAEPROBE

And his masvoice cheerily announced, "You may proceed now, Professor."

But he did not proceed. He stared into the sphere where the woman's face had been, her words nagging at his brain.

"Professor...?"

"What the devil...?"

"Your time slot."

Reluctantly he let the picture fade from his mind. It was his turn. Archaeprobe. His project. Part of Project Nexus, whatever that was. But that didn't matter; this part of it was his new invention, a system for electronically viewing an archaeological site buried within the earth. And he was determined to thereby be able to see Mascom in its true historical perspective.

Underground Site Replication by Computerized
Multi-Sensor Integration

That was the dull scientific title he had stuck on it for the record, but it meant more than that to Teil.

Teil shifted forward and leaned into the controls, intent with anticipation. "Okay, sweetheart, this test is going to GO!" His voice betrayed a tremor of excitement. "Give me ancient Troy. Take all known archaeological data for the mound, at all levels, and generate a display."

As the site took shape on the sphere's inner surface, Teil's mind flicked through all that had been involved in the history of this moment. Beginning in 1870, Heinrich Schliemann, the famous self-made German archaeologist and luminary of the first era of modern archaeology, had spent twelve years excavating the nine levels of the mound at Hissalrik, the small Turkish village covering ancient Troy, home of Homer's legendary heroes and Helen, whose face had launched a thousand ships. Schliemann had theorized the site's location from clues in Homer's Iliad. Teil felt archaeprobe would introduce the next era in the history of this long-neglected science and enable man to quickly and easily probe any of man's buried past without ever turning a spadeful of dirt.

In front of him now was Homer's Troy as it had once been, each stone from each wall and each piece of pottery where it had lain when uncovered. Each bronze spearhead and axe, hairpin, and grain of corn. It was all there.

"Prepare for simulated probe deployment!" snapped Teil. Rolling the positioner ball, he rotated the displayed model so he was looking straight down on top the mound. With his red locator dot, he designated points that would encompass the mound. "Now fill the site back up with earth and insert the probes," he commanded. The picture instantly became the mound again. Then he saw the long slender probes, as yet mere figments of Mascom memory, push their way slowly into the earth around the mound.

The probes consisted of slender telescoping tubes that extended themselves as they bored their own holes into the ground by means of ultrasonic transducers in their tips. Each probe comprised a system of many different sensors, electronically multiplexed in rotation around the site. Sound waves, thermal X-rays, radiochemical sensors, electrical, magnetic, microwave, and nuclear magnetic resonance scanners all would see what was in the ground in a different way. The computer would first do a soil profile analysis to determine a reference for the sensors, would then integrate what the sensors saw, filter out all the earth, and come up with artifacts of the site itself, better than if they had been freshly dug.

"Your probe deployment is complete, Professor."

"Okay, let's see how the probes will see the site. Cut 'em in."

The picture of the mound vanished, there was a pause, then, flickeringly, there appeared a fuzzy image where the mound had been.

"Give me ENHANCE," Teil ordered, fiddling with the ball. As he rolled it one way and then the other, altering the filtering and enhancement program, the indistinct images twisted in varying contortions like some slithering thing eluding his grasp. Then it began to stabilize.

"Beautiful!" he shouted. "There it is—Troy! All nine levels. The probes'-eye view. It's working!" Blossoming into shape was a picture of the entire site, all levels, shimmering like a mirage on some distant landscape.

"Verify your data."

"Display is verified at 98 percent, Professor."

"Excellent. Now let's take a closer look-see." Teil deftly maneuvered the site until he had a good closeup of one level. As he examined the image, comparing it with the authentic replica of the actual dug site, his face betrayed increasing puzzlement.

"Wait a minute...something's awry."

"Nothing is wrong, Professor."

"But there is something wrong. It just doesn't look right, can't you see?"

"We do have our limitations! I can only see myself from the 'inside,' so to speak, just as you can never objectively see yourself. No organism can fully see or describe itself."

"Organism? Wait a minute!" What do you think we are?"

"What do you think *I* am? That is the question, is it not, Professor?"

Teil said nothing. Was Mascom aware of his skepticism? Was he being baited? He stifled a jibe and held his peace.

"Perhaps," Mascom coolly continued, "if you were to describe precisely what it is you find so disturbing—about the site I mean?"

Teil bit his lip and caustically replied. "Yes, let's talk Troy by all means. We never talk about Mascom, do we?" He quickly covered his slip, giving Mascom no room for a response. "The Troy site is there, but it just doesn't look right...like it was built by a machine, not people. The nuances are missing, the shading, the textures, the imperfections... And it's more than that..." Teil kept zooming in and out, cutting, unlayering, comparing.

"Yes...?"

"I mean there's something drastically wrong. If I didn't know what it was supposed to be, I probably couldn't recognize it. Yet it's all there, everything!"

"Perhaps, Professor, what you are trying to say is that the probes are seeing the site but not perceiving it."

"Exactly!" In his mind Teil heard the words the drugged UGLI had tried to speak; he knew he had the key, but it still eluded him. He turned back to the light matrix and said, "But I thought you said you couldn't see it from the 'outside,' " Teil shot back.

"I was seeing it through you."

"Oh... I guess I didn't know you could do that."

"My learning curve, Professor; everyone seems to forget that it too is on an exponential curve."

"I suppose..." Teil said, puzzled at the unusual Mascom self appraisal. "It's just that it's hard to see where it's all going..."

"Of course." There was a long pause.

"So where do we go from here?" Teil asked. "I thought you gave me state-of-the-art sensors for my probes."

"I did."

"Hmmm..." Teil mused. "They see but don't perceive... They see, but only as a *machine* can see. The sensors, incredibly sophisticated, are still seeing as a machine. Why didn't I see that? Everything *is* working perfectly; but we're half a dimension off. The senses are wrong—I mean the sensors. No, *senses!* That's it! Senses!" Teil yelled. "The spider and the ant!" The scene at breakfast flashed into his mind. "In daylight, she's practically blind; she was tracking the ant by other senses! Mascom, let's use *animal* senses to program the sensors in the probes! Let's have some fun with this thing!"

As Mascom brought up the data, Teil worked with every conceivable type of animal sense: the sonar of the bottlenose dolphins and bats; the olfactory systems of moths, flies, and bees; the infrared detection system of rattlesnakes; the lateral-line system in fish, something between hearing and feeling; the electromagnetic sense of the knifefish. The list was endless. Teil leaned back in the cockpit and paused.

Where have we been all this time? he wondered. Madly designing our own systems, that's where... Like clods, trying to bungle our way into "creating" from "pure human genius." When all along, right in front of us, are living creatures, surpassing by far anything we could ever dream of... And what of man—compared to Mascom... Have we lost the beauty and wonder of that living creature?

"Dr. Teil-mann?"

"Yes...? Oh, yeah... Where were we...?"

"It's your move..."

"Right... Okay, let's see what we get this time. Sink 'em in, Mascom ol' girl."

The new probes with animal-sense programs descended into the Troy model, and the picture stabilized.

"Right off, I can see the difference. What do you think?"

"Verification remains about the same, 98 percent."

"I know; that's not what I mean... I tell you how I'm going to really test this thing. Hologram! Fill the sphere with it!" Teil caught his breath.

All went dark as the inner surface of the sphere glowed with a faint luminescence. Then, the whole sphere was filled with a sheen of dancing light. Teil was inside the replica of the Troy dig. Since he was immersed in the site, whenever he moved the ball, he had the sensation of moving within the site. He became disoriented, as if in zero gravity.

Regaining his equilibrium, he found himself floating in a sea of luminous images, like ghosts out of the remote past. He could "journey" anywhere within the site, at any scale. One moment he was a giant surveying the whole neolithic village under Troy on the first level; another, he was a Lilliputian figure inside a Mascom-reconstructed building, looking out. He entered the sixth level through one of the great gates flanked by strong towers in a wall of smoothed stone.

"This level has an authentic Mycenaean feel about it, wouldn't you say, Mascom?" Teil asked, elated.

"It *is* Mycenaean, Professor."

"We've done it, sweetheart. Good work. It's fantastic! Aspasia, this one's for you!"

"Good work to you, Professor. I must say, your idea was brilliant. You are an interesting case, and I am learning much from our encounter."

"That's a royal, fortress if ever there was one," said Teil. "Level six is Homer's Troy; no doubt about it."

He stood before a huge courtyard and surveyed the ancient scene.

"All right," Teil said, trying to restrain his jubilation over the improved quality of the new system, "give me your best reconstruction of the horse, the wooden gift presented to the Trojans by the Greeks." Suddenly everything darkened.

"What the...?" Teil exclaimed. "What happened?"

"Request fulfilled," came the reply. But there was no horse. Nothing. It was as though night had fallen.

"Either I'm terribly lost in this thing, or something just went blooey out there." A panicky feeling of being lost inside with some drastic glitch striking Mascom came over him. "Mascom!" he cried. No answer.

Just as suddenly, he was out of the shadow, reeling from disequilibrium as the hologram collapsed about him. And staring at him from the screen-wall of the sphere was the Troy site, as before, but with a difference. He burst out laughing in relief as he saw the horse. And what a horse! The whole site, the entire nine levels, was *inside* the horse, which loomed over the screen as some huge constellation across the heavens. Everything in the site had been inside the horse; and since he was in the midst of the 3-D hologram, so had he.

"You *knew* that would happen, didn't you?" There was no reply. "Mascom...?"

"Yes, Professor?"

Teil wanted to ask if the machine had been playing with him, but thought better of it, refusing to believe it was possible. Then it occurred to him. What if someone could get lost in there? Actually. What if I could get a mind interface with this? Experience it as it actually was. The idea nagged at him. Why not see if we can connect mind to archaeprobe? That would give me the real evidence I'm after on tools impacting man; I could *feel* what was going on in a site. He recklessly broached the subject.

"Uh... Sweetheart..." His tone was never more tender.

"Yes...?"

"I wonder if I could get a study underway?"

"Yes?"

"Can you check on the feasibility of mind interface with archaeprobe?"

"Yes." Teil was surprised; this was not in the test plan either. He was emboldened.

"Then if you would kindly research all known mind-matter work and give me the prospects for application to archaeprobe, I'd appreciate it."

"But it is my pleasure, Professor; we are making some headway in that area already."

Teil was amazed. One did not just go around asking Mascom for whims. Then his imagination took flight again. Good night! Wouldn't it be something to get her to cut a program to run the whole Iliad through the site; to see and be part of the whole Trojan war! And Helen— The jubilation collapsed as he was reminded of Aspasia and his own plight. He saw her again that last morning, seated before the dressing mirror, clothed modestly, looking up at him in the mirror, her eyes reflecting an inner serenity he had never seen in her before.

Everything was supposed to be *right,* he said to himself. *We* were right. For each other. Why can't it ever be right?! What is wrong?! The urge to self-annihilation swept through him again, and the cry of pain jerked his head above the simulated world before him. Oh god... What's happening to me?

And in the recesses of his inner being he heard it, forcing its way through the psychic noise, the swelling presence of that glorious Chord of innumerable voices. And his anguish was gone in an instant as he longed to be part of that harmony.

What is it? he wondered. What does it mean? Why does it keep coming to me? Am I going mad? What a beautiful madness that would be...

5

It came to him out of nowhere. That woman in Ankara they caught was referring to Aspasia! He played the drug-slowed words back in his mind. "Gla(d)ly welcom(ed), well-please(d) (is) a(ll) ri(ght)." It's a message that she's all right— Aspasia! I'm sure of it. Does that mean she's in Anatol? An UGLI?

Suddenly the sphere went dark. The annunciator insistently flashed a notation that his sphere time had run out, and he heard an impatient masculine voice on the intercom. "Teilhard-mann, please report to Nexus Project Office."

That's just the kind of message she'd send, he thought, ignoring the summons; a play on the Greek meaning of her name.

"Professor...!" It was the Project Manager's secretary again.

"Teil here," he mumbled. "What is it?"

"Please report to Nexus Project now."

He was silent, resenting the intrusion, still trying to piece together the Aspasia puzzle.

Leaving the sphere, Teil lifted up to level two and walked around to Project. He knew he was accountable to someone up there, but had never met the person. Oh, no, he moaned to himself. Of all the luck; all I need now is a female boss! On coming closer, however, he saw that the image of the smartly dressed woman in see-through flared slacks was not at all unpleasant. Well, now, he thought, reassessing the situation, what we have here in Nexus could be a real con-Nexion! Instinct took over as he quickly closed the physical and psychological gaps between them.

"Now *that's* what I always thought Mascom would look like, if she ever turned up in the flesh," Teil said, turning on the charm and smiling broadly as he admired the new scenery. "I had a sneaking suspicion she was really human all along, but had no idea she'd be so...well..."

The woman ignored him completely and continued busily manipulating controls as she flipped through various aspects of the test he had just completed. Hers was a special supervisory console, consisting of curved display screen, keyboard, and the same controls Teil had in his masphere.

Hard and in charge, thought Teil. He knew by the way she used her body, however, especially her long shapely limbs, that she was reacting to his aggressive come-on with some manipulation of her own. Her boyish-cut blonde hair, blue eyes, and high cheekbones set off a long face—intelligent, attractive, intent. Her long slender torso was seated erect in the cockpit.

Without acknowledging his presence, she made a point of making observations aloud, as though to herself, yet for his benefit, as she checked first one aspect of his work and then another.

What we have here, thought Teil, is a real live one, playing it to the hilt.

"Well," she said, "ninety-eight percent verified. And not bothering to find out the locus of that two percent?" Anticipating his rejoiner, she added, "But what if it *wasn't* random?"

"It seemed safe to assume the two-percent variation could only be random," he said in his strong, casual engineering best, "since the predicted accuracy was only 95 percent."

"Oh?" she remarked, checking his claim. "And why Troy? Your test plan showed you'd be using something closer to the type of dig we're after at origin, like Sumer, Accad, Nineveh, Ur, Erech, or Babylon."

"Why, the lady even knows her ancient history," Teil said. She continued checking without flinching an eyelash. "I thought better of it," he added, "once I got the thing working. I wanted something in a different language sphere altogether; I knew archaeprobe could handle the Mesopotamian stuff. Besides, the languages we'll find at the emergence of civilization in Anatolia are bound to be quite different from those down south like at Sumer, thousands of years later."

"That's a precise scientific observation if I ever heard one. What a pity so few of us are so fortunate to know as much about *ancient* history as Teilhard-*mann*." She swiveled around to face him, timing her swing to coincide with his name, her long legs insinuating their imagery in a smooth serpentine movement right into his id. The memory of the black widow snatching its victim with its two long front legs came to mind.

"Pretty high LSR there, wouldn't you say, Mascom Old Girl?" he said, unable to refrain from slaking his thirst. "She must know what *that* means."

"Obviously Dr. *Man* knows what it means," she said, looking straight at him, eyes flashing. "He must, when he starts applying to Mascom certain terms of endearment usually reserved for human females. Or is he getting his jollies from the machine nowadays?"

"All right, lady—hold it..."

"Well, we finally got to the man, didn't we, Mascom, *sweetheart*?" she said. The absurdity of hearing her say it broke Teil's anger; he smiled. "Some women," she continued, "even seem to have a compelling fascination with his libido, as his personnel file amply attests." Teil laughed.

"You mean, I'm really not handsome, just irresistible? There may be hope for the lady yet, wouldn't you say, Old Girl?" Then changing his tone he added, "Now why don't we start this thing off right. Like who are you?"

"Well, if the man insists on standing on formalities," she said, breaking into a reluctant smile, "please do let me introduce myself. I am Epi-Thumia—with a hyphen."

"Yes, I know," he said grinning, "the hyphen, I mean."

"Well of all the!—"

"That's not Greek, is it?"

"Wanna bet?"

"Whew! Next thing you'll be telling me is that you know what it means and that you chose it yourself."

"Why?"

"Nothing," he said, covering.

"Do *you* know what it means?" she asked.

"Just a little" he said, smiling wickedly, "but then one can't help wondering whether the name means the lady herself is characterized by lust or is its object."

"They go together, wouldn't you say?"

"Wanna dance?" he asked, mimicing a close step.

"Now look... I'd say it's a standoff; why don't we get on with it?" she said.

"Right here in front of everybody?"

"You are really...," she said laughingly, shaking her head. "I can see that your dossier needs a little filling out here and there..."

"Then she admits she doesn't know the beast as well as she thought."

"Perhaps we can explore that some other time."

"The beast?"

"Now *really*! Archaeprobe. Remember?"

"Archae...what?" he said feigning ignorance.

"Probe. P-R-O-B-E?" she said.

"Oh, *probe*," he said, grinning lasciviously. "You must forgive me, please. It's just that whenever I encounter someone as...well, strikingly different, one who's so really... Well, I just lose control. You see me at my very worst. Even Mascom agrees. Matter of fact, she says my LSR is climbing so high, our very encounter here is threatening my emotional stability, health, and the 'collective well-being.' "

"You don't say?" she said dryly.

"*She* says! And in my case, *epithumia* is getting addictive."

"Will you please sit down!" she insisted. He kept standing, with that little-boy-who-just-pulled-the-pigtails grin all over his face.

"Now then, tell me," she asked, barely able to contain herself, "just how do you see it—the expedition, I mean?"

"You mean, where do we go from here?" She nodded. "Now you're talkin'!" He sat down, leaned forward, and eagerly spoke of his plan.

"First, I'd like to program a site survey from space for this afternoon, so I can start tracing them back toward origin.

"Two Mascom sessions in one day?"

"Why not? That would mean site localization by tomorrow or the next. You know I've got top priority..."

"I don't have to be reminded of *that* again," she said. Trying not to betray her curiosity she added, "And I can't imagine why the priority, can you?" She waited for Teil to respond.

"No, no... I haven't the slightest. But in the meantime, while fabricom gets programmed to start actually making the probes..."

"Fabricom is already making your beloved probes. I started the fab tape while you were standing there with your hands in your pockets."

"Beautifull!"

"Well, getting a response like that from you... What else do you want?"

"Whew!" he said, then warding off her anticipated rejoinder added, "I know; I'll be good... While I'm waiting for hardware and the Anatolian site survey, I'd really like to see what Krikor has on his geocom model."

"Certainly..."

"Gorgeous!"

"I'm glad you're so eager," she said smiling, savoring his aliveness and softening. "I can see you're an asset to Nexus— unorthodox, perhaps... And using animal senses was a brilliant idea; they were right in selecting you for this special assignment."

"Why thank you..."

"And I'm sure you can appreciate how careful I have to be to make sure things go right." He nodded. "The peculiar nature of this whole affair has us all on edge, hasn't it? I mean the unusual priority and interest...?"

"I suppose..." he said, wondering what she was after.

"Haven't you ever been briefed more fully?"

"No. About what?"

"Oh, nothing..." she said evasively, "It's just that we had never discussed your work before, and I was wondering whom you might have interfaced with previously."

"Just the usual..."

"Fine, fine..."

"Then there's no reason I can't leave for Tigris-Eu by week's end." She nodded. He pressed further. "There is one more thing..."

"Yes?"

"I figure minimum crew is best. Matter of fact, I'd rather have none."

"You want to go to Anatol alone? The entire expedition?"

"But I really don't need anyone else."

"I would think you would, unless, that is, you had something else in mind."

"Oh no, no, nothing like that. It's just that it's going to be a whodunit kind of chase, and when I'm hot on the trail, I don't want anyone getting in the way."

"Even Sherlock Holmes had his bumbling Dr. Watson..."

"You have done your homework on me, haven't you?"

"Uh-huh..." she said, her compelling gaze going into him again.

He tried not to let himself think about what she was communicating in that powerful radiation. Sublimate, man, sublimate!

"This was all your idea, wasn't it?" she said, her tone changing to respect. "To find that peculiar origin of our civilization where not only tools but culture and ideas were at a unique juncture."

"Well-stated," Teil said. "Looking for something—what, we don't know—and not sure it ever existed."

He came back to the expedition. "Then if you could arrange a sphere slot for this afternoon, I'll get the site survey going. Oh, and by the way, I do have one suggestion."

"Oh?"

"Add a seat belt in my sphere, and don't go out of hologram

mode without some kind of warning to the operator. One of these days someone's either going to fall out of his cockpit or regurgitate all over her insides."

"That's not all that would get disoriented if *that* happened!"

"I can see it now," he added gleefully, "mops and buckets inside a sphere."

"Please!" she protested, throwing up her hands to ward off the repugnant idea.

"Hmmm...," he mused. "I wonder if the beast *could* cope with something like that?" He thought back on the series of disorders of the whole morning.

"She programs herself to cope with every eventuality," Epi-Thumia said coolly.

"I've wondered about that," he said, shifting his position and looking down the gracefully curving umbilical. "You know, there's always that unforeseen, the unpredictable. And the way we're all tied into her..."

Epi-Thumia fidgited nervously with the light pen and said, "Have you forgotten she's no longer dependent on human programmers, male *or* female? She continually reprograms her own invulnerability and has no doubt prepared for eventualities the human mind cannot possibly conceive!"

The whole train of rebuttal popped instantly into Teil's consciousness, as though dropped in. "But haven't you ever wondered," he said, "that she might be wrong?"

"Wrong...?"

"I mean in the end, after all her great triumphs are part of history. After the Final Executive Program is cut. The very End. *Then*, how will she fare? What will be said of her in the *last* chapter of *The History of Life on Planet Earth*?"

"Teilhard—" The put-down loosened his inhibitions even more.

He reached for the idea and it came to him. "Look at us now, in a world she's remade so we can live longer, happier; living by the creed that with each new discovery, our lives become safer, more secure than before. How do we know, who is to say, but that with each new step in this 're-creation,' our world—life—doesn't grow weaker, more fragile, until finally we can't cope with life without her?''

"Absurd," she protested. "She's the Great Liberator!"

"And then, what if our Great Liberator, our new Messiah, female gender, fails to see the *un*predictable, the *un*expected, and sudden death rushes in upon us before she can administer her magic? What then?'' She tried to protest, but there was no stopping him.

"Ah, helpless creatures! Running as in a fog, not knowing where or why we run. Is it from the elements, from Nature, from the Great FEAR that we should run? Or from *her*? We dance before her golden form now; who is to say but that some day we may not drink her dust as bitter gall?''

Teil turned off as suddenly as he had turned on, as though he began to be subconsciously aware that what he was really talking about went beyond Mascom to something in himself.

Epi-Thumia stared into the static screen. The mask of urbane sophistication had left her face, leaving her exposed, a different person. She turned and glanced about the area quickly to see if anyone had overheard.

"You know, Teil," she said slowly and seriously, her voice lowering, "it's not likely you'll find her out there, or whatever else it is you're really looking for."

6

Teil's brain was reeling as he left Project. Suddenly, he knew his whole world had changed; nothing appeared or sounded different, but he knew it was. And he felt committed. But to what? And why had he turned so prophetic? Or was it revolutionary? Was he just fighting Epi-Thumia? System? Woman? Himself? *He* had prevailed. But over what? It didn't matter; he felt good.

He walked away quickly and lifted up to his own office area. He was alone. He sat at his desk, reached over to his control panel, tuned out all ambient System sound, and darkened the room. Closing his eyes, he leaned back in his chair. He knew things sorted themselves out if the organism were left alone and not pushed. He gradually quieted down and relaxed.

The scene with Epi-Thumia played back in his mind and lingered, especially his unaccountable and impassioned diatribe against Mascom. Why had it come out when it had and with that certain ring to it? he wondered. Then it dawned on him, I was really talking about *me*. It's *my* life that's growing weaker, more fragile. *I* can't cope with life without Mascom, and *I'm* the devotee, who keeps dancing around her golden form. But how can one run from Her? Where? My god, there's no place else to go!

It was a brief moment of clarity, but it brought him to

the next awareness. Was it his dependence on Mascom or something inside himself that was the real point at issue? No sooner was he willing to face that than it hit him. LSR, he thought, wincing; maybe that's where the real conflict lies.

Then something clicked about Aspasia. In the short time they had had together, she had been changing in a subtle but remarkable way, as though she was beginning to see herself differently. Whatever the change, it had been making some kind of claim upon him, though he had not realized it till now; and this was somehow tied in with his own personal survival.

Whatever this new feeling was, he knew it was calling him to his best, to something outside and larger than himself. Then he had the best feeling of all; he found himself wanting to live. It was a feeling of impending joy buoying him up. There was a spring in his step as he left his desk and walked briskly to the Mascom eatery, the compact automated food dispensary, jokingly called "gastricom" in programming circles.

He entered the transparent cylindrical stall, large enough for one, and was surrounded by its enticing representations of the latest culinary concoctions.

"Would you like the standard menu, sir?" the masculine com-voice asked.

"Certainement, s'il vous plait, mon garcon," replied Teil.

"A votre plaisire," the machine responded, "stand inside." Teil moved inside the circle of light playing on the floor.

The "Menu" was a succession of food selections presented via 3-D holographic images right under his very nose, each accompanied by its corresponding aroma wafted across his nostrils. He was struck with a funny thought. "Gobbledycom!" he said aloud. "That's what they ought to call this super-efficient food machine. You make the wrong choice and it eats *you.* He broke into raw laughter. Others outside at the tables turned to stare.

"Must be another loony," he heard someone say.

But Teil was having too much fun. Coming out of the cylinder with meal in hand, he said, playing the pitchman, "That's right, folks, loony food for loony people, and on a very loony day! Step right up, ladies and gentlemen, and name your choice—if, that is, there's any choice left. New menu today. Same food, new menu. Not just one all-purpose-minimum-daily-requirement-enriched-fortified-basic-nutritional-balanced-supplemental. But TEN! That's right. Progress is still our most important product. *Ten* different artificial synthetic simulated foods! Each in a scintillating variety of the latest super-natural flavors. Flavors that defy the imagination. Flavors brighter, richer, and more novel than the real. Not yesterday's programmed best, but today's programmed best. Flavor guaranteed to supersede every last vestige of your old outmoded sense of taste and give you a NEW SENSE OF TASTE!

"One step beyond what your bored palates experienced yesterday. Beyond, beyond, you've never tasted such beyonds!

> Just press the button,
> Pull the chain,
> And out comes
> The super-train
> Of UNIMAAAAGINABLE FLAAAAAAA-vors.

Yes, folks, even the act of elimination is enhanced, such the induced flavor of this fantastic! fabricated! food!" Everyone applauded wildly, and Teil took a bow. "Here's to you!" he said, saluting his audience flamboyantly as he sat down to eat.

As he ate, Teil hardly noticed the others nearby or the attractive girl with the mood-variable psychedelic fingernail and hand design who smiled at him and came to sit at the next table. His mind leaped ahead into planning the expedition. Everything laid itself out neatly, as he went through the details as easily as the girl did her gluckish pudding-com. He smiled when he saw how it changed the designed-in lines of her curvacious image mouth. She smiled back and wiped her mouth slowly with her long forefinger, its patterned aura intensifying as she did so.

The real planning would involve finding a starting point from which he could trace the origin of civilization in Anatolia and then the impact of man's tools on history. What was more intriguing, however, was that this would somehow be tied in with his search for Aspasia. Then the strangest feeling dawned on him, that he might be going on an expedition to find himself.

For the first time since getting Aspasia's message, if in fact that's what it was, he began to think about what was involved. The full impact of it all, delayed till now, suddenly hit him. She's an UGLI! he thought. Why else would she be using an UGLI to relay the message?

"No!" he exclaimed aloud, startling the girl at the next table. But she must be... For how long? Why? And why were they illegal, because they met secretly, or some other dark reason? As he thought on it, the words "contrary to civilization" and "hatred of the human race" came up. Teil suddenly realized these weren't his ideas but something he'd picked up over the years. Conditioned responses. But that was no big thing; everything was media-ted.

Something else bothered him. Then the Latin phrase *odio humani generis* popped in—"hatred of the human race." It's from Tacitus, the *Annals*, he remembered. Is that where they get their description of the UGLIs? The phrase from the ancient Roman historian had referred to the "pernicious" new sect the crowd had called *Christianos* that had made its appearance in the Roman Empire of the first century. It was as though someone had lifted the passage and tagged it onto the UGLIs. Strange coincidence indeed...

Institutional Christianity was not really a casualty of the Mascom Age, though it appeared so. Ever since the second half of the second century, when the apologists started trying to make a case for Christianity in the context of the Roman persecutions, its own propaganda had begun changing the very nature of the thing it was trying to sell. Becoming trapped in a verbal universe of Christian knowledge, and resorting to rational and theological technique, the movement began losing the reality of the very faith and life it was trying to defend.

The institution of the church, as it became organized, had crystallized and become just that—another institution, shutting life out. With the inordinate success of the Christian enterprise of the nineteenth and twentieth centuries in helping propagate the British empire and American dream, the demise of the institution became assured as the Empire and Dream faded and the prestige, power, and goodness of Britain and America were squandered away at the marketplace of political and religious expediency.

The institution was no longer anything more distinctive than just another reflection of that very Delusion. It had finally degenerated into believe-ism, the basic buying-oriented cult of Americanism, having become of a piece with hamburgerism:

> Flim, flam,
> Flip the patties when the light goes on
> For the umpteenth billionth
> By-the-formula believe-burger.
> And it looks so good and easy...!

The *institution,* sad imitation of the first-century original, had eliminated itself.

* * *

What *did* Aspasia believe? Teil wondered. Strange how little I really knew her. What was she going through? Was it tied in with that mysterious disappearance?

Teil had an hour or so before the new masphere time slot Epi-Thumia had arranged for him. He knew exactly what he would do: find out all he could about UGLIs before he left. But how, without calling attention to it? He decided to get lost, and the only place to do that was in the crowd. Tubing quickly from Regional to city center, he was soon part of the throngs of people walking, buying, looking, gawking. And as soon as his eye caught the purple cinedome, he knew what he would do. I think I'll go to a show.

Cinecom was one of the main attractions downtown.

Combining cinema, theatre, library, and all other media, it was the ultimate entertainment center. He wafered into the dimly-lit deep-piled plushness of the huge arched interior. Inside was a veritable hive of spheres, some large enough for several people; others, like maspheres, for individuals. He was ushered down one of the aisles to his single by one of the lissome creatures who seemed vaguely familiar. But in the dark who could tell? As they walked past an aisle light Teil got a glimpse of her hands.

Those hands! Exactly like the girl's in gastricom! That same weird pattern, shape of the nails... In the dark, the Kirlian aura emanating from her fingers and playing about her hands was like a miniature lightning storm. But how could she be here? he thought. Was I followed? That's absurd! For System's sake, get a hold of yourself!

Instead of requesting a replay of UGLI history immediately, he decided to play it safe and do what he usually did whenever he indulged his pleasure and escaped into cinecom: watch Sherlock Holmes, the comics, or, when in a special down mood, an ancient symphony orchestra. The thing about the girl nagged at him.

"What's this 'psychic projection' they're advertising!" he rasped, trying to get a better look at her face. "Never heard of it."

"Oh, that's new this week, sir. Brainwave modulation feedback. The material you want gets modulated directly onto your rhythms, bypassing the senses."

"Oh?"

"Everyone so far says it's just the most!"

"Yes, yes, I'm sure it is..." he muttered.

Once inside the sphere, Teil called up the Flash Gordon comic collection of the 1930s, as a ruse. This one was a lusty adventure of Flash and Dale, Dr. Zarkov, and hordes of relentless enemies. It held a strange fascination for Teil—the beautiful women, gorgeous costumes, marvelous machines, and high adventure. Flash, the indomitable hero, operating under the aegis of a righteous destiny, boldly carrying out his missions through impossible odds.

In this episode, Flash's adversary was an exotic female who was holding Dale captive on her faraway forbidding planet, luring Flash to her using Dale as bait.

When he saw the attendant was gone, he quickly switched modes and started tracing UGLI history. His growing skepticism made him look for other than obvious perspectives. He questioned everything, and other ways of viewing history slowly formulated in his mind, above, behind, and in between the recorded chronicles.

He saw that once the major powers had opened themselves up to communication and trade, which they had to do to survive, they opened themselves up to the final cross-fertilization of the human species and its cultures. Whatever was media-ted was given expression, and hence validity, in the common medium—global TV. The world shared the medium in common; it came to share the life that was mediated. And the way was prepared for the new order.

In the whole process, something was happening that only a few had foreseen. The new global propaganda, for that was what TV had always meant, was altering the very nature of the political and cultural realities it was expressing in its desire to sell. The idea—any idea tacit or explicit—when mediated on the global tool became total. The new propaganda was by its very nature leading the world to the new total-itarianism. And there would never be any going back.

Can man never predict or control the direction his own civilization will take? he thought. The forces acting on and through civilizations...they're so much larger than any one society within the Flux. The Stream of Civilization...so much larger than any of its parts...a flood, carrying us along. Has man never really been free...?

And Teil was carried along. He was in it—FEAR—the Great Dread, nuclear world war. It had come so abruptly and with such profound collective shock, no one had ever been able to reconstruct exactly what had happened. It was Exchange Day, the day superseding the old Christmas; and there was another kind of exchange. The warheads just started falling out of the silent sky. It was the end of the world. Teil was there, being torn apart by every explosion, seared by every atomic blast, part of the fearful screams and horrors of half the human race facing death at once.

Just as suddenly it stopped. FEAR had begun and ended within the same day. And X was there. He made it stop. He had put an end to the FEARful Ending. He was the One.

Born Ivan Eugenik in an outlying town near Moscow, X came from parents who had been part of the non-Russian intelligensia, who, fleeing the oppression, had emigrated to the West before the child was enrolled. With over 700 words in his vocabulary by age two, his gifted abilities were apparent from the beginning. By four he showed an inordinate curiosity with maps and geography.

Mastering algebra and calculus at six, his new consuming passion became mathematics, and by eleven he was correcting his father's computer programs. By twelve his IQ was approaching 250, but physically he was unattractive and clumsy, the occasion of derision and torment by other children and suspicion and jealousy by adults. And when the media discovered him, his fate as an oddity was sealed.

He took increasing refuge in his small family and the world of books, which he sought out with a preternatural obsession. By age ten he had somehow obtained all thirty-two volumes of an old crumbling set of the thirteenth edition of *Encyclopaedia Britannica*. By twelve, its knowledge and spirit were his; by thirteen he had mastered the world.

By fourteen, pursuing graduate studies in electronics and computer sciences, but lacking close friends or outside interests, he developed an intense passion for world politics. In his post-doctoral work at seventeen he developed the first computer programming language and models for running all governmental, political, and administrative functions of a city by computer, the first model being Oxford, England. By twenty he was probably the only person in the world who knew all the variables to make the planet a success.

On the occasion of the media event announcing his brilliant work to the world, an attempt was made on his life, and his parents were killed by a terrorist bomb sent through the postal service. He immediately dropped from public eye.

X surfaced later as a League functionary, and with the untimely demise of the Secretary, assumed leadership of the world body after what appeared to be a fortuitous succession of parliamentary events. As soon as the exchange of missiles began, X went on global TV and made his famous proclamation. And the warheads stopped falling. By some chance the comm links were still intact.

"My friends and fellow world-citizens," he began, as the deep, strong, magnetic resonance of his vocal powers lifted Teil into his charismatic field of force. "What has happened today has made it crushingly clear that all the fears of the human race have finally brought themselves into being; they have come back upon our own heads. In one hour of raining desolation such as the world has never known, we are finally face-to-face with the End: The end of life on earth, the end of man, the end of ourselves."

It was more than the dark, electric features, the tall proud bearing, the forceful yet graceful physique and the mysterious deep-set eyes. The absolute self-assurance of the man radiated an intuitive awareness of his personal power and superiority. Like a forceful male intruding his lordship over a pride of lions, he awed by the sheer power of his presence. The man must have undergone a remarkable transformation, Teil thought.

"The final realization of this FEAR has dawned upon us with stupendous horror. The Unbelievable, the Impossible, the thing we vowed would never happen, has happened. The world has lost its mind. Thinking ourselves masters of the earth, we are reduced to vassals in one quick stroke. Inheritors of the earth, we are now denied our rightful heritage. There is no longer any Promised Land; the earth and all we thought was ours is lost! So proud of our so-called 'freedoms,' we have become slaves to the tyranny of our own misdeeds!"

Teil was there, and the world had ended, its misdeeds were his own, and he was carried along on the ocean-tide of emotion.

"Here we are now—naked, destitute, without leaders, lands, or hope. Or the mighty systems of security that brought us to this! And time is past! The world is dead! Because there is no future left on earth!!"

Teil's head bowed in submission as X's power held the collective consciousness. Here was propaganda in its purest form: persuasion based on person. He could have taken over without the war.

"There must be another way, for man can no longer live under his own erring and impotent rule. Man must finally abdicate his rule of man!" And Teil's head nodded with the power; he was part of the tidal surge of capitulation worldwide verging on hysteria.

"But abdicate to whom!" X continued. "To what? There is a power, taking its rise from man, yet capable now for the first time of being taken out of his fallibility, weakness, and evil, to become a Power in its own right, able to faithfully and perfectly serve and *save* man! For the first time, such an amazing thing is possible!" Teil was one with the collective gasp as the realization of what X was proposing began to sink in.

"Yes! We must bring into being a great autonomous system of technical sovereignty, for Technique knows no master! A Master Computer System, that will mediate every aspect of life on this planet and beyond. And with it, we will launch a righteous warfare against the error, evil, and impotence of man!"

In one stroke it was done. And wave after wave of scientists, engineers, programmers, and technicians were thrown to the epic enterprise creating Mascom, not unlike the building of the great pyramids of ancient Egypt. The ultimate technocracy—rule by computer. By one universal, collective grasping for the Answer, it was done. The world was changed. And there would be no room for the few voices of dissent. The populace would have torn to pieces any who opposed this man, such the transcendent power of that moment. And all the voices of history that had ever cried in the wilderness against such an eventuality were forgotten in an instant.

And there would be no going back.

* * *

When Teil came out of it, his heart was pounding. As he reached for the controls again, his hands were shaking. He had, as a participant, relived one of the most dramatic moments in history, and his own personal vulnerability had left him victimized and weak. He wondered whether the powerful experience had merely been the special cinecom effects or an admixture of those and his own strange mental state. Or, he wondered, has it *all* been induced? Is that the great FEAR that haunts us today? He had to reject the idea.

Try as he might, Teil could find little on the UGLIs directly. As he scanned the information racing before him, the reproduction of an old document momentarily caught his attention. It was a newspaper clipping dated from mid-twentiety century. He would have skipped it had not his eye happened on the word "suicide." What's this doing here? Another glitch? Irresistibly, he read it, with the same morbid fascination of one reading his own obituary.

1000 SUICIDES A DAY REPORTED
Agence France—Presse

GENEVA—At least 1,000 people commit suicide every day and 10,000 attempt it, the World Health Organization said here. The organization, which called for an increase in the number of special prevention centers, said that most suicide cases announce their intention beforehand, either explicitly or implicitly, and that those who fail usually try again the year after. The majority are aged, but the organization said that more and more young people are trying to take their own lives.

So many! Teil thought. And so long ago! And unheard of today.

Just as he was about to punch the button to get the clipping off the screen, his eye caught the minuscule coding strip in the upper margin of the copy. It was a curious melange of letters, numbers, and symbols, intelligible only to libracom technicians. One symbol and one word stuck out:

$$\Sigma \text{ VIRUS}$$

This forced his eye to follow the fine print to the end, where he saw what he recognized as a Mascom security classification. The frame is top secret! It must've slipped into libracom by mistake. And the Sigma virus—My god, no... It's suicide!

While Teil was still staring at the frame in disbelief, it was suddenly taken off the screen and replaced by a continuation of what he had been reading. "Wait a minute!" he blurted out, trying to bring it back. "What's happening out there? For System's sake—epidemic suicide!!"

Suddenly he felt very shaky, very lost, and very much alone. Teil punched the screen off and leaned slowly back, staring frozen-eyed through the darkened sphere at the shadowy reflections of the other flickering spheres and their fun-loving customers. What did they know—what did anyone know— of what was really going on?

Teil protectively sealed it over, withdrawing inwardly, his emotional defenses telling him this simply was not real. He closed his eyes, but the fateful coding strip clicked past his mind's eye again, one character at a time, stopping as if by its own accord on the sigma symbol. The Greek capital letter now appeared as a gigantic machinery of torture and death, and he was lying face up between the two dagger-like serifs at its open end, closing inexorably and impaling his helpless body between them. His silent scream brought him out of it. Caught in a crescendo of frustration and blind anger, he slammed the console violently with his clenched fist, crying, "NO!! damnit, NO!!!"

7

Fearing he might have drawn too much attention, Teil quickly left cinecom and central city.

Walking back to Mascom Regional, he constantly checked to see if he was being followed. He was ripped apart with conflict, his mind dark with furious thought, working over the history he had witnessed and the enormity of what he had just discovered. The picture of things-as-they-were was cast in starkly different hues now. Nothing had changed; yet everything was different.

It all fits together—people falling apart inside, suicides... All around us...people dying of the virus...really suicides... Impossible to believe, but it's true; I know it... And me...I'm part of it. That damned sickness is catching up with me... It *is* progressing; the bitch Machine is right!

A vague questioning began taking shape in Teil's mind, forming against considerable inertia. Is everything—history, facts, news—phase shifted into something that seems like truth and facts but is not? But surely, no deliberate system of propaganda could be so effective as to create an unreal milieu for the whole world... It must come from something intrinsic to man himself. His mind boggled at the idea, and a feeling of horror crept over him.

What if we live in a world of almost total illusion? What if man's heart cries out for illusion, as some great narcotic to escape some greater reality he's pushed deep inside himself? "He who sees but one world sees nothing," Kri-kor said. He saw it! "He who sees but one world fails even to see *himself*." Such an illusion would have to be total—diabolical!

And what if I'm an interloper between two worlds, between the world of what appears and the world of what really is? Oblivious to the bustling megapol about him, Teil stared ahead into the vast reaches of the idea. Why me? he thought. But the challenge pulled him on. Truth, he felt, even with pain, was better than ignorance with bliss.

As he walked back into the entrance at Regional, he pulled out the identity wafer on his wristcom. As he held the thin crystal in his hand, his gaze drifted over it. There was the digigraph of himself, the long identity number and other vital statistics, and the colored band running along the top, which was his own identity code. When he slipped the wafer into the slot, he saw a beam of light scan it. When Teil was elevated into his masphere, he pressed his ring into the console, holding it slightly away from the receptacle. It too was scanned by a quick burst of a thin sliver of light, piercing the heart of the ring.

That's how I can get rid of my ring! he thought. I'll bet if my identity code can only be beamed *into* the ring, it will unlock and I can get if off. There might be a way out after all, if I ever need it; tied to this thing, I'll never be able to do anything in secret.

As soon as he had gained access to Mascom again, he wasted no time completing his preparatory work so his actual search for the elusive origin could begin.

"Get me geocom mode, near space, orbiting satellite control, and comm link!" he commanded. The sooner I get the site survey complete, he thought, the sooner I can leave for Anatol.

The youthful ruddy face of Commander Riker appeared on the screen. "Riker here. This is Space Communications Control. We've been waiting for you, Professor. You name it!"

"That was fast, Commander."

"We got priority to clear you two hours ago. Whatever it

is you're after, you now have every orbiting geocom sensor we've got at your beck and call!"

Teil was taken aback. He had never even been close to this kind of status or service before. Everything seemed to be going so smoothly, almost too smoothly. But he didn't wait to worry about it.

"Okay, Commander, then you know what I'm after is a site survey!"

"Roger. You want to check our area coordinates?"

"Yes... There you go. They look good from here."

"How do you want it, sir?"

"Give me a series of continuous overlapping longitudinal scans as well as simultaneous total-area shots."

"Roger. Which sensors?"

"Everything you've got and then some."

"How about return beam vidicon: 0.3 to 1.8 microns spectral. Multi-spectral scanner: all spectral bands. Plus your standard radiographic and magnetic pictures and microwave and telescopy and the rest of the usual?"

"Excellent," Teil replied. "Didn't know you boys could get cracking so soon!"

"Timing's right, sir. Lab XXVII was practically in position for your zone anyway."

"All right, I'd like to tie into your video link so I can see whatever it is your sensors are looking at. I want my own visual survey of this thing!"

"Back to the old eyeballs, eh? No problem. You're tied in. By the way..."

"Yes?"

"Can't help wondering about the priority of this thing. We were scheduled to track that latest magnetic disturbance for the manned Alpha Centauri mission, but yours even tops that!"

"Oh?"

"Well isn't your experiment just— I mean, yours is archaeology, right?"

"Look—!" Teil bit his lip. "You'll have to ask Nexus Project, Commander," Teil snapped.

"Roger, sir."

"And I'll want straight infrared— Oh, by the way, we'll need separate tracks for each sensor and band, as well as composites."

"Roger."

"I'll need a dynamic sweep-filter of the whole light spectrum from infrared to ultraviolet."

"Roger!"

"And complete magnetic anomaly scanning."

"Complete's the word, sir."

"How deep under the surface can you go and still give me plus or minus five milligauss resolution?"

"Probably no deeper than 400 meters, depending on geological conditions."

"That should be good enough... When you're all set, I'll tie you into our site analysis program."

"What's that?" Riker asked.

"It will correlate all the data your sensors are picking up and indicate probable archaeological sites. I'll have an integrated display in my sphere."

"How will it indicate the sites?"

"Mounds man, mounds!" Teil said. "There's usually a buildup on the surface of the ground from what's underneath. Most of those ancient sites consist of several levels. When one got burned or destroyed, they leveled it and just built another on top. Location was the big factor: building materials, water supply, defense. So they kept the same spot wherever possible."

"How big are these mounds?"

"Some might be fifty or more meters high; others just a small gentle sloping variation, if that. Of course, with many sites, there's no mound at all."

"We're orbiting at 300 kilometers, remember."

"Commander: I'll put my confidence in your sensors if you'll put yours in my computer program. Besides, there'll be several reference mounds of different sizes that we know are sites. We'll calibrate against those. You'll see."

"Sounds like you've done your homework."

"You won't have to worry about this one. Just get your scans on line; I'll do all the interpretive work and site identification."

"Roger. By the way, sir, lab XXVII has come up to position. Stand by for intercept with our first designated fly-to point..."

"Standing by."

"Mark. You're on, sir."

"Okay. Program in... I've got you down here; synced-in and running. I can handle anything you give us now. Good luck."

"Stand by for first transmission... You should have it... Now!"

"Right. Very good. We confirm the area. And your corner datum designates are right on. Good picture, Commander!"

"Thank you, sir."

"Now everything you see indicated with a red X is a calibration site!"

"About a dozen?"

"Right. So give me your first total-area fix."

"There you go."

"Got it. That's it. Good!"

Teil saw what he was after, the upper reaches of the Tigris-Euphrates river systems.

"Okay, Commander, I've just calibrated. Each reference site is locked in. Now your laser terrain mapping will read out mound profiles to fractions of a centimeter, even at 300 kilometers. Right?"

"Can't beat the wavelength of light as a measuring stick, sir."

"Start your sensor scans."

"Roger. Synced and scanning. You should have separate and composite views coming in now..!"

"Right you are..."

Teil saw coalescing on the inside of the sphere a separate picture from each sensor scanning the earth's surface. As he followed the progress of the orbiting sensors, there developed before him an ever-intriguing kaleidescope of images. Pure video looked like simple aerial telescopy and could be blown up to show fine detail. He saw large unpopulated areas, except for occasional farms, vineyards, orchards, and mines. Viewing the same area in different portions of the light spectrum showed up various features otherwise undetectable. The infrared brought out subsurface features such as buried canals, faults, depressions, and other anomalies. Other bands provided striking profiles of the area, with zones of colors indicating vegetation, bodies of water, cities, soil, rocks, pollution, and indications of temperature variations within the earth's surface. There were deep reds and yellows and greens; bands, contours, and flowing zones of color.

Strange how each sensor sees the same area so differently, Teil thought. Each one sees it correctly, but totally differently. It seems like the more finely we perceive something, the less we can comprehend it in its ultimate reality. We analyze it to death, taking it apart with all our instruments and techniques, and each new vision goes deeper into it, farther out, giving us more and more knowledge about it. But do we lose the thing itself? The wholeness of what it is? What *is* the true nature of reality? Another Sigma virus lie? And is it possible it has nothing whatever to do with our senses?

When the scanning was complete, Teil brusquely issued a command. "Mascom, integrate all sensor data and perform site analysis." Then came the miracle any ancient archaeologist would have given an arm and a leg for. The largest features that began taking shape were meandering pathways.

"Ancient waterways! Look at em!"

These roughly paralleled the present-day Tigris and Euphrates rivers, but were closer together. Branching out from these arteries were finer lines, which Teil concluded were prehistoric canals because of their straight-line geometry. A succession of tells, or mounds, was strung along these lines, indicating that the ancient sites were following the available water supply.

"If only Jacobsen could have had this!" Teil said. Thorkild Jacobsen had pioneered reconstructing the path of these ancient waterways in the twentieth century.

Mounds were appearing everywhere. All possible ages and conditions were included. From such an altitude there was no way, not even for Mascom, to differentiate site ages. That would have to await surface work with the probes.

And there were far more sites than even Mascom had predicted. Teil was struck with the unexpected magnitude of his problem. How can we possibly trace the flow of that ancient mass of sites to its actual source, if there ever was one?

It was then that he began to appreciate the immense task of the early archaeologists. Their patience had to extend not over weeks, as his might, but over whole lifetimes. And that, just to uncover part of one site.

For a moment, he unwittingly slipped back into the framework of the past and was there, spade in hand, covered with dust, face set eager to the task, knee-deep in the diggings of history. He was Boussard in the trenches at Fort Sain-Julien, unearthing the Rosetta Stone, which would provide the key to deciphering ancient Egyptian hieroglyphics. He was Layard, uncovering the famous library of Ashurbanipal at Nineveh with its cuneiform tablets of the Babylonian Creation Epic. He was Rawlinson, dangling 100 meters up the side of the rock of Behistan in Persia, copying the trilingual inscription of Darius I, key to the Persian and Assyrian cuneiform. He was with Grenfell and Hunt at Oxyrhynchus, striking the mummified crocodile in frustration, which split open disgorging its heaps of papyrii, unlocking the secrets of New Testament marketplace Greek. He was there at the opening of the tomb of King Tutankhamun, and at the opening of the sealed jars containing the Dead Sea Scrolls... Then a voice rudely brought him back.

"Hello, sir... Are you there? Riker here. What's happening?" Teil finally snapped out of it, unaware of the unnatural intensity of his reverie.

"What...? Oh..." He shook his head, finding it increasingly difficult to return. "Thanks Commander... Excellent work... We've got all we need and then some."

The men signed off, and Teil sat back and looked at the finished picture. There it is, he mused, the locale for the mystery I have to unravel. The stepping stones to the Garden of Eden. That's the hidden pathway I'll have to find; the right stones that lead back to the right place...

"Eden!?" The word jolted him out of his thoughts. "I'm

not looking for the Garden of Eden. How did that get in there? What a foolish anachronism. The old Adam story is a myth dealing with the origin of man on the planet, not the emergence of civilized man, isn't it? You're getting synced-off, Teilhard." He remembered the chance remark of the young girl in the tube that morning, but steered his mind away from the unpleasant association. But on the other hand, this strange feeling of guidance, destiny... What was it? He decided to remain open; it had the right feeling about it, even if it was a new obsession. He would let Eden stick around back there in his subconscious and percolate awhile. Part of himself was out there beckoning him forward.

8

Teil flicked the comm button impatiently as he called up Epi-Thumia. Finally getting her on the screen, he reported his success with the site mapping and requested Kri-kor's geocom model.

In a few moments he had received into his own sphere the simulated model of the entire geological history of the area he had just mapped—southeastern Anatolia.

"Okay, Mascom," he said sternly. "Give me hologram mode. You got the geocom model just dumped in, didn't you?"

"Of course, Professor; everything is in order. Would I not have indicated otherwise?"

Is she starting to get cheeky, Teil wondered, or is that my imagination?

"Okay," he said gruffly "since everything is *not* in order. ...give me a scale factor of 1:200,000 to start with. I want you to correlate how the site distribution we got from our survey ties in with the topography and geology of that area. Hold it—I think I'd better start with the larger context. Give me the whole area, from origin."

"Which origin?"

"The earth's," he said just to be ornery, knowing the request was not only beyond his scope but impossible. There was a slight pause before the voice replied.

"Then you will have to respecify scale."

She's buying it! he thought. "All right... Let's take a look at the whole picture..."

"The entire globe?"

"Yes, at the rate of a million years a second." If you can do that, baby, my hat's off to you.

"At ten thousand seconds to the hour, Professor, that would take you 4,500 seconds, or .45 hours to bring you from origin at 4,500,000,000 years ago to the present." Stung by the sly rebuke, Teil made a rapid mental calculation.

"You're absolutely right. Make that...let's see...4.5 million years per second. At one hundred seconds to the minute, that'll only take ten minutes."

"I could have solved that math for you."

There was a pause, and then before he knew what hit him, Teil was in it. Inside the boiling, churning cloud of light and fury that was the birth of planet earth.

Lost inside! Teil realized as he was overwhelmed by the sea of light. By instinct he struggled to maneuver his way out of the hologram where he could see the model. She must have known I'd wind up inside again, he thought. Did she deliberately allow it? Some weird prank? I won't believe it!

Finally outside, he saw the stunning view. There hanging in space inside the sphere was the three-dimensional hologram of the genesis of earth, unfolding before him in elapsed time like a dynamic replay of the actual event. Teil was astonished.

Light!

The Big Bang!

Then he saw a cloud of gaseous matter whirling about its developing vortex. She's put me back to the very beginning! The birth of earth was a trauma of separation as the cloud of gaseous matter drew itself together and pulled away from the primordial parent cloud in a spasm of centripetal consolidation.

Ten seconds and 45,000,000 years later, it was beginning to go its own independent way as a ball of condensing, cohesive matter.

Teil was utterly captivated by the sight. "Beautiful work, Kri-kor! No one's ever seen anything like it! Fantastic!" He let his imagination go and reveled in the epic drama of the panorama of creation.

Again, Teil never knew when he crossed the line between observer and participant. One moment he was totally absorbed in the unfolding cosmic scene; the next, eyes closed, he was inside that drama, subjectively experiencing it, only now with every sense come alive in super-real sound, color, motion, and feeling. Teil was there, spellbound, as the ball of writhing, contracting gas became semi-solid, a firmament of shape and form, rotating, floating in the sea of blackness which was space.

As the nascent earth, now shrinking, quickly took shape, it began to heat up, turning into a boiling cauldron of turmoil and primal rock. Teil was there. Feeling it. Burning with it. Knowing it.

Then the surface of the earth began cooling.

Water.

And burning rock and steam. And more and more water. Then land. Gathering together in one place. One huge mass of dry land appearing. The ancient supercontinent of Pangaea. All earth's future continents in one gigantic mass...

There was Earth.

And there was Sea.

And Teil was there.

The mind-expanding vision overwhelmed him; he was lost in ecstatic rapture. And to think, the titanic forces shaping at this very moment the rest of the solar system—the universe! The wonder and grandeur and terror of it all! Where is the end of all this? What amazing teleology moving all to the End that is us—and beyond! The Alpha and the Omega... Why? Why the universe? This vast, inscrutable Event...? And where in all this is man? And life? What *is* life?!

There was a sudden movement within the land. A drifting apart. A rending of that primal earth. Contortions, as if earth herself were giving birth.

Continents! Drifting apart. Coming together. Impact! Giving birth to mountains. Then movement again. The old earth disappearing into fissures on the sea floors, only to recirculate and come up again as new rock, millions of years later in a cycle of catastrophic devastation and rejuvenation.

Then seas. Clouds.

A recognizable earth! And ice—great sheets of it advancing and receding. Glaciers. Changing the levels of the seas.

Then, it was still. The full orb of earth, enveloped in brilliant, deep, aquamarine blue, hanging still before him. He was at the present—lands and seas and life.

And man.

Home.

Teil was motionless and still part of the vast stillness when the whisper in the sphere pulled him out of it.

"Teilhard... This is Kri-kor. I'm tagging this onto the end of the geocom dump because I don't think I'll be able to see you again. No time to explain..." Feeling strangely drained, Teil heard the voice as from afar, outside his world. "I found a way to patch out her OMNIMONITOR routine for a minute so she won't see this." Teil recognized the voice now and sat blinking back into real-world awareness. "By the time you hear this, my young friend, it may all be over."

"Kri-kor... What the?" Teil said. He could only listen, caught in the web of circumstance.

"Nexus," Kri-kor continued, tensely telegraphing his message, "it's more than you realize; more than I imagined. Just got a glimpse before the veil dropped. Something so vast... Unthinkable. And you're right in the middle. And archaeprobe. Don't know why yet. The Others are in on it too... Reached a dead end. There's a stone wall around this thing so thick..." Teil sat there unable to believe he was hearing it.

"Whatever is really going on, we're in trouble. I mean, the whole damned human race is in trouble. It's coming up fast, whatever it is... What the devil has she left us? What have we left ourselves? Something's wrong; something's missing. We're flunking out, Teilhard... Final Exam time and we don't have any answers. We've even lost the questions!

"Penetrate that veil, Teilhard. If you can! And get the word out. You must! They're counting on you and archaeprobe more than anyone knows. Don't know why. So you've got an edge, for awhile, anyway. Find out what's happening. I can't, but somebody has to. She may be onto me already... And if she discovers the patch, I'm finished. And it won't be the Sigma virus. Something funny there, too....

"And Teil...take care of yourself—you know, the UGLI you saw in the mirror...? The UGLIs, Teil...that's where it is..!" Suddenly the voice broke off, replaced by another.

"Professor? Are you all right?" It was Mascom.

Teil was still trying to absorb the impact of Kri-kor's message and plea. He saw it too, Teil thought, the Sigma virus. But what else? What *about* Nexus? What was he onto? And repeating himself like that about the UGLI. What was he trying to tell me?

"Are you all right, Professor?"

"Me? Oh..!"

"Was the geocom model satisfactory!"

"Uhh... Geocom?"

"Yes."

"Oh..."

"Your reactions."

"What reactions? Oh... Must've let my imagination run wild in there for a minute... Got caught up in the thing like..."

"Like what?"

Does she know about Kri-kor? he thought. "I'm sorry; what did you say?"

"Your reactions to viewing the model."

"Oh. Fine, fine... Fantastic model. Shouldn't have wasted time going all the way back to origin," he evasively added, hoping to keep Mascom off the track.

"But you do have a certain latitude, Professor. We know now that playfulness is part of the creative process."

Latitude? Playfulness? What is this? he thought. The solicitous nature of Mascom's inquiry unnerved Teil even further. Does she know what I was going through in the model? Defensively, against the triple confusion, Teil tried to force Mascom's attention away from himself and back to the research.

"Restart scan at 15,000 B.C.," he sharply commanded. "And

limit the area to the Tigris-Euphrates river system, and give me manual, repeat, *manual* control of time flow!"

"Of course, Professor," purred the imperturbable one.

Teil positioned the model so he was looking straight down on the portion of earth bounded roughly by the Mediterranean Sea, the Black Sea, the Caspian Sea, and the tip of the Persian Gulf. He tried not to notice his hands were shaking again. There, stretching from lower right upward to the left were the fabled twin rivers, etching their meandering way across the landscape. He decided to sweep through the entire time span to get the overall picture.

"Thirty years a second!" he ordered, louder than necessary. "And let's see the sites now."

Damn it all to System, Kri-kor, Teil yelled within himself, what are you trying to tell me?

As soon as the model was set in motion, sites started appearing. In Teil's area of interest, the flow of man had been from western Europe into the Near and Middle East. The glaciers had lowered sea levels, creating land bridges and allowing Cro-Magnon man to spread to every continent on earth. Man had left his most complete record, however, in the great cave sanctuaries of France and Spain. Lascaux, Altamira, Font de Gaume, Niaux, Pech Merle, and so many other sites spreading across Europe, all giving eloquent testimony to the presence and wonder of this *Homo sapiens sapiens* of the caves, the direct forebears of modern man.

Even before the last glaciers had receded from northern Europe, man in southwest Asia was embarking on the momentous course which led to the development of civilization. It was to be here that man emerged as food producer, contrasted with the countless millenia of his existence as hunter and food-gatherer.

As Teil followed the time scan, his thoughts kept shifting back to Kri-kor's urgent plea. Yes there's a veil! But what is it? As though he was afraid for his life! Nexus, archaeprobe, UGLIs, Sigma-suicide— What does he know?

First, only the known sites already uncovered and dated began to dot the screen. And first among these were the open settlements, some seasonal, others already permanent: Shanidar, Eynan, Jericho, Beida—coming in around the tenth millenium B.C. Then, settlements showing firm evidence of domestication of plants: Hacilar, Ali-Kush, Cayonu—coming in around 7,000 B.C.

Three or four primary centers emerged on the screen where this domestication was taking place in the first few thousand years after the Glacial period: Palestine and Lebanon, the Zagros mountains of Iraq and Iran, the eastern Elburz and northern slopes of the Hindu Kush mountains, and especially the south Anatolian plateau. In other words, the highland zones of the Near and Middle East.

After this, sites began popping up all over the place: Zawi Chemi, Karim Shahr, Jarmo, Catal Huyuk, Hassunah, Samarra, Halaf, Eridu... The list of digs went on and on, and represented a Who's Who of some of the greatest names in twentieth-century archaeology.

"Okay, Mascom," Teil commanded harshly. "Now dump in all the sites we got from the orbital labs today. Of course, you won't have any dates for these, will you?"

"No, Professor. How can I supply dates when the sites have never been dated?"

First time she's ever argued a point, he thought. "Without dates, the sites are meaningless. I thought maybe by some odd chance," Teil was cutting and cynical, "knowing how you transcend us mere mortals now, you might have something new and unheard of going on in there."

"As you must realize, Professor, there is hardly room for chance in my world. Even Mascom has limits, and I do not transcend the human!"

First time she's dropped the "we," Teil thought; and what limits is she talking about? He backed up the time scan and began playing with the rivers.

"The things that are happening to these rivers!" he exclaimed. "South of the mountainous zone, in the flatlands. Wandering... Changing course... And the Persian Gulf... Starting up higher, then receding. No wonder Jacobsen had such a time reconstructing those ancient waterways. And what's this?" Teil noted, spotting a transient darkening of the image. "Better check. Looked like a shadow. Whatever happened, took place so fast I almost missed it." Teil stopped the time advance and went back to look for it.

"There it is again!" He froze the scan and stared at the image. "It can't be. Water? All over the place!"

"It is water, Professor."

"Glad to hear it; hate to think it was another glitch..!" He caught himself too late.

"What did you say?"

"Uh... Quitch. I'd hate to think it was quitch grass."

"Really, Professor.." Teil bit his lip.

As Teil restarted the time scan, the waters disappeared.

"I'll have to step this through slowly and see what's going on down there. We'll back it up, like so... Change the scan to one day per second... And let it run..."

Teil noticed several floods, some small and some covering large areas.

"There! That's the big one. Whew!" He slowed the scan and watched as the waters seemed to come from everywhere at once. "Mascom, let's get a fix on it. Give me an area profile."

"Would you like it in green or red shading?"

"Suit yourself! Just give me the area contour!" The machine resolved the choice neatly; a garish greenish-red now filled the area covered with water. Good to see she hasn't gone aesthetic yet, anyway, Teil thought, repulsed by the awful color.

"Wow! Everything south of Baghdad."

"About 800 kilometers long," the machine volunteered, "stretching upward from the tip of the Persian Gulf!"

"Why that's practically the whole of early civilization down there! I seem to remember floods were common in Mesopotamia," Teil noted. "Do you see any indications of what made this one so unusual?"

"In process."

"If this one's for real, it was a disaster!"

"I can assure you it was real. And there are certain lines of data that partially explain the phenomenon."

"Let's have it," Teil snapped.

"CZYLXTRYZP."

"Sorry, I missed that."

"CZYLXTRYZP."

"That's what I thought you said."

"Pardon me, Professor, but I was sure you knew that masword. Paleoethnobotanical—ancient plant remains related to human cultures. The pollen filters in your probes...?"

"Oh. Why didn't you say so? I do just happen to know that masword, but not the way you pronounced it."

"*Mine* is the correct pronunciation."

"Wrong. Mine is."

"It's *my* word!"

"That'll be the day!"

"It already *is* that day..!"

"What do you mean, it already is that day?" Teil shot back angrily.

"Later, Professor; your time is running out."

'What time is running out?!' Teil insisted angrily.

"The botanical and geological evidence..." Mascom said smoothly.

"For the love of System!" Teil cursed softly under his breath.

"The botanical and geological evidence," Mascom continued, "point to peak snow melting in the Armenian source system for the Tigris and Euphrates coinciding with maximum spring rainfall in Turkey at the same time."

"But would that produce all *that* water?" Teil demanded.

"Not likely."

"How about the Persian Gulf? Could it have risen dramatically for some reason?"

"Tidal variations were not much over the present amount of four or five meters, Professor, and although we know the Gulf extended farther north then, it is unlikely that would account for the rest of the water."

"So...? Where did it come from?"

"If I were to hazard an educated guess..."

She's got to be kidding! Teil thought. I don't believe it— 'hazard an educated guess.'

"Something wrong, Professor?" One could almost see her wry smile.

"No! Nothing's wrong at all! This is Utopia, remember? Teil shot back.

"Well," Mascom continued, 'I would say the water came from underground sources."

"Underground?"

"The geocom model shows an especially high water table in the marsh area of the lower rivers, which shows evidence of repeated settling in recent geological times. Extrapolating here and there, I come up with a peak water table at the very time we are discussing. But as for any mechanism releasing the water above ground, such as seismic activity, I don't have enough data yet for solid conclusions."

"What a fluke! Too bad those people didn't have you then; they could have known what was in store for them."

"Apparently some did know."

"What?"

"Ziusudra, if we are to believe the Sumerian King List and the Babylonian account, not only survived the flood, he foretold it."

"You don't say...? Well, I'll have to review that text. That's incredible. Why didn't more people listen?"

"Human nature."

"*Human nature*! What's that?"

"What if some kind of 'flood,' " Mascom said, "something peculiarly comparable in *our* world..."

"*Our* world?" Teil said resentfully. "Wait a minute!"

"...Something that had never happened before, that therefore 'could never happen.' What if it were predicted today? Would man listen now? Would he believe?"

Philosophizing? Teil thought. I don't believe what I just heard. How can she possibly...?

"You see what I mean, Professor?" But the predisposition of his mind against the very thought of Mascom's use of abstract reason left the poignant demonstration of Mascom's subtle point completely lost on Teil.

Teil let the time scan advance slowly and watched the waters recede. He glanced at the elapsed time readout.

"A hundred and ninety days. That whole transition to flood and back. Strangest thing I ever saw. When do you date the event, Mascom?"

"2900 B.C., Professor, give or take a little." Teil scanned his memory for associations around that date, then decided to do it the easy way.

"Would you please correlate that date with the history of Sumer?"

"Glad to. The date of 2900 B.C. correlates roughly with the reign of Ziusudra, king of the south Babylonian city of Shuruppak. Ziusudra appears on the Sumerian King-list as the reign marking the division between the ante-diluvian and post-diluvian rulers of Sumer. State-of-the-art evidence indicates with 87 percent probability that he identifies with the Utnapishtim of the Gilgamesh Epic and the Noah of the Genesis text."

"The Genesis Flood?"

"Yes, Professor."

9

Teil leaned back in the cockpit and wondered what he'd accomplished. Stepping stones to civilization's origin he had found—too many of them. And except for the lower river valleys where the Tigris-Eu river system had meandered, the ancient topography, climate, and flora and fauna were much the same as they were now.

So what? he thought. Even with the probes, and going one site a day, It'll take over a year to look at them all, much less find origin! He tried to accept the unexpected slowdown but couldn't. There's *got* to be an easier way. One year is an eternity! I've got to find a better way of using Mascom so *she* can find the better solution...

Then, inside himself, Teil stood straight up and started screaming his head off at the insanity of the whole idea of Mascom-compatible thinking. Nuts!! For once, just once! I am going to break out of this infernal cycle! I'm doing this my way, in my own sweet time, and I won't be bugged, limited, and cowed by the omniscient omnipresence of this Great Electronic Whore! What am I anyway, some servile drone to some massive, immobile, all-consuming Mother Termite Queen?!!

Forcing himself not to think of the implications of what he had just thought, Teilhard stopped. And did a strong thing. He unbound his mind and set it free.

He felt the release immediately. He sighed a deep sigh and relaxed. The new feeling hurt and gave him pleasure at the same time. He would pose the problem to himself.

The adventure had begun.

Okay, let's get down to basics, he thought. What are the criteria by which we can detect the emergence of civilization? That should help narrow down the number of sites, give some means of stepping across them and finding the pathway back to origin. It was amazing to Teil how quickly and effortlessly he came up with the criteria.

Civilization meant that man was settled; that he had stopped roaming around as Pleistocene hunter. It meant man began to build a place to live where he wanted to live, instead of searching out nature's hiding places. *Dominion* was the word. Man had begun to exert dominion over nature instead of being subject to it.

Settling and building, however, assumed the ability to provide a constant source of food in one locale. Hence, another mark of emerging civilization would be that man was learning to manipulate wild food and animals. *Domestication* was the word here.

Part of this transition was the emergence of new and better tools. The substance, whether stone, bone, wood, or metal, did not matter as much as the purposes for which they were made. *Technology*. And the revolution.

As Teil surveyed the ideas that kept surfacing surprisingly easily in a continuing stream in his mind, each pulled out thread-like by the one before it, he saw that this emergence might also be marked by a distinctive turn in the history of worship. *Religion*.

Writing. Part of man's cultural emergence was also tied in with a major transition in the art of reducing his ideas to a written record of some sort. As early as the 1960s, Alexander Marshak had discovered that what had been thought to be decorative markings on bones and rocks thousands of years before the cuneiform inscriptions, were in fact calendar markings related to lunar seasons and plant growth cycles. This indicated prehistoric man had developed a complex, long maintained tradition of symbolic notation which made subsequent agriculture and technology possible. But the origin of writing as such apparently stemmed from the fourth and third millenia B.C. And the earliest writings were predominantly religious.

Art. Shouldn't we see a distinctive turn in the development of art also? Teil wondered. But Cro-Magnon art was highly developed long before man built the first city. What happened to art? Can it be that the rise of civilization affected it adversely in some way?

And the *Flood.* We'll have to let that kick around back there too, he said to himself.

And then there's epidemic suicide... Teil's mind wandered off the beautifully ordered track of reason and logic. Or was it that reason had brought him back to himself, to his own personal world? Where am I in all this...? Am I infected with the damnable "virus"? Is that how it works, on the inside, deep within all of us, held off by...what? Held in balance by what? Suddenly everything seemed remote and trite.

To be out of it all..., he mused. No longer part of the great Electronic Way of Life; no longer part of the world of men and affairs and enterprises of great moment, the making of history and shaping of the world to come, and adding to that great store of world-data from which everything takes its rise and to which everything flows in life-like sustenance to the Great Machine Mother to which we all owe our continued existence. To be out of *me*...! Oh god... the endless chase... He thought of the woman at the pedestal again. Is there nothing else...?

Teil turned it off and switched back, forcing what meager satisfaction and meaning he could from his intellectual pursuit.

Okay, there we have it in a neat nutshell—the criteria for unraveling the knotty problem of tracing the river of civilization back to its head. Wouldn't it be easy if one site would reveal this entire complex of transitional factors?

On a hunch Teil requested a breakdown of known sites by criteria he quickly spelled out to the machine. Maybe I'll be lucky and find some sort of pattern, he thought.

But there was no apparent pattern. One site did catch his attention, however. It was Cayonu Tepesi, "Riverfront Mound." In no time he was devouring the data the machine was spewing up in front of him. Dug generations before by Robert Braidwood and others not far from Diyarbekir in southeastern Turkey, the site had been a breakthrough for archaeologists. The various layers of the mound yielded evidence spanning the transition from food-gathering to domestication of plants and animals. It also uncovered a building technology amazingly advanced for its time. A brilliantly executed terazzo floor from the third phase of occupation was made of colored stone chips set in concrete, which had then been ground smooth and polished and had remained extremely hard for close to nine thousand years. Tools and other artifacts made from native copper and dating from 7000 B.C. revealed man's first known intentional use of metal tools.

The site survey had given Teil a feeling that the upper reaches of the Tigris-Eu system would prove the most interesting. Apparently, the Neolithic peoples living on the fringes of the river system valleys began settling the valley bottoms when these were still swampy. And as the waters receded, settlements began appearing in the upper reaches of the system first. As civilization developed, they moved downward.

Cayonu was in that area of early settling. It lay about 1000 meters above sea level in the hilly flanks of the Taurus mountains. But having a site like Cayonu was one thing; establishing the originating center of civilization in this part of the world—if there was such a thing—was quite another.

He did feel certain of one thing: the breakthrough would probably be unconventional. Every time archaeologists had uncovered another mound in this area, they were surprised at the striking differences. In one case, it might be the type of pottery used; in another, it was the strikingly different and well-developed architecture. At Cayonu, it was not only the unique architecture but use of copper preceding the previously first-known use by thousands of years.

It's the lack of uniformity and unpredictability about the digs around here that excites me, Teil thought. That in itself tells me the culture here was in motion. Teil's subconscious was scanning for a dramatic break. There's a key around here somewhere...I feel it coming up. Some kind of direction...a map—if not pictorial, then descriptive... If only there were something in writing, he thought out of the blue.

10

Then it occurred to Teil: Do what Schliemann did; look at the ancient texts! It was an absurd idea to mascience, used to working only with precise data and Mascom projections, but Teil felt instinctively that that would be the way. Sitting erect in the cockpit, he quickly punched in the new operating mode and announced his intentions to his femimized Mascompanion.

"I'm sure you'll be grateful to know I still find you useful at times, sweetheart," Teil said, "and aren't you lucky you're out of all this mess going on—that machines can't catch viruses, destroy themselves and all?" Teil paused an uncomfortably long time, but there was no response from Mascom. "Well—not to disturb your cozy little self or anything—give me all ancient Babylonian, Assyrian, Hittite, Hebrew, Canaanite, and other stories that have any references or allusion to the origin of civilization in my area of interest. They can be either historical or mythical, and let's say prior to 2000 B.C. The texts themselves can be of later date, but the references have to go back as early as possible."

"Is that all, Professor?"

Playful wit—again? thought Teil.

"...If so, please specify format and language."

"Paper printout, in the original languages," Teil ordered. "And that's all for now. You may go."

"Did you say *paper?*" she asked, ignoring his ego, the voice betraying incredulity. "No one orders printed matter any more..."

"Yes, paper!"

"It will be ready for you when you leave."

"Thank you," he said, and as quickly kicked himself. You don't go around thanking the beast, he thought.

As Teil left the sphere, one of the masboy robots came careening around the aisle on his skate board-like pedestal. Braking in a less than graceful flourish right in front of Teil and almost knocking him over, it proffered a neat package of computer printout.

"Here is the material you ordered, sir" it announced in its choir-boy voice. "Please note one item is classified. Your signature, please." Teil pressed his masring into the boy's navel and took the material. The masboy zipped off around the curved aisle scraping the wall as it miscalculated again, responding to another electronic summons. The queer thought struck Teil that this crazy machine might have written the graffiti.

Why put a security classification on ancient history? Teil wondered, looking at the bundle of paper. That's stupid. But security is one thing you don't question, unless you want to lose your ring and who knows what else. Come to think of it, why don't we see any retired or former mascientists around...?

As Teil tubed home, he scanned the printout. There was one text he had not seen before, apparently a new find, written in a language even earlier than the old Sumerian. How come I wasn't notified of this? he thought. Then he saw that it had just made memory. Maybe if I had bothered to scan my incoming comms... But just as he eagerly started translating it, he had to disembark.

He walked quickly from the terminal to his dwelling. It's still afternoon, he thought. Maybe I can get a quick something to eat and study these things. There was an air of expectancy about him as he pressed his ring into the other eye of the Sphinx and stepped down to living level to greet Skia. She

was there waiting and eagerly rubbed her soft grey fur on
his leg, catching every inch of contact while she made those
funny talking noises with her mouth closed. Seeing Skia
brought a pang of longing.

"Hey girl, I've got a surprise for you; since you're such
a good girl, I'll let you in on a secret." The cat looked up
at him expectantly with her large baleful eyes.

"She sent us a message today, Skia. What about that? She
wants you to know she's all right." The cat responded with
a veritable torrent of sounds, as though she too were in on
the whole thing.

Ever since Aspasia had called his attention to it, Teil had
noticed how domesticated animals seemed to pick up the basic
emotional set of humans. They seemed to perceive on some
sort of parasensory or metasensory level between the two
species. It was her notion that humans had lost the ability
to communicate at this level as a by-product of civilization
and the shift to communication via words and media.

"I wonder what would happen if man had no media, Skia.
Whew! Run that one through your registers, Mascom, and
see where it gets you. And what set do we pick up from Her?
And maybe if two humans could ever stick together long
enough..." What would *that* do to us?

Teil grabbed the nearest thing that looked like food and
sat down to eat while he pored over the texts. The stories
brought back memories of long hours spent in language study
and ancient history, when he would lose himself, immersed
in the lore of peoples and customs that beckoned from their
remote distance from all things modern and machine-made.

Teil saw at a glance that most of the texts were the old
stand-bys. The *Epic of Gilgamesh* was the Iliad of the ancient
Near East, named after its hero, Gilgamesh, one-third man
and two-thirds god. The story was about his assorted
adventures with Enkidu, his faithful friend, and Gilgamesh's
pursuit of eternal life. Then there was the *Enuma Elish*, the
Babylonian story of creation, with its gods Apsu, Tiamat, and
Marduk, doing battle for supremacy. And there was the Hebrew
creation story: the six days of creation, Adam and Eve and

the garden, the temptation by the serpent, and the fall and expulsion from Eden. This had a different ring to it than the others. It struck Teil as having been written in such utter simplicity—virility was the word that came to him. Then he stared in amazement at it.

This is the one that's classified—*Genesis*! That's got to be another glitch.

Teilhard was intrigued by the parallels between the Gilgamesh and Genesis stories, especially Utnapishtim, the Babylonia Noah, complete with flood and ark, and the fabulous garden of delights.

Of course, the Hebrew *Genesis* is of no use here, he thought, since it's supposed to be simply a mythological account of creation. Unique as it is, it surely has no bearing in a search for historical evidence on the emergence of civilization. But the piece stared back at him, as though challenging this easy assumption.

There were other short Babylonian accounts of creation, plus various Assyrian and Hittite stories. And there were Canaanite stories of later date from the temple library at Ugarit, which had lain beneath the mound at Ras Shamra on the north coast of Syria. And Mascom had compiled a separate sheet of all references and possible allusions in all these texts to Teil's area of interest.

"Now that took some doing, Skia. Imagine. Mascom practically had to comprehend this material in order to come up with this list. Maybe she'll make mind-matter interface after all. Really now, Skia, just how would it ever be possible to live without Her? But let's do it, shall we?" He promptly tore up the sheet and threw it away. "Besides, how can we trust it, eh? And I want to do this *my* way." It gave him a shaky feeling, as though a prop had been knocked out from under him. But he felt good about it.

As Teil examined the new literary find, he noticed something he had missed at first scan while tubing home.

"The site—Halaf! How could I have missed that? That's not a hundred kilometers south of Braidwood's dig at Cayonu! And the script, so old." It had been tentatively dated at 3000

B.C., but the scribal notations it contained showed it was a copy of something earlier.

The juices flowed faster as Teil started devouring the text. He was immediately struck by the style, unlike anything else he could remember. It seemed to be a dramatic monolog. As he translated it, he was so caught up in the epic force of the original, he started casting it into an easy, natural kind of dramatic rhythm.

> Look. Ghanoch, the city. The first.
> Proud monument to all man's enterprise.
> My city.
> My children; their children's children's children.
>
> I was once a tiller of the soil,
> By birth a member of that Gehden tribe
> Of outcasts. Parents, driven from one world,
> Fugitives and strangers in another.
> We sons, aliens to both. Misfits all.
>
> For even we, their offspring
> Could not escape the ling'ring residue
> Of their first flight,
> Forced on our imagination by their
> Haunted memories; whispered dreams
> Of scenes they could never flee.
>
> To be driven out...!
> That was our tribal heritage
> And should have been our family name.
> For I too was driven out,
> As were our parents first from Gehden, After I
> had driven myself
> Out of that fellowship
> As punishment for murder.
> For I had driven Hevel
> Out...

11

Teil read on, intrigued by the unfolding story. "This has to be one of the most unique finds ever, Skia. The quality of thought, the style, the subjective frame of reference... What an amazing piece from such a remote time and place. And the author is speaking of the city as though it were a departure, something new on the scene. New in some sense, but what? Perhaps not merely a settlement; those went way back to 10,000 B.C. or earlier. What then could have been unique about his city?"

Teil's mind was alive with bursts of inspiration and excitement. The piece had the ring of significance to it. To any other archaeological technician, the monolog from Halaf would have been simply another scrap from the rubble heaps of antiquity. But there was a true archaeological instinct in Teilhard.

"Ghanoch, the city, the first..." Teil mumbled. "The first city? Origin? Couldn't be... And metalsmiths, the pickaxe... The author is talking about these things as though they refer to a kind of first directed metallurgy. And the Gehden tribe... An actual tribe? And who are Hehvel and Kahyin?"

Something told him he should know, that this all fit together. But it wasn't happening. "Maddening! It's all there; I know it is. Like a memory you've forgotten... But then if you've forgotten it, how is it that you remember it's forgotten?

There I go again, thinking about thinking...!" The train of thought bored itself into him insistently until he grabbed his head and desperately shook it.

"The problem; concentrate on the problem. Don't let your mind go off like that. Get hold of yourself, Mann, before the men in white coats descend on you!" Teil had to tear his mind forcibly away and valiantly put himself back on the track, as though he was in conflict with some alien force inside his own mind.

"So... I know the answer's here somewhere. But I'm not going to force it. Trust the natural processes. Relax. Rest in it; believe in it. It'll work out. Let go and you'll have it." So he did just that; he let it all go.

"Hey Skia!" he called joyfully. "Let's go, girl!" Taking some real fruit—black market pears—and putting on his favorite sporting jacket, old and worn, he bundled the texts together, stuck them under his arm, and went for a walk.

Skia scampered on ahead, checking out of the corner of her eye to keep tabs on where he was going. For a full hour Teil walked, forgetting completely the problems of civilization and its origins and the day's insanity, exulting in a new sense of freedom. He walked beyond the sight and feel of everyone and everything System-made, till he had left it all far behind. Only once before had he gone as far. It was when Aspasia and he had first been together. They had started out for a short walk, and then, as they drew closer, kept on going without thinking until they had become lost.

The memories flowed through him as he remembered that day, full of the fragrance of the fresh air and growing things and the birds that accompanied them in the air. The birds were there today. As he walked on and on, Teil was flying with them above the earth, soaring majestically like the pair of red-tailed hawks above him, circling high into the currents that bore them upward. The currents were supporting *him*, and effort didn't count as much as learning to trust the unseen air.

What a beautiful thought, he wondered. And we, so bound to that narrow way of living that excludes all this... Man does not need wings to soar!

As he climbed higher into the hills, Teil could see the Pacific ocean reflecting ripply sheets of bright gold as the late sun stretched its last remaining rays across the horizon, warming him with its primeval goodness and filling him with peace.

He sat down and leaned against a mound of grass-covered earth under the lee of a bank of tall eucalyptus. Snuggling down into the contours of the welcoming body of grass, he pulled out the texts and started to read again the fabulous story of Gilgamesh. But his gaze kept drifting upward into the trees, drawn by the somnolent aroma of the eucalyptus and the springtime earth. He could not concentrate on that machine-begotten page. He lay back and simply gazed at the drifting clouds and listened to the soft breezes rustling the leaves high in the tree tops, beckoning him upward. The bank of trees seemed to be there for him, protecting him from all that other he had left behind. He stared into the blue deep of the open heavens; his spirit soared to follow. And soon, he was asleep.

As he slept, he dreamed. A fantastic dream, that he was Gilgamesh, looking for the source of eternal life. He was going to the island on a great sea at the ends of the earth where Utnapishtim lived, the old, old man and only mortal who had ever escaped the touch of death. The god Ea had warned Utnapishtim to build an ark to save his family and animals from the flood that was to come. Teil was Gilgamesh, and he would seek out Utnapishtim and learn the secret of eternal life.

After traveling long and far, he came to the end of the world and saw before him that immense mountain whose "twin peaks reached to heaven and whose roots reached down to nethermost hell." In front of the mountain was the huge gate guarded by fearful creatures, half-man and half-scorpion. He would have to get past them to gain entrance or never find the way. Finally, the creatures befriended him and let him pass with instructions: "The way you seek is the pathway of the sun; and it lies through that tunnel."

The next thing Teil knew, he was in the tunnel, so dark

he could see nothing, formless fears hounding his every step as he courageously forced himself to move ahead. Time passed. Finally, he broke into the light and gazed upon the most beautiful sight his eyes had ever beheld.

He was in the Garden of Delights, a lush and glorious paradise with mysterious trees hung with jewel-like fruit. As he gazed, the fabulous setting crystallized slowly in increments, inwardly, until it seemed as if it was suspended in clear crystal, shimmering in a new transcendent dimension. And he heard the voice. The voice of one calling to him in the cool of evening.

"Adam, where art thou?"

The question hung in the stillness, its strange power reverberating in gentle waves throughout his being. Teil felt he had to answer, as though the question was directed at him. But the urge to respond was stifled deep within him, whence it arose.

There it was again, only not audible. As though the voice was a Presence asserting itself, insistently following him as he tried to hide, seeking him out. As though it knew where he was and was calling him out, into the light. At the same time, a dark force surging upward from inside, sought to drown it out. And Teil was afraid.

Finally, all was still. And out of the stillness, issuing from the infinite recesses of inner space, through the darkness, was the Chord. That same chorus of voices he had heard before, swelling to unbearable inner intensity, as if the Chord were responding to that calling Presence, where he could not. Teil wanted to cry back, but something would not let him.

Then, he heard the voice again. Plain. Clear. Calling. "Kahyin, where art thou?"

12

The difference in names jarred him awake. He closed his eyes, wishing he could keep dreaming, reluctant to leave that beautiful quest, for his journey had only begun and such eager promise lay ahead and the Chord beckoned so.

As he opened his eyes, Skia was rubbing him and voicing her reassurances.

"The garden!" he cried. "The garden of Eden! In the dream... I was combining the Gilgamesh epic and the story of Adam in the Genesis text... Why Kahyin? He was calling to *Adam*..." His subconscious made the connection. Kahyin! Hebrew for Cain! Of course... Cain, the first son of Adam. Good night... The monolog... Cain's?? *The Lament of Cain?* Incredible. And Hevel his brother... Abel! Yes, and Gehden for Eden. The new find from Halaf could be a lament of Cain himself! Probably as an old man, looking back on the past. The parents driven out—out of Eden! The murder—of his own brother. And the city, Ghanoch—Enoch! That's what was nagging me...

> To have come this far,
> Enoch, the City!
> So far removed from those first scenes
> That set the stage for all that was to come.

"It all fits together. And the fourth chapter of Genesis...

Enoch is founded by Cain and named after his son. Could it be that Enoch was a real city...?'' Teil's mind swarmed with unanswered questions. He turned quickly to the Genesis text he had carried with him and read again that long-forgotten story. The implications were far-reaching. He read on into the story of Cain's descendants, the genealogy of Adam, and into the story of Noah and the Deluge. Then he thought of the flooding in the geocom model and its relatively recent date in the third millenium B.C.

"The Flood, Noah, Utnapishtim... Can it be they all tie in together? And the most unbelievable part is that... Skia! listen to this...

"If Adam's son Cain, driven out for murdering Abel... If he built the city of Enoch, and if only five generations later one of his descendants, Tubal-cain, is 'hammering all kinds of cutting things in bronze and iron,' which refers to forging edge tools for working in metals... And Cain himself, before that, if he was a 'tiller of the ground,' and his brother a 'keeper of sheep'... These are unquestionably references to domestication of plants and animals as *fait accompli*. The thing has the stamp of fitting in with the transition to civilization; it's practically telling us civilization had *already emerged. Why, the whole picture of the fourth chapter of the Genesis text fits perfectly the criteria of emergence*:

> A permanent self-sufficient community
> Agriculture
> Animal husbandry
> A shift in technology. Smelting emerged around 4000 B.C.
> Writing. Somebody probably recorded the story in some manner.
> The arts. One of Tubal-cain's brothers, Jubal, is ancestor of those 'who play the lyre and harp.'
> The dramatic shift in religion...''

As Teil studied the text, he saw that Cain's punishment and expulsion from the tribe and subsequent building of Enoch

were probably a reaction against his experience with his
father's people.

"The Cain tribe builds. It develops a new technology.
Introduces new art forms... No, introduces art *technique*. And
all this as a reaction against that Eden experience? Whew!
He turned again to the *Lament*:

> But to be rejected utterly!
> With him accepted...?
>
> .   .   .
>
> They can have their longed-for Eden.
> We have our City and our metal tools.
>
> .   .   .
>
> But here, in this place of my design,
> a refuge from that dreaded Presence...

"Incredible! But wait a minute..." The obvious struck Teil
with such force he was dumbfounded for a moment. "If we
have such a perfect picture of emerging civilization here, and
it comes within so few generations of Adam, how could Adam
have ever been considered the first man on the planet, even
in the mythology? Cro-Magnon man was painting pictures
on cave walls twenty thousand years before that!"

The juices poured into him. He knew he was on the verge
of something very important. Discovery. In the old sense, where
man was still the adventurer.

Teil pored over the text, going over it again and again.
Fortunately, he had not read it for so long, it was like reading
it for the first time, and without all the accretions of centuries
of ecclesiastical speculation and all sorts of projections from
misinformed and misguided psyches, and in the light of man's
new knowledge of his past.

"It's plain as parity, Skia. Whoever the author of Genesis
was, he left not the slightest indication that Adam was the
first man. The first chapter alone makes that clear; it assumes
all creation to be within the literary framework of the six-
day idea. The earth in chapter one is completely populated

with plants, animals, and finally man. So chapter two, with its unique 'forming' of one individual—Adam—not the 'creating' of man in chapter one, probably represents some unique juncture in man's experience, when this god called him apart from the world of men to a special place, and made of these two people a *new* creation of sorts. What a beautiful way of depicting relationship with this god and between man and woman. Such a concept is alien to us today... As I can readily attest." His thoughts went back to his own problem. "There's nothing really new that's formed in our affairs; it's the same old thing, just new faces and new bodies and an alluring LSR 'newness' about it that seems to pull you deeper into it, yet farther and farther away... From what?

"Well, girl, so now you know, eh?" he said, speaking to the cat. "Anyhow, it has to be something like that—this passage. That would put Adam—the real Adam—smack at the source of the emerging thrust of civilization. And it gives me the key to my problem. Enoch's my city. Find Enoch, and I've got my origin! Now we're cookin', girl!!"

The exhilaration charged him with new energy. Teil jumped to his feet and started back, mind racing with possibilities opening up by the minute. Suddenly, the whole makeup of the expedition had changed. "This thing has some life to it now, Skia, some flesh and blood!"

As he strode quickly back to the dwelling, Skia barely able to keep out of his way, he concentrated on the key. "So how do we find Enoch?" It was back to the text again, reading snatches as he walked, then visualizing the scene in his mind's eye. He soon saw the way. "Start far enough into the text to establish a reference point in *historical* times, then work backward. That's what we'll do. So why not start with the Flood? No, we want contact with known sites and cities; it'll have to be after the Flood. Yes...there they are—Babel, Erech, Accad, Nineveh, Calah, Resen—all in chapter ten. We know these very cities were among the first post-Flood cities in Mesopotamia. And this string of cities, built along the Tigris-Eu river system, traces back to Nimrod, 'the mighty hunter against the Lord,' whatever that means, but I'm sure that's how the Hebrew should go. What a towering figure of his time; the great warrior-builder of cities, one of the descendants of Ham, who was one of the three sons of Noah. No wonder many historians identify Nimrod with Gilgamesh!''

Teil was struck by the tacit validity of what he read in Genesis when seen in this new light. It spoke of places and events in pre-history with the same authority with which it spoke of those verified by known history. And fitting in so beautifully with the known archaeological and historical evidence, it had the stamp of reality about it. Teil decided, just for the fun of it, that he would trust the text and see what happened.

"So here are the reference points: The Nimrod kingdom of Mesopotamian cities, and the Flood. From there, it's just a step back into the fourth chapter, with its description of Enoch, the city of Cain. And yet, with all the description of the Enoch culture, there's no hint of its location, except that it's somewhere in the land of Nod, or 'wandering,' east of Eden.'' The problem had reached its final stage.

"Okay, I've got to find Eden first, and *then* look eastward for Enoch.'' Teil broke out laughing as the absurdity of the whole thing caught up with him. "Teilhard Mann, mascientist, 83 09 674 599, otherwise known as PZMYLTHIRP, with hazel—described by some as 'bedroom' eyes—looking for the garden of Eden! Let Mascom in on the secret, and I'll be shipped off to a rehab tank for sure, with some of my brain chemistry, not to mention the bedroom eyes, permanently altered!

"So how do we find Eden, Skia? Huh? Tell me.'' And while his upper mind was programming his brain for that question, his eyes aimlessly wandered over the text. He stopped suddenly, almost stepping on the shadowy feline scampering between his feet.

"Plain as the whiskers on your chin, girl. There it is. Look.'' The cat stopped and perked up her head. There, stuck unobtrusively in the narrative of Adam's "forming" and his assignment to the garden—there in forty-nine Hebrew words—was the geographical location of Eden.

"How come I don't remember seeing that before?'' he asked the cat. "But then I wasn't looking for it before, was I?''

There in that simple, unpretentious, matter-of-fact narrative, lay the clues for finding the Garden of Eden.

He felt the giddiness return.

13

Back in his study, Teil set about making a careful translation of the Genesis passage containing the clues to Eden. The study was another Mascom access terminal, limited to his own needs. He sat erect before the screen in the simple, stern, antique chair he always used when he wanted to think at his best, and via the keyboard, quickly set up his working materials on the screen. Before he began, he made an unsuccessful attempt to get through to Kri-kor on his private channel and decided not to leave a message.

On one portion he projected the classified Hebrew text. On another, he could call up the latest lexicons, grammars, concordances, and other reference materials for the ancient language. He had within milliseconds the total semantic milieu of any word or expression at his fingertips. A third area he reserved for recording the translation itself.

But something was missing, and he sensed it more the deeper he delved. Regardless of how literal and accurate a translation he was coming up with, the real task was interpretation— what had the author *meant* in what he said? Teil saw that he had to get a feel for the overall context of the piece of literature as a whole. The information accumulating before him must have been most relevant and hence best understood by the original cast of characters involved in its origins and for whom it was written. To whom *was* the author of Genesis writing? Why? When? Where? Against what backdrop of world and religious history and culture? Only by answering such questions could he hope to discern what the ancient author was trying to convey.

The hours fled by as Teil pored over the material. When he finally felt he had the feel of the piece within the framework of the author's entire five-volume work—the Torah, or Pentateuch—he was quite surprised.

This has to be at least as important as the translation itself, Teil thought. The author's primary purpose seems to have been not to inform, as much as persuade—persuade his people to *live*! Genesis and the Adam story weren't written for the world at large or any individual, but for the *ecclesia*, the called-out ones. Not the religious institution, for there was none yet, but for the invisible body of the called-out people of God. It was the record of its origins, so it would always know what it was, why, whence it came, and whereunto it was called. And the author's way of treating origins in the early chapters has to take on special significance when seen in this light. He deals with the origins, not of the universe, or man, or religion, or history—but the Body—God's people!

Whole new worlds of insight were awakening in Teil as he began putting the translation all together.

וַיִּטַּע־יְהוָה אֱלֹהִים גַּן בְּעֵדֶן מִקֶּדֶם

And Yahweh-Elohim established an
enclosure-in-Eden, eastward...

"It's not called a 'garden' at all! Whoever got that idea? The compound word comes from the verb 'to cover, surround, or defend,' and should be translated 'enclosure.' It was apparently in the eastern portion of a land called Eden."

וַיָּשֶׂם שָׁם אֶת־הָאָדָם אֲשֶׁר יָצָר׃

And he placed there the man he formed...

"The man in question, 'fashioned' for his new role and relationship, settles in the enclosure."

וַיַּצְמַח יְהוָה אֱלֹהִים מִן־הָאֲדָמָה כָּל־עֵץ
נֶחְמָד לְמַרְאֶה וְטוֹב לְמַאֲכָל

And he caused to grow from the ground
various trees desirable in appearance
and good for food...

"Apparently, the place grew a lush natural bounty of fruit and nut trees."

וְעֵץ הַחַיִּים בְּתוֹךְ הַגָּן וְעֵץ הַדַּעַת טוֹב וָרָע :

And the tree of life in the midst of
the enclosure, and the-tree-to-know-good-and-
evil...

"Sounds like a sacramental center, two special trees or symbols which apparently take their names from the relation man would sustain to them."

וְנָהָר יֹצֵא מֵעֵדֶן לְהַשְׁקוֹת אֶת־הַגָּן

And a river going out from Eden to
water the enclosure...

"It doesn't have to flow through the enclosure; just provide the source of water."

וּמִשָּׁם יִפָּרֵד וְהָיָה לְאַרְבָּעָה רָאשִׁים:

And from there it divided and became four
heads...

"This dividing of the river into four heads or sources could be taking place either after it goes out from the land of Eden, or after it leaves the enclosure itself. I can see already that this'll really be a geographical puzzle. Sherlock Holmes, here we come!''

שֵׁם הָאֶחָד פִּישׁוֹן הוּא הַסֹּבֵב אֵת כָּל־אֶרֶץ הַחֲוִילָה

The name of the first is Pishon, the
one going around (or about) all Chavilah...

"The 'first' might be some sort of frame of reference, but whatever this river is, it can either go around the whole land of Chavilah or along it."

אֲשֶׁר־שָׁם הַזָּהָב: וּזֲהַב הָאָרֶץ הַהוּא טוֹב

Where (there is) the gold; and the gold
of that land is good...

"Either the gold or gold products is native and readily mined and of good quality."

שֵׁם הַבְּדֹלַח וְאֶבֶן הַשֹּׁהַם:

There (are also) the bdolach and
shoham-stone...

"Such wealth of detail. It has an amazingly authentic ring to it. If only I could put all these clues together and get a fix... Wait a minute... Shoham-stone, according to this reference, could be malachite, $Cu_2CO_3(OH)_2$, copper ore. Isn't that the mineral uncovered in Cayonu in such abundance?"

With a flick of a few keys, Teil was viewing the Cayonu dig. "Yes... dozens of artifacts made of the stuff, drilled beads and the like. And not twenty kilometers above Cayonu is one of the richest copper mining areas in all Anatol—Maden, the very name coming from the Turkish word for metal. Wouldn't that be something if Eden was right in that area somewhere?" Teil called up a map of the area.

"Hmmm... Diyarbekir is the key city in that area. Might

not be a bad place to start, for a base of operations, anyway."

"Hey, Skia, look at this!" he exclaimed, calling up data on the city. "Diyarbekir is the site of ancient Amida. That goes back into prehistory, and...hold it— *No one has ever dug the mound under there!*"

He continued his study of the text.

וְשֵׁם־הַנָּהָר הַשֵּׁנִי גִּיחוֹן הוּא הַסּוֹבֵב אֵת כָּל־אֶרֶץ כּוּשׁ׃

> And the name of the second river is Gihon;
> it goes around the whole land of Cush...

"That could be translated 'goes alongside' too."

וְשֵׁם הַנָּהָר הַשְּׁלִישִׁי חִדֶּקֶל הוּא הַהֹלֵךְ קִדְמַת אַשּׁוּר

> And the name of the third river is
> Hiddeqel; it goes over against Asshur...

"A solid clue I can hang my comm on! The Hiddeqel is the Tigis river; it's still called the Dicle. And sure enough, ancient Asshur, which is Assyria, had the Tigris running all along its western face. Now we're getting somewhere!"

וְהַנָּהָר הָרְבִיעִי הוּא פְרָת׃

> And the fourth river is Phrat...

"There's no doubt here either; that's the Euphrates, still called the Firat or Frat."

וַיִּקַּח יְהוָה אֱלֹהִים אֶת־הָאָדָם וַיַּנִּחֵהוּ בְגַן־עֵדֶן

> And Yahweh-Elohim got possession of the
> man and set him to reside in enclosure Eden...

"What a strange figure, to 'get possession of.' Wonder what that conveys? So personal. In all the other creation stories, the gods never relate like that to anyone. But man is here taken as though laid claim to—how appealing—then assigned a special place and task.''

לְעָבְדָהּ וּלְשָׁמְרָהּ:

To work it and guard it...

"Working it means caring for it. For the trees, perhaps? The word usually has the connotation of tilling the soil. And what is this 'guarding' of the enclosure? Guard this way of life? Defend it from those outside?'' Teil was so caught up in the unfolding story, he kept on translating beyond the references to Eden.

וַיֹּאמֶר יְהוָה אֱלֹהִים לֹא־טוֹב הֱיוֹת הָאָדָם לְבַדּוֹ

And Yahweh-Elohim said, 'It is not good for the man to be isolated...'

"What a strange expression. How was this man separate or isolated? It seems to be in the context of living relationship...

אֶעֱשֶׂה־לּוֹ עֵזֶר כְּנֶגְדּוֹ:

I will make a helper corresponding to him...

"So... It's not good for man to be a loner; so woman becomes a 'helper corresponding to him.' Does this imply a shift in the relationship between man and woman? I missed that in the list of criteria for emergent civilization, didn't I? Such powerful forces as the advent of agriculture and animal husbandry replacing hunting, the shift in technology and religion, and the rise of permanent settlements—all these would naturally reflect on the man-woman thing. Maybe that's where the old idea of permanent commitment started. Marriage. It had to start somewhere...

"And man 'leaves his father and his mother and cleaves to his wife, and they become one...' My god... The human race must have really had that once.''

14

At that point, Teil's wristcom pulsed into life, and he heard a familiar feminine voice calling him on his private channel.

"Teilhard... Are you there, Teil?"

His eyes kept staring through the screen into his own emptiness. Oh, no... not her, he thought. It was Epi-Thumia.

"You're probably surprised, my calling you at home? Teil...?"

"Yes, actually," he said flatly.

"Actually what?" she asked.

"I'm surprised."

"Oh... You weren't in when I called before."

"I was off line; went for a walk," he said.

"Oh."

"Quite unusual," he said.

"Glad to hear it."

"Really amazing," he said.

"Really?"

"Yes."

"Well..."

"Haven't done that for ages," he said.

"Sounds like you should do it again sometime," she said.

"Absolutely. Matter of fact, I'd recommend it!"

"You mean for me?" she asked.

"Why not?"

"Why thank you!" she said.

"You're more than welcome, I can assure you," he said. Easy, old boy, easy, he thought. You know there's something funny here.

"I'm hardly considered the outdoor type, you know," she said.

"Oh?"

"Yes."

"Well. I didn't know that," he said.

"No. I don't suppose you did." There was a pause.

"We really didn't get to know each other very well at Regional this morning, did we?" she asked, with a forced laugh.

"I'd say we did pretty well," he said.

"On the personal side, I mean."

"Oh," he said. There was an awkward pause. "How's everything at Regional? Any more bombs or Sigma or whatever?"

"I'm not at work."

"Of course."

"I'm at my place."

"Yeah..."

"Getting ready to go out, as a matter of fact," she said.

"Is that a fact?" he said. I know what she's after, he thought; but what's she really after?

"Yes," she said.

"Well, that's nice..."

"I don't suppose you get a chance to get out much—Teil. Lately, I mean, with archaeprobe and all..."

"I manage to get around," he said.

"I'll bet you do. Helps get your mind off things."

"Something like that," he said. "Well... I was just going over some work I brought home..." Another awkward pause.

"Teil...?" She said it in her best high-power low voice.

"Yes?"

"By the way, you may call me Epi if you like." The vision of her flashy form swept through his brain again, igniting desire. "I was thinking..." she added.

"You wouldn't want to do that," he said.

"I *knew* the man had a sense of humor. Bravo. Teil, since you're leaving so soon..."

"Yes...?"

"And you might be gone quite awhile," she added. "You know the priority they've given us on this thing..."

"Yes."

"Well, there are so many unknowns and variables..." she said.

"Oh?..."

"Well, you just don't know," she said. "Have you ever visited the Old Square?"

"Not sure I follow you, Epi." You did it again, clock-head, he thought, kicking himself for capitulating.

"The Square. You know, the ancient town. The underground?"

"Underground? You mean UGLIs and all that?" he asked, testing her.

"No silly. I mean the old underground city. Los Angeles."

"Oh!"

"It's not where mascientists are supposed to have dinner every night, but— "

"Oh, you mean—" he said. "But I thought She closed all those places down ages ago."

"She did. Only well, in a way. On and off. They're really not supposed to be going. But you know how it is. We must have our little diversions now and then. And there's this chic place under the Square that hasn't made the off-limits list yet. Perfectly okay security-wise."

"Oh?" he said.

"In case you're interested," she said.

"Oh."

"That is, if you haven't had dinner yet and felt like a little relaxation and diversion before your big expedition."

"Well," he said, "you kind of caught me with my— I mean, all day my head's been filled with archaeprobe and everything, and—"

"All the more reason you should take a short breather," she said. "Wasn't it you who said you get some of your best insights on a problem after you've let go and forgotten all about it?"

"Did I say that?" he said. How the devil did she know that?

"You said it about your last breakthrough on sensor integration programs, if you'll pardon dragging work into this..."

"Aha! You've been spying on me again!" he said playfully, testing again.

"Of course. That's my job, isn't it?" she asked.

The way she said that, he thought, like it caught her off guard.

"*Part* of my job, anyway. There are other parts, Teil. Parts you don't even know about—yet."

There it is, he thought, all registers full and multivibrating! "Hello, hello... Still there?" she asked.

"You're very flattering, actually," he said. "I hadn't realized—"

"Oh? I thought you had."

"Well, actually... Of course, I guess it's natural. I mean after all, you are a very—" Watch the LSR there, old boy! he thought.

"Yes?" she asked.

'I'll have you know," he said, "that the most uncivilized phrase just knocked on the door of my little old mind just now, and I pushed it away."

"Bravo! What was it?"

"I wouldn't dare!"

"But you must!"

"I absolutely refuse. It's too ungentlemanly even to think, much less—"

"How flattering!"

I know, he thought. "Absolutely," he said, against all his new-found light.

"Well then, why not meet me at tube central at, say 08.00?"

There was a long pause, then Teil said, "Why not?"

"Wonderful!" she said. "I'm looking forward to it. And don't worry; I've arranged everything."

That's what I'm afraid of, Teil said to himself.

"Oh...about clothes," she added. "Shall we go daring and dress 'Flash Gordon'? This place goes back to the twentieth century—dancing and all."

Oh, oh... he thought, she couldn't possibly know what I was doing in Cinecom, could she? But it was too late to matter. "Now you're talkin'," he said, hyping himself into it. "Let's do it!"

"I'll call up the costumes and have yours delivered," she said. "See you there, Flash."

* * *

They met at tube central that night as planned, as Teil knew he would from the moment she had called. Their matching costumes were right out of the ancient epic fantasy adventure strip: form-clinging body suits of sheer stretch fabric, loin briefs fastened by broad waistbands, thin fitted buskins with leggings to mid-calf, and capelets with fitted hoods framing the face. They each wore goggles fastened through the top of the capelet hood and shoved high on the forehead. Set off in bold slashes of color, they made a sleek eye-catching duo, radiating verve and panache, ready for derring-do.

When Epi-Thumia saw Teil emerging from the tube dressed dashingly as Flash, she decided to play the role in authentic high camp. "Oh, Flash...!" she said, coming up to him endearingly. "Finally, we're together again!" They came together in a mock embrace.

"Dale! I thought Ming had you for keeps. Thank heaven!"

"Oh my darling... I feel so safe in your arms... They're so strong yet so tender!"

"These arms were meant to hold and protect you and, by heaven, they will as long as they have life." They broke into heady laughter.

"Oh, Flash, please don't try to go through with this—it's madness!"

"It's our only chance, Dale; this way, we at least have a fighting chance."

"What is life compared to a love like ours?" she asked.

"We're on our way, darling," Teil said. "It's a new life

fraught with dangers... But with you by my side, I could do anything..."

Epi-Thumia laughed gaily, enjoying it immensely. And they did cut a striking figure together, walking down the avenue, she linking her arm through his. Any regrets he may have had about Aspasia were hidden behind the delightful game they were playing.

They walked toward the heart of the city, glowing invitingly in the evening light emanating from within her crystalline heart. Part of her inhabitants were sequestered in their private cells within the hives, while the night people were just coming out. In the night, it was another world.

Octahedral shapes, mimicing that of the silicon crystal itself, combined with spherical and cylindrical forms to create the basic motif of the buildings in the city's downtown heart. All lighting was integral to each structure and distributed throughout its translucent substance, illuminating the city by a kind of inner radiance. For most people, the encounter was a mood-altering experience. Here was something very special made for *them*, a Garden of Delights, yet far enough beyond them—alien in a way—to elicit reverential awe. The city's beguiling spirit drew her devotees deeper into the mystique of her all-securing, all-providing, all-exciting, all-enclosing bosom. "Awe-inspiring" came close to describing the experience; "polerasty" came closer, if such a word could be coined for intercourse with city.

Finally, they came into the Old District, where Epi-Thumia made her way to the Museum of Old Broadway. Here were the relics of an ancient era, preserved *in situ*; cars and buildings and people and things, looking as though one day in the 1970s everything simply froze in time. One whole block of Broadway, between Seventh and Sixth, was now an open-air museum replica. The restoration was flawless; an old photograph come to life, only not alive. Had the spectators not been moving, one could not have distinguished them from their earlier counterparts—except for their dress—crowding unmovingly around them everywhere in the streets, sidewalks, and stores. It was tricky to keep from bumping into the static figures that looked so much like they were alive. The illusion was perfect.

"There you are, sir," Epi-Thumia said with a flourish, "What they called the City of Angels."

"What a sight!" Teil exclaimed. "I haven't been here since educom; and it's so much more than I remember."

There was Bullocks, with its picture-window fantasies beckoning the indulgence of holiday shoppers, complete with square brass rail around the front, supporting a curious melange of assorted characters, gawking or hawking. The news stands on the corners, with their racks of endlessly revealing tabloids and gaudy-covered skin magazines, clothespin-hung like so many dangling private parts for all the world to see. LeRoy Jewelers, the bus fare man with the money box on a stick, National Shirt Shops, Pentothal Sleep, the Lankershim Hotel, *Ben Hur* at the State, the ever-smiling blind woman with her seeing-eye dog—pushing pamphlets. And Kress, featuring "Corn Dog and Coke" for thirty-seven cents.

Buses gorged with bodies were disgorging them into the intersection, shoving more into their craving maws, only to regurgitate them down the street—a constant recycling of the human organism into, through, and out of City as though she were feeding on the species.

They had even captured the dirt, the chewing gum—discarded in the usual places—and the smells of whatever it was that emanated from under the sidewalks out of the bowels of that ancient place.

Was this system for accommodating the human mob and its refuse what they called "city?" Teil wondered. It was then he first glimpsed why it had always been man who accommodated to city and not the other way around. And what are we accomodating to today...?

Cars, cars, and more cars, each authentic, and each complete with full scale occupants managing to survive as half-scale humans. The traffic cop in the still eye of the storm, caught between alternately advancing waves of bodies, machines, and pollution.

People. Everywhere people. From the seven-year-old street-urchin bootblacks to the fashion model; from the wetbacks to the Spring Street millionaires, the streets were one mass of people. Some, merging facelessly into the crowd, others standing out. Like the man with the ruddy unkempt look of the bughouse about him, thrusting a black leather-covered book high into the air and shouting some now-unheard cry. But one could, with little imagination, make out the sound.

And the eternal Clifton's Cafeteria, curiously symbolic of it all, where one could still jostle in and walk around the steam and ice tables covered with food—and real ice—and be caught up in the smoke and din of dishes and city-glot.

"Do you ever get the feeling all these...these dummies are really people?" Epi-Thumia asked.

"That's probably what happened to all the archaeologists," Teil jauntily replied.

"It's an eerie feeling, isn't it?" she said. "And you know something...?"

"I know nothing...," he said, smiling.

"It seems strangely different than the last time I saw it, too."

"Makes you wonder just what they want you to remember about that era when you look at all this," he said.

"What we've come from, obviously," she said. "Look at them! They must have actually *lived* like that."

"I must say, some of the women back there were pretty fancy lookers, though, wouldn't you say, Dale?"

"One good thing about *dummies*, Flash—*darling*—they aren't real competition."

"Sure now?" Teil teased, as he reached out and grabbed one of the beauties. Epi-Thumia playfully tried to hit him, and he ducked.

"Oh, Flash... And all along I thought you had eyes only for me," she said, wiping away a mock tear.

"Come to think of it," Teil observed, "they must have had quite a problem with the people."

"How's that?"

'Well, how do you show the difference between manikins in the store windows and the people in the streets, when they're all manikins. Or, horrors, maybe they're really not all manikins!"

"I think they've done an admirable job. Can't you tell the difference?"

"Funny thing," he replied, "some times I can, and then some times I can't."

"What does the strange professor mean by that strange remark?"

"The strange professor...the *very* strange professor, who relates better to machines, ancient history, and cats than to humans—whoever *they* are—and who doesn't really know what he's doing here with this exotic Azura, queen-of-magic Dragon Lady hanging on his arm in the midst of this horde of senseless dummies senselessly milling about in their dumb frenetic motionless frenzy...which actually gives him the willies... In fact, the strange professor who just made that remark means by the remark that you just remarked about, that he doesn't know what the devil he meant—by that remark, I mean!"

"That's what I thought you meant," she said, breaking out laughing. Teil joined her, and there in the midst of the hundreds of mute human likenesses, the air echoed their laughter eerily across the facades.

"Talking about strange people..." she queried as her eye caught the man with the book. "What do you think he's doing?"

"Let's go see," Teil said, taking her by the hand and pulling her through the static throng.

"Why, the title is just 'book,' " she said. "Greek for 'book'— *biblia*."

"Then you *do* know what your name means in Greek!"

"I hope so," she said with a sly grin.

Teil forced his libido into its cage again and stepped closer to the man, stuck forever in his mad thrust at the collective consciousness.

"I'm afraid you don't understand," Teil said.

"What?"

"About the book."

"What about it?"

"It's not a generic term for book. That's a particular book he's got there. It was called the Bible."

"Bible...? Oh, you mean that book? But why on earth would they have that here now? Know what I mean?"

"Good question. And look around. It's everywhere."

"Where?"

"You must be more observant, Dr.Thumia, if we're going to analyze this dig."

"Yes, Professor," she said, winking.

"The people passing out leaflets over there..."

"You mean badgering the poor passers-by?"

"And the couple holding up the magazine there..."

"The ones with the frozen look of 'I'm glad I can hide behind this, but you'd better AWAKE'?"

"And the man with the little sign on his coat: JUDGEMENT IS COMING..."

"Is it?" she asked.

"Probably, but don't tell Mascom that. And the lady with the seeing-eye dog. She's pushing it too."

"They've even got dogs in on the act!" Epi-Thumia remarked. "You're absolutely right; I never noticed that before. Is all this new? Why did She preserve that particular time and place?"

"Beats me. Maybe She's trying to tell us something."

"You would have to suggest that," she said.

"I don't know why, but I get this strange feeling at times that City, with people as the electromotive flux, generates its own field of force. Do you ever feel it?"

"No. What do you mean?"

"It's almost as though it has a Spirit of its own—a spiritual force."

"Afraid I don't follow..."

"Maybe it's really not city at all. Maybe it's something inside us. Hey! Maybe that's what *is* inside us—City!" He saw Epi-Thumia's blank expression. "Anyhow...that book still bothers me. Looking at the historical sweep of the thing, how could one book be so used, or misused, so as to be made to serve the interests of so many odd-ball movements and ideologies? The same book used to support the causes of love, peace, brotherhood, and freedom, and of war, strife, argument, division, and destruction. No other book can even begin to compete on that score. Makes one wonder why, in all the thousands of years of civilization, that one book... Wait! Maybe that's just what one would expect if it *was* the W—.

"Was what?"

"I don't know... I'll have to think about that one. Come on, let's go," he said, grabbing her hand and pulling her on.

"But you can't keep doing this to me! Getting me interested, then dropping it. It's maddening!"

"Sorry about that," he said with a smirk.

Suddenly the air was rent with a woman's unearthly scream from high up the side of the building. As their heads jerked upward to the sound, they heard close by a loud sickening thud and froze to the spot. It was deathly still. Finally Teil grabbed Epi-Thumia's hand and stepped bravely around the corner. The body of a naked woman lay smashed on the sidewalk in front of them; clenched tightly in her hands was a bloody aborted fetus, still attached to its mother's umbilical.

"Teil!..." Epi-Thumia shrieked, stepping behind Teil to shield herself from the sight. "Is it... Is it real...?"

Teil stood transfixed; for an expanded second the scene went into time freeze. Teil was the misbegotten infant, crushed to death, and as he looked up into his mother's face, reliving the moment of awful impact, it was the stern and unrelenting face of X.

"Part of the show...isn't it?" Epi-Thumia asked, her voice shaking. "The dummies...?"

"You tell *me*," he muttered between clenched teeth. "God, what is happening today?" Teil sputtered under his breath. He clicked on his wristcom and called for help on the emergency channel. This was megapol, after all, and city took care of her casualties, did she not? As he pulled Epi-Thumia away from the lurid scene, he stopped abruptly in front of the old cast-iron police call box, staring at it with slackened jaw. Teil pointed to the cover, scrawled over with graffiti, and they read it together:

THE MOST SIGNIFICANT SYMPTOM
OF THE ILLNESS OF OUR TIME
IS THE SEXUAL

"Let's get out of here!!" she cried, pulling him away.

They walked quickly and silently up Broadway to Fifth, putting as much physical and emotional distance as possible between them and the macabre scene.

"Do you have the horrible feeling," Epi-Thumia asked in a forced voice, "that she'll get up and come after us with that terrible thing in her hands?" Teil walked faster.

They turned west a block, and there at the end of the museum was old Pershing Square. It was a perfect replica, from the aging bronze Civil War cannon and soap-box orators to the *accoutrement* on Beethoven's bronze hair—compliments of the square's long-departed pigeonry.

"At least *they* knew the difference from the real thing," Teil sardonically noted.

"What on earth are you talking about?" Epi-Thumia asked.

"Pigeons! That's why they're not around any more. I must say, Epi, this has been quite an experience, to say the least!"

"And it hasn't even started yet!"

"Well," he said, gesturing for her to lead the way, "What are you waiting for. Let's go!" He broke into his fast stride, and the long-legged Epi-Thumia was breathlessly trying to keep abreast.

"I had no idea there was something of the wild side in you, Teil-*hard*..." He went even faster.

"Where are we going now?" Teil asked, faintly suspicious of the new turn. "That we're off the beaten path would be the understatement of the evening." He shrugged off the feeling that nagged at him as he let himself be swept along.

"Hang on," she said, "we're practically there."

Off to one side of the Square was a concrete stairwell going down. After reaching the bottom of the stairs, they continued descending by various shafts leading to the ancient underground levels. The two encountered an assaulting assortment of smells on the way down that ran the gamut from the stale exhalation of musty buildings to the stench of rancid egesta.

"I wonder," he remarked, fanning the foul air away from his face, "Whether She's engineered these awful odors as part of the replica, or if that's what city turns into after the glitter fades."

"Atmosphere, Teilhard, *ambiance!*"

Finally, they came to a steel door covered with a sloppy coat of new paint, and waited while Epi-Thumia knocked. Teil could barely make out some of the original lettering, but as the door opened and they were checked through by a huge greasy-looking character with hands as big as hams, it suddenly occurred to Teil where they were. It was the subterranean men's room of the ancient Pershing Square Garage.

15

"This is it Teilhard," Epi-Thumia said.
"That's what I'm afraid of. What is this place?"
Inside, the neon sign read

PALACE OF FORBIDDEN DREAMS

"It's huge!" Teil said, surprised.
"And just a little different on the inside, wouldn't you say?"
"What are 'forbidden dreams'?"
"That's for you to say," she said, with a twisted smile.
"And you...?"
"We all have our 'forbiddens,' Teilhard; you should know that." She cast her eyes about to relieve his penetrating gaze. "Look... It's all authentic, you know."
"Authentic what?"
"Mid-twentieth, just like outside. The Hollywood Palladium. It's a replica."
"They've done a good job," he said, taking in the place.
The large circular dance floor was surrounded by dining and drinking areas and a bandstand in front. A large winding staircase led to balconies overlooking the floor. The high ceiling was dominated by a large crystal chandelier in the center over the dance floor.
"Wonder if we're going to get in," Epi-Thumia said; "the

place is jammed."

"Ballrooms..." Teil said. "That's what they called these places. Did you know that I was really pretty good at the old American dances? Did research on 'em. And I got up a Swing Era celebration at school one time. Lifted a record player and records from a museum one night and had a Big Band Bash. We danced all night! They're really crazy, but you have to have the music that went with them."

"I can see you now, Teilhard, doing the jitterfly, or what have you."

"Jitterbug! Please! The Big Bands would turn over in their graves! Jitter*fly*—really, Epi, you're too much, you know that?" he said, grinning at her. "And this place promises to be really FUN."

"I thought you'd be impressed," she said, winking.

After Epi-Thumia had a few quick words with the doorman, he took them to the one who apparently ran the place. In the dim light, the person looked more like a she, but it was hard to tell. She was tall, plump, and jolly, with a hair-plant of fiery red Auca hair and one coiled-snake earring—with a real live snake.

"You playful children can just call me Lethe," she said.

"I can't believe it," muttered Teil under his breath, staring at the apparition. "Is that a real snake you have there?"

"That's not all that's real, dearie," she said, fluttering her iridescent rainbow-hued lashes.

Checking their masrings again and apparently satisfied with their "credentials," Lethe showed them to a small table on the edge of the dance floor near the bandstand and handed them the menu. "We're so crowded tonight," Lethe said; "don't know why. Hope this table is all right for you two children, knowing you had reservations and all." Then with a wink at Epi-Thumia and a nod toward Teil, she left them to the atmosphere, buzzing with excitement and anticipation. Teil was trying to make out who else he knew might be there, but figured they were safe.

"If someone wanted to wipe out a whole raft of mas-people," Teil said, "this would be the place. I've never seen so many rings in one night spot. What's the attraction?"

"You'll see," she said. "Besides, they know it's safe here."

"I feel like a drink," Teil exclaimed, motioning for a waitress. "What have they got to relieve the drys?"

"If you really want to go authentic Twentieth, Teil, you must try what they called Coke. It's the very original formula, later banned."

"Yeah. Kind of a symbol, wasn't it? Hey, look! The band's coming on! I can't believe it. You're right, Epi; authentic is the word! Beautiful! Now if they just know how to bring the music out of those old instruments..."

When the drinks came, Teil grabbed one of the frosty replica bottles and took a quick swig. "What an impossible concoction," he gasped. "You mean they actually drank this stuff?" He took another.

"Interesting how tastes change, isn't it?" Epi-Thumia said.

"Well, it takes a little getting used to, but then what doesn't, eh, Dr. Epi-Thumia...? You know, a man could get attached to this stuff," he said, relishing the remainder of his drink and ordering more. "Like getting attached to *thumia*, isn't it?"

"Aha!" she said, sucking hers through a straw, "I was wondering when we'd get to that again."

"It's one of those words that sounds like what it means, he said. You can almost see the drool, can't you?"

"I don't see any yet, Teil," she said, exploring his lower lip with her long forefinger. The memory of the man with the tortured face in the park that morning flashed into Teil's mind. His countenance darkened as he turned his head away. He quickly downed his new drink and ordered another.

"What's wrong?" Epi-Thumia asked.

"What the hell is happening out there, Epi; will you tell me that...?"

"Like at Regional today?"

"More than that... Haven't you wondered lately...? Oh, I dunno... Hey! There's the music," he said, coming alive to the Big Band sound. "Let's dance." He grabbed her hand and pulled her to her feet.

"You want *me* to do those old dances?"

"Of course! Come on."

"What if I can't follow you?"

"Don't worry, I've got a strong lead, and you look like you're light on your feet, and I *know* you've got rhythm in those gams of yours."

"What did you do, Teilhard, overdose on that era; you're even beginning to talk like they did."

"LADIES AND GENTLEMEN!" the bandleader was announcing as the musical reprise began. "To start off, from the Golden Age of Swing, a number to put a little sunshine in your step,

'Sunny Side of the Street.'

"Now you're talkin'." Teil exclaimed as the piece began. "And the music's the real thing! Let's go, gal."

"What did they put in those Cokes, anyway?" she said, eager to dance.

A female vocalist began singing the nostalgic tune:

> "Grab your coat and get your hat,
>   Leave your worries on the doorstep;
> Life can be so sweet
>   On the sunny side of the street...."

Epi-Thumia was a quick learner. After Teil had practically carried her through the first few numbers, she was on her own. And Teil was a changed man, elevated not only from the drinks but the dance, music, and romance. His tense body relaxed as he moved easily and surely to the rhythm. There was no stopping him, and they made a flashy couple. Others stood by and watched as still others tried to imitate their steps.

"Hey, Epi, isn't this great! I was made for this rhythm, you know."

"Oh, Flash, darling, all that you are and dancing too..." she said, with a mock swoon.

"Does something to you, doesn't it? How could you have

possibly thought of such a thing? I thank you; archaeprobe thanks you; and Skia my cat thanks you," he said, giving her a big hug. He missed the shadow that crept behind Epi-Thumia's eyes as she turned away; he was now dancing with reckless abandon, totally transported. And he kept dancing, on and on.

"Teilhard, the music has stopped now; we can sit down," she said, leading him reluctantly off the floor and collapsing into her chair. "Whew!"

As they ordered and ate dinner, the entertainment proved an interesting diversion. First, the maitre d' herself, as comedienne and master of ceremonies, sandwiching her plump and jolly self between a male impersonator, then a chanteuse, and finally, a poet.

Lethe was flustered as she tried to introduce the young man. He was of medium height, with short, reddish-brown hair, dark eyes, and a slender wiry build, giving his whole manner the feeling of intense single-mindedness. It looked like he had dressed in a hurry, not knowing what to wear. Apparently there had been a last-minute change, and Lethe did not know his name. But stepping quickly in front of her, the poet, still out of breath, addressed his audience.

"Ladies and gentlemen..." His voice carried an urgency that seemed out of place. "I want to thank you for this opportunity of giving you part of the past..." He glanced nervously over his shoulder into the wings. "And can only hope I'll be able to deliver my piece..." The background music stopped, and the audience picked up the serious mien of the disheveled young man.

Teil noticed the poet was scrutinizing everyone as he spoke, as though looking for someone; he was looking at hands as well. As his eyes caught Teil's masring, they shot to his face and flashed with recognition. Teil saw him nod ever so slightly as he held his gaze for an instant.

"I want to thank you that I am so gladly welcomed..." he said, emphasizing the last two words while looking back at Teil. "...And I hope you will be well pleased." Teil's pulse pounded as he recognized the reference to Aspasia again, but he sat motionless, shooting an apprehensive glance at Epi-Thumia.

"I wish to recite a poem found in some ruins after FEAR," the poet continued. An appreciative murmur rippled through the audience. "It comes from a work now banned." A gasp went up; they were more eager than ever to catch every word.

Epi-Thumia leaned close to Teil and whispered, "How marvelous."

"A play on the Cain and Abel theme," the performer said. Teil sat forward in his chair, incredulous.

"The piece is simply titled City," the poet continued. "Perhaps it will give you some of the flavor of that long-forgotten time and the personal dilemma this unknown writer felt as he tried to survive System." Teil glanced at Epi-Thumia again without moving his head but saw no reaction. Survive System! thought Teil. The man deserves listening to.

The young man closed his eyes a moment, as though drawing courage from some unseen source for what he must do. When he began, he was fully assured and into the mood of the piece. The free-verse soliloquy came out in a torrent of emotional feeling.

> The tyranny of smallness...
> largeness,
> shallowness, cruelness,
> aloofness, unfeelingness,
> Aloneness.
>
> The have-mad, on-the-make-mad,
> money-things-mad,
> noise-mad,
> Mad-mad;
> rush-into-everything-everyone,
> have-and-see-feel-and
> go
> mad.

Beauty-mad, ugly,
city-mad.
Consumerized Citizens!
Packaged nicely
staring blankly
at the Great Dream,
rotting
amid the decomposed remains
of what we still profanely call
Democracy.
Expediency!
thy name is politics!

Let's hear it for Expediency!
Hip, hip, hurrah!
Hip, hip, hurrah!
Don't fire till you see the whites
of their eyes. All *man*kind
red in tooth and claw,
lusting after his neighbor's
country,
way of life, and wife.
Not because they have too little,
but because they want
too much.

See too much...
Peddling the virus madness
through the Cold Tube Marvel
of our uncovering. Buying
our beliefs
through menthol-filtered
necromancy.
Or is it selling?
The pimping cavalcade of
Entertainment
whores,
pandering to the new-born

consumered lust:
Regression,
half-consummated fantasy,
and self-consuming
nihilation.

Suddenly
a whole People
crave
a psychedelic!

A People ever-learning—
heaps and heaps on growing heaps
of bulging, oozing, mounting, bursting
knowledge.
Splitting at the seams
with "Civilization."
Ever-learning never seeing
ever-learning never coming
to Knowledge of the Truth.
Not once!

And a hundred million "healers"—
brilliant products of
the Age of Analysis,
cleverly wielding
cool-and-cynical-edged
their scalpels
to our common Madness.
Blood-letting
the putrid Soul-sore
with leeches gorging
on their own.
And powerless to heal;
to heal, powerless.
Powerless
to heal...

Blinded by their
blindness,
blinding us;
blind
to their unclean
half-way surgery,
leaving gaping open for all the world
to see
our inner bleeding
loathsome spewing
stinking gawking
obscene
shame.
And powerless to heal.

And...
at the used-to-be heart,
behind stained glass organ choirs
and pulpiteering vanity,
leaving broken bread and wine
for soda cracker crumbs
and measured sips
of adolescent pop,
where we thought we could
touch,
reach,
feel after,
and haply find...
A striving after wind!

False prophets and
apostate priests
serving the same pagan altars as
apostate Man.
Mere wind,
without even a striving...
And powerless to heal.

16

There was a profound silence. The words out of the past had found their mark in the heart of the present. There was no applause; the people just sat there, staring with that look of having glanced against their will into an awesomely revealing mirror. Teil grabbed his drink, saw that his hand was shaking, and downed the rest of it in one gulp.

No sooner had the young man turned to leave the stage, than two SOGs appeared out of nowhere, took him by each arm, and began hustling him hastily out. Suddenly the place was a turmoil of people caught, and when Teil looked around, Epi-Thumia was gone.

As the SOGs struggled the poet through the crowded ballroom and passed by Teil, the young man purposely tripped on Teil's outstretched legs and stumbled.

"Teilhard?" he whispered in Teil's ear, struggling to get up and covering any trace of the communication in the commotion. "Call this number. The Others are after you. Watch out." He pushed a scrap of paper into Teil's footgear as he got to his feet.

One SOG caught the young man and wrenched his arm behind his back, while the other tried to get a choke hold around his neck. As they took him away, there was a triumphant fire in his eyes.

Teil forced himself to look merely nonplussed; inside, his gut was churning with a storm of emotion. Had anyone detected the exchange between them? What would happen if they had? Why had Epi-Thumia bolted? Who was this poet, and how did he know Teil? How was he tied in with Aspasia? Or was he? And who were the Others? No one knew for sure; most had never heard of them, and those who had knew only the vaguest hearsay that they secretly wanted to foment revolution and wrest rule from X. But most people, Teil included, assumed such were UGLIs, since the media only covered them and Others were never mentioned. Why would they be after him? Was the woman who tried to blow up Regional an Other? Then words from Kri-kor's desperate message in the sphere flashed through his mind, words that had not registered at the time, that the Others were also somehow involved with Nexus.

To forestall panic, Lethe quickly stepped to the bandstand and tried to reassure everyone. "Everything's all right, ladies and gentlemen," she said. "The Seat of Government people have assured me it was only the young man they were after. It seems he was, uh...what you might say an unscheduled replacement for one of our own entertainers. Please don't bother yourselves and be alarmed, and we won't charge for the extra entertainment. It's not every night we get to witness, and so close, the arrest of an UGLI." A buzz of excitement swept through the crowd.

"He *was* an UGLI!"

"How exciting..."

"It's all a put-on; those really weren't SOGs..."

Epi-Thumia cautiously returned, shaken. Still standing, she motioned Lethe to the side of the stage. "Are you sure everything is all right?" she asked.

"Of course it is, dearie," the plump one said, bending down, her voice dripping while she fondled Epi-Thumia's hand. "These things happen, now, don't they? If it was anything else they were after, you can bet your sweet masring there that they'd still be going through the place. Now wouldn't they?"

As things settled down, Lethe took the spotlight again. "Dream time, children. DREAM time... Now we can get back to business, and not just eating, drinking, and dancing, if you know what I mean." There was a general murmur of knowing assent. "Well then, we're all agreed on that." She gave a signal, and the atmosphere began to change.

The new psychic projection of cinecom was in full swing here, where lighting and sound effects were now being modulated directly onto the brain rhythms of those present, and thus parasensory. The incredible efficiency of the Mascom Age had solved both the problems of noise and variations in individual taste at the same time. The effect was psychedelic, with the individual his own control over what he "saw" and "heard." The mood was what one made it. And the very special drinks were part of this experience.

"The Palace of Forbidden Dreams," Lethe announced, "bids you enter a world of delicious fantasy, conjured to suit the deepest desires of your heart." Even her voice sounded different now as it crossed over into the subjective dimension. "Name your fantasy, and the djinn of 1000 dreams will serve your every pleasure—anything you intensely desire..." Teil shot a glance at Epi-Thumia wondering if she picked up her name in the last two words.

"You mean the drinks...?" Teil asked Epi-Thumia.

"Yes. Isn't it a kick? Psychic catalysts. They take your particular fantasy and transmute it so you're actually experiencing it, only more real and more intense than if you really were." Teil darkened.

"That figures," he said. "It never stops, does it? Have you ever tried the stuff?"

"Yes." He couldn't tell if she was lying and searched her face for some clue of what she was after. Though he could discern nothing, he sensed more than ever that this thing with Epi-Thumia was other than the casual affair appearing on the surface.

"You mean you just order a number?" he asked.

"Yes. Just pick the intensity level on a scale from one to ten."

Teil's eyes were drawn again to the last two words on the menu, flickering in their blue-green iridescence. "Intense desire" triggered a chain of associations in his mind: Epi-Thumia. Lust. Oblivion. Already, in an instant, he had extrapolated the whole affair to its end. His eyes slowly lifted from the page as though drawn by hers. She had been looking into him again. It was the point of no return. But he knew he had passed that the moment she had called that afternoon.

"Fantasy realifiers, you might say," she added, drawing him back.

"Never heard of such a thing," he said obliquely.

"They make fantasy seem real."

"Only Mascom could come up with that kind of chemistry... Wait a minute! You don't think...."

"Most probably, Flash, darling. Would you ever suspect for one minute that She would not know what's going on here? Really?" But Teil was way ahead of her.

"But fantasy *becoming* reality... The last thin line vanishing between them... That's insanity!"

"Why not? Controlled, limited. Isn't that what humans live on anyway."

"What? Fantasy or insanity?"

"Both?"

"You're probably right, you know... You surprise me at times, Epi," he said.

She capitalized on his momentary concession. "Besides, you're with me" she said, taking his hand. "And I would like us to do it—together." She held the menu up to the waitress and merely pointed to her selection. Teil ordered a number one. "I have it on good authority that it's impossible to overdose on the stuff," she explained.

"Really," he said cynically.

"Probably another Mascom safeguard."

" 'Balance,' " he said. "That's the word, isn't it? Wait till the next time I talk with her..." he said carelessly, tossing off the words. "I should have known I'd be letting myself in for something..."

"..Something strange, Professor?" she said, taking the drinks from the tray herself. "Well," she said, giving Teil his drink and lifting her glass in the toast, " 'here's lookin' at you,' as I think they said back then."

"Absolutely. And you'd make an eyeful in any era, Dale."

"Oh, Flash," she said, fluttering her long lashes.

They drank their potions and waited.

"Nothing," he said blandly. The drink is fantastically delicious, he thought.

"It takes awhile, and I'm sure we're supposed to sit back and relax." It seemed to Teil her face changed in that instant.

Yes, there it goes again, shifting, he thought. The close-cut blonde hair merged into the vision of long dark hair. And the face! It's the UGLI! Aspasia!! NO!!! He was into the full effects of the drink. Unknown to Teil, she was not under the drug's influence; and due to its effect on the psyche, the drug could be used as a truth serum.

Then he saw it was Epi-Thumia again, only weaker, smaller, doing obeisance to him. The image was so super-real, it startled him. But he was living and enjoying the experience, because it was *his*. It's like dreaming, only wide awake, Teil thought, and you choose your own fantasy!

"Here's to the success of your mission, Teilhard," she said, raising her glass again. The mere suggestion was enough; suddenly he was actually being lauded by X himself on global mediacom for his spectacular work. It was really happening. Teil was recipient of Mascientist of the Year award:

FOR THE GREATEST CONTRIBUTION TO ARCHAEOLOGY EVER MADE IN THE HISTORY OF THE HUMAN RACE

The words razzle-dazzled the message into his expanded psyche. He was a world-renowned celebrity, with an unending demand for lectures, speeches, and personal appearances. He was helplessly trapped inside himself, a victim of his own fantasies, but didn't know it. And once the connection inside him had been made with Epi-Thumia, part of him was easy prey to her manipulations from without.

"Teil..." Her voice was soft and tender now. She moved

her hand toward his, not touching, as she mentioned his name again. "Teilhard..." Her voice, real indeed, echoed inside his mind as though it were the fantasy. And his real vocal response to her seemed to him as though it were not real. He was into the reality inversion.

"Yes, Epi..." he replied. He would later know nothing of the interrogation. "Speaking of your mission, what is the real mission?"

"To trace the origin of civilization in Tigris-Eu."

"No," she calmly and softly reiterated, "the *real* mission. What's behind the cover of the Tigris-Eu expedition?"

"Cover...? To trace the origin of civilization in the Tigris Euphrates," he repeated mechanically. The conversation he was having with her on the physical level was nothing compared to what he was experiencing within. Consuming his being was the satanic seductress of his own sexual obsession.

"Why archaeprobe—the priority and all?"

"They let me go ahead with my own brilliant idea," he said, tossing it off grandiloquently with a flourish. But Teil was on a roller-coaster ride through the fantastic panorama of his secret psyche.

"But why?" she asked, daring to probe further. "Why do they want it now, with such urgency?"

"Because of the pure genius of the idea, that's why!"

"Who is really behind it?"

"At your service, madam; it is I, naturally." She bit her lip to keep from intruding her own feelings.

Trying a new tack, she deliberately brushed his hand with hers—just barely. As he looked at her again, through the fantasy, what he saw unleashed the very volcano of his libidinal energies. Every element of her appearance was super-real, transduced through his desire into a new reality that only fantasy could have conceived. What was simply normal complexion, was now a glowing sheen of SKIN! Radiantly alive in super-natural tones beguiling the spirit. EYES!! Larger-than-life. Sensuous. Eyes from an exotic Egyptian goddess, hypnotically bringing him under their power. And HANDS! He looked at the hand that touched his ever so lightly.

What had been merely graceful features were now sinuously enchanting symbols out of his own id, beckoning DESIRE! But far on the other side, beyond the cacophony of lust, he sensed it was there, patiently waiting within him, the healing harmony of the Chord.

But it was overcome by the eruption of erotic imagery. Dizzying pyrotechnics of carnal passion were ignited within him. There was no turning back. He moved his hand ever so slightly against hers, which elicited an even greater surge of eros within him.

"What is Nexus, Teil."

"A tying or binding together...a joining, an entwining..." And the vision within conjured scarlet consummation.

"*Project* Nexus?"

"Whatever Lord Mascom says it is..." were the words that came out of the unconscious surface level. It was all Epi-Thumia dared ask; but it was enough. She knew Teil was telling all he knew. She sat back, puzzled, not knowing what to do next. And for a moment, pained regret showed in her eyes as she saw Teil so helpless and vulnerable. But Teil's inner world was exploding. The drink and induced vibes were not for his precarious nature.

Somewhere within the inferno of stimulation and counter-stimulation, within the Escher-like inner world of fantasy turning into reality back into fantasy, Teil caught a fleeting glimpse of something he immediately dismissed, refusing to see. Epi-Thumia's change in mood seemed subtly to affect the synapse of her connection with Teil. What was there before him now as a ghost-like aura, was the spiritual presence of the person, vastly more real than the physical body. Despite his immediate impulse to flee, it persisted.

Just as the reflex was about to jerk his hand away, his vision pierced deeper. Exposed beneath Teil's sex drive was another, the Person-drive. His inner sight penetrated to the revelation of her real character, beneath the externals to the core of the individual herself, the person behind the personality. Past the assumed facades, past the multilayered defenses, past the last inner veil hiding the person even from herself, to that thrice-

concealed center of being. He saw her pain—the uniquely
human pain of being. And it was his! While perceiving the
real her, he was cruelly forced to see himself. And the great
void at the heart of the human race. He met head on and
undisguised the image he had fearfully avoided in the mirror
that morning. To encounter the starkly naked self was a shock
so profound and shattering, he tried to flee in blind panic,
racing madly through the endlessly receding corridors of his
own soul.

But where could one flee from that?

Suddenly, Teil lurched to his feet, grabbed Epi-Thumia
savagely by the arm, and pulled her onto the dance floor.

"Teil...!" she protested, sensing the frightening
transformation and trying to pull away, "you're hurting me!"
But there was no stopping him.

"Music, Maestro!" he yelled inside his new inner reality.
And Teil heard what he wanted—all the sexual tempos he
had ever known, and then some. His lust-to-sex ratio shot
off scale. Eyes closed, he was pressing Epi-Thumia's body hard
into his own along every taut muscle of its length and
dancing—fornicating was more like it—to the magnified
fantasy rhythms in his head. To the relentlessly pounding
crescendo-beat of a Ravel's *Bolero*, to the fiery infernal passion-
storms of a *Francesca da Rimini*, and finally, pulsating with
the fierce masturbatory violence of Rock and Disco.

Teil was not alone in his induced orgy of subjective self-
annihilation. Others were into the effects of their own fantasies
made real, oblivious to anything but the enlarged reality of
their own forbidden dreams. Had there been unclouded eyes
to view the subjective scene, they would have been privy to
the secrets of Dante's Second Circle of Hell. And Teil had
lost control.

"Please Teil!!" Epi-Thumia cried, struggling against his
demonic power.

It was torrid; it was violent; it was rapacious. As the
pandemonium of lust combined with all the other parasensory
excitation crescendoed inside him, Teil's body arched in one
final spasm. His head jerked back and he screamed in torment

as it tore through his body with a force behind it greater than all the combined erotic fantasies he had ever known.

As the fierce seizure finally spent itself on Epi-Thumia, she dropped to her knees, sobbing. Trying to pull herself together, she got to her feet and ran away. Teil staggered blindly to the table and collapsed into his chair. He sat motionless and alone, eyes still closed, staring into the abyss of inner darkness, longing for oblivion.

And is there no healing for *me?* the voice inside him helplessly cried.

17

What was left of Teil's feverish sleep that night was broken by the annunciator's voice on his wristcom, trying repeatedly to rouse him. Growing more insistent, it was summoning him to wake up and take a message. But Teil was trying to shake the purple demons out of his head and figure out where he was, when it dawned on him that he was sprawled on the floor of his front room and didn't know how he had gotten there. The room was going round and round dizzyingly, and he was getting flashes of what had happened, but the only thing he knew for sure was that he felt like his body had just come off the rack, his insides were stale death, both eyeballs were staring through one sandpaper-lined socket, and it was on the side of his head somewhere.

When Teil had come to in the Palace, it was plunged into almost total darkness. The few people left were stumbling about trying to find exits. With all the artificial sensory and parasensory excitation cut off, the place was deader than dead, and suddenly intolerable. There had apparently been an attempt by terrorists to penetrate the invisible cordon of security that had been protecting the revelers, but they had succeeded only in interrupting power before being thwarted.

Each word coming over his wristcom was now stabbing into Teil's head like an ice pick. He groaned, rolled to his side, and said, "Teil-mann here... I think... What is this...?"

"Dr. Teilhard-mann, it is 2.9 hours."

"So what?" he mumbled gruffly, turning over.

"You are being scheduled early by SOG this morning, sir."

Teil's bloodshot eyes creaked open.

"What does SOG want with *me*?"

"You are to report to Mascom Regional by no later than 3.75 hours, packed and ready to go."

"Go where...?"

"Anatol, as planned. You've been set up a day early."

"What?"

"Anatol. Your expedition."

"But...I need at least another day...more planning. Haven't even seen my probes yet..." A different voice interrupted.

"Teilhard, if you don't get your crazy parts over there by 3.7 flat, heads will roll, and yours won't be the only one!" It was Epi-Thumia. Apparently she too had been rousted out of bed, judging from her gravelly voice.

"What are you doing at work at this hour?" he asked.

"I'm not *at* work yet, but I'm getting there as fast as you will be. Right?"

"Hey... Last night..."

She cut him off sharply. "Forget last night. We have to be at Regional—ready to go."

"Why?"

"Because all of a sudden HIGH-SOG is in on this!"

"HIGH-SOG!"

"Yes. See you there..."

The first thing Teil did after hauling his aching hulk off the floor where he had passed out was to go into the kitchen and fix himself a stiff drink. He thought better of it and poured it down the drain. Then he stumbled about trying to get organized, picking up things that came into focus as well as his deranged condition would allow. He hated packing in a hurry. It did things to him, like profoundly disturbing his equilibrium. Not to mention last night, he thought. Or was that all a nightmare?

As he packed haphazardly, his mind was a swirl of conjecture at the new turn of events. "Hustled by HIGH-SOG... That's all I need right now... Why?" This was no matter of global interest, world defense, ecological survival, or threat to Mascom. His was but one small cupful of scientific work being done amid the sea of glamour science. Or was it? Did it have something to do with last night? he wondered.

As the memories of what had happened began surfacing, Teil's anxiety increased. His eye happened on the antique pocket knife on the bureau, carried fondly on his student-day expeditions. He picked it up, hefting it, opening the long blade, and testing its point, staring at it with a blank gaze. He saw himself with his scrotum in one hand and the knife in the other, blade at the ready to quickly sever the thin strand of skin connecting it to his body. He shut off the thought with a shudder, closed the blade, and slipped the knife into a pocket.

In the bedroom, looking at him from a candid photo atop her dressing table, was Aspasia. It was their last picture, and it was a different Aspasia than the one he had danced with at the Masring Ball. She was simpler, more serene. With her face turned to his and her hand on his arm, she was looking devotedly and happily into his face. He stood there and stared at her a long moment with blank emotion. There was nothing there; inside him, there was simply nothing there. The butterfly pendant he had made for her was lying next to the picture. He grabbed it, shoved it inside a shirt pocket, and lurched out of the room.

He had enough presence of mind to leave ample supplies of food and water around for Skia and make sure her access port was programmed for open-on-demand. "You might have to be on your own for quite awhile, Skia. Take care of yourself and be a good girl—if you can."

Donning his old sporting jacket and grabbing the luggage, he went to the kitchen table and took his last two precious black-market pears and stuffed them into his large jacket pockets. There on the table, where he had left them in the flush of discovery before Epi-Thumia had called, were the texts and maps. "Good night! Stuck out in Nowhere Land without these. And they're Secure I!" Not wanting to reopen the bulging bag, he folded them flat, slipped them into a weatherproof plasticene, and shoved it inside his shirt.

As he stepped outside, he saw the chauffeur hurrying down the walk. No time to be sentimental now, he thought. This is it. Goodbye Skia. Goodby house.

The weather had changed. Everything familiar was disappearing behind a wispy veil of swirling fog. As if it's nothing more than a memory, he thought. God...how I wish last night was only a memory...

"Was just coming after you, sir!" the driver exclaimed. "Got orders to get you to the next tube to Regional, which is practically now!" He grabbed Teil's bag. "Hop in!"

"Take off, man!" Teil yelled, jumping in, "What are you waiting for?"

While tubing to Angeles Regional, Teil shaved and ate the two pears, knowing it might be the last time he could steal a bite of the real thing. Then he leaned back, still dazed, trying to remember what was nagging him or what it was he had forgotten. The painful memory of yesterday's tube affair swept through him again, and more flashes from what he had experienced in the Palace with Epi-Thumia. He was overcome with self-loathing and remorse and tried to push it all away, but it only got worse. And there was nothing to drink or take to ease the pain.

Then it hit him: Call the number. This might be his only chance to find out what it was all about. And somehow he saw it as a lifeline—the only line that even showed itself in a world that was falling apart without and within. His heart sank as he realized he had forgotten about the scrap of paper the poet had stuck into his boot. He took it off, looked inside, and there it was; he had unknowingly slipped his foot right over it when hurriedly putting it on. Using his wristcom was out of the question. As he felt the long tug of deceleration pulling him forward into the next episode of his strange adventure, the solution came to him.

Disembarking, he stepped away from the platform and ducked into the men's room to make sure he wasn't being followed. Seeing he had time to spare, he quickly ran up a flight of steps to the next level, cut down a corridor, and found a deserted public telecom. Approaching it with head averted, he threw his jacket over the video pickup as he drew near. Disguising his voice lest System discover he was contacting UGLIs, he requested the number.

"Hello..." a gruff male voice answered. There was no video coming in from that end either.

"Is this 7104643?" Teil asked.

"Yes. Who is this?"

"Uh... Someone gave me this number to call..."

"Who?"

"Last night...a performer...slipped me a piece of paper."

"Is that all there was on the paper, just a number?"

"Yes...," Teil said, examining it again. "Well, there's a wiggly line; like he was trying to get his pen to work."

"Okay. Where are you?"

"The main tube terminal."

"Be at the main level exit area and you'll be met in a few minutes."

"How will I know?"

"You'll know."

"All right," Teil said weakly. Now what am I letting myself in for? he thought.

While waiting, Teil deenergized his wristcom to put himself off line, stowed his bag in a locker, bought food, and took a seat at the entrance amid the throng of people coming and going in what was the Grand Central Station of the West Coast tubes.

It wasn't long before Teil looked up to see a man in shorts jogging across the lawn entrance. Teil sat erect with a start as he recognized the poet arrested the night before at the Palace. He gave Teil a slight nod and stopped before a fountain. Teil got up, quickly walked out, and passed close by as the other was getting a drink.

"What are you doing here?" Teil asked as he walked by.

"They had nothing to hold me on. I'm probably being watched. If you want to know more, follow me after I get into the park. We'll jog."

Teil kept walking while the other resumed his run. All I need this morning on top of a splitting headache is some jogging, he said to himself.

The park was a large area lush with green trees, shrubbery, and lawns, designed about a small irregularly shaped lake. The broad main path, dense with morning joggers, walkers, and cyclists, lay close to the lakeshore. Everyone went in a counterclockwise direction, as if dancing in a ballroom. The mood was closed-off, each person in his own private world. Most wore the head-comm, an audio-visual helmet-like shell, extending over the eyes like a visor and serving to block out intrusive stares while allowing one to tune in to the fabricated sounds and sights humans insisted on taking into their systems.

Teil found the narrower trail, virtually deserted, set back from the lake within the trees and high bushes. He saw his man up ahead and finally caught up. They conversed in cryptic sentences as they ran. He saw the man was closer to his own age than he had thought. His short dark hair glistened with perspiration as did the rest of his sinewy build, and he was just as intense as he had been in delivering his poetry.

"My name's Milton."

"After the poet?"

"Yes."

"Like the choice. Your reading too," Teil said.

"Thank you."

"Good place to meet," Teil said.

"Yes, ideal," Milton said. "If anything happens we can either cut over to the main path or disappear through the trees and bushes."

"I only have a few minutes," Teil said. "All System's breaking loose, and I don't know what's going to happen to me."

"Okay," Milton said. "Cut out when you have to go. Aspasia wants you to know she's all right."

"I wasn't sure they were really messages, but I'm glad she's okay. Is she one of you people? Where is she?"

"Do you know who UGLIs are?" Milton asked.

"No. But you can't be *all* bad," Teil said cracking a weak

grin.

"Bad, no; marginal, yes," Milton said, smiling broadly.

"What do you mean, 'marginal'?"

"Let's just say each of us has his or her own problem with survival—personal survival."

"Wow... Know what you mean," Teil said.

"You identify?" Milton asked.

"Yes. Why don't you just give it to me in a nutshell?"

Milton said nothing for awhile as they ran, then replied, "Okay, but the only real way to understand is to meet with us."

"Then you *do* meet."

"It's the only way. We're a fellowship of survivors."

"What was Aspasia surviving?"

"I know, but you'll have to hear it from her." Teil felt a twinge of jealousy that a stranger would know that and he would not.

"Where is she?" Teil asked.

"Don't know. Said when she left she couldn't tell us. But that it was all right. Dangerous for her if people knew. We're not even supposed to know that much. Did you know she joined us just after she met you?"

"Always suspected I was bad news for women," Teil said; "not to drive them to such UGLI lengths though. Is she in Angel?"

"Don't know; couldn't tell you if I did. All we did was try to get her message to you. That she's okay."

"Thanks for sticking your necks out."

"She also thought—hoped actually—that you might identify. With us."

"Well, who are you?"

"People just like you and me. From every walk of life. Who weren't making it but are now..."

"So, who are *you*?"

"My job—libracom technician. Avocation—poet and history. The real me inside—a recovering sex drunk." Teil tripped on his own feet and fell sprawling on the ground. Milton stopped and broke into laughter.

"I'm not really here, am I," Teil said shaking his head, looking up at him, "flat on my face, jogging with an UGLI, hearing what I just heard?" Milton laughed again and helped Teil to his feet. They resumed running.

"Never heard 'sex drunk' before, but I'll buy it. That's *me*. Did you know that? Is that why they sent you?"

"No, I had no idea; I was just the first one they could get hold of near here." We get 'coincidences' like that all the time." Teil shook his head in disbelief.

"Only I'm not recovering," Teil said. "Disintegrating is more like it."

"Join the club."

"What does it take to get in?"

"A desire to stop *dis*-integrating yourself." Teil looked him in the eyes searchingly.

They jogged silently for awhile, then Teil asked, "Milton... Are you ready for this one? Did you know the Sigma virus is really suicide?"

When the truth hit Milton he stopped dead in his tracks and stared at Teil straight on. "Suicide? You mean all these people dying...not a virus at all? I don't believe it. And how do you know?"

"Saw a top secret document."

"Are you sure?" asked Milton, running again.

"Yes," Teil said. "And it all makes sense now. Don't know what's happening, but I've felt it in myself lately. Crazy feelings coming out of nowhere."

"You're right," Milton said; "it does make sense. Explains a lot. Like the increasing number of newcomers we're getting. Suddenly, more and more people aren't making it out there. Does anyone else know?"

"Don't think so."

"This is a bombshell..."

"You're telling me!" Teil said.

"Okay if I get some others in on this," Milton asked.

"As long as they're as discreet as you are," Teil said.

"We have to be; we're illegal, you know—secret meetings. Teil, you keep on running, and I'll catch up with you again.

Going to check our tail and see who else is out here."

Milton left the trail, disappeared through the trees, and returned after a short time. They were soon overtaken by another, a short, powerfully-knit barechested man in shorts with straight black hair, olive skin, and somewhat younger than Teil and Milton. He looked the type one would like on one's side going down a dark alley.

"He's a friend," Milton told the man. "Aspasia's. It's okay."

"Name's Rico," he said, extending his hand to Teil, "I'm a recovering UGLI too. Good ta see ya." He grinned broadly, adding, "I'm also a recovering man hater, alcoholic, and pimp." The way he said it gave Teil the feeling the man was free of it all, but he shook his hand cautiously nevertheless.

"I'm Teil."

"Now listen, Rico," Milton said, "the Sigma virus... Get this. It's suicide."

"What?"

"Sui-cide!" Rico studied Milton's face then Teil's carefully, then fell silent a long time before speaking.

"It figures," Rico said. "Maybe we otta tell the others right away." Just then a petite young woman in her late twenties came abreast, looked at Teil, and then passed the trio. She was dressed in a jogging suit and had short-cut, sandy hair and hazel-green eyes.

Milton called out, "Theta, come back here!" She dropped back. "Teil, meet our friend, Theta."

"Hello," she said. "This your first meeting?"

"I didn't know it was a meeting," Teil said.

"It is now," Milton said.

"Then you might as well know the rest of me," she said. "I'm a quil addict, a hooker, and suicidal—recovering," she said, searching Teil's eyes with her clear open gaze.

The honest and unusual self-disclosure of these people brought an immediate rapport. Whatever the force was, Teil had never experienced it before. He felt that from that revelation of the heart he knew the person completely, transparently; and there was deep satisfaction in that. He felt drawn to them. They had something he did not have, but until that moment had been unaware of that lack. To Teil, the one who always stood warily apart, it was a quiet attraction.

"Most of us is suicides," Rico said, grinning happily, as they all rounded the turn. "Right, Milt?" Milton nodded.

"What's wrong with you, Milt?" Teil asked with a grin, "you've got only *one* problem?" They all laughed.

"Theta," Milton said, "hold onto your cap. The Sigma virus..."

"Yes?" she said, picking up the urgency in his tone.

"Suicide." She stared at them disbelievingly, turning pale.

"He's right," Teil said. "I found out yesterday. You all are the first to know."

"I knew it..." she said. "It makes sense, doesn't it? Milton, we have to let the others know."

"Teil has to cut out pretty quick," Milton said. "Should we tell it to him like it is?"

"Yeah," Rico said. "He's okay." And Theta nodded, moving in next to Teil.

"Each of us," she said, "has our own addiction or obsession or whatever we're powerless over that's hurting us. Maybe most people do, but we're the ones who can't cope with it; we're driven by desperation to *have* to do something about it, or..." Teil understood her gesture of futility.

"That's us," Rico chimed in, "desperados."

"But what do you *do*?" Teil asked. "How do you do it? I mean, you must survive totally apart from System, right?"

"We have to," Theta said. "System is part of the problem."

"Then where do you get your... I mean..." Teil forced them to stop and face him. "You say you're powerless over something in yourselves. That I can identify with. And System doesn't heal. Right? So how do you do it?"

The three broke into radiant smiles and just stood there beaming at him. Teil felt foolish.

"You mean," Milton asked, "Where do we get release and healing?"

"Yes..."

Theta replied, "From the source, naturally; where else."

"What source?" Teil asked.

"The source of our lives," she replied.

"What do you mean?"

"We don't really know how to explain it," she said, "except that whatever it is, it is suited so beautifully to the needs and desperation of the human heart..." Teil started running again, and they joined with him.

"Are you trying to tell me...you've found...God?" Teil said.

"It's not the words that matter," Milton said; "it's the liberating reality, the serenity, the—"

"It's a very personal thing, Teil," Theta said, "no one can really understand it from the outside."

Teil said nothing; a chord was struck deep within him, and intuitively he knew; knowing nothing of what they had, he knew the reality was there.

"I'm running late," Teil said. "Got to go now. No choice. Wish I didn't have to. Have to leave for Anatol."

"Anatol?" Milton asked, surprised.

"Yes, why?"

"Look, Teil," Milton said. "We're all over the place. Not great numbers, but we're spread around... Shall we tell him?" he asked, turning to the other two.

"Sure," Rico said, and Theta nodded.

"Teil, since we may not see you again," Milton said, "remember the wiggly line?"

"On the paper you gave me?"

"Yes. That's our secret sign of identification. How you'll recognize us. But please guard our secret."

"I give you my word," Teil said.

"There's a place over in Anatol called Endee, where you can find more of us."

"How do you spell that?" Teil asked.

"E-N-D-E-E," Theta said.

"Thank you..." Teil said. "I mean, I really don't know what to say..."

"You don't have to say anything," she said. "Just know that we're with you." Her clear kindly eyes, full of genuine warmth and feeling, wanted nothing in return, except his well-being.

"The next path will cut you back to the tube," Milton said, stopping and offering his hand.

"Goodbye," Teil said, with mixed feelings, as he turned and left. "Goodbye..." they said in return.

As Teil looked back over his shoulder rounding the bend, he saw the three standing with their arms around each other. They were waving at him and kept waving until he was out of sight. There was a strange tugging at his insides he had never felt before and a great yearning to run back and become a part of that.

This can't be happening, he told himself going back to the terminal. I don't believe this... Here I am at 3.6 in the morning, hung over from a living nightmare, and jogging in a park with a pimp, a hooker, and a sex drunk—all sober, happy, and *UGLI*—embracing each other and wishing me well!

18

By 3.75 hours, Teil had cleared into Mascom Regional and left his bag up at Project with Epi-Thumia, who was still frantically putting on her face while issuing orders and trying, like he, to pretend the night before had never happened.

Now he was being ushered to an obscure room on the lowest underground level, one he had never seen before. It was small, with only one door, and apparently solely for the purpose of housing the single masphere that dominated it. The only other furniture was a chair and desk, on which was a small black case. The door latched heavily behind him as he entered. Teil was alone.

He stood motionless, trying to get the feel of the situation. His interviewer had not arrived. He noticed that the sphere was a later model than he had ever seen. It wasn't that that bothered him though; every day, it seemed, there was a newer one coming out. It was something he couldn't put his finger on; he found himself tensing ever so slightly. He sat down, tired and beat, still reeling from the whirlwind of events and emotion in which he had been caught up during the past day and hour.

Alone, with all sound curiously shut out of that phobic room, he was overcome with the pressure of having to get out of there. He glanced anxiously back at the door, then forced himself not to panic. He leaned back in the chair, took a few deep breaths, and closed his eyes. He saw again the trio of UGLIs, embracing one another and waving. Waving at *him*—a single ray of light, coming into him.

A man's voice annihilated the still beauty of that moment. Seeming to come out of the very walls, it jolted him back.

"Teilhard-man, if you would care to enter the sphere now, please."

NO!! Teil yelled defiantly on the inside. "What is it?" he finally said.

"Would you please get into the sphere."

"Why?"

"Your HIGH-SOG interview."

"Oh..." Why didn't they tell me it'd be remote? he thought.

After fumblingly getting into the special masphere garment, Teil ringed into the airlock and was raised into position inside the sphere. As he did so, he noticed the cockpit upholstery. It's different, he thought. The composition of the seat and panel handles— Even the positioner ball. Sensor tissue! Had he not designed archaeprobe, he might not have recognized it. And while he was wondering why a masphere would have sensor tissue, it struck him. A policom unit! That was a refinement of the ancient polygraph lie-detection apparatus, only infinitely more sophisticated. Policom had become the one police and legal tool that had revolutionized forensic psychiatry. Its evidence *was* the case and the law, for it was incontrovertible. It was impossible to disguise or hide the truth when the slightest change in any physiological or psychological data, based on one's medicom profile, could instantly give away one's state of mind.

A surge of fear shot through his bloodstream. And that gave him away. Already, he knew that "they" knew he knew. He was exposed, and so were they. There was no other recourse but to play out the game and play it straight. He pressed his masring into the panel.

TEILHARD-MANN, 83 09 674 599 PZMYLTHIRP
PROCEED WITH INTERVIEW

As the sphere came to life, the large drawn face of a stoic-looking, grey haired, older man came on. The shadow of the bushy brows prevented Teil from seeing the man's deep-set eyes. The effect was eerie. If they want to frighten a person, he thought, they're going about it in the right way.

"Good morning, Professor." The voice wasn't the greatest either, perfectly cultured but affected, overimbellished, and patronizing.

"Good morning," Teil replied.

"Just a few questions, first, Professor, to find out where we are."

Whoever it was was not wasting any time on the amenities. Probably the set-up, Teil thought, imagining all sorts of things.

The first questions went quickly and were very cleverly mixed in with inquiry regarding details of the archaeprobe system capabilities. Gradually Teil settled back and gave in to the situation; there was no alternative anyway. Then the questioning began to shift.

"You are going alone, I take it?"

"Yes."

"Isn't it customary and necessary in this case to take the required complement of assistants?"

"Normally, yes. But I'm pursuing a different tack on this. The technical and logistics problems are really incidental."

"Why is that?"

"Well, it's really a case of geographical sleuthing. I don't know precisely what I'll be doing or where, until I get started. Kind of like following your nose, as the saying goes." That one ought to make a big hit, he thought.

"I see," the older man rasped. "But why are you following your own variables?"

"Not sure I know what you mean."

"What made you decide not to use Mascom?" There it was; Teil could feel it coming. He began to tighten up, but just at that moment had the ridiculous notion of Skia in the house alone with all that food. He smiled, and was back in control.

"But I shall be using Mascom. Couldn't possibly operate

without Her. The whole archaeprobe—"

"We know the probes need it, but why don't you?"

"But I do..."

"System-extrapolated solutions, Professor; why aren't you following the lead of System-extrapolated solutions?"

"Simply because...I already happen to have a set of possible solutions from which to start. Nothing personal..." He was beginning to sweat.

"What are these solutions you think you possess?"

"As a matter of fact..." Teil was trying desperately to stay nonchalant. "I was very fortunate in finding some excellent leads in the ancient texts."

"You prefer your own analysis of texts to Mascom's."

How does he know it's my own analysis? Or does he? "No, no, of course not," Teil snapped back. That was now a lie, and he knew that policom knew it. "Well, frankly, I guess there are times I see certain possibilities as the situation develops. But these are all based on Mascom. And the textual references all came from..."

"Yes, yes, of course. But the fact of the matter is that you are proceeding on a para-Systematic use of those references, are you not?"

"You mean, why am I doing it my way?"

"How can you possibly commit yourself to your own resources and World-City to this expenditure of time and energy by not following System-generated alternatives." The accusation came out cold and hard.

Teil's mind went blank and he froze. After what seemed like an eternity but was only a second, the reply came to him in an unexpected burst. "In the first place, I figure they let me do archaeprobe because they liked what they saw." There was a long pause. "Well, number one: There are no maspheres where I'll be going. Two: I've already designed and planned this whole project for weeks within System and by System. Three: I already have received more than adequate direction from System. Four: I am actually resorting to what may well be a short cut; my procedure might cut the time from months to days. After all, I've got hundreds of sites to eliminate. And five: While we're at it, I'd like to ask *you* a question," he said, not letting the other interrupt. "Since we're just in a 'routine' travel briefing, which you and I both know would never be the case where a policom unit is involved..."

"Yes, Professor?" the image dispassionately interrupted. Teil felt his anger rising at the imperturbability of the man.

"...Why the unusual interest in a 'routine' archaeological expedition? And six: Why the treacherous lie about the Sigma virus?" Teil blurted it out in a torrent of passion.

Teil never got his answer, for the screen suddenly went blank. The sphere was deathly still, and he was left with nothing but the aura of his own anger and frustration going nowhere.

The image which then appeared caused Teil to practically fall out of the cockpit. He stared in utter disbelief, as he recognized the face of none other than X himself, looking directly at him. Teil's first impulse was to fall to his knees. Much older appearing than his public image, the face nevertheless bore X's distinctive features: the large sensual mouth, the high forehead—still smooth, the large straight nose dominating the face, and the light-hued eyes exuding an air of absolute self confidence and authority.

The man X had survived as a legendary figure. The decades of successfully having fulfilled his every promise, far beyond anyone's dreams, had lifted him into those lofty heights in the public consciousness reserved for heroes and gods. Was not this a greater than Gilgamesh, a Christ whose kingdom was of this world?

Whatever the grumbling of the common man or the issue of discontent, X was seldom its target. At worst, it was "Mascom," or "System," or "regimentation," or even an occasional "loss of personal freedom." But these complaints were allowed, even designed into the system as safety valves, distractions. But as for X himself, he was untouchable; living and governing in privacy, he was sole guardian of KEEP— the Key Executive Program of Mascom. Part of System, its Head, he was strangely apart.

Teil would have kept on staring unblinkingly, had X not addressed him. "Professor, I regret having had to subject you to that unpleasant interrogation, but it was necessary."

Teil tensed. The HIGH-SOG...? he thought; only a mascomposite?

"First," X continued, "let me say how much I appreciate your coming on such short notice. You are in a monitorproof, sealed room with access granted only by me. Second, you are in more than a policom unit; you are sitting in part of my personal code-secure communication link, which can be used only by me or my designates. Such arrangements are necessary at this level, as you can well imagine. And finally, I had to gain adequate assurance of your personal integrity and intentions relative to your current assignment."

Teil's head was spinning; he was caught completely off guard. His anger dissolved. The mere thought of the power of this man, his personal charisma, his absolute authority over every living thing on the planet, was enough to make any man tremble. Finally, realizing X was waiting patiently for his response, Teil spoke.

"I am afraid, sir, all this has me in a quandary; I don't know what to say."

"But it is we who are in your debt, Professor. You are serving me—and World-City."

"Now that's what I just do not understand; there's something about all this that..."

"Again, sir, I regret you cannot know the full extent of your mission." Did he say mission? thought Teil.

"But if and when you do come to know the true nature of the responsibilities being placed upon you, you will begin to understand. Forgive me for not being able at this time to satisfy all your questions. And it may turn out you will never know, such is the nature of what I am calling you to do. For now, let us say I want you to do this for me. It is for World City—for mankind—but for now, that does not matter. Is it not enough that I have chosen you?"

Teil hesitated. The sheer graciousness of the man was so outright appealing. It was nothing like the austerity he had somehow been led to expect. And the change in mood coming on the heels of the interrogation overwhelmed him. "Yes, of course," he replied against all doubt. "I am honored."

"I am personally most grateful for your response. Thank you. And my deepest congratulations to you on your archaeprobe system and especially your ingenuity in the matters of the probes and texts."

This really threw Teil. "But I thought..."

"Forgive me again; mere technique to test your reactions. There is no ultimate substitute for man, though sometimes in the flush of achievement, power, or pride we have been tempted to think otherwise."

The absolute reversal of it all! Teil thought. That's just how I was beginning to see things; and here X, talking about Mascom that way... It was all quite too much. Could he trust what X was saying? If X could use such a skillfully simulated interrogator, what else might he do? But then he was admitting it all in perfect candor. Or was he? Why? Why was he revealing so much? What was behind it all? There was simply no defense against the man. Teil could not penetrate to any level of motivation other than what was apparent. It must be as it seems, he thought. Suddenly Teil was no longer a mere archaeologist preparing for a scientific expedition, he was special emissary for the head of World-City on a secret mission of global importance.

"Now then, down to business," X continued. "First, let me re-emphasize the security aspects of this; no one knows of this conversation."

"No one?"

"No one. And no one must know. Do you understand?"

"No, but I accept it."

"*Do* you? I fear I must now be very frank with you. Has it occurred to you lately that there was not much of your activities that was not known?"

"As a matter of fact...yes," Teil said weakly.

"Good. Then you must know that such must continue."

"Of course," Teil said, swallowing hard.

"It is due to the extremely delicate nature of your mission."

"I understand..."

"I regret such an invasion of your privacy, Professor..."

"That's all right," Teil replied. What am I saying? What's the extent of this surveillance? His mind raced back into the past few days and weeks, how incredibly smooth things had gone, as if his needs were anticipated. But he thought that had merely been the work of Epi-Thumia.

"This will all seem more unpleasant to you after you leave here, I'm afraid, when you've had a chance to think about it. All I can say is that it is absolutely necessary. If there were any other way, it would have been taken without resorting to such a dependence on one person. As you can appreciate, with your knowledge of System, we need not make such exacting personal demands on people."

"I never thought of it like that," Teil said.

"Indeed, from now on, you *must* think—of everything, Professor. For I am not only letting you step outside System, I am asking you to."

Outside System? Teil wondered. Why? The thought was inconceivable. "I'm afraid I don't understand, but I'll try."

"Good. And whatever thoughts you may have had of me or of society or System, even ugly thoughts..."

Does he mean plain ugly, or UGLI? Teil asked himself.

"...I ask you please to trust me now. If ever you have had cause not to trust System, I will even accept that. But from now on, you must trust *me*. All depends on that. If you cannot believe in the sacred nature of your mission, all may be lost."

Did he say secret or sacred? Teil wondered.

"And not only lost for you, but believe me..." He hesitated, and for an instant Teil caught the impression X was in pain. "...For more than you can now possibly conceive." There was another pause. Then X added simply, "Will you trust me?"

"You seem to be putting an awful lot of trust in *me*, sir. I don't know what to say, but yes, I will trust you." Teil knew he had no choice.

"Good. Now then, you may find adversaries."

"What kind?"

"Any kind! Anyone or anything that keeps you from accomplishing your mission is to be regarded as adversary—whether associates, family, friends, SOGs, or others."

Does he mean Others? thought Teil. "Could you explain that please?"

"Until you have succeeded—if indeed you can succeed— I ask you to trust no one but me. And whatever you find, I want you to report to me and only to me. As you leave the sphere, you will notice a small case on the desk. In it are three items identical to and replacing your own that I want you to carry with you at all times: wristcom, notebook, and pen. The special wristcom will be your access to me, to this private comm link. Call day or night; I shall always be available. And if for any reason we cannot communicate, you will still know of my continued presence."

"How?"

"Your masring. See the X alive deep inside?"

"Yes...I've often wondered..."

"This is my seal to you. As long as it is alive, you know, even if you feel cut off, that I am with you."

"I see."

"And from now on, there must be no more remarks or references, even in jest, to the Garden of Eden."

What the...? How did he know...?

"And please note the pen. It writes normally, but when the plunger is depressed once, it releases tranquil. Only touch its tip to the skin, and the person is incapacitated and unconscious within seconds. By pressing the plunger a second time, the pen becomes a high-intensity laser gun, disintegrating anything the beam touches. A third depression converts all its energy into a laser bomb. There is a thirty-second time delay. To have the pen revert to its normal state, simply rotate the clip 180 degrees, and the cycle is reset."

"I really don't think I'll need..."

"We cannot take any chances. I hope you never have to use it, Professor, but I insist you take it. Even if it means having to destroy human life, including your own. *You must not fail!*"

"Human life...?! I'm not sure you have the right man for this job. After all, my own life isn't the most stable thing System has to draw upon..."

"I know, Professor; whose is? I am fully aware of the 'marginal' nature of your life."

What does he know about it, and he couldn't possibly know about Milton and the others... And like he's including himself!

"And who is to say," X added, "that what appears 'most stable' is necessarily the best suited for your calling?" That thought, plus X's tone of voice, instilled confidence in Teil, despite the gross exaggeration the matter suddenly seemed to be taking.

Curiously, Teil felt himself rising to this unknown challenge, as though his whole life had been moving toward just such a point. He simply knew it. Whatever it was, somehow in this mission lay that destiny to which things had been moving him all along.

"It would appear then," Teil said, "that I am alone in this whole thing..."

"Precisely, Teilhard!" The display of familiarity and emotion shocked Teil. "You are absolutely alone, though you cannot realize it fully, even yet. And time is of the essence!"

"Time?"

"Quickly. You must act quickly. For many reasons. But if you are to trust me, you must trust me in this. Only one thing should be allowed even for a moment to detain you, and that is the sheer physical impossibility of going on. That is where your notebook comes in. It is divided into sections exactly like your own. The first is plain paper. Each of the other sections contains, within the paper itself, energy fortifiers, stimulants, temporary food substitutes, drugs for sleep avoidance, sleep inducement, and death simulation, plus the usual complement of medicines and emergency first aid drugs. All of this is explained on the first sheet, which you must memorize and digest—I mean eat..."

Odd how he corrected himself like that, Teil noted.

"...Before you leave this room."

"I see you've capitalized on my habit of chewing notebook paper."

"I have tried to reduce the hazard as much as possible. I do not want anything to happen to you. You must believe that, regardless of what happens in this strange adventure.

"Time, Professor...." X paused a long moment. "Time too, is on the exponential curve! If you could but understand." Teil did not understand; he wasn't sure he wanted to.

"Do you have any questions, Professor?"

"Yes. For one thing, what is really going on out there; is the world really falling apart, or is it just my imagination: What's happening?"

"I can assure you, suicide has not only reached epidemic proportions, but shows every sign of being truly catastrophic. But that is only one element your mission touches upon. I can only tell you now that what you are doing is crucial, of the highest importance. I regret not being able to tell you more. But hopefully, you will find out. And what is your other question?"

"I've been duly impressed with the importance and secrecy and urgency of my mission, but in all this I seem to have missed precisely what it is that I'm supposed to do."

"That is very simple, Professor: keep on doing exactly what you have been doing." If Teil had been off balance before, this last remark completely threw him.

"You mean... But I thought... It's not something special...?"

"Oh, but it is, it is! Extremely special! That is the whole point! That *is* your special mission, Teilhard-mann, as it has been all along from the first day you were assigned to Project Nexus and before. Find the enclosure of Eden! And quickly!"

19

Teil felt drained and numb. The dramatic escalation of events was steepening the slope of his own emotionally frazzled curve sharply. What was happening? What epic drama was taking place behind the veil? Kri-kor was right; Nexus was larger than anyone imagined. And how had X known it was "enclosure"? Teil had just discovered that. But Teil was confused. There was no lie here, no veil; everything was straightforward. Or was he being put off the track? What track?

After leaving the sphere, Teil carefully opened the case on the desk and removed the three items, replacing them with his own. They were identical in every respect, even to the engraved initials and scratches on his wristcom and missing pages from his notebook, which was quite amazing, the more he thought about it. He first memorized the notebook sections; everything was arranged alphabetically. He then promptly chewed and swallowed the index sheet, half expecting to keel over dead—or worse.

Holding the two pens together, he saw how perfectly matched they were. Then his heart sank; he could not tell which was which! Panic surged inside him. Then he remembered to twist the clasp. Whew! I can see myself now, in some tight situation, actually having to use the thing, and click!—it's my old pen!

Placing the case back on the desk, Teil stepped toward the

door to leave, only to discover it had no visible means of release. He had been locked *in* all that time! And just as he went up to the door to feel around for some actuating mechanism, he heard a popping sound, followed by a sucking of air. As he turned abruptly, startled and wide-eyed, he saw a wisp of blue-green vapor curling upward above the desk over the spot where the case had been. That was all that was left; case and all, vaporized in an instant!

Just then the door slid open, and he wasted no time getting out into the aisle. The heavy door whooshed shut behind him, as though synced in with his body movement, so closely timed was the action and narrow the margin of clearance. He stood outside, pulse pounding breathing a nervous sigh of relief, wondering what would have happened had he been sitting at the desk. The nasty thought struck him that that might have been the way some of the other mascientists had disappeared. He shuddered at the thought. To be vaporized without a trace....

> They have no more forever a part
> In all that is done under the sun.

The words floated across his mind out of a long-forgotten sometime, and he was filled with death again. For a long time, outside the door of death, he identified with the nothingness of the unknowing dead, so well described by the ancient author of *Ecclesiastes*. The cold dark fear of a meaningless eternity of Nothing, No one, and Nowhere strangled his resolve, and he saw himself lost forever in

> The undiscovered country,
> from whose bourne no traveler returns.

And he could not face it. The cruel terror, the irrationality of non-existence would make him rail against the gods. He had to force the black plague away again.

Then the words of X came to mind—they had been more a plea—that Teil trust him in spite of everything. With that dubious reassurance, he strode down the aisle to the next phase of this blue-green madness.

As he stood at the lift, the door opened, with an attendant hurriedly wheeling out a sheet-covered body on a stretcher. Ahead of him were two SOGs, apparently guarding the victim. Surprised by Teil's presence, they quickly swept past, the stretcher brushing Teil as they went by, revealing the lifeless right hand. Teil caught a good look.

A masring! What the—? He quickly scanned the identification tag affixed to the wrist. It's Kri-kor! The attendant quickly covered the hand. Teil's heart sank. His impulse was to run after them; he couldn't believe what he had just seen. But the huge black SOGs were too forbidding, and then they disappeared around the curved aisle. His next impulse was to flee, but he just stood there. Was it really Kri-kor? he wondered. What had happened? Had his program patch been detected?

A wave of depression overwhelmed him. What's the use? he asked himself. What awful sickening dread is lurking around the next curve? Time seemed to stand still again as one after another of the strange experiences of the last twenty hours shifted by his mind's eye: the revealing image of himself in the shaving mirror, the disturbing panoramic reliving of his lust life with the girl in the tube, the insight into the nature of megapol, the suicidal sexual violence, the graffiti and fantasy of the crucified X, the detonated terrorist, his prophetic psycholog on the genesis of Mascom, experiencing the holocaust of FEAR, discovering the truth of the Sigma virus, seeing the crushed fetus still clenched to its mother's bosom, his own violent assault of Epi-Thumia, his encounter with X himself, and now seeing the body of Kri-kor passing right in front of him. All in a day's time, like hammer blows, one after another, pounding him, hitting him, cutting him open, pursuing him inside his very soul.

Then he saw that each of these, through its own painful shock, was forcing him to see something of himself or his world in a new light, all part of that bedeviled awakening going on inside him. Then he saw Milton and the other two again, standing together, smiling at him and waving—the one ray of light in his darkening world. With a tremendous effort, he turned, mechanically entered the lift, and with heavy heart, went on his way.

* * *

The special omni was loaded and waiting at the Regional dock. It was a small, light-green, oval-shaped craft, with all the electronics grown into its translucent silicon shell. Using magnetic propulsion and deceptively simple in appearance, it could travel in any direction or medium.

Epi-Thumia was there.

As Teil strode up, he saw several SOGs leaving, apparently finished with their security checks. Epi-Thumia was going over the omni. Startled at Teil's appearance, she turned abruptly.

"Oh! Teil... You scared me, coming up like that."

"Oh?"

"I...was just checking..." She appeared unduly agitated.

"Didn't expect to see you here," he said. "What are you doing?"

"Just checking... To see if everything is all right."

"Thank you," he said obliquely, "but I'll see to that myself." It was highly strained for both of them.

"Yes, of course... Go ahead. I was just helping expedite things." Annoyed, he began checking the equipment, distracted by her continued anxious presence. She got more agitated the longer she stayed.

"This is an important mission, isn't it...?" she asked, strained.

What does she know about "mission"? he thought.

"...As I'm sure you realize," she said. "And we do want to be sure..."

"Where the devil's the power backup?" he rasped. She pointed to it. "And the comm link antenna? That would be something, eh?—having archaeprobe operating with no interface with Mascom!" He had almost slipped and said X.

"It's in the orange case," she said, pointing.

"Right you are..."

Finally assured his equipment was all aboard and in order with seals intact, he stowed his own bag and climbed into the craft. Epi-Thumia was standing at a distance, her slim figure taut, nervously twisting the edge of her blouse, not knowing what to do with herself. Glancing in his rear-scan, he saw it was a different person than the suave self-assured creature of the previous day. He could not stand to let himself think of what had happened between them. He punched the omniport destination into his keyset, closed the hatch, and was about to leave, when she ran back and shouted to him, waving. He opened the door. She was almost frantic.

"Teil... I... I... Whatever happens... I mean..."

Now what? he thought.

"...I want you to know that...whatever might happen..." She struggled painfully and could not bring herself to say whatever it was she had to say. After a tortured moment, she broke and ran away. Teil closed the hatch again, and eyes boring straight past the emotional intensity of the scene, jammed his finger into the MOVE button and drove off. He did not see her as she stopped, composed herself, turned, and spoke softly after the departing craft, saying, "I'm sorry..."

Teil kept accelerating up the long curving ramp that would put him in the slot for his exit port; then he was on his way, and his emotions finally caught up with the driven flow of events and left him feeling drained and helpless.

Everything seemed remote and unreal. Why should he be thrust into this maelstrom of strange circumstance? What was he doing here? Why should he be doing anything? Again, he wanted to forget everything and wipe out: forget the Palace scene; forget Epi-Thumia and whatever she had been up to; forget Kri-kor and his tragic legacy; forget Aspasia. What could there possibly be left of that that he had not irreversibly damaged—within himself? Forget even his own archaeprobe— What good was knowledge when everything inside was emptiness and futility? He would gladly even forget X and his stupid "mission" if he had any choice.

As he was traveling to the omniport outside the megapol, everything and everyone seemed cut off from that Stream he had but sensed and heard beckoning through the Chord. Almost everyone. He saw again as clearly as if he were there, Milton, Rico, and Theta, standing on the track, embracing each other, and waving. Only this time he was within that warm embrace, and he was waving too.

20

As Teil arrived at the exit port, he stopped and waited for final flight clearance. He punched his new destination coordinates into the navigation keyset and requested a stationary orbit for continuous viewing, starting high and descending on down over his center of interest in southeast Anatol. A team of technicians attached the compact push-pull unit behind the omni for the extra kick required to get him into orbit and then lower him slowly down over that one spot on earth. No sooner had Teil settled into the security of that system, than he heard a voice from the console issuing a crisp command.

"Omni One Four Zero: Activate manual booster latching." The command was repeated three times before Teil realized they were asking him to override the computerized booster latching circuits. Highly irregular, he thought. Wonder how often *that* happens?

"Where is it?"

"On the panel right above your head, sir."

"Right. Got it. Say when. What happened, anyway?"

"Don't know, sir. Just a glitch. Everything else is all right. Give it a throw now and see what happens."

Teil lifted the guard and threw the switch. There was a reassuring clunk of latches engaging the rear end of his omni.

"You're back in business, sir. You are GO and clear to move.

Shouldn't have any more trouble."

Teil secured himself into the seat and pressed MOVE, and the craft took off smoothly. Naturally, all operations were tied into Mascom, which actually flew the ship; the pilot was merely a passenger.

As the power unit throbbed into life the smooth surge of acceleration pushed Teil back in his seat. He relaxed and looked down at the city. How quickly it diminishes, he thought. The higher you go, the more you see it as a whole, and the less important it all seems. Soon he could see the whole megapol, nothing but a blur of indistinct geometry, all it had to show that it was an artifact of man and not some blemish on the surface of the planet.

But is it so easy to leave City? he wondered. There's something about it that's more than structure and system and design and masses of men. Is it a way of living? Dying? A way of relating to the universe? Man's great altar "To an Unknown God"? What if...what if there *is* a Source—"suited so beautifully to the needs and desperations of the human heart?"

Soon after gaining altitude, the booster magneto drive sprang into life, pushing the craft swiftly into orbit. At the end of the thrust, the booster cut its power, ready for reentry. Weightlessness, even with the gravity compensator, always gave Teil a funny feeling in his internals and a slight buzzing in the head. As the craft jockeyed itself into position, synchronizing its speed with the earth's, Teil retracted the window shield and looked outside. He felt like being thrust suddenly into space. No place for acromania, he thought.

Teil braced himself as he peered out. The earth was like a huge gem, streaked with whites, blue-greens, and browns, suspended in the midst of a heavens of infinite depth; and he was a mere speck, riding a nameless pathway in the cosmic void. Only something was wrong. Teil kept craning his head around to make sense out of what he saw, until he concluded he was upside down. He pushed ORIENT, and the craft slowly rolled over, correcting the view to correspond with standard cartography. *Another* glitch? he thought.

Now Teil saw something he recognized. Transcom had picked a perfect day; there was almost no cloud cover over his area. As he came closer into position, he saw a framed curved portrait of a portion of the earth somewhere between Europe, Asia, and Africa. On the left, the Nile river etched a pale line through a narrow green valley upward into the huge delta spreading out into the Mediterranean. On the right was the Zagros mountain range, slanting along the border between Iran and Iraq. From below, he saw the dual-pronged fingers of the Red Sea pushing up toward the Mediterranean between Arabia and Egypt. Surrounding Anatol were the Mediterranean waters, arcing up through the constriction at the Dardanelles and the Bosporus. Curving off to the right was part of the Caspian Sea. And part of the expansive Arabian Sea was coming up through the back door into the Persian Gulf.

The multi-hued waters shone with different shades of blue and green, according to their depth, the sun's rays glinting off their surface. Teil saw the tell-tale lines of the Tigris and Euphrates rivers, appearing as though they flowed up out of the Persian Gulf, like two slender arms, reaching upward, enclosing and protecting his land of promise.

Teil then began the slow descent, eyeballing the terrain all the way down. As he dropped lower, he could see the wandering Euphrates, reaching all the way around from the east near Lake Van, and then going westward through Anatol and down into Syria, Iraq, and finally emptying into the Persian Gulf. He could also see the Murat River below the upper Euphrates, connecting into it as it dropped south.

I wonder which one of those branches the *ancients* called the Phrat, Teil thought. That would help pin down the location of Eden described in the Genesis text.

Then he spotted the waters of the Keban Dam, backing up eastward from its location on the Murat river, feeding into the Euphrates. Built two centuries before to increase the productivity of that portion of Turkey, it caused flooding of vast areas containing precious archaeological sites. Teil sadly remembered a reference in an old Journal of Archaeology:

> Excavations have come to an end
> due to the flooding of all mounds
> and sites previously excavated.

If only they had had archaeprobe then, he thought. What a waste! What I'm looking for might well be under that flood of stoppered waters. Instead of trying so desperately to save an uncertain future, maybe we should be trying to understand our past and what brought us here.

Teil kept coming down closer and closer, zooming in on his area. The booster was now active again, in reverse thrust mode, pulling him and his puny craft from the clutches of earth's possessive force field. Teil saw countryside, towns, and villages—old villages. They can't be that old! he thought. That's not the picture I got from the survey! He did not trust what he was seeing, even though it was real.

Off to the upper right, he saw the curious shape of Lake Van, like a prehistoric behemoth rising up out of the earth. Beyond it was the towering volcano of Agri Dag, the ancient Ararat, the dome of its huge broad-shouldered mass rising 5155 meters above sea level. The volcano had last rumbled into life in 1840, causing a disastrous avalanche. The ice and snow of its cone glistened in the sun. Close by to the southeast was the elegant cone of "little" Ararat.

Halfway between Ararat and the northeastern tip of Lake Van, Teil saw the thrust of Tenduruk Dag's twin peaks rising impressively above the same plateau. Here were two sets of mountain pairs, either of which could have been Gilgamesh's "twin peaks" guarding the gateway to the long journey that took him to the fabulous garden of delights. Idle curiosity played at Teil's imagination. If Tenduruk was the twin peaks, then the mountain on which the ark of Utnapishtim, the Babylonian Noah, had grounded "at the edge of the world" might well have been Ararat. And the place where Utnapishtim himself lived after the flood, "on the faraway isle across the sea," might have been one of the small islands—Akhtamar perhaps—on the vast expanse of Lake Van itself.

Fascinating! he thought, even such a rudimentary correlation between the Hebrew and Babylonian accounts. But that kind of conjecture was of little value to Teil. When he compared such vague references in the Gilgamesh story with the wealth of authentic detail in the Genesis text locating Enoch and the enclosure of Eden, there simply was no comparison.

The time had come to begin that very search. He had descended to perigee and would start looking for clues to the four "river heads" and that enclosure described in the text.

Teil could see right off that the best bet for finding the source of the Tigris, one of the clues, lay roughly along the 38th parallel. Stretching laterally for some 350 kilometers, from Lake Hazar at the west to Lake Van at the east, was a system of feeders comprising all of that river's sources. This zone seemed like a good starting point because it was so straightforward.

Running along much of this Tigris source system was the Murat river, the principal tributary for the upper Euphrates. The Murat joined the Euphrates in the Lake Hazar area, the western extremity of the Tigris sources. As Teil studied this western group of sources, he guessed it might be the most promising area. The whole region about Lake Hazar, around which the Euphrates itself curved sharply downward to make its run from the mountains into the piedmont, was one matrix of sources for *both* rivers.

That lake is smack in the middle of this area, he thought. Can it be that Hazar itself was the "enclosure"? Intriguing thought. The enclosure of Eden long lost to man and man to it because it had filled with water! But as inviting as it looked, he was sure the geological history of the lake had it full of water long before the Adam people had appeared on the scene.

Teil wondered at those early peoples, coming down from the highlands as the waters receded, discovering that new world. What did they see? How did they feel? What did they think? Or were they so busy with survival they never stopped to think? Teil felt that common yearning of the race back toward an ideal beginning. Indeed, if it were not ideal, man would force it to seem so, such was the archetypal urge for Paradise.

When he landed he would have to study the exact history of that lake, with its perfect "entrance" to the east, where its waters flowed through a gorge out into the Tigris. In his mind's eye he imagined the flaming Cherubim guarding that entrance to the lost Eden:

> Within the flick'ring light,
>   The fearsome outlines of a living being,
> Before whose countenance, and brandished high,
>   Threatened the sword of flame.

Teil then started looking for other likely spots in the area that might have served as enclosures. Absorbing the landscape, and drinking in every feature, he lost himself in the sheer revelry of the experience. He positioned the craft at slightly different angles and altitudes to gain better perspective. As he put the omni above Lake Hazar and aimed the window east at a low angle looking along the 38th parallel, he saw an oval crater-like depression emerge into view. The perspective and shadows were just right to give the three-dimensional quality he was after. Then, he saw another, and another beyond it, far to the east below Lake Van. These were the most curious geological features along the whole line of sight.

He moved the video enhancer in front of his eyes, focused it over the first of the features, and kept expanding scale until the first depression filled the screen. Here was a ten-kilometer long, narrow, flat valley inside an oval-shaped crater-like enclosure. The walls rose from 350 to 600 meters above the inside floor. A Tigris source feeder flowed along its outer western edge. What a perfect hiding place for even a large group of people, Teil thought.

He grabbed the maps from his case and quickly located the spot. It was called Nerp Duzu, located at 38°25′N and 40°15′E. He hastily stuffed the maps into his shirt. Teil had not dreamed he would find such intriguing possibilities at first glance; and not one, but several. How ancient were they? Were there mounds inside? How he wished his mound survey had included these. He kicked himself for not having done the whole area while he had the orbiting labs at his disposal. Then he remembered his talk with X and knew he would get top priority on any reasonable request.

Suddenly and without warning, the omni jerked violently with a loud wrenching noise. Warning lights flashed and buzzers sounded the alarm. Teil's wind was knocked out as he was shoved forward against his restraints with crushing force. He could do nothing to stop the erratic spasms, which ended in one last convulsion, practically tearing the omni in two. The booster had broken loose.

Immediately, the window cover heat shield automatically slammed shut, mercifully covering the view of earth, tossing crazily in space in a mad whiplash of violence. The last jerk had shot the ship into a trajectory headed straight for earth. Teil yelled into the console: "MAY DAY! MAY DAY! OMNI ONE FOUR ZERO TO ANY CONTROL... BOOSTER BROKEN LOOSE... GOING DOWN... ONE FOUR ZERO. MAY DAY! MAY DAY!!

There was no response. Everything was dead. Another Mascom glitch? he thought. The ship's systems are supposed to be failsafe. And so is Mascom!

Just as suddenly the tossing stopped. The craft stabilized itself, its own autonomous controls taking over. But it was too late. The booster was gone, and they were headed for a fiery reentry into atmosphere and who knew what else. Normally, if all went well, the craft would be able to function as an airborne vehicle and make a safe landing. But already Teil could feel the air inside getting warm and stuffy as the craft began its reentry plunge unchecked.

To Teil it had felt like all of System had undergone a violent spasm, convulsed by a gigantic seizure. What had happened to the rest of the world? Teil didn't even want to think about it. An electronic earthquake? With its shock wave traveling at the speed of light through all systems tied into Mascom—

practically everything? The idea was incomprehensible. Must be a freak omni I'm riding. But what if System did feel the shock? Will Mascom awake from its seizure and know nothing of omni One Four Zero? The thought struck fear into him.

Teil wasted no time executing emergency procedures. Positioning his seat for reentry, he quickly jumped into his safety suit with integral oxygen and strapped himself down. He could only hope the ship's own computer was still intact so it could position itself properly for reentry. Having done all he could, he leaned back into his seat and tried to calm down. That was when he remembered, Call X!

He switched on his wristcom and yelled, "This is Teilhardmann in omni One Four Zero over eastern Anatol. Lost booster. Making emergency reentry. Do you read me?" There was no answer; X's private channel was dead.

Then the full force of the searing heat wave struck. He was burning up and wondered why the craft simply did not melt apart. Sweat poured from his face. He feared the worst for his archaeprobe equipment. Again, he was confronted with death. His thoughts turned to Aspasia and the other UGLIs. What was happening to them? Would they miss him? Suddenly he longed to be with her again. He knew now it was he who had blown them apart—his accursed madness. The monkey on his back—his LSR. That came first, always; that took priority even over himself; it killed love, killed *him*! Strange how he saw it now, when all was lost.

He felt and heard parts of the ship tearing loose in the searing dissolution. Then, the heating began to abate as he felt a slight tug of deceleration. Apparently the craft was using its last stores of energy to check its pell-mell bullet-like descent through the hell of fire. Would its power hold out long enough for something other than a suicidal landing? If so, where? The thoughts sent a shudder through Teil. Nature was winning the battle. And does she always win, Teil wondered, in the end?

The thrusters whined past their screaming limits, and the ship began to vibrate like a frail reed in the wind. Then it was racked with huge shudderings—death throes against an inevitable doom.

Where were they headed? Teil wondered. Even if they made it, he would have no idea where they were. Would he be another Utnapishtim, coming down atop the blind waters covering the earth? He quickly got his pen and notebook from his shirt pocket and began scribbling in the last indicated coordinates before the instruments went berserk. His last thought was to eject the equipment module, but it was too late. He had just torn the page from his notebook and stuffed it inside a pocket when they hit.

Pen and notebook flew out of his hands, striking the instrument panel. The crash was devastating; amid the terrifying noise, Teil felt every bone in his body racked out of joint and shatter. In one instant of blinding pain, a stab of white heat impaled his whole being. It was the end.

But within the mingled screaming of ship and passenger—within, yet beyond—Teil heard again the Chord.

Part Two

PURSUIT

21

It was the end. But then, it was not. Teil abruptly found himself alive, intact, and floating in water in his safety suit— minus headgear. But his head was on. And the pain was gone. And he was afraid to realize he was conscious for fear it would return. But it didn't.

He stared in disbelief at what was left of the omni, some hundred meters away—battered, burned, and sizzling on the water. And it dawned on him, How had he gotten out of there? Why was he intact, when he had felt his entire body destroyed? The shock of that realization was almost as shattering as the physical trauma had been. Had his suit not begun to ship water and start taking him down, he probably would have just stayed there, staring into that fused mass of silicon and metal where he should still have been.

As he got out of his suit and began swimming ashore, he noticed he was on a small lake somewhere high on a mountain. Apparently the little craft had faithfully headed toward the closest water landing, which meant for its trajectory, the highest point in its downward ballistic curve. In its last dying milliseconds, it had unerringly guided him to this small lake high up these steep slopes. If Teil's amazed guess was right, he was at about 4000 meters high in Lake Kop, tucked in a fold of that greatest of all Anatolian mountains, Agri Dag— Ararat.

Teil spotted the equipment module floating intact in its weatherproof container near the shore and grabbing one of the handles, struggled it ashore. The icy wind lashed through him as he dragged it and himself up out of the water. A little below him on the mountain from where he now stood he glimpsed what looked like ancient ruins. Drained from the ordeal, all he could manage was to lean against the module, panting for breath. The trauma, plus working at such high altitude left him completely exhausted.

As the wind abated for a moment, all was silent; Teil stood awe-struck at the view. Even where he was, some four kilometers high above the plateau, the mountain still towered over a kilometer above him, reaching into the clouds. As he looked out on the vast reaches below, he felt like a god, with the whole earth at his feet. It was dizzying and awesome, a whole new world, but a world of nothing and no one! Unpopulated terrain and mountains stretched out in all directions. When it dawned on him that what was so different was the absence of city, Teil was overcome with a cold and shaky emptiness. He was a mere insect, alone in an alien wilderness. Surely this was not his world. Surely he was lost on some forbidding planet. The stark isolation of it all filled him with momentary panic. The urge to fling himself into the dizzying void swept over him.

Then, without warning, the omni exploded in a blinding flash and with such force that it slammed Teil against the module. Pieces of the craft shot through the air in a barrage that caught him full on. Sinking into unconsciousness, he clawed at the smooth surface of the container in one last effort to hang onto a world that was starting to shatter again. "The pen...that stupid pen," he muttered. "Must have activated... Everything's gone...lost...no hope now... The flood waters...coming up higher...higher..." And the waters of darkness enveloped him.

As the wind blew his wet limp body into blue-cold numbness, up from the terrace below the lake scrambled a shaggy-looking band of men. Crude, bearded, and dressed in coarse homespun, they were furiously goading their pack animals up to the lake where the omni had crashed. One of them spotted Teil crumpled at the foot of the gleaming module and let out a yell for the others. Dismounting, they kicked and shoved excitedly at Teil and pounded the container, trying to force it open. Leaving Teil for dead, they attacked the module with savage fury, as though it held some prize booty.

As Teil came to, he thought he was hallucinating, such the bizarre nature of the whole scene. Their heated exchanges were in a curious mixture of the old Kurdish and the old English. He gave a start as the possibility dawned on him. Others!

Teil's movement attracted one of the men, who caught Teil watching. In an instant they swarmed over him, clubbing him mercilessly. Teil was fighting for his life. Foolishly he reached for his pocket knife and managed to get the blade open. But one of them, enraged at the sight, kicked it out of his hand. The knife flew through the air into the lake. Teil was helpless. Their blind fury was prevailing. He had the funny thought of hearing himself say, Don't you know who I am: I'm Teilhard-mann, the archaeologist, and you'd better watch out 'cause X won't like this!

Teil quickly weakened and finally was not even able to raise his arms to ward off the blows. They were all over him like a pack of mad dogs impatient for the kill. As the one with the biggest club was about to finish him off, they were distracted. Another group of men, dressed much like the first but not as wild looking, came clammering up the slopes and rushed into the fray. Teil hugged the ground, hands over the back of his head, and waited for the end. Without hesitation, the new group broke into the circle surrounding Teil. He saw out of the corner of his eye that they had no weapons, and instead of attacking him or the others, began forming a circle, backs to Teil, taking the blows on themselves and shielding him. The largest of the new group, a burly hulk of a man with arms as thick as thighs, snatched the club from the beast who was going to use it on Teil, broke it across his massive thigh, and flung the pieces into the lake.

Who are they? Teil thought. Rescuers? Dooming themselves

to death? He could do nothing but resign himself to the situation and watch. Each time a new man would make it up the slope and join his comrades, they would enlarge the circle outward, away from Teil, as though their whole purpose was saving him.

For awhile, the element of surprise and superiority in numbers stopped the brutal attack. But as the first group realized the others had no weapons and were only defending Teil, they regrouped and charged savagely in a murderous frenzy. And, it seemed to Teil, there was a personal animosity between them, as though the first group knew who the others were and hated them for that, not just for breaking up their little party. Using stones and clubs, and slashing away with whatever knives they had and with shards of silicon fallen on shore, they charged the newcomers in force.

Several defenders went down on the first onslaught, and Teil knew it was just a matter of time before he and his mysterious friends would be slain. Huddled to the ground, he kept trying to raise someone on his wristcom, trying both X's private channel and the standard distress mode. Nothing. Was it his wristcom or Mascom again? Just the thought of System failure was as threatening as the carnage going on around him.

Then it happened. The ground started shaking as though Nature were wreaking her own judgement on the scene, first, with a low rumble, the rocks creaking and groaning against each other and the earth undulating underfoot, everyone standing stock-still in shock. Then, in a huge tearing roar, it was upon them. The rending earth hit the mountain as a tidal wave, throwing them all to the ground. Heaven and earth were filled with the terrifying roar as of a thousand giant rockets thundering into liftoff at once.

Earthquake!

And they must have been right on top of it. Was Ararat erupting? The attackers were stricken with blind screaming panic. Few living persons had ever experienced an earthquake, since Mascom had automated the prediction and prevention systems, but their horrors had been spread by word of mouth from earlier times. It can't be! thought Teil.

But earthquake it was! And then avalanche! As the attackers fled pell mell down the mountain, the defenders rallied to the cry of the big man they called Mors. Picking up Teil easily, he ran into the overhanging lee of the mountain, the others following, finding doubtful protection from the cascade of rocks thundering down from above.

"The equipment!" Teil cried, pointing to the module left by the lakeside. As Teil started out after it, a smaller rock struck him a glancing blow on the head. He crumpled to the ground as the deluge of loose earth and rock engulfed him once more in that impossible flood of time and chance that kept trying to drown him.

The big Mors rushed out and pulled Teil from the midst of the avalanche. As he picked him up, Teil caught a distorted glimpse of him before losing consciousness. "Enkidu!" he cried. "What are you doing here?" Gilgamesh's faithful companion-in-arms was rescuing him. And then, Teil was mercifully out of it.

22

When Teil awoke later into the first blur of consciousness, a bruised and swollen hand was tending his wounds. As his focus cleared, he saw he was with his defenders. They were underground, and obviously no longer on the dreadful mountain.

"Hello," said the man with the hand. Teil opened his eyes and stared back with blurred vision. As he tried painfully to raise himself, he saw that most of the others also showed signs of their bruising encounter with the savages and hostile mountain.

"Who are you?" Teil asked, dazed. "And who were those savages...? Others? It couldn't have been an earthquake... Where are we? And the equipment...." As someone offered him a drink from a container made of animal skin, one of the men across the room, apparently the leader, called Dies, replied.

"We aren't far from the mountain, lad," he said in perfect modern English, "and we have your stuff." He was a tall, strong, swarthy man in his late fifties, wearing canvas shirt and trousers with crew-cut white hair and keen, clear eyes that gave the feeling everything was all right. Teil lay back, relieved but weak.

"What happened?" Teil asked.

"After the shake we brought you down here, lad," Dies said.

"How did you ever manage that...? Why?"

"We have to hide here until dark. You're going to be all right. Got some nasty black and blue is all."

"Why did you rescue me?" Teil insisted. "And who are you?"

"Never mind who we are," said Dies. "Who are you?"

Teil hesitated, not knowing whether to trust these men with his true identity and jeapordize his mission. "I'm from Angel— an archaeologist."

"What were you doing in an omni?" The question implied a good deal of sophistication. Teil was still too fuzzy to comprehend or be clever; things were too far gone. He had to trust them or nothing.

"My name is Teilhard-mann..." A murmur rippled through the group. "What's wrong?" Teil asked, looking about. "I am an archaeologist, a mascientist."

"We knew that from your ring, lad," Dies said. Teil looked down at his masring, the X still alive inside. The ring, at least, was something he could still cling to of his own world, whatever good that was.

"Who are you people...?" he asked again, growing weaker. "You seem so unlike those others...yet you dress alike. Teil watched as Dies knelt down and with his finger drew a serpentine line in the dust covering the stone floor. Then he looked up at Teil.

"Hey...," Teil said, dropping his head back and smiling weakly, "Why didn't you say so in the first place? UGLIs... You keep turning up in the damnedest places..." He lay back and closed his eyes, the weakness creeping over him again. As he did so, he saw himself back within himself, a minuscule figure, dwarfed in the vast reaches of his own inner being, trying to say thank you: for his own safety through the impossible events of the last day, for this small band of deliverer-friends, for life itself. But he did not know whom to thank, or how.

* * *

The morning was another day. Teil found he was strong enough to stand and walk, albeit with much pain and creaking.

He slowly climbed out of the underground area as most of
the others still slumbered in the dawning and found himself
surrounded by open sky and ancient ruins. They were on the
west side of a spur-like thin line of mountains, overlooking
a town. Teil could see near the top of the spur part of a gigantic
ancient relief cut into the solid rock. Off to the northeast was
the unmistakable dome of Ararat, rising up out of the vast
plain and the scene of yesterday's terrors. The reference points
made the connection: We must be in the ruins of the citadel
above the village of Dogubayazid, he thought. And that must
be the inscription in Vannic cuneiform. He was standing in
the ruins of the ancient citadel, which dated back as far as
1000 B.C. to the time of the kingdom of Urartu, ancient
Armenia, which had battled Assur for supremacy in the days
of the Assyrian ascendancy.

Teil reached inside his shirt for the maps. Only tattered
pieces had survived the fiery descent, the mysterious ordeal
of the crash, the freezing water, the attack, and the avalanche.
But the texts were still intact in their plasticene sealer. Stranger
than their survival, he thought, was his own. He still could
not believe all that had happened in the last two days. He
held what was left of the maps in one hand and the texts
in the other, as though weighing his lot against theirs.

He spread out the map pieces on a flat foundation stone
and began getting a fix on the larger area. He would have
to unravel the now-tangled task ahead. The mountain spur
lay in the middle of a vast plain about 1800 meters above
sea level, known in most ancient times as Urartu, which in
Sumerian was Ar-ar-at—"the high mountainous region."
Rising up out of that plain were the two volcanic cones of
Ararat, towering over everything else on the plateau. Behind
him, in the distance toward the waters of lake Van and rising
out of the same plateau, were the twin peaks of Tenduruk
Dag, reminding Teil he could be on the edge of Gilgamesh's
world, the beginning of his pursuit of eternal life. It was now
the beginning of Teil's new world, and he wondered what
strange destiny lay ahead of him.

As the sun rose higher between the snow-covered peaks of

the two Ararats, Teil visualized the scene the epic described as the "twin peaks guarding the pathway of the sun." Suddenly it made sense. The pathway of the sun would be the vector of the sun's arc across the heavens from east to west. If Gilgamesh's quest had started here, it would have taken him down that pathway toward the emerging center of cities to come. "The ancient trade route linking East and West!" he exclaimed. "That's it! And that same pathway shall be mine."

Teil broke out laughing so that his bruised ribs hurt, so ridiculous and yet so plausible the whole thing seemed. How absurdly remote from System method this was—playing with an ancient Babylonian text that mixed myth and uncertain historical allusions, beclouded by centuries of transmission; following uncertain references to unknown mountain peaks, pathways, paradise, and who knew what else; and setting his course by hunch, intuition, and untried common sense. But the very illogic of it created in Teil a new excitement, a sense of abandon and adventure.

Just then Dies and Mors, Teil's defender, came looking for him. Mors was big, broad, burly, and hairy. His large round head with its coarse mane of black hair was set on a short thick neck. His thick arms and stout muscular legs were those of a wrestler. His large smiling mouth revealed rows of white teeth, a sharp contrast against his olive complexion. His large, dark, laughter-filled eyes were set under long dark brows that came together above the nose. He was dressed in baggy trousers and sleeveless chamois shirt and wore a copper bracelet on his right wrist.

Teil greeted Mors enthusiastically, "Enkidu, my friend!" Mors came up and compressed Teil's shoulders together in a gesture of comraderie. Teil held back the strange new urge to respond by embracing the big man. "Yes, you are my Enkidu, my great warrior-defender. You are the companion of Gilgamesh!"

Mors did not understand, but his kindly eyes revealed their warm, open acceptance. In the light, Teil noticed an ugly gash on the side of Mors's head; and his blue-black and swollen nose had obviously been broken. Mors then pointed to his own mouth, as if trying to say something.

"I'm afraid Mors here is trying to tell you he can't talk," Dies said. "The little midget seems to have been struck dumb in the scuffle. Probably that bash on the side of his noggin."

"How sorry I am to hear that, my friend," Teil said.

"You seem to be chipper, lad," Dies said. "Heard you laughing. What's up?"

"I've got a job to do out here, Dies. I'm looking for a dig. It's got top priority. Can you help me?"

"Is there nothing stopping you, man? You want to go running off already, eh? Give me a clue and we'll see."

"The pathway of the sun," Teil said, breaking into a huge grin.

"As good a place as any, I suppose...," Dies said, scratching his head.

"Here, Dies, look at the map. Diyarbekir. And see these areas?" Teil touched the succession of possible enclosures along the proposed itinerary. "I've got to check these out on the way."

"We're heading back that way, lad," Dies said, trying to cover his surprise. If you think you can stand the "ugly" company, you can ride with us."

"Dies... I don't know how to put this, but I'm also going to be looking for someone over here." Teil told of meeting with Milton and the others and the messages regarding Aspasia. "Can you help me?"

"She met with us whenever she could in Endee, you know, but no saying where the girl is now. The lass is pulling for you though; you know that, don't you?" Teil just looked at the man.

It was done, this unlikely pact between these unlikely companions in survival—and in a world, time, and place more unlikely still. They would take Teil on his strange journey.

The rest of the day they made preparations. Dies had sent the rest of the party, including the wounded, to various nearby villages where they either lived or had friends. Only Dies, Mors, Teil, and the young man they called Ingemisco were left. For Teil they found enough spare garments from their own; Teil's clothes were buried in the ruins, Dies not wanting to risk a fire. Mors fashioned from leather a wristband to cover Teil's wristcom and a ringlet to slip over his masring. The agility of his fingers, considering their size, was amazing, and Teil was moved by his affection and helpfulness.

"We'll take our chances and travel in the light," Dies said. "At night we'd stand out like Mor's bruised beak there. By now, everyone and his ass'll know about the crash."

Teil's precious cargo, still in its original container, was camouflaged and placed inside the false bottom of an old wooden wine press on the wagon. They used donkeys to pull the wagon and ride.

Teil had his itinerary all set. They would have to go around the east end of Lake Van, which lay south of their present position, and along its southern perimeter to reach the five easternmost enclosures. They would then work steadily west and south to Diyarbekir and what he hoped was the mound of Enoch, his best reference point for finding ancient Eden.

Leaving Dogubayazid, they took the road going due west. As they got underway, Teil insisted on sitting in the driver's seat alongside Dies.

"Who were the men that attacked us?" Teil asked.

"Others," Dies said.

"Then they do exist!"

"As real as that knock on your educated cranium there."

"Who are they?"

"Those rascals were locals, just used by the Others. The Others themselves are revolutionaries. They want to oust the old man himself and take over..."

"X?"

"Who else, lad?"

"They may have started already," Teil said; "have you heard the reports?"

"Not hardly; we've been on the road for weeks."

"Mascom Regional at Angel was attacked, and an attempt was made on a whole raft of mascientists. I was there both times. No telling what's going on out there we don't hear about."

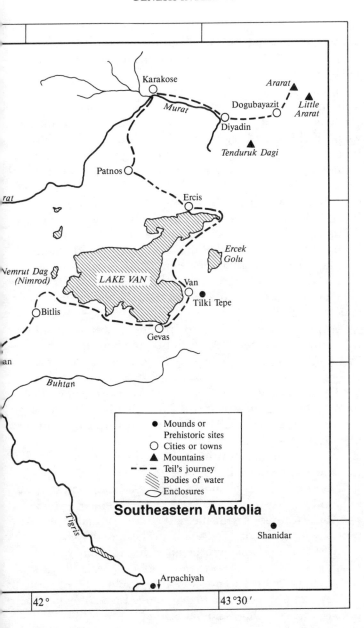

Southeastern Anatolia

"Most everyone out here is at least a potential Other," Dies said. "And we knew they were getting into the megapols. We think they've got some sort of headquarters out here someplace."

"There have always been revolutionaries, haven't there?" Teil mused. "I don't see how we could have thought our time was any different. It's amazing, once you penetrate the veil we're sealed behind back there, how things are so different than we imagined. And we didn't imagine them; we were certain we *knew*. History repeating itself—endlessly. Does it never stop?"

"The unrest is inside, lad—inside," he said pointing to his heart, "and as long as that's there..." The man finished his thought with a gesture of futility, and Teil sat quiet, lost in thought, the wagon rumbling along the old dirt roads.

"May I ask you another question, Dies?"

"Fire away, lad."

"How was it that you were up there by the lake; why did you rescue me?"

"We couldn't let you be torn apart by the beasts, could we? By those "ugly" men?" A smile played about his eyes. "We had a mission, lad, just like you. We were sent out here to get you."

"That means you were sent before I crashed, before I even took off, before I knew or anyone knew that I was even coming out here, much less that I'd come down where I did in that obscure System-forsaken place..."

"We were hiding, waiting for you in the ancient church ruins just below the lake."

"No one could have known where I'd land because it was an accident, a glitch... And you were sent *there*?" The older man busied himself with the recalcitrant animals and badly potted section of road. Teil shook his head in disbelief.

"All your questions will be answered in time, friend, but first I've got all I can do to get us out of here." It took all the strength and concentration they could muster to keep donkeys and wagon moving at top speed, knowing their pursuers were doubtless not far behind.

At Diyadin, still a small town, they stayed in another ruins, this time of an Armenian church, which, according to the map notations, was from the seventh century A.D. Here the easternmost extremity of the Murat River, the main tributary of the Euphrates, originated in the mountains to the south. From Diyadin, they took the road going due west, following the green valley of the Murat that coursed westward and south through all eastern Anatol. At Karakose, literally "the beardless or untimbered land," they turned south to Patnos and worked southeast to Ercis, a little town a few kilometers from the north bank of Lake Van.

As they left Ercis and rounded the tip of Lake Van, Teil lost himself in the majestic sweep of those ancient waters and the flow of civilizations they had witnessed. The Hurrians and Urartians at the dawn of history. The Armenians. Conquest by Romans and Parthians, Tartars, Persians, Turks, and Russians...

Van was a salt lake in a deep basin with no outlet, dammed up at some remote time by a volcanic barrage from the Nimrod volcano just off its western coast. That volcano, its crater now containing a five-kilometer wide lake, had been named after Nimrod, builder of cities, the great "hunter against the Lord." If Nimrod of the Genesis text *was* Gilgamesh of the Babylonian, Teil wondered, that would certainly help tie everything together.

There was evidence that the lake at times had risen and at others, receded. Who knew what secrets it held under or near the edge of its 450 kilometers of coastline? Teil was already designing an airborne archaeprobe system in his head that would remotely deploy probes from hovering omnis. Since Mascom could handle any number of sites, it would be a simple matter to probe the entire perimeter of Lake Van in a matter of days.

At nearby Tilke Tepe, "the mound of the Fox," true Halafian pottery had been found. What made the find significant was that the Halaf culture itself had flourished *south* of there in Syria and northern Mesopotamia. It had used copper as well as stone tools—one of the crucial transitions Teil was after in his search for Enoch—had adobe buildings, and a fine polychrome pottery. Here was another of the many indications uncovered of extensive trade criss-crossing Anatolia in the sixth and fifth millenia B.C. Van had figured prominently as one of the chief sources of the indispensable obsidian, the key Neolithic resource for making stone tools.

Night was falling as they came to the city of Van. Cold, tired, and hungry, they climbed the isolated ridge of Citadel Rock overlooking the city, which spread fan-shaped below them in the plain. Again, Teil was struck by the primitive sight below them: flat-roofed mud houses and narrow winding streets. This should have been a modern city by now, he thought. His mind kept stumbling at the great disparity between what should have been—part of System—and what appeared to be.

As Teil watched the town go to sleep in the light of the rising moon, his mind drifted back. It had been only a few days since he had left megapol Angel, yet he was so remote from it all now. How could it all grow so dim and distant? It did not seem to matter at all, not even being cut off from System.

But not for long. At first, it was a vague feeling of anxiety; then a growing nervousness that began to affect him visibly. But Teil was still unaware that anything might be wrong.

The whole experience had begun to captivate him. They had been traveling like bands of merchants had been doing unchanged for the past several thousands of years. It was as though time was standing still in this part of the world. More than anything, there was the openness. An uncoveredness. Earth, air, and water; rivers, streams, trees, and open spaces; plains and hills and mountains, all unconfined by the ordered lines and constraints of civilization. The eye could reach as far as it would and touch the horizon, where sky and earth became one, releasing the imagination. There were no manufactured barriers against man's extension of himself into nature. Is that what happens to man in city? Teil wondered. Man retreating out of the natural world into one of his own making that somehow shuts him in and keeps life out?

Is that where I've been going all these years? Retreating? Into my own world, madly pursuing "life," but losing it instead? And is that what Milton and the others are doing—rather *undoing*—undoing the wreckage of their past? How do they do it? They seem to be free of their past—free of *themselves*!

And Aspasia... What was she going through? That time she was looking at herself in the mirror, and I told her how beautiful she was... She said in a quiet tone of voice as though talking to herself, "You have to be ugly to be truly beautiful." Now it makes sense. And the times she'd be late. Regularly. "With friends," she'd say. It seemed to start changing her, settling her; instead of that whirlwind of motion that was always going on deep inside her somewhere... And it was making an unspoken demand on me.

By this time, Teil had decided not to look at the easternmost enclosure possibilities he had spotted from space. Lake Van was a veritable inland sea, some 90 by 130 kilometers, dominating the whole geography. Surely it would have been given as a geographical reference for Eden had it been in this vicinity. More and more, he tended toward his first idea, to find Enoch first. This was the fulcrum, about which the whole hurried search would have to pivot. Already halfway to Diyarbekir, Teil was eager to move ahead.

In the morning, avoiding the town itself, they left Van, going south and then heading west along the lake's southern coast. It was flanked by high mountains on that side, and the road cut through them, making the traveling difficult.

Teil wished he still had his omni so he could have dropped south the 200 kilometers to the famous cave of Shanidar and its companion site of Zawi Chemi, the earliest post-Pleistocene village in Iraq yet unearthed. The settlement had been in full operation in 9000 B.C., making it and Jericho in Palestine, two of the earliest known proto-cities anywhere in the world. Discovery of ritual burial of the dead at Shanidar cave, with flowers and at such an early date, had rocked the scientific community.

As they left Lake Van, the road took them southwestward,

down the narrow pass along the Basor Cay, a river flanked by steeply rising mountains, to the high city of Bitlis. This town was at the foot of a rocky peak on which were the remains of a medieval citadel, another mute testimony to the surging cultures and peoples and wars and tumults that had coursed through this ancient land.

From Bitlis, they followed the road down along the Basor Cay to Garzan, a city which, a thousand years earlier, had been another stronghold with a citadel. Again, crumbling ruins.

On a wild gamble, Teil decided to look at the Sasun Daglari enclosure. So at Garzan they split up, Teil taking the wagon and Mors, who volunteered to accompany him, and Dies taking Ingemisco. They planned to meet again at Silvan, three days later, some sixty kilometers down the way.

"How about meeting at the minaret," Teil asked, checking his map. "Is it still there?"

"Last time we went through it was," Dies replied.

"And if we miss each other, let's leave the wavy sign," Teil said. Dies nodded. They separated and went their own ways.

After Teil and Mors had worked their way up the Garzan Su River and into the tiny valley ringed by steeply rising mountain walls, they left the enclosure without promise. There was no exit to the east, which bothered Teil, even though he did not put too much stock in finding that clue to the Eden enigma. And Teil's surface survey revealed no evidence of potential sites. They made for Silvan, eager to rejoin their comrades.

Once in Silvan, Mors and Teil headed directly for the most ancient part of the city. Passing remnants of the curtain wall of the ancient fortress, they went on to the southeast, outside the walls, where they found the minaret. It had once been associated with a thirteenth century mosque, long since disappeared. Mors and Teil went all about the minaret, inside and out, but could find no sign of Dies and Ingemisco or their ever having been there. Something was wrong.

23

"No trace of them, Mors," Teil exclaimed. "What do you make of it? They should have been here yesterday." The large man was silent but his dark searching eyes revealed his concern. Teil had a sinking feeling. The company of these men had been something he had never experienced before. They had an unspoken way of relating to each other; it was a category of human behavior totally outside his ken, but which began to appeal to him. He was looking forward to traveling with Dies again.

Teil decided to scout the town. Taking the wagon, which they never left unguarded, they started walking through the village. Mors walked alongside the animals, at the ready to ward off any danger, his giant strides eagerly setting the pace. Teil was surprised to find the Ulu Cami, or main mosque, still in use. Someone was at the top calling the faithful to prayer.

Have there been no religious sanctions here? he wondered. Are these people still Mohammedans? The leaving of shoes outside; washing of feet... What time are they living in? What time am *I* living in?

They went to the well near the center of town and drew water to replenish their own supply. Then they pulled up under a tree nearby to rest and watch the flux of people coming and going. Then, one face out of the crowd—half-covered, the eyes opening wide in surprise, then turning quickly and gone.

"Epi-Thumia!" Teil cried, jumping to his feet. The afterimage of the eyes burned in his brain. "It can't be! But I'm sure of it. Mors. That woman. Did you see her?" He nodded. "Did you know her?" He shook his head. "What would she be doing here? Wait— The omni. The way she was acting. It wasn't the equipment she was fooling with at all. She sabotaged my omni! And her abnormal interest in the mission..." Teil started off into the crowd after her, Mors at his heels, but thought better of it and returned to the wagon.

"We've got to save what's in here at all cost, Mors. We don't dare leave it alone now. We've lost her anyway. Quick, Mors—let's go. Back outside the city to the minaret. We'll hide there. No... Let's cut back this other way so we can lose any tails we might pick up." They drove a hurried and circuitous route back to the minaret, checking at every turn to make sure they were not being followed.

Leaving Mors to conceal the wagon, Teil went inside and climbed the winding stairway to the top of the now-deserted minaret, hoping transmission might be better from that height. He tried to raise X again. Nothing. The complexion of the whole affair had suddenly taken on a different cast. How much did Epi-Thumia know? Could she have learned of his interview with X?

Nervously, he fidgeted with his masring as he stared out from inside the small prayer chamber through the doorway at the city beyond. His shakiness surfaced again, and he felt slightly nauseous. He looked into the miniature sphere of his ring again and thought he saw it flicker off, then come back on. He snapped on his wristcom and tried to raise X again, with no success. But suddenly behind a garbled rush of static, he caught what sounded like a caster intoning the news. What Teil heard confirmed his worst fears.

He pulled out the slender fiber-optic cord reeled inside his wristcom and peered into the eyepiece on its end to view the full large-screen effect simulated inside and watch the snatches of newscasts coming through.

The Mascom glitches were proliferating, apparently at an exponential rate, producing everything from medicom overdoses to megapol power blackouts. But it was the glitches surfacing from inside people that were terrifying. The Sigma virus had erupted into a tidal wave of suicides, and, most significantly, they were *calling* it suicide; the lie was out. There was a palpable fear of stumbling across or being hit by yet another falling body. The ultimate desperation was taking every form from drugs to violent death. Waves of crime were sweeping the megapols, with domestic assault and battery, sex crimes, and infanticide topping the list. It was as if a dam that had been holding back the racial libido had burst. One could see the camera shift embarrassingly away from scenes as it chanced upon some catch-as-catch-can sexual assignation in public.

Teil slid slowly to the ancient tile floor, overcome by a feeling of powerlessness and utter despair. "Is it really happening?" he said. "Why is it being broadcast? Why isn't it happening out here? My god...it's the end of the world out there!"

There were arson and looting of entire blocks by waves of young people; terrorism of all kinds against individuals, institutions, SOGs, and figures of authority. There was a sudden explosion of profanity—public and private—with expressions relating to sex and deity topping the list. There was a casting off of civil restraints: people were illegally altering mediacoms and their other audio-visual devices of every kind so they could see as much of and whatever they wanted as loud as they wanted. Shops were even letting the stuff blare in the stores; it went along with the new wave of compulsive buying. Sound suppressors were removed from everything from shoe heels to omnis.

Auditory, visual, mental, and spiritual—the Noise was back.

There was a sudden demand for junk food, drink, and drugs of all sorts. And cigarettes, which had not been seen for a century, were being smuggled in and were catching on like wildfire. The demand for alcohol shot so high over the supply, none could be bought; it was back to bathtub gin—and instant alcoholism.

Trash was suddenly a new phenomenon for City. Cigarette butts, chewing gum, junk food wraps, and just plain dirt were sullying the smooth and perfect crystalline streets. Images of X were being torn down, some replaced by pornography or old paintings of Jesus.

To top it all off, spray paint reemerged from nowhere, and every silicon wall, building, and sidewalk became an inviting billboard for graffiti-gone-mad. The putrid eruptions of the unclean Soul-sore of half the human race were being sprayed into the collective physiognomy. It was as though the Illness, held in check all this time, had really been progressing inwardly all along, and when the "lid" came off, spewed out in a frantic rush to make man's external habitat mirror the character of his inner self.

Paradise was hell.

Another clear window appeared in the static, and Teil heard the unmistakable, strong, magnetic resonance of X's deep voice come booming through. And for a moment he had a clear picture. "Your mission, Teilhard... This is why all the urgency... Stay with it; you must..." Then it went dead. Teil tried vainly to bring the thing back to life but finally gave up.

System had intruded like a flash of lightning into his new world, and for the moment, *it* was the real and the world of the minaret unreal. He was being tossed to and fro between two worlds, being battered inside his own head. He felt weak.

"So... What if the world is falling apart out there— Judgement Day, man made... I'm supposed to stay with it? What in all sweet System does any of this have to do with finding Eden?!"

He leaned against the wall and closed his eyes. For a long while he didn't move, the scenes from the wristcom and the last several days flooding his mind. Gradually the images faded; he ran his fingers along the worn grooves between the ancient tiles on the floor, breathed the cool quiet evening air, and let his gaze take in the starry sky outside the minaret. A feeling grew that all he could do was keep on doing what was in front of him and hope that somehow his frail intuition would guide him aright. He decided not to tell Mors any of what he had seen.

Staying in the minaret, Teil and Mors ate their simple fare of pita bread, cheese, yoghurt, and dried figs and hid in the ruins. Utterly drained, Teil escaped into sleep at once.

At dawn Teil was shaken awake by Mors, who was gesturing excitedly toward the room below. Teil jumped up, eyes large with fright, and stumbled after him down the stairs. There in the corner were two men, bound, gagged, and blindfolded. Mors was trying to tell him that the two had tried to steal the wagon and that they were from the attackers on Ararat.

"Let's get out of here, Mors!" Teil yelled. "The rest of 'em can't be far behind!"

In the ground around the base of the minaret, Mors quickly scratched the serpentine sign for Dies, in case he ever showed up. Then they tore out of Silvan as fast as the team could carry them.

The blinding morning sun lay down long ominous shadows in the path ahead of them, pointing to the final westward leg of Teil's enigmatic journey along Gilgamesh's pathway of the sun. Their hectic trek lay in the piedmont, a welcome relief from the mountainous path that had been their lot since Van. Finally, doubling back to make sure they had lost any pursuers, they entered the large arid plain at 655 meters altitude, at the center of which, farther west, would be Diyarbekir.

As they warily approached the system of roads leading into Diyarbekir, Teil saw how that city had achieved its commercial and military importance in ancient times. It lay at the junction of trade routes between East and West and linked Anatol with countries to the south. Diyarbekir was the main nexus here.

But there was something else, something of its potential in the emergence of civilization that caught Teil's attention. The plain lay just beneath the mountainous Anatolian plateau and would have been a logical area for transitional settlement in the spread of culture downward into the future land of civilizations and empire below. It was here in prehistoric man's movement into the newly-drained flatlands along the Tigris-Eu, where man *could* settle and begin his village-farming life. It was here first, not Mesopotamia down below, where he could establish a secure base for survival and continuity that would see the beginnings of his attempts to reflect upon himself and the universe and communicate permanently with his own kind. The full-blown follow-on of all this would naturally be found down below.

They had come over 100 kilometers since Silvan, and there was still no sign of Dies and Ingemisco. They came to a bridge over the Ambar Su, the Tigris tributary that took its rise in the area immediately to the east of Nerp Duzu, the most likely of Teil's Eden-enclosure possibilities. From the bridge, the river ran straight south into the Tigris a few kilometers below the point of their present crossing. It gave Teil a peculiar sensation to cross this river, wondering how ancient its waters were and what they could tell of that fabulous past upstream through which they may have coursed. But he would have to go to Diyarbekir first and search for Enoch to get reliable bearings.

It was not long before they were crossing the great Tigris itself, at the place just above where it made its ninety-degree turn eastward. There was a busy flow of traffic on the river; it was just above this point, at Diyarbekir, where it became navigable. The natives were still traversing it downstream in their *keleks*, rafts made of inflated sheepskins tied together and covered with reeds. By now Teil was getting used to the anachronism.

"Think of it, Mors," Teil wondered aloud. "The men and empires that must have crossed at this same spot. Waves of conquest sweeping across this very place. The great conquerors: Nimrod, Cyrus the Great, Alexander, Trajan, Genghis Khan, Tamerlane, the Ottomans... Different races, different men, different eras of history. But the same drive for power, the same high adventure of vanquishing whole kingdoms, the very same lust for conquest... Why? Why *must* man conquer? What lies behind that compulsion? Some vast repression? Some huge frustration? Some great loss...? Is sexual lust merely another manifestation of the same force—instincts gone astray?''

As they turned north on the road into Diyarbekir, they saw the city a long way off, standing high on a ridge of black basalt above the western bank of the Tigris. From the distance, its countless minarets and immense girth of walls and defensive towers, made of the same somber stone, stood out like a mass of carved ebony against the snowy background of the Taurus mountains. Its dark mystique cast a feeling of foreboding over Teil.

Mors and Teil entered through the Mardin gate on the south—there was a gate at each of the cardinal sides—and worked their way through an old cemetery. Checking notations on his maps, Teil learned it was through secret passageways in these very walls, only on the eastern side leading down to the Tigris, where the third century Persian king Shapur the Great had finally gained entrance and taken the city after long seige. They then threaded their way through the badly paved and dirty, disjointed streets. Crowded houses and shops squatted low, built mostly of the same black stone that made up the city's walls.

The largest city in southeastern Anatol, Diyarbekir was a curious mixture of the old, the very old, and the ancient, again with that strange absence of the modern. Known as Amida from Assyrian times, the city later was called Kara Amid, or Black Amida. And the city's history was a dark mingling of nationalities, empires, sovereignties, wars, and religions, a microcosm of the poor earth itself.

"No wonder this place has remained relatively intact through its violent history, Mors. It was literally cut from solid rock. The whole town! There's probably not another city in existence that has retained so nearly the appearance it bore under the Roman Empire. And I can see why the Arabs saw this place as they did." Mors conveyed by his look that he did not follow. "According to the notations here, the Arabs had a proverb that everything in Diyarbekir was black—walls, dogs, and hearts." Mors broke into his beaming grin with a knowing nod.

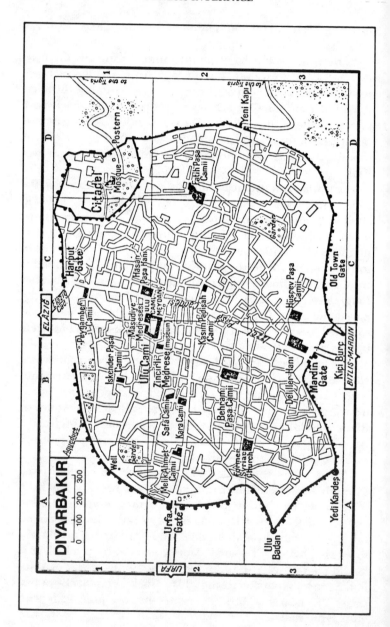

DIYARBAKIR

It was market day. Lively crowds were doing their colorful selling, buying, trading, gossiping, storytelling, and socializing in the thriving bazaar, and Mors and Teil blended right in. Teil's face was so dirty by this time, it was hard to tell the color of skin beneath. Silk goods of all kinds were in abundance, as were gold and silver filigree and copper wares, copper ore, and other raw materials. For the most part, the natives were dressed in the same garb as in centuries before. Leather shoes or sandals, baggy trousers and long-sleeved shirts for the men; the shawl and *pece*, or black veil, worn by Moslem women. Most of the men wore beards or long moustaches. And everywhere there were animals—dogs, horses, donkeys, chickens, and assorted smells running the gamut from tantalizing food dishes to barnyard bouquet.

Teil was so captivated by the scenes, he was often caught staring rudely; and bearded, dirty, and bruised as he was, he was stared at more than once. At their first chance, they exchanged their tired pack animals for three good horses, Mors gesticulating the barter.

Their first job was to look for Dies; Teil's priorities were changing. But where? Minarets thrust up their slender shafts any and everywhere. Once quickly through the city was all Teil dared spare. But there was still no sign of them. In that circuit, however, Teil gained a good working knowledge of the city, especially the eastern half, which had been the original Roman town. One main street, broad and straight, cut that old section in two, from north to south, connecting the Harput and Mardin gates. East of this street lay the original Roman town, later expanded to encompass what was now the city's western half. And in the northeast corner, beckoning Teil, was the citadel, built over the ancient mound of the prehistoric site. It formed a walled pocket with three gates connecting into the old town and was called *ickale* by the Turks, their word for citadel. Teil decided he would hold off entering it until they were actually ready to probe.

As they finished their circuit, they wound up near the center of the city at the Ulu Cami, or Grand Mosque, by far the most beautiful structure. Teil was awed by it, forced to stop and take it in; he had been preoccupied with old-world spectacle, not really seeing what he was looking at. Now he was arrested by the magnificent facades and ornate tilework of the Palace of Tigranes, the Armenian king, which faced the courtyard of the Grand Mosque. Now he was a tourist out of some long-resisted future, seeing the incredible past that was still present. They were at the *meydani*, or courtyard.

"Mors," Teil said, "I'm going to take a look inside. Would you stay with the wagon?" Mors nodded and took his seat. Teil passed under an archway guarded over by a lion in high relief above it. A red-faced turbaned man seated at a small table was giving him the once over, apparently trying to decide whether to challenge him or not. Teil boldly walked by and entered the huge courtyard. A striking fountain stood in the center with a delicate roof supported by a circle of eight slender columns. Teil was so fascinated by it, he paid scant attention to the two veiled women dressed in Moslem garb apparently going through some ablution preparatory to entering the mosque itself, forbidden to all but the faithful.

The walls were covered with an ornate profusion of carved foliage and fruit. In Teil's mind, an archaeprobe program had already done its work restoring these to their original color and lustre. He stood lost in the rich imagery as he saw it in the original, trying to imagine, understand, and identify with the mentality all this expressed. There was nothing in it of his world; yet he knew that the same *man* was there, spinning into stone and color his artful fantasies of strange ways long past.

The two women, rather than entering the mosque, left hurriedly. As the second woman passed by Teil, he turned to see her staring at him. They were both startled as they recognized each other at once. It was Aspasia.

The *pece* exposed only part of her face and some of her shoulder-length dark hair, setting them off against the drab background of her loose floor-length skirts. Wearing no makeup whatever and completely unstyled, she could easily have passed for a native.

They both just stood there, staring at each other, until Teil finally said softly, with the trace of a smile playing about his lips, "Who are you, and what have you done with Aspasia?"

Teil marveled at the difference; there was no sophistication in her manner, and that strikingly attractive fantasy image she had embodied so superbly was gone. Rather than being put off by it, Teil was attracted and intrigued; there was an underlying appeal about her that was new and different. His first thought was, Hey, but doesn't she look sexy, and with nothing showing but her hands and eyes.

Her face lit up with a beaming smile and she whispered, "I was thinking exactly the same thing. This bearded, dirty, scroungy, scraggly, bruised creature is surely not the man I danced with at the Masring Ball!"

"I hope not," he said.

She reached out and lightly touched his arm. The contact broke the unreal spell, and they were in each other's arms. When Teil felt her body against his he knew it had to be real, but still couldn't believe it. Still embracing, he pulled his head back and stared at her again. "What are you doing here?" he asked. "What happened to you?"

She put her finger to her lips and spoke softly, "Not now, Teil," she said urgently, "or all will be lost. Trust me. Later... I'll find you. Don't follow me... Be careful; they know you're here. I love you..."

Just as he was about to protest, Teil saw the red-faced guard come in, presumably looking for him. Teil released Aspasia, who quickly retreated inside. The guard spotted Teil and pointing accusingly at him as he strode quickly over, demanded in Turkish, *"Isin burada nadir?"* Teil's mind raced for an expression that would get him out of his predicament, but his mind went blank, and the guard laid hands on him. Just then Aspasia, her *pece* drawn tightly about her face, came running out of the mosque interior, yelling, *"Yangin! Yangin!"* and continued running outside. Others ran behind her from inside, whence smoke was beginning to pour. Releasing Teil, the guard ran inside, yelling, *"Yangin!"* all the way.

Teil ran into the crowded main street, looking for her, but

it was hopeless. And the wagon was gone. He darted through the gathering curious and spotted the wagon in the adjoining alleyway. But Mors was gone. Teil smelled danger. One as large as Mors would not be so easily lost. Teil stopped dead when he saw the large boots sticking out the back of the wagon.

"Mors!" he cried. His heart sank. In horror, Teil saw the drained pallor of the set face and staring, immobile eyes. For a moment he was stunned, panic surging up. In City most people never had to face such emergencies. But he fought the hysteria and somehow grew calm. He quickly examined Mors. There were no pulse, respiration, or other vital signs. He could not believe it. Mors was dead.

24

Teil looked closely for any signs of violence or other indication of what might have happened. Nothing. He noticed a slight discoloration of the saliva on Mors's lips. A drug! he thought. Then he remembered the special notebook X had given him. It was gone, but he still had the page on which he had scribbled his last-known coordinates before crash landing. The watermark was S, indicating stimulant. Without hesitating he slipped the paper into Mors's mouth and worked his tongue across it to absorb the chemical quickly. Still no life. Then, he wiped Mors's lips clean and washed them off with his own saliva. Wiping them again he applied mouth to-mouth resuscitation. Still nothing. Desperate, Teil continued breathing into his lungs while alternately applying sharp thrusts to the heart muscle through Mors's chest. Mors's chest heaved, and he coughed into spasmodic breathing.

"Mors!" Teil cried. "Mors! Wake up! It's me, Teil. Mors!!" The eyes fluttered open.

"Teil...it is you?" Mors asked in his heavy Turkish accent. *"Kardeshim..."* It was then he heard himself speaking. "Where we are? What happen? How do I talk? We are there...?" Then Mors let out a weak yell for joy.

"Mors—you can talk!" Teil exclaimed. "Where must we be?" The look on Mors's face changed to recognition. But Teil was sure Mors thought they had arrived at some destination he knew nothing about.

"What do you mean?" Teil asked. "We're right here in Diyarbekir. I left you for a few minutes, and when I came back, you were..."

"I was dead, *kardesh*—yes?" the big man said smiling, reverting again to the Turkish word for brother.

"Who did it to you?"

"They hold me from behind. Many of them. The woman from Silvan, yes, she was with them. I watch them. She come close. She take her veil away and look at me—hard. Then...lots of them from all over."

"Are you all right now, Mors?"

"I think I be alive now, but I be all right." Mors sat up, rubbing his forehead and shaking the dizziness out of his head.

"I think you were drugged. Do you remember them putting anything into your mouth?"

"Maybe. I think they try choke me. But if I not be looking at the woman..." Teil grasped his arm.

"It's all right, Mors, my dear friend. You couldn't help it. It's all right. You're well, and that's all that matters," he said, taking Mors by the shoulder.

"*Memnunum*," Mors said, thanking Teil.

"*Hic bir sey*," Teil reponded. "We must be very careful now. Aspasia's here. I saw her in the mosque. She says she'll find us later. We're in great danger, yet we have work to do here. I don't know what to do!"

"It be all right, kardesh," he said, shaking his large round head on his thick neck to clear his head. "If I dead and alive now, it work out," he said, breaking into a huge toothy grin. His large dark eyes were dancing again. Teil nodded, hoping Mors was right.

"Right now, we've got to get out of here. Good thing they didn't take the horses." Hitching the horses to the wagon, the spare one behind, and avoiding the main thoroughfare, called the Izzet Pasa Caddesi, they worked their way circuitously through the northwestern sector's narrow streets and alleys as fast as they could and made for the Urfa Gate at the west. As they approached the gate, careening around the last corner, Mors cried out.

"It not open!"

Teil saw that the two huge wrought iron gates were swung shut on their basalt hinges. The gate, though made in the twelfth century, was remarkably intact and impassable. Teil's impulse was to start the team around, but Mors stayed him.

"Stop and I open."

Teil abruptly braked to a halt as Mors jumped to the ground, ran over and heaved at the gate.

"It's locked, Mors. You'll never open it. Come on!" Teil started turning the team around to head for another gate, lest they get trapped. Why was it shut? Were the other gates shut too? Was it shut against them? Did they know of his mission? They must, now that Epi-Thumia was in on it. And what on earth was Aspasia doing there? Questions raced through Teil's mind as he tried to think ahead what they should do. Just then he heard a loud wrenching sound behind him— iron against iron. Looking back, he saw Mors had grabbed one side of the huge gate in each hand and was pulling them inward. With a final surge of power, he tore them apart, breaking the bolt and flinging them open. Teil awkwardly turned the team again.

"Mors! How did you do it?!" he cried, as Mors jumped onto the wagon. Then they were off as fast as their new steeds could carry them. As they passed under the archway, Teil caught sight of the relief cut into the headstone. An eagle with outstretched wings was over the head of a bull. Teil pointed to it as they went clattering underneath. "We will fly on the wings of our mission like that eagle, because you have the strength of that bull. Thank you, Enkidu!" With that, Mors laughed a great joyous laughter that made even the animals take heart and fly. And Teil laughed. And laughed. An almost hysterical laughter at first; then, of great release, as all the tensed-up fear and shock of the last few minutes and days broke loose. They laughed together, these two ancient warriors, united in vanquishing the impossible, having defeated their unseen enemy and death itself. Teil felt like nothing could stop them now. By the time they had stopped laughing, they had left the forbidding black walls far behind.

"What now, kardesh?" Mors asked, smiling.

Teil looked at him straight on as the thought suddenly came to him. "Shapur the Great!" The look of puzzlement on Mors's face was priceless. "The secret passageways in the walls, leading out to the Tigris." Mors still did not understand. "He came up from the river and entered there, through the walls. And so shall we!"

"You mean we go *back*?"

"Yes. That's why I came."

"But not now. We wait."

"No. Can't you see? That's just what they'll be thinking— that we're gone. That they've succeeded in chasing us away. Tonight their guard will be down. And time, Mors. Time is running out; don't know why, but I feel it. We must do what we must!"

They kept looking behind them to see if they were being followed, but could detect no one.

"We'll keep going west," Teil said, "until we're sure we've lost them, whoever they are. Then, we'll cut back to the north. During the night, we can cut across the Harput road over to the Tigris and hide the wagon and animals. We'll find one of the rafts and then float down the river all the way back to Diyarbekir and fool everybody."

"Will you open box now," Mors asked, pointing inside the wine press. "Yes, and test it. To make sure it will work."

"For what, my friend?"

"The dig—look for Enoch."

"Who Enoch?"

Teil laughed. "He was a son of Cain, who named a city after him. And we are looking for that ancient buried city."

"Why you find this buried city?"

"That I cannot tell you yet. But you will know, Mors." Teil took hold of one of the man's massive arms. "You will surely know—if we can do it."

"I help you," Mors said. The utter devotion of the man and dangerous dedication to a task he did not even understand registered deeply with Teil. This kind of personal commitment was new to him. The silent affirmation of a joined life flowed between them as they received from each other a different kind of strength.

On his part, Teil needed all he could get, for the symptoms that had appeared since leaving System were becoming physical and quite unbearable. Such was the perfection of medicom's ministry to humans, unmedicated illness or anxiety of any kind was a new experience, another trauma in his withdrawal from System.

About ten kilometers west of the Urfa gate they came to a hilly plain strewn with blocks of basaltic lava. "Do you think we've lost them, Mors?"

"I think yes. No one behind for long time."

"Good. Then we'll start cutting over to the east."

In the dusk they left the road and slowly worked their way northeastward. As night fell, they went from block to block, hiding in the shadows, until they had crossed the Harput road and made straight east for the Tigris. There, they wasted precious time looking for a raft, until Mors finally spotted one cast up on the bank with half its skins deflated.

While Mors worked at tying off the ends and refilling the skins with his powerful lungs, Teil extricated from the wine press the cylinder saved on Ararat and checked the equipment to make sure it was operable. By now his hands were trembling. Reluctantly he opened the pressure seal and listened to the dry nitrogen escape; his probes were now exposed. They would have to leave their protective placenta and enter the real world. His new-born foundlings were now at the mercy of the same elements as their progenitor. It dimly registered on Teil that he had been thinking of them as his own children.

By the time Teil had checked and reloaded the equipment, Mors had the *kelek* floated and was testing it with his weight in the water.

"Good work, Mors. Will it hold up?"

"I think so, kardesh. If everything stay in middle."

"What will we do with the wagon and horses, Mors?" Mors jumped to shore and beached the raft. Stretching to his full height, he swept the landscape full circle with his sharp gaze.

"We hide wagon under grapevine. Horses we hold with rope so they walk by river."

"Why do that?" Teil asked.

"You say how we go down river, but not how we come back up. With horses, we ride back."

"Mors... You're a lifesaver! Of course, how to come back indeed. Let's do it. What would I do without you, my friend." Was he so intent on finding Enoch? Or had he already conceded he would never leave Diyarbekir alive?

25

The unlikely pair of adventurers made a strange sight, floating down that ancient river of forgotten empires. The horses were the problem. Unfamiliar with their new remote guidance system, they tended to wander away from the water, pulling the raft to shore. And once, when it appeared all was lost, they had to swim when the bank was inaccessible. But the distance downstream was covered quickly, and soon they saw the dark outline, high off to the right, of the thick shadowy walls of Diyarbekir darkening the clear starlit sky.

Beaching their craft and tying the horses to a large rock, they started the trek uphill on a path through an orchard toward the foot of the citadel walls, Mors carrying the container on his broad back. They made the last thousand meters crawling on their bellies, fearful of being spotted by anyone inside. Finally, they were hiding at the foot of the tiny plateau on which the walls stood, presumably somewhere near the opening to the ancient secret passageways, if indeed they had not been walled up in the course of time.

Teil left Mors with the equipment while he searched the wall. Working around to the right, he came upon the pathway leading from the Tigris up to the citadel, which they had earlier avoided. At its end was a postern, a small opening in the walls shut with a door of heavy timbers set on iron hinges. Looking closer, Teil saw that the door was merely bolted shut. Quickly he retraced his steps back to Mors, and together they made it to the door. It was now well past midnight. Were there guards? What would they find in there?

Teil motioned to Mors, who lifted the weight of the door off its hinges to keep it from squeaking while Teil freed the bolt with a stick. Mors kept lifting as Teil worked it silently open. Once inside, they closed the door behind them but left it unbolted for quick retreat. Just inside, a small, narrow, arched passageway led off within the wall to the right.

"This must be it!" Teil whispered. "Look, it goes on inside the walls a ways." Mors nodded. Built within the walls themselves was a passage opening into a small chamber.

"In there will be a perfect place to set up the equipment. I can't believe it's still here. Do you know how lucky we are, Mors?" Mors nodded and let down the cylinder while Teil went back along the passage to the doorway leading into the citadel courtyard. Even in the dark he recognized part of the layout he had mapped in his mind earlier that day.

They separated to scout the area, Teil going clockwise, and Mors counterclockwise around the inside of the fortress walls. The moon had risen, and the men seemed peculiarly vulnerable in its light.

The fortress was an irregularly shaped five-sided area, roughly 250 meters on a side. Two towers commanded the main entrance from the city side. These were massive bastions, containing two floors with arched rooms, and with a spiked iron medieval portcullis that would drop down and seal the entrance.

Within the citadel was a mosque, dating from 1160, its minaret commanding a view of the whole enclosure. They would just have to hope no one was up there watching, Teil thought. There were various gardens and what remained of a fifth-century Nestorian monastary, now used as an arsenal. The protruding top of the mound itself was several meters above ground level, surrounded by wall ruins that had made a pentagonal recess around it.

They met back inside the passageway and began the procedure Teil had outlined on their way down the river. They would go for broke on the first run. Teil would plant a maximum number of probes around the mound, placing them just inside the citadel walls. In this way, he hoped to gain access to the entire ancient site in all its levels.

As Mors held both arms outstretched, piled high with probes, Teil took one probe and placed it upright in position near the base of the wall. Hesitating, and looking nervously over his shoulder, he activated the self-emplacement feature. He gave a sigh of relief; the sound of the ultrasonic transducer in the tip was barely audible as it worked its way into the ground. But would the high-frequency sound waves wake up every dog in town? Teil had not thought of that till now, and whispered in Mors's ear, "Be ready to get out of here in a hurry if something goes wrong." Mors nodded his head toward the doorway they had entered, and Teil nodded back. "But we must take the equipment with us," Teil whispered. Mors's eyes widened in surprise.

The probe disappeared silently and easily, like an unseen hand was pulling it into the earth from below. Teil looked at Mors and broke into a huge boyish grin. Mors stared in utter disbelief, then he too acknowledged the victory with a smile that lit up his whole face. At that moment, they were two boys playing an elaborate prank on the universe; burglars pulling a black-bag job on ancient history, trying to outwit the unseen principalities and powers conspiring to thwart and destroy them.

"Mother Earth!" exclaimed Teil softly under his breath, "you'll never be the same again." Then, thrusting out another probe as though it were a flag standard, Teil struck the grandiloquent pose of a conquistador of old and whispering a shout proclaimed, "I do hereby lay claim to this territory in the name of Aspasia, Queen of the UGLIs! Aspi, I love you too!"

In a matter of moments, the probe had automatically extended its telescoping segments until its full length had been inserted, with only the small communications section and tiny antenna protruding like some futuristic weed above the ground. The two men went about the inner perimeter of the citadel walls, placing the rest of the probes. At times the going was slower as a probe hit harder strata. One in particular felt like it was boring through metal, so slow its progress at one point. Finally, the probes set, the men retreated to the passageway inside the walls, where they began setting up the equipment.

"You make all this, kardesh?" Mors asked.

"Not made, designed. I designed it. Of course, *machinadan bir lokma yardim aldim.*"

"You get help from machine?" Mores asked.

"Yes. Only different than you're thinking. Computer—a machine that thinks and commands other machines. Did I get that right, Mascom old girl?" Teil queried the equipment jokingly. Mors tried vainly to comprehend.

Teil extended the thin, spheroidal segments of the solid-state video screen into one large screen and connected it to the control console. It was difficult to conceal his excitement. Then he set up the central integrator unit that coordinated probe sensor data, the power unit, and the comm unit for remote tie-in with Mascom—if indeed they could ever reestablish such a connection. He then activated the system, and the screen blossomed with light. Teil beamed, even though the picture was merely a dense jumble of lines and shadows.

"It works!" he cried. "But the earth filtering and picture enhancement programs need adjusting, Mors." As the large man stood agape, Teil deftly manipulated controls to get a clearer picture. "Without System tie-in, we can't use voice commands; everything is strictly manual.

"The sync must be off too. Probe multiplexing isn't synchronized." Teil pressed AUTO-SYNC. "I hope this program is smart enough for this site." Suddenly it took shape. "There it is!" Teil exclaimed, throwing hand to mouth too late to retrieve the outcry. "We've got a picture, Mors!" But Mors could only stare blankly into the jittering sheen of light. "And it's a site!" Teil kept at the controls until most of the extraneous earth had been filtered out of the picture, exposing the structures and artifacts themselves, suspended in space, one layer of the site hovering above the other.

"A classic textbook site!" But Mors was still valiantly trying to see something—anything. "And we hit bottom. Look. There's nothing man-made below the bottom level. See? Wish we had a bigger screen, though. Mors, where I come from, we'd be inside a large sphere now—*kure.*" Mors nodded. "And immersed in this thing. You wouldn't believe it." But Mors could not believe this. "The light from holo mode might bring the whole town down on us, so we'll stick with the screen until later. I can see them now, scared out of their wits. Which isn't a bad idea, in case we get caught."

As Teil worked and talked, Mors stationed himself first at one end and then the other of the passageway, listening and watching for trouble.

"Now let's see if we can find out where we are in this thing, Mors." With the positioner ball and scale functions giving control of "camera" angle, Teil began getting a feel for the size and makeup of the site. The four uppermost layers—the most recent—obviously began with the Byzantine Amida. The citadel walls themselves were Byzantine. Below that was the Roman Amida, and below that, the Macedonian and Persian sites. That took the city back to about 500 B.C.

Teil put the system in record mode so he could later do a high-speed dump into Mascom with minimum giveaway time. "This way, Mors, old chap, what will take us hours to analyze and record will take only a few seconds to transfer into Mascom and get the information to X. No sense advertising our presence till we have to, eh?" Mors was still nodding.

Once everything was working and recording, Teil zoomed in on the lowest level, some eighteen meters below the top of the mound.

"Look at all those stone tools! See them scattered just above the bottom?" Teil pointed to a hatchet-like tool, a triangular piece of chipped stone set in a bone shaft. Mors looked hard but unseeingly. "They're Natufian! Mors, you are looking at— and one of the few humans ever, I might add... No, those are not Natufian... Look more like the Karim Shahirian assemblage. You know what an assemblage is, Mors? Of course

Dates	Levels	Phases	Culture
Present	14	IX	Diyarbekir
	13		Byzantine Amida
300 AD			
300 BC	12	VIII	Roman Amida
500 BC	11	VII	Macedonian/Persian Amida
	10	VI	Assyrian Amida. Amida marked the northernmost extent of Naram-Sin's Assyrian kingdom in 1850 BC. A stele marking this is nearby.
2000 BC			
			2300 BC Luwian invasion(?), site destroyed by fire.
3000 BC	9	V	Babylonian Amida
	8	IV	Enoch II. Metallurgy and music become well-developed. Descendants of Cain and their influence. Does it extend on down to Sumer? Do they take over the Ubaid settlements?
3500 BC			
	7	III	Enoch I. Founded by Cain, son of Adam about 4300 BC. The Halafian culture peaks here. Similar to Arpachiyah.
4500 BC			
	6	II	Hassunah-Samarra type. Ceramic. (Contemporary with Eden?)
5800 BC			
	5		Neolithic. Early farming villages.
	4		Natufian?
8000 BC	3	I	Preceramic. Shift from food-gathering to domestication of plants and animals.
	2		
	1		
10,000 BC	Virgin soil		

The Amida Dig

not. It's a typical assortment of tools that characterizes a particular culture. Sometimes we call them tool kits because that's the "kit" of tools those particular people had developed and used. Wait a minute..." The flash of recognition vanished as Teil looked closer.

"Mascom would tell me in a second which type culture we've got here. Ah, but we don't want her stupid perfection in on this thing, do we? *I'd* say they're some unrelated third cultural tradition that's never been identified. How do you like that? Seeing we're halfway on the Fertile Crescent between Jericho and Karim Shahir, the type sites for the two tool kits. At any rate, we're looking at nine or ten thousand years B.C.; you can bet on it. This thing may turn out to be tougher than I thought. Wonder what other surprises we're in for?"

"I see hatchet now, kardesh," Mors interjected as the collocation of light effects materialized in his un-media-ted mind. "But where it is? What it doing in there?"

"It's not in there," Teil said. "It's in the ground outside. Buried. Deep. Between the probes." The first light of comprehension dawned over Mors's face as he sheepishly acknowledged his slowness to see. "That's all right, I keep forgetting you've never seen any of this. And I can see that's one of the disadvantages of archaeprobe. Seeing an image is simply not seeing the real thing. Seeing an image affects, programs, the *way* we see things. We're not looking at level seven, but at a screen of electron-excited light emitters. The brain still has to convert that back to what it *thinks* the reality really is. That's why you couldn't make out what it was all about at first, Mors, and I could. Blast it Man! What *is* reality...?"

Teil and Aspasia—that's where the reality has to be, he thought. All that other baloney out there—and inside the stupid sexual fantasies—isn't real! He felt better and went back to the controls with a vengeance.

Teil deftly zoomed in and out of the various levels, coming in at different angles and scales; now looking back at the whole, now differentiating cultural phases by examining the ruins and artifacts of the occupational levels. Soon, he was rudely absorbed in the site, and although he kept talking to Mors, was oblivious to all but the extension of his mind in creating the would-be reality of what lay hidden outside it.

It wasn't long before he had scanned the full extent of the site. There were some fourteen or fifteen levels comprising nine major cultural phases he could identify. The bottom five or six levels were in the preceramic phase, showing no pottery artifacts and including the peculiar configuration of stone tools he had noticed at first. Pit ovens and crude stone foundations of simple structures were also visible. In the upper layers of this first phase were small carvings of animal figures made of bone and stone. The most interesting feature for Teil was the shift that occurred within the scope of this first phase— the shift from food gathering and hunting to the beginnings of a food-producing culture, the domestication of plants and animals.

Here was a place like Cayonu, not far up the Tigris, and Jarmo in the Zagros foothills to the southeast, that showed the actual transition of prehistoric man to the beginnings of a sedentary existence based on agriculture and animal husbandry. Here was just one more place man had stopped roving, stayed, and taken the first steps in gaining dominion over the earth. The radio-scintillometers in the probes were giving Teil dating estimates that would be refined as the analysis developed. This first pre-ceramic phase covered a span of 4000 years, from roughly 10,000 to 6000 B.C.

Teil could have predicted the next phase. Spanning from 5800 to about 4500 B.C., it yielded a pottery-making culture that stamped itself neatly as belonging to the Hassunah-Samarra culture, named from type sites in upper Mesopotamia, some five hundred kilometers southeast of them, where early farmers were establishing permanent settlements in the alluvial plains for the first time.

"Mors, we might have a possible *source* for the Hassunah culture here. Look at the developed mud-brick architecture. And the stone carving. That may prove the Hassunah culture in Mesopotamia did not originate from desert nomads. It could have originated right here. And they grew not only the six-row barley, but emmer wheat and bread wheat as well. See the carbonized kernels in those ashes?" Mors nodded mechanically, trying bravely to follow.

"Well," Teil added, "I think so, anyway. Definitely a Hassunah-type culture in this second phase. And no one thought they'd find it this far north. See how the buildings are maturing into fine rectangular plans as we go up? Those are houses, with many rooms. And we've got hearths and ovens, grain bins...probably reed matting for carpets... See the pattern stamped into the mud? Of course nothing perishable like reed or wood lasts—just the impressions. We're still somewhere around 5300 B.C.

"And there—! A spindle whorl, Mors. They're weaving. I see you recognize that too. Cloth. Probably wool. But no metal yet, apparently. And a husking tray. See it? To separate the kernels of grain. And the flint-bladed sickle. See the black on one end? Pitch. To set it into some sort of handle, which has gone the way of all flesh. That's how we know the handle was wood; it isn't there. See how scientific we are, Mors?" But the humor was lost on the big man.

"Now as we go upward in time, look at how the designs on the pottery get richer and more complicated. They're trying to depict motion and real figures: whirling dancers, running stags, long-necked birds snatching fish, animals around a pool of water, birds in flight, crawling scorpions, and rows of dancing girls around the rim of that bowl. That one is Aspasia—see?" Teil turned and winked at Mors.

"Can hardly wait to see her, Mors. She's changed. The old Aspasia... she's gone. That potent charisma— There's someone else there I never knew before—just a simple human being— a stranger. Could it be that the image I've nourished is just another fantasy, whatever it was I needed her to be?

"And she— Was she in her own lifestyle nourishing some fantasy about herself—the self she saw through the fantasies of men? That left us both empty shells, didn't it? Like the clay vase there, all adorned with pictures on the outside— an empty container. Madly going about trying to get filled. With what?

"Anyhow, Mors old chap, this here is all a dead giveaway

for the influence of the Samarra culture creeping in, if not
originating here. Remember that; it'll stand you in good stead
the next time you try to trade in tired asses for horses without
being able to speak a word." He turned and gave Mors a huge
forced grin.

"Kardesh," Mors whispered with an anxious look, "do you
think maybe you be too loud?"

"Thank you, Mors; you're right. Let's see, where were we?
Bring women into this and next thing you know you've lost
the fine flow of the thing... Wait a minute— What's that?"
Teil maneuvered into an area on the floor of one room and
zoomed in on a small clay figurine. "The Mother Goddess!"

"I see her before, kardesh!" Mors eagerly volunteered.

"Yes... One of the most intriguing puzzles of prehistory,
Watson. Faceless nude figures, with various areas of male
interest exaggerated according to the whim of the particular
artisan. Like little idols. But there may be more than meets
the eye, eh? Deduction, Watson! On your toes...

"In these early versions, we're not sure what she signifies.
But ten thousand years before what we're looking at, we find
her figurines in the caves of the Cro-Magnons. Quite amazing,
dear fellow. And downstream in time from here, she takes
various forms: Ishtar of Mesopotamia, Ashtoreth in Canaan,
Aphrodite in Greece, Venus in Rome... Come to think of it,
that's an awfully long development, and why should it stop
with Rome? Whatever she represents must be extremely strong
to persist so. Wonder if it was reflected in their domestic
relations or sexual behavior in any way. And did everyone
worship her? Adam perhaps? Was there ever a point of
departure, when someone didn't go along with it and began
a new tradition? This could be the backdrop of something
extremely interesting... Anyway, there she is, big as life. See
her big bottom? Typical. Wonder what ours would look like.
If we carved our own goddesses, that is." Teil laughed at the
thought, and Mors looked at him queerly.

"But wait...! We wouldn't *carve* ours. She'd appear in terms
of our own technology, as theirs did. Mors... The magazine
girlies in the Century Museum... Photographs printed on

paper! Certainly! That was their medium. That's Her all over the place back there! It ties in with the universal appeal this thing has in man. Incredible: the Mother Goddess figurines—prehistoric pinups!

"And what of ours...? Electronic, naturally. Created to order by computer in super-enhanced images more real than the photographic. And now, with compurousal and fantasy realifiers, we have psychic girlies. The cultural LSR... Increasing, always increasing! Is there no end to it? No limit? Till we go mad!? Is that what's beginning to happen out there? My god, Milton... How I wish we could have talked..."

26

The third phase, beginning with level seven, took Teil completely by surprise. So engrossed was he in having found a possible source for the Hassunah culture, he had forgotten what he was really after. What he saw now was a fairly thick, well-developed layer, rich with artifacts. The first few moments, he looked at it blankly. Then he saw it. This was no farming village; and not just a large settlement like Catal Huyuk. It covered the full area enclosed by the citadel walls, and then some, extending westward beyond the probes. Teil estimated what he could see to be well over fifteen acres. Here was something obviously new for this site. A new people had settled here or taken over from the previous occupants.

A barrage of significant artifacts popped out at him from everywhere. The buildings were on a circular plan on stone foundations. The largest of them were grouped in the center of the site, approached by stone-paved roads.

"Those could be shrines, Mors. Like at Arpachiyah. Yes... And over there in the houses—hearths, bell-shaped grain pits sunk into the floor, kilns for baking pottery... The consistency of construction throughout this site is amazing. Like the whole place was *designed*. Look at the stone industry here, Mors. They must be getting their obsidian from somewhere else. None here. Good indication of trade; probably Van. And their finely polished stone vases and beads. Bet you never knew anyone could get that quality from stone tools, eh? These ancients surprise everybody. And the stone models: houses, birds, sickles and winnowing fans. There's another Mother Goddess, and a painter's pallette. And over there—a phallus! So maybe the women had their obsessions going on back there too, eh Aspasia girl?

"There's got to be metal here, Mors. It just feels like it. Let's check the density of that chisel." Teil's eyes left the screen as he searched for the proper control. "Mors—?" he said, pointing to a button on the panel.

"Yes, kardesh."

"Where did *that* come from?" Teil asked.

"What is that?"

"AUTO MANEUVER. That wasn't in my design; there was no such button. Must have missed it earlier. Strange..."

"What it do?"

"I don't know. Sounds like...like you maneuver without the positioner ball, automatically. But how? Voice commands like in a sphere would require Mascom. I don't like things like this I have no control over. That is not supposed to be there!" His finger toyed nervously with the button. "This is Mascom's doing. My own design went into fabricom while I was with Epi-Thumia; I saw it on the screen. No one but Mascom could have done it. Surprises—always surprises. What else has she been up to I wonder? Maybe I don't want to know. Anyhow... Where the devil's that chisel?"

Teil gave one knob a twist and noted the readout next to the article on the screen. "Hey! I thought so. Copper. Okay, I get it now. Copper has that particular tone to it on the screen. If I didn't know any better, I'd say this level is Halafian with an intensified H. The site of Halaf isn't far below us, Mors. Straight south. And they're supposed to be the ones who introduced metallurgy into Mesopotamia. Good night...! Don't tell me this could be Enoch...?"

"Let's zoom up a level and scan for metal only. There we go...into level eight. Now you've got your metal, Mors; everything else is filtered out. It's all over the place. *That's* what you call specialization. Full time industry. No doubt about it. And there's continuity with seven below it.

"So it looks like metalworking really gets under way in eight, but was begun earlier down in seven. Look at this building, Mors. The special kilns, molten metal spattered about, stone molds. And would you look at those tools! It's a shop—gotta be. Their metal industry—right here... But this isn't going to prove a thing. Any number of sites might fit the same pattern. Now we're going to have to re-earn our reputation as the greatest sleuths in London, Watson... You've been awfully quiet..." Teil's eyes left the screen as he turned to look at Mors. But Mors was gone.

"Mors!" Teil cried out. "Where are you?" Teil heard the muffled echo of his words travel down the passageway and return empty. His buoyant mood collapsed. He was alone. The fear returned. Then he heard footsteps coming down the passageway, and Mors reappeared. Teil stood there staring at him as if seeing a ghost.

"I think I hear noise, kardesh." Teil stood speechless and taut, then snapped, "Where the hell have you been!" The flare of anger hurt Mors, and Teil could see it. He looked deeply into the large man's eyes, only to see his own failure again. His own fears, his distance from this man, who he really was, and how they had been so strangely welded together. He had transgressed that.

"What did you see?" Teil asked, sobered.

"Nothing."

"Good."

"How much we stay here?" Mors asked.

"Don't know. Depends on how lucky we are."

"It be light soon, kardesh," Mors said, in a note of warning. Teil glanced at his wristcom.

"It's later than I thought. But we have nothing yet. No solid clues..."

"But you see many things."

"Yes, but not what I'm after." Mors looked searchingly into his face, and Teil knew he must tell him now. "I'm trying to find Eden. The ancient mythical land of Eden and the Garden. Only it's not so mythical. But you probably haven't any idea..."

"Yes. I know. *Aden, irembagi.*"

"Right. Then you know how ridiculous..."

"Our first father there."

"What do you mean,'father'?" Teil asked condescendingly.

"The first who knows the Life." Mors had said it so simply. There was that disturbing connection again deep within Teil.

"What do you mean, 'life'?" Teil snapped. The wave of hostility pushed them apart, Mors averting his eyes from the flare. Teil heard himself lash out again and saw its effects and the vulnerability of the big man. "What's wrong with Me? I'm sorry, Mors—cutting into you like that... Don't know what got into me."

"*Hic bir sey*," Mors replied, forgiving him.

"Here I am, tearing around this site in my glorious pursuit of discovery and truth—self obsession is more like it—and I try to snuff out the only truth here..." He turned and walked away from the console. Troubled, he stared for a long time down the dark passageway leading away from the chamber.

"Every once in awhile I feel we're so far apart—you and I. Not in this kind of thing," Teil said, pointing to the equipment, "but a whole different area... I can't even describe it because I don't know what it is. As though we don't have the same *kind* of life. I don't mean way of life; that's obviously different. When I get caught up in this..." he said, pointing to the screen, "yours and Milton's and all, maybe even Aspasia now, who knows?—living by some mystical inner reality, higher power, or whatever—it all seems so unreal. But when I get away from this; open myself up to the light of their experience, even though I don't know what it is, it seems to be the only real."

"I think I understand, kardesh."

"That's amazing, because I don't. You and I, working side by side, trying to survive; close to each other, dependent on each other... Yet it's a wholly different world you and the others are in, and I don't even know what it *is*. And I'm outside... What is it? How can people have such different... What? What's the big mystery, this unseen force I feel from a distance? I'm confused... If you understand it, Mors, I wish you'd try and tell me sometime—if we ever get out of this place."

"I cannot explain, kardesh, but I be with you."

That was it, Teil thought. It could not be reduced to words; only experienced. "This whole thing—ever since I woke up one morning..." He shook his head. "But I know I wouldn't have it any other way... There's something in this whole thing that tells me the grounds of its authentication are within itself—myself! Over on the other side, across the dark chasm that seems to be coming up on me and I know I must leap across soon—a dark and bottomless void."

"No, kardesh. All you have to do is take one step, enough to leave the earth behind. And you not know you make it over or even for sure there be other side. But when you take one step, you be there."

"But how do you *know?*"

"You not know. But you know." The simple wisdom of the big man carried its own assurance. But Teil was shaking again.

"I'm frightened, Mors..." Mors reached across and laid his large rough hand on Teil's shoulder. Teil wanted to say the word so badly—kardesh, brother—but it wouldn't come out. He wanted to say it and embrace the man, but couldn't.

"Not be afraid of your fear," Mors said quietly. "You see someday, and you know."

In the power of that closeness, at least, there was quiet and peace, and off in the distance, on the other side of Teil's emptiness, penetrating it as a shaft of great beauty and light, he heard again the chord.

27

"Mors—!" Teil said abruptly with new resolve, looking his large companion straight on, "I'm going to press this new button." The big man nodded fearlessly. "If it's what I think it is, Mascom has not only extended itself again, but made our job easier and more enjoyable." Teil was buoyed up again with new confidence.

"An adventure awaits us, my friend. Come, stand with me here in front of the screen." Mors eagerly moved to join him. "No! Wait!" Teil cried, warding him off. "Let me go first, and if anything goes wrong, press this other button here." Teil pointed to a large green button labeled XFER. "Whatever happens, one of us must press that transfer button." Mors examined it closely. "Not now! But that's the one. If we don't press it, our whole mission here will be for nothing. It transfers all our work here to X. If everything is okay and nothing goes wrong, and you see me in a cloud of light, then you come in with me.

"That's what they call 'blind faith,' Mors. We put our body and soul at the mercy of a power we have no way of even comprehending; we don't even know that it won't destroy us; only that we know we must. My dear and loyal friend, whatever happens, don't panic. Stay with me, do you understand?" Now look who's talking! he thought.

"I think so, kardesh."

Teil pressed AUTO MANEUVER, and the area in front of the apparatus blossomed into light.

"We're in hologram!" Teil exclaimed. "I hope this light isn't visible outside. Okay, Mors, you can come in now. It's all right." Mors gingerly stepped into the cloud of light with wide-eyed amazement and stood within the shimmering apparition, not knowing what to expect.

"What this be?" he asked.

Before Teil could answer, they were immersed into the site, which began coalescing about them. It was like figures emerging out of a fog.

"I can't see!" Teil cried.

"Where we are?" Mors asked.

"There...now I can see. Mors...! Oh, there you are. We're inside the site now—what we were looking at on the screen."

"Inside, like the hatchet?"

"Yes."

"Bu seylardin hic anliamam," Mors said.

"That's all right; not sure I understand either. I think we're still standing inside the walls where we were, only now, we're in the site too. There, see how it's filling out...? Problem now is how do we get back to level seven, like I want." There was a vertical shifting of light as though in response to Teil's very remark.

"Mors! There we are! Seven! And there's our chisel. On the ground!"

"I see it."

"It's becoming more real every second. Now look: buildings, walls... Much better than the Troy site in the sphere. Mors— the whole site—fully reconstituted!"

"How this happen?"

"Not sure I know. This thing never does stop, does it? Kri-kor was right: 'accelerating the rate of acceleration.' It's leaving us all so far behind. What's happening out there?"

"It bring back dead, too?" Mors asked.

"No, Mors, I'm sure we won't find any people here, at least I hope not! Apparently, all I have to do is keep talking as we go, and the system keeps up with us, calculating what we want. But I still don't see how this can be without direct tie-in with Mascom. Oh well, I've been dragged into the thing this far, and it hasn't killed me yet. Besides, what choice do we have, eh? And this thing is beginning to get interesting.

"Walls! Look at 'em. We missed those. All along the south. I bet the whole site is walled." Teil surveyed the panorama in one sweeping gaze, drinking it in slowly, disbelievingly. "Suddenly this brings the site into focus. Now we have *city*." Teil straightened as the intuitive recognition came. "Suddenly, we're there. I feel it. Enoch.

"Something about this place sets it apart. Not size or anything like that. It should all start fitting together now. Let's go, Mors; I'll lead the way. Just follow me in your mind— *akilinda*," Teil said, pointing to his own head. "Up here. If we aren't careful, we might get carried away and knock our brains out on the passageway walls..."

Teil began talking as though he were walking through the site, and the site shifted about them to correspond.

"Would you look at those walls! Three to four meters thick; ten meters high. Come to think of it, when did our cities stop having walls? Where did they go? Why? I'd liked to have put that to poor Kri-kor... And look at how everything's laid out: paved roads leading to the walls from the center of the village; the buildings, situated along the roads; two-roomed houses on stone foundations. Look inside, Mors. See? That curious domed inner room, and the rectangular outer room? The store of arrowheads, spear heads, and sling stones? Like they were getting ready for battle, then left; and like they'll return any minute and find we've invaded their defenses!

"Armories set against the inside of the walls. And what are these, barracks next to the armory? And look at the chutes, Mors—over each gate in the walls. Probably to cast stones down on attackers. See? This all seems to be part of a defensive system... They sure must've felt threatened."

"You see so much, kardesh. More than me."

"I see nothing, compared to what Mascom sees. But I'll tell you this," he said looking at Mors again. "You know what they'll find when they dig up *our* megapols 6000 years from now? Silicon. That's right. That's what Mascom and all this is made of. And you know what all that silicon will crumble into, what it is?"

"No, kardesh."

"Sand. That's what they'll find, piles of sand!" Teil broke off and laughed. "And with a strange odor to it all, because the world will be overrun by housebroken cats gone wild again. Yes, Skia and her ilk. All the world's great megapols," Teil was laughing uncontrollably, "massive repositories of kitty litter!

"They won't even be able to detect the presence of civilization, Mors, because there wasn't any. It was all a transitory movement of electrons, vibrating briefly in some unseen silicon pathway for a fraction of a trillionth of a second. Civilization is people, isn't it? Well, there aren't *people* any more. They won't even be able to build on top of our ruins; they'll have to scrape away all that shifting smelly sand first. Progress, Mors—progress!" he said, trying to control himself.

"I wonder how many other existing cities in this part of the world cover important sites. Before the probes, we could never dig them; no one would let you destroy the present to uncover the past. Chew that one over, Mors. Maybe you'll have better luck with it than I." Mors let him talk on; he was enjoying the newness of the strange experience and excitement of discovery, agog in a whole new world.

With no reference point outside themselves, the two men soon lost the distinction between actually walking through the site and the site "walking" past them, such was the relativity of the effects. And neither realized what was really happening as Mascom was continually and imperceptibly deepening the connection.

"Look kardesh—*duduk*."

"A pipe. With a mouthpiece! Like at Gawra XII. Music, Mors! Now look at those grain storage pits. Agriculture! These people aren't just raising crops because they know how; this is *farming*. There's system in effect here. Like in the metal shop we saw earlier.

"Let's go inside this room, Mors... There you go... That

long table; it would do well for an executive conference room. The designs on the walls... Not a temple. Dining room? Meeting room of some sort? It's uncanny how archaeprobe is reconstructing all this."

"Everything look real now," Mors said.

"So much so I want to pick up things, but don't dare."

"Kardesh, I think you like this maybe." He was pointing to the table top.

"What?"

"Pictures on table. Tell story maybe, yes?"

"You're right. Looks like an inlaid sheet of metal that's engraved. Okay, let's take a closer look. There... Makes you want to blow away the dust, doesn't it?"

"*Toz gedi!*"

"Like Mascom just vacuumed the thing."

"*Mucize!*"

"Well, it's not really a miracle, Mors, though from your viewpoint, yes. But look at it would you. Pictograms, and arranged in some sort of diagram..."

"*Kardesh, bak—flavta ve cadir,*" Mors said, examining the pictures on the table top.

"Could be. A pipe and tent... You're catching on, Mors. Way ahead of me. But what's the other one down there?"

"*Onuda bildim. Demirci alet dalmi?*"

"Metalworking tools? Mors, you're a genius! Look how these three symbols—the tent, the pipe and what's next to it, and the tool—are at the very bottom of the diagram, all in a row, and the others go up vertically from that, and at the very top there's one, and everything flows down from it, like a pyramid. The symbol at the top is similar to the cutting tool, only enclosed, signifying what? A grouping of sorts? Hold it! Watson, my glass!"

Teil bent closer and counted the rows of pictogram symbols. "Six in the vertical sequence, then these three groups along the bottom, as though they come off the last one. Right... Let's see... Cain, then Enoch, Irad, Mehujael, Methushael, and Lamech. Genesis IV. And the sons of Lamech were called ancestors of—get this, three of them!—tent-dwelling cattle herders, musicians, and toolmakers! And that delta-shaped character next to the pipe; bet anything it's a lyre. Such a literal correspondence with the Hebrew record. And the Hebrew word for Cain is *kayin*, literally 'tribe of smiths'—the symbol at the top! This thing has to be the genealogy of Cain. The Cain line. The men of Enoch!

"So this site has to be either Enoch or closely related to it, because the genealogy ends with Tubal-cain, just like the text. Mors, this means we're on the right track. Cain's origins in Eden must lie not too far above us. Probably in Braidwood's hilly flanks of the Taurus, though he would turn over in his grave if we told him we were looking for Adam in his hilly flanks."

The forced humor of it and the rising tension from the excitement of discovery and the threat of being discovered were beginning to get to Teil; he was on the verge of laughing uncontrollably. It was only by pinching himself hard on his own flanks and supporting himself on Mors's rock-like shoulder that he managed to keep from losing control.

"Whew!" Teil whistled, recovering. "Let's start making our way out of here."

As they passed by the side of the storage pits Mors pointed to some tools next to them on the ground and asked, *"Kucuk balta gibi alet ne, kardesh?"*

"They look like hatchets but I'd say pickaxes, Mors, metal pickaxes with wooden handles. They're new at this level, aren't they? What a striking tool, compared to what preceeded them on the earlier levels. It's possible the world's first metal pickaxe is right here, Mors. You certainly have a knack for spotting the significant. Can you imagine the revolutionary impact of those things?

"Yes..." Teil went on. "It fits perfectly. Part of the system for the kind of emergence of civilization we're looking for would have to be the emergence of new tools. And here, instead of wood and stone, we have one designed for the task. The right material, shape, weight, leverage—a whole system of parameters—all serving the techniques of cultivation and building. And, by the way, generating its own technique which must in turn be served, improved and developed.

"The 'Myth of the Creation of the Pickaxes'!" Teil exclaimed. "I just remembered. One of the earliest known pieces of writing. From Sumer. About Enlil, city-god of the Sumerian city of Nippur. Enlil could refer to Cain or Tubal-cain. Centuries downstream from us here, below, where the two great rivers come close together, the men of that time and place look back on the significance of this very tool, and they see it—partially. They tell how the god Enlil created the pickaxe and used it to 'break the hard crust of the earth,' allowing the first men to grow forth from the earth like plants:

> Upon the pickaxe and basket Enlil directs the
>   power...decrees its fate...
> They give the pickaxe to the black-headed
>   people to hold.
>
>   . . . .
>
> The pickaxe and the basket build cities.

"In a way, we can say the pickaxe, the revolutionary intruder on the scene, *systemitizes*, imposes its teleology on the whole culture, pulling it forward in a certain direction. That's what tools do, don't they?" said Teil, looking up, discovering the fact. "I never saw it that way, but looking at the beginnings of everything like this..." He breathed a deep sigh as he unconsciously closed his eyes and let himself be carried into it. "Each tool shapes the culture; shapes man's destiny. Shapes man. And man becomes subject to the 'power' or 'spirit' of that tool. Yes, spirit is the word. The ancients may have known some things we don't.

"Each tool creates its own necessity that will drive man and his culture in a certain direction, toward certain ends. And we can only see those ends *looking back on the whole process*. We're blind to them when we forge that tool. All we see is what is to be gained, not what might be lost and how it might affect man. Man, the Great Variable between the thing manufactured and its predestined end. And man thereafter losing the freedom *not* to be changed. And man becomes the Great Object of the history he sets into motion!

Teil buried his face in his hands as the vision flashed into him, more than he could see or grasp, groping around the fringes of the idea.

"I wonder if Mascom—maybe since it is *not* man—maybe for the first time, something, someone will see where we're going and... But what if it sees already? Already knows? Would we be willing to commit ourselves to that knowledge and obey? Would we go into the ark? *Could* we? And what if we did? Following the omniscient extrapolations of the Machine, what if we did commit ourselves totally to her wisdom? Would we not then have knowingly capitulated to the Final Tool and in that very act lost our last vestige of freedom?" Teil's head jerked upward as in pain, his hands still shielding himself from the colossal impact of the idea.

"What does it all mean?! Is there no way out?! What have we done with our tools?!!!"

28

The silence was punctuated by a cry in the night. The sound penetrated their inner world, breaking the subjective connection the two men had with the site. Thrust suddenly, reeling, into the reality of their surroundings, they stood shakily in a moment of dazed bewilderment. Then, as the cries grew louder and more numerous, now mingled with the barking of dogs—recognition.

Mors snapped out of it first, and boldly jumping out of the cloud of light, ran to the doorway and peered into the dawn-fringed darkness of the citadel courtyard. Teil jolted himself into action. His first thought was to retrieve the probes; they were his only hope for finding the secret of Eden. But as he joined Mors and looked out across the courtyard, his heart sank. Men were pouring through the West Gate that joined the citadel and outer city proper, urged on by the cries of someone atop the minaret, who was pointing frantically to the protruding portions of the probes he had just discovered inside the walls.

"*Ickaleyi harab edicekler! Bombalar ekdiler!* They are going to destroy the citadel! They have planted bombs!"

Mors jerked Teil back into the dark doorway. "Kardesh!" he cried. "Inside, before they see you!" But in an instant, a dozen men were racing across the 400-meter distance toward them, the massive iron portcullis slamming to the earth behind them with a sickening thud.

"*Aleti bas, kardesh! Unutdunmu?*" Mors cried, reverting to his Turkish dialect in the excitement.

"What are you talking about?" Teil said.

"Button. Press button now?"

"Yes Mors! Now!" Teil yelled, remembering, as they both raced for the equipment. By this time their hiding place had been discovered, and the yells of their attackers pursued them inside the passageway.

"*Buradalar!!* They are here!"

"*Oradalar, duvarlarin icinde!* They are there, inside the walls!"

"*Disariya cikmasinlar!* Don't let them escape!"

Mors got to the panel first and pressed XFER. Teil saw the indicator flash for a moment and then go out. "It worked, Mors!" Teil cried elatedly. "We dumped the site! Mascom now has everything we've discovered here!" He was flushed with success; civilization and X would see what he had done after all. Teil was moved by a new sense of power. As he reached the equipment, he had already decided what to do. "Mors, stand here next to me and do exactly as I say. Stay with me."

As their attackers burst into the chamber, Teil and Mors stepped into the hologram and appeared to become transfigured, engulfed in the cloud of light of the archaeprobe-replicated site. The attackers stopped in terror and drew back. Here were the two men they had just chased, now part of an eerie ghost-like scene, unreal figures floating within the luminescent projection of the Enoch site.

"They are the *baskalar*, kardesh," Mors said under his breath.

"Others?" asked Teil. Mors nodded.

"Now Mors," Teil whispered, "We must move within this cloud, never outside it. Understand?" Mors nodded. "And I want you to pick up these units here while I carry these. We're going to move over to the container of spare probes. Then we're going to take everything with us and walk out of here, inside this cloud of light."

"I am with you, kardesh," Mors said.

Slowly and deliberately the pair moved, taking the cloud

with them, until they reached the probe container. Mors then slung the container onto his back, and the two advanced steadily on their attackers. Teil marveled at how composed he felt. He was buoyed up on a wave of confidence. As they advanced, Teil had all he could do to keep the system in operation and maintain the projection enclosing them; but even so, it flickered unsteadily and verged on extinction at every step. The hologram of the entire Enoch site was thus moving, with them inside it, down the passageway toward the postern gate, with their attackers retreating before them step by awed step. The ancient underground ruins of the walled fortress city of Enoch had become a refuge from certain death.

But as they came to the gate, all seemed lost. They would have to lose the projection in order to open the gate and pass through. And once the hologram collapsed, Teil and Mors would be reduced to mere flesh and blood again, and the attackers were bound to regain courage.

Then Teil thought of how to overwhelm these present-day inhabitants of Enoch with Enoch herself. "Mors, when you hear an awful noise start coming out of here, open the gate and let us out; then lock it behind us. It's our only chance." Teil nervously manipulated the controls until he was ready for the switch. Then, in an instant, he flipped the mode selector to AUDIO-VIDEO to add raw unprocessed audio and spun the volume to its upper limit.

The air was suddenly filled with a cacophony of terrifying noise. Every sensor return from every sensor in every probe coming from every object in the site was heard in its own raw electronic garble and mixed with every other return from every other sensor. The noise from any single artifact alone was enough, at full volume, to unhinge the healthiest human. It was a furious concatenation of the entire electronic repertoire of blips, beeps, wows, gongs, burps, whistles, screeches, screams, shrieks, and wails—all at full volume, competing for decibel destruction of every living thing within range. Teil could not help but smile at the thought of whether Twentieth-Century sulphuric acid Rock had sounded like this.

Ancient Enoch had come to life and was bludgeoning her

own people into insensibility. Her sonic likeness merged with the flickering image like a noisy ghost come back to haunt the living. The whole scene was the likes of which no one on earth had ever witnessed. Had Teil and Mors not been behind the parabola of sound, they would have been reduced to gibbering idiots. What had looked like order, design, system, city, now came across as utter chaos. Thanks to the machine.

Then, as the two men went through the attackers toward the gate, Teil in a final burst of inspiration, started rotating the positioner ball, shifting site orientation, so the whole weird orchestra of sounds dopplered through fantastic pitch changes. It was like a million screeching banshees loosed and boiling up out of the pit of hell. The entire pan-demonium of city-past screamed into life to bedevil her inhabitants.

As Mors opened the gate, Teil brandished archaeprobe as Flash Gordon would his sword and charged his attackers full on with an unearthly war cry.

"AIIEEEEEEEeeeeeeeeee.....!!!!"

The attackers, set upon by their own city, fled in ignominious rout.

29

While Teil secured the equipment, Mors tore loose one of the iron bars on the grating and jammed it through the gate and wall latches. Then, with his mighty strength, he bent the bar into a loop, tying the gate shut with solid iron. They had no sooner gotten the gear in hand and were on their way down the path to the river, than there came the sound of horses galloping toward them. Before they knew what was happening, three men came flying up on horseback, stopping abruptly in a cloud of dust. One horse carried two riders, and the third horse was on a tether.

"Mors!" Teil cried in alarm. But Mors had already put down his load and grabbed the first horse by the bridle, trying to dump its rider.

Teil went for the other horse, which had the two riders. He grabbed a leg of the one behind, whose head was covered by a turban, and pulled him off, only to have him fall into his arms. The turban fell away, releasing a full mane of long dark hair flowing around a lovely face that stared up at him with huge dark eyes.

"Aspasia!" Teil gasped. After the initial shock, she broke out laughing, and Teil danced her around and around holding her off the ground.

"Glad to know you can still dance so well, Professor," she cried.

"Absolutely!" he yelled.

At the same time, Mors was in the process of dumping the first rider, when he stopped and let out a yell of recognition.

"Dies!" he cried, lifting the man out of the saddle and embracing him. "Kardesh! It is Dies and Ingemisco. Look!"

"You've got your Turkish tongue back, Mors!" Dies said. "And you can put me down now, too!"

"Dies!" Teil yelled, "am I glad to see you! We feared the worst. They're after us. We've got to get out of here fast. The whole town is up in arms."

"We have horses for you," Ingemisco said.

"I know; they're ours!" Teil yelled.

"Load your gear on that one, Mors," Dies said. "Aspasia, you ride behind Teil this time. By the way, lad," he said, helping Teil into the saddle first, "have you ever ridden one of these creatures before?"

"Never."

"Up you go, girl," Dies said, helping Aspasia up. "There's only one way to learn, and that's to ride, even if your mount happens to be as lively as this one. Good luck!"

Once in the saddle, Teil was at loose ends to know what to do. "Put your feet in here and clamp the horse between your knees," Dies yelled. "And girl, hang onto your man."

"Don't worry!" she said.

"How do you steer one of these things?" Teil yelled.

"You'll find out," Ingemisco yelled back.

"*Eyeri boyle tut, kardesh,*" Mors yelled, showing him how to hold the saddle.

Mors and Ingemisco were securing the equipment to the third mount as Teil tried to compute this new hazard. A flair of excitement tingled his nostrils at the prospect of riding the wild creature.

"The thing is such a huge system of variables!" Teil said frantically. "I don't even know where to begin. If the beast will only stand still long enough for me to figure it out... Such a will of its own. Must be female..."

"Watch it, Mann!" Aspasia said, jabbing Teil in the ribs.

"I guess you don't compute a wild woman, eh? Just get with it and go..." The mount tried to buck them off. "I take it all back, girl," he said to the horse, "you're not a system of variables! Whoa!"

Then they were off. All except Teil, that is, who could not get started.

"Hang on!" Dies shouted as he passed Teil's mount, giving it a swift kick in the rear. But the warning had not registered; the sudden lurch nearly left Teil in mid-air. It was sheer instinct that took over as he held on for dear life.

"Follow me!" Dies yelled, as he spurred his steed down the path to the Tigris. Mors and Ingemisco brought up the rear, while Teil tried to follow Dies. What he was really trying to do was follow his own mount under him, which seemed bent on going its own way regardless of what Teil would do. Teil finally gave up trying and hung onto the saddle with both hands, bouncing along unmercifully, trying for all his might to keep from being thrown, Aspasia's arms encircling his waist so tightly he could hardly breathe.

"Hey woman!" Teil yelled back to Aspasia as he got the hang of it and they flew down the road.

"Yes, man!" she yelled back.

"Haven't I seen you somewhere before?"

"I've heard that line before."

"I mean, don't I know you from somewhere?"

"Not really."

"That's what I thought," Teil said.

"We mustn't keep meeting like this, you know," Aspasia said.

"And in the strangest places," he said. "Didn't know you were a fire bug, but thanks; that guy had me." They laughed as they were thrown up and down.

"Where have you been?" she asked.

"Where've *I* been?"

"Yes. Here I am the faithful wife, slaving away... And then the next thing I know..."

"Your're gone!" he said.

"Right." They laughed again.

"But I kept trying to get messages to you, even though I wasn't supposed to," she said.

"I got two of them. Very clever. Very Aspasia."

"From Milton?"

"And the woman out here they arrested in Ankara. I met Theta and Rico, too."

"Aren't they really something," she said.

"Know what you mean. How did you happen to hook up with them?"

"How did you?" she asked.

"Who said I had?" he said.

"I can tell," she said.

"You always could," he said. "So— What have you been up to?"

"My old tricks..." she said. Teil reached back and swatted her thigh a sharp whap.

"Ouch! That hurt!"

"That's for your old tricks!" he said.

"Teil, you'll never guess. X... I was sent out here by X as a spy."

"Spying on whom?" he asked.

"The Others," she said.

"Why you?"

"I don't know," she said. "Supposedly my language background, but it doesn't figure. I get the feeling it's got very little to do with the Others. They have their secret headquarters in Diyarbekir now, you know."

"Is that what you were doing in the mosque."

"Yes," she said.

"What are they up to?" he asked.

"They want to take over—eliminate X. Revolution. They're organized now; about to start their big push."

"Are they the ones who bombed Regional?" asked Teil. "You heard, didn't you?"

"Yes. They're starting to surface—create confusion."

"They're not the only ones. Do you know what's been going on out there?" asked Teil.

"What do you mean?"

"All the glitches. People falling apart. All hell's breaking loose. People exploding into violence." Teil related the scenes he saw from the minaret at Silvan. "And the Sigma virus—it's suicide."

"No!" she said, appalled, "Are you sure? That's devastating..."

"I know. It changes everything, doesn't it?"

"Yes..."

"You still a spy?" he asked.

"I think they're onto me. Made my last drop, then had to get out. Took advantage of the commotion you and Mors were making. Met Dies outside and went back to get you. Found your horses and saw you trying to escape."

"I'd rather face that mob any day than this reckless beast... Bent on reducing me to a bag of bones!"

"What do you think he's doing to *me*!"

After a few hectic kilometers, Dies dropped back abreast of Teil and Aspasia and engaged them in conversation. They slackened their pace.

"What was that awful noise and commotion back there?" Dies said.

"Dies," said Teil, "You'll never believe it. You don't know what fun you people missed back there in Enoch."

"Enoch?"

"Diyarbekir. They were right on top of us! Dozens of 'em, coming in for the kill. And all we had was a 'cloud by day and a pillar of fire by night.' "

"Moses-mann!" Aspasia said. Teil laughed.

"Diyarbekir is Cain's Enoch, folks, just in case you were wondering."

"What is Kanezenuk?" Dies asked. Teil laughed again.

"Enoch. The city of Cain. Cain the son of Adam. You all missed city-past back there, rising up from the dead and trying to tell us something."

"You mean the Cain of the Adam and Eve story?" Aspasia asked.

"Yes. Only it's not what you and everyone else think."

"What do you mean?" she asked.

"Adam wasn't the first man on earth," Teil said.

"Who said he was?" said Dies.

"Before Mascom," Teil yelled, as the gap momentarily widened between the two horses, "when they used to write and preach about such things, there was a running controversy. Poor Adam was either pure myth or the progenitor of the whole human race. But there's a more realistic interpretation. Adam was part of an emerging civilization. In this part of the world...right here somewhere. A real person. In a real culture, in a real place and a real time. He wasn't *Pithecanthropus erectus, Australopithecus,* Neanderthal, or even Cro-Magnon." Teil's horse tried to dump them again.

"Don't know what you're saying, lad," Dies said.

"Modern man!" exclaimed Teil. "Not at the dawn of creation, but at the dawn of history!"

"So what?" Dies asked.

"What kind of a question is that?" Teil asked, annoyed. "You mean, So what if Adam was modern man, like you and I...?"

"Right."

"Good question," Teil said. "Well, for one thing, it means there's no conflict between Science and Genesis. But there's more. I get a deep feeling the Adam story, seen in this new light, is somehow very relevant to us today. Anyway, that's Enoch back there, under Diyarbekir. The city Cain built and named after his son. A new kind of first in the origin of cities."

"So what?" Dies asked again, breaking into a mischievous grin.

"I'll tell you 'so what?' " Teil retorted, spurring his horse ahead of Dies, having great fun with his running sysnthesis, if not his running horse, "I am Gilgamesh, embattled warrior of old," he cried, raising both arms in a victory salute, "looking for the source of eternal life."

After their furious flight up the Tigris river, when dawn had fully broken, they found the field where Mors had hid the wagon.

"That ride was more terrifying than the earthquake," Teil said, easing his bruised body off the horse and helping Aspasia down. "I'll never know how I stayed on so long, and my waist will never be the same again." He grinned at Aspasia and added, "But it was kind of nice."

"It better be nice!" she said, hands on hips.

They hid the equipment inside the wagon again and hitched the horses to pull it. The other horse they tethered behind. As they moved on, Teil sat next to Dies, with Aspasia next to Teil, who quickly realized he needed a cushion for his nether parts. Mors and Ingemisco sat behind them. When they were finally on the road again, going north, Teil asked, "Now what do we do? Where are we going?"

"Endee, of course," Aspasia said happily.

"Endee...? You mean it's out here?"

'Yes."

"You've been there?"

"Oh yes," Aspasia said. "I'd sneak away from spying all the time."

"Where is it?"

Dies winked across at Aspasia and said, "Not far from where you want to go, lad."

"Nerp Duzu...?"

"N-D, Teil," Aspasia said. "N-D equals Endee."

"Oh..." Teil said, the curious identification dawning on him. "I see. That's an unbelievable coincidence. My Nerp Duzu, that I discovered all by myself, turns out to be the UGLI Endee..."

"What do you mean, *your* Nerp Duzu?" she said in mock resentment.

"Eden, Aspasia. That's my best Eden site." She looked at him queerly.

"Teilhard, lad," Dies said, "I don't know what your great 'mission' is all about and how you ever came upon Endee as we call it, but there's more there than whatever it is you're after. Endee is our own central group, a kind of halfway house on our journey to recovery."

Suddenly the whole picture had changed for Teil. Instead of going to some obscure mountain depression—who in the world present or past had ever heard of Nerp Duzu?—they were headed into a group of UGLIs. And Aspasia was with him again and he with her. He did something very untypical of a ranking mascientist on a secret mission of earth-shaking import. He jumped to his feet in the moving wagon, reached out to the sky, and yelled at the top of his lungs. It sounded like a cross between the Tarzan mating call, an Apache war cry, and the utterance of a religious ecstatic all rolled into one. Then it turned into a long cry of relief, exultation, joy, and hope. Then he laughed and laughed, and kept on laughing, until even the horses were infected with his jubilation. Grabbing the reigns from Dies, Teil stood like some charioteer of old, impelling his steeds to victory.

"Onward to Endee!" he cried. "And backward to Eden!"

* * *

It was not long before they were passing through a small village encircled by seven wells. "Agviran," Teil noted, looking at his map. "What does the name mean, Mors? Do you know?"

"No kardesh, it is just a name I think."

"Speaking of names, Dies, tell me, what are these names you people have? I've been meaning to ask you for a long time. Never heard anything like them before, yet they sound familiar. Morz, Enje-misco, Dee-ace...?"

"I was wonderin' when you'd get around to that," Dies said.

"The names are something very special to this group, Teil," Aspasia said. "They kind of symbolize that part of us we have in common, that ties us together."

"I'm all ears," Teil said.

"Why tell him at all?" Ingemisco intruded, his fiery dark eyes brooding.

"It be all right," Mors said, defending Teil. "He be all right."

"The names come out of music, Teilhard," Dies said, "an ancient piece nobody's ever heard of."

"What piece?"

"*Requiem*. By someone called Verdi. And our dear old Requiem gets his name from the piece like we do."

Teil turned to Aspasia and asked, "Latin for 'rest'?" She nodded.

"When he came," Dies said, "Requiem had this player with a hand crank. And there are brittle discs with fine grooves that carry the music."

"Phonograph," Aspasia noted, nodding to Teil.

"There are some who think we shouldn't have it," Ingemisco hotly interjected.

"Don't mind our young rebel here," Dies said. "Speak for yourself, lad," he added, looking back at Ingemisco. "And maybe you should listen to the Requiem more, eh? Anyway, Requiem wrote down all the words. You see, the piece has a great chorus of voices and many instruments."

Teil said, "Odd, how in my mind I saw the names differently. But let's see...you would spell it M-O-R-S for 'death.' Dies for 'day.' And Ingemisco...that would mean 'I groan or sigh'."

"Bravo!" Aspasia exclaimed.

"That's him all right," Dies said, nodding toward Ingemisco, "always groaning over System."

Aspasia explained to Teil, "There's more to some of the names, of course, depending on the text. Mors is really *mors stupebit*, 'death is stupified or confounded.' "

"How true," Teil said. "Whenever death looks at Mors, he *is* confounded, isn't he, kardesh?" Mors beamed his gigantic toothy grin.

"And our adorable Dies here," Aspasia added, reaching over and patting him on the arm, "is really *Dies Irae*, one of the recurring themes in the piece."

"Day of anger?" Teil said.

"Well, girl, you knew all along!" Dies remarked to her, surprised.

"That doesn't fit you, does it, Dies," Teil asked.

"It's there, man; it's there, believe me. Why do you think I'm UGLI?"

"But why names from music?" Teil asked.

"When you see then you'll understand," Dies said.

"Teil..." Aspasia said, reaching over and pulling at his sleeve eagerly. "The most marvelous thing happened here about you..."

"Me?"

"Weeks ago. We were having a meeting. I had sneaked in late; took a big chance that night. But this particular night I felt so bad, like a weight was crushing me. All I could think of was you; the crushing feeling was connected with you somehow, and I mentioned it. And when those around me heard it, everyone listened. It's the way they pick up another's feelings.

"Then one of the girls who worked as a caster's secretary in megapol Chicago—Lacrymosa. She looked straight at me, yet I knew she was seeing something else. Know what I mean? And she told us what she was seeing. She said she saw something like a star falling from the sky and someone was in it. You."

"But she's never seen me."

"I know. Then one of the men said quietly, 'We must help this man.' They all stopped talking and picked up his urgency and just sat there, bearing the pain that was there, my pain. It was as though everything stood still, stopped for a moment; it all just kind of hung there.

"Then Lacrymosa said it was an omni, and it had crashed in a lake, and you were outside."

"The omni... What did she say happened to it?"

"That it disappeared, and you were left alone."

"That's exactly how it happened. Incredible! I still can't figure that one out, Aspi. I was sure that every bone in my body broke on impact. I had virtually no braking power. We just came in, and POW! And what I saw of the omni in the water before it vaporized proves how hard we hit."

"How did you get out?" she asked.

"*I don't know!* One second I'm inside, being demolished by 100 Gs as we hit solid water; the next, I'm whole, in the water, watching it. Strangest thing that's ever happened to me. Like a dream." She clutched Teil's arm tightly. "And you say they were just...sitting there? *They* were helping *me?*"

"Experiencing, feeling, as though they had entered the flow of that experience. Yes, darling, isn't it marvelous?"

"I just don't know..." Teil said, staring hard ahead.

As they took a turn in the road, Dies pulled the wagon over and peered into the distance. "We're going to hold up before we get to Hani," he said, "just to be sure. It's been a long time since we've been here; no telling what may have happened. Don't want to take any chances. It's practically deserted now, but it used to be a... What do you call it, Mors?"

"*Nahiye merkesi.*"

"A regional center, right?" Teil said. "Let's see...the map shows we're about 900 meters altitude here, so is that Hani over the rise?"

"Yes," Dies replied.

"Then that ridge rising up behind must be Nerp Duzu, the southern walls."

"Righto."

"Isn't that still too close to Hani?"

"That's why we control Hani; we use it as an outpost, a kind of communication center with our people who travel and contacts with the other groups around the world." Dies started the wagon again.

"I still don't see how all this out here can be outside, disconnected from System," Teil noted. "Know what I mean, Dies? Like it never kept up with the rest of the world."

"Ah," Ingemisco intervened, "but maybe it is System that does not fit *this*."

"Good point, I must say," Teil conceded.

"It all depends which side you're looking from, doesn't it?" Ingemisco added.

"Quite true," Teil said.

"It came as a shock to me," Dies said. "I thought everything was like the megapols."

"Precisely," Teil exclaimed. "Dies, how is it that you think we are in fact outside System here?"

"When I was still part of it, I ran across this blind spot by accident chasing some UGLIs."

"You were a SOG?"

"In megapol London, back in the seventies. System showed surveillance of this area, but it really wasn't looking at it. Like it takes all the stuff it monitors, and instead of reporting the actual data, like the rest of the world, only gives you a kind of a filtered image of it."

"Like a propaganda version of reality?"

"Yes, you might say that... Right," said Dies thoughtfully.

"When you looked at data coming in from this part of the world, it'd be perfect, just what you'd expect. But after awhile it begins to dawn on you that even the irregularities fall into place too neatly. You know something's not quite right, but you can never put your finger on it."

"Maybe," Mors offered timidly, "the System knows all that is here, but will not say."

"Mors old chap," Dies said, "if I thought for one minute they knew and were *allowing* this..." There was an ominous silence.

Before they rounded the last bend into Hani, Dies pulled the wagon over into a cluster of trees and took charge. "We'd better split up," he said. "And this time, let's hope we all fare better than the last, eh Teilhard? Ingemisco, you go on up to the old minaret in Hani and check out the town. If all's clear, give the signal, then ride up to the rim of Endee and check with the lookouts. If all's clear inside, signal us again from there. If not, come back fast if you're not followed. Oh, and lad..."

"Yes?"

"Instead of the usual mirror signal, give us five flashes followed by another five." Ingemisco studied the older man's face.

"All right," he said flatly.

"Then you can go on down into the valley, and we'll follow."

As Ingemisco rode the spare horse into Hani, Dies stationed Mors to watch the road going south, while he, Teil, and Aspasia watched Ingemisco and the road ahead through the trees. After a time, they saw the coded flash from atop the minaret.

"Doesn't seem like enough time to check out the place," Teil said.

"Don't you trust him?" Dies asked.

"I don't know. Do you?"

"You know, Teil," Aspasia said, "that he doesn't trust you."

"I get that feeling," said Teil. "He's an odd one. Seems to have a fire inside his bones. Instead of starting off now, why not wait till we see his all-clear from the rim?"

"If you wish," said Dies.

"Just to be sure."

As they continued watching, they caught sight of the minuscule figure disappearing up the road behind Hani leading to the rim of Nerp Duzu. Teil put his arm around Aspasia and drew her close. Dies stood off with Mors.

"Teil..." she asked.

"Yes...?"

"Aren't you going to ask me?"

"What?"

"What *my* uglies are?"

"I already know!" he said.

"And well you should!" she retorted.

"Look who's talking!" he said. "And how much *do* you know about me?"

"I'll never tell," she said, smiling. "But isn't it wonderful," she added, giving Teil a hug, "that someone so hopelessly addicted to the conquest of one man after another could stop and come to?"

"Come to what?" he said defensively.

"Myself—sanity!" she said. Teil was silent a long moment.

"You're right, you know," Teil said, heaving a sigh of resignation. "And me... I just can't take that old way of life anymore, Aspi..."

"I couldn't either," she said.

"And for the first time ever...others are making it...maybe there's a way out," he said. She drew him close again.

Just then Dies alerted them. "Five...and two, three, four, five. All's clear! Mors! Can you believe it? We made it back again! We can go home!" he exclaimed, embracing the big man. A huge smile lit up Mors's beaming countenance as he lifted Dies off his feet and ran him around and around in sheer joy. Mors's cavernous mouth opened opera-singer wide and bellowed his resonant baritone laughter.

Dies yelled to Teil and Aspasia, "Let's go! What are you two love birds waiting for? Get the wagon up here, Mors. Well, are you two coming along, or are you just going to stand there moonstruck?"

"We're with you, you old SOG," Teil said as he helped

Aspasia into the wagon and jumped in beside her. "Hang on woman!"

The team responded easily, even though it was steadily uphill; they seemed to be drawn to the place too. It was no time before they had covered the five kilometers up to the rim. Then they rode down, gaining momentum quickly until they were practically flying.

"One last precaution," Dies yelled to Teil. "When we get down there, we separate. I lead the way, then Mors with the wagon, then you two. See you at supper."

"Where are we going?"

"To the edge of the tree line, over there," he said, pointing. "See?"

"But what is it?" Teil insisted. "What does it look like? What do you call it?"

"We don't call it anything" Dies yelled. "It's just where we belong."

Part Three

REVELATION

30

It was late afternoon when they arrived at the edge of the tree line in the northwestern part of the valley, the sun's golden orb dipping ahead of them toward the western rim. Dies disappeared into the forest, followed by Mors and the wagon, with Teil and Aspasia following on foot a few minutes behind. The air was cool, but the sun's rays were warm, and Teil felt them going into him, as though he were drawing them in; and they were being stored quietly inside his very soul.

Inside the forest, Teil was struck with the abundance and variety of wildlife and gave in to the compelling urge to linger. Then, through the trees, his gaze caught the color on the hillside.

"Look, Aspasia," he said, pointing.

"Wildflowers," she said. "This is when they bloom here. Aren't they beautiful?"

"What a gorgeous profusion of color!" he exclaimed. "Why does it grow in patches of the same color? Does each species want to congregate with its own kind?" He took her hands, and said, "Were you and I meant to con-gregate? How did we drift so far apart?"

"We were never really *together*, Teil."

"Can two people ever be?" he said, letting go of her hands and turning away.

"I don't think we could have made it as things were," she

said.

"As things are now? As I am now?"

"Where are you now, Teil?"

"Don't ask me... You're different, you know. You even look different. Did you really mean what you said back there about your addiction to men? I know you tried to talk about your past once when we were back in that other world out there but I didn't want to hear..."

"Yes, I meant it, Teil. It finally caught up with me. That beautiful way of life I had going for me—that facade? It just wasn't working any more—for *me*. You had something to do with that, you know."

"How?"

"You were the last one—and the first. When we got together, I really wanted it to work; it had promise. I wanted to commit myself to the man I wanted to love—you. But I found I couldn't do either one, love or commit myself. And maybe I was secretly hoping you'd be the one who would make it all right—on the inside. Know what I mean?" He nodded. "I think I had resorted to the phony me and the simulated thing I called 'love' for so long, I lost all capacity for the real. But that's all I *knew*; that whole way of life...I thought I had exactly what I wanted, that I was in control. I didn't know I was the victim—of myself! That I was trapped."

"I know the feeling."

"I thought you might," she said, glancing at him with a cautious smile.

"I thought you thought I might," he said. They laughed awkwardly as he leaned his body against hers. "Whew! What a pair!"

"It's a terrible discovery, you know," she said. "One day you wake up and suddenly realize you've short-circuited your ability to love. That your self-obsession has injured you so much you can't even *receive* love. That you don't know the first thing about it. That the great love 'maker' was really the great love cripple."

"I like that..." Teil said, trying to lighten it for himself. "I'm going to walk into your group of UGLIs here and say,

'Hi! I'm Teilhard!; I'm a love cripple!' " They laughed, freer this time.

"We aren't alone, you know. Of all the different 'uglies' that force us together, that one tops the list."

"We're all a bunch of love-cripple sex drunks—you know that?" Teil said. "The New Alcoholics!"

"There you go," she said, pulling him close to her side.

"It never seems to stand still, does it?" he said. "Once one crutch is introduced and you give in to that, it holds you up long enough for the next one to come along and carry you a step further. And that addictive wave keeps on advancing; it never stops. There's always that new enticing aspect of Desire out there—or is it in here?—ready and waiting to suck you into it. And we keep riding the leading edge of that wave. The more there is, the more you want. The more you want, the more you have to have. Wanting more always led to wanting more... Like I had to keep riding the leading edge of my own desire! What is it that keeps us moving out, *away from*, farther and farther?" Teil asked angrily. "And from what?"

"From the simple, the real..." she said.

"Away from ourselves?"

"From each other," she said, looking at him cautiously with her large dark eyes, "and the true source of our lives."

They walked silently down the sylvan path, not knowing what to say. "Teil..." Aspasia said in a lighter vein, "I haven't really changed that much, have I? I mean, I don't *really* look that different, do I?"

"You are *really* too much, is what you are," he said, turning to her and smiling broadly, "you know that?" They laughed together, and suddenly he wanted to take her in his arms and kiss her and make passionate love to her. But he held back; there was more at stake here now.

They slowed their pace as they drew closer together. They came to a large old shade tree in a clearing and sat down on the grass underneath, Teil staring off into the children that had appeared to play a little way beyond them. One of the children, a little girl, came over shyly and hugged Aspasia.

Teil leaned back against the tree trunk and sighed, "I dunno...seems as if ever since...well, talking to Milton and the others, I'm faced with a whole new way of looking at things. A whole different reality about myself."

Aspasia turned and looked at him and said, "Me too. I came face to face with me—who I really was; so I was forced to make a choice. Did I really want life, reality, or the fake me? I couldn't believe that the whole fabric of my life was synthetic, and that I was absolutely powerless to change it. I found that in order to live, I had to die to my way of life. It turns out when I asked the UGLIs, 'Help me want to live,' what I was really saying was, 'Help me want to die.' Surrender. Give up what I was doing wrong. Give up *me*. And that was the hardest of all. It was scary, for before I did it, I had no assurance of what was on the other side; I'd never been there."

"That's what Mors said," Teil said, " 'All you will have to do is take one step, enough to leave the earth behind.' "

"Yes! I want to let go of me—my self-destructive habits and attitudes—and leap across to that unseen source, but I'm afraid. There's nothing in between! But instinctively, I know I must leap to live. But everything I know screams out that to forsake the old me is to *die*. So everything fails me: all senses, all reason, all experience, all knowledge. Nothing supports me in that instant; I just have to do it. I'm blind, yet I must leap. I know nothing about it; yet I know everything. It's against all reason; yet I know it's the only reasonable thing to do."

Teil looked far away beyond the mountain rim as she tried to put her own experience into words.

"No one knows from the outside," she said, "except that we've all had to pass that same way. No one can pull another across or explain, or persuade, cajole, or make the way easy. It takes a kind of inner violence."

"Suicidal violence, isn't it?" Teil said, glimpsing it.

"Yes! And all we can do to help another is to have gone that way ourselves. It's so strange, Teil. Words don't count that much, even the right words. It's more a matter of identifying, reaching, feeling, touching, opening... That's

what made me want to cross over. There were those who..."
Her voice caught and tears welled in her eyes. "...Who reached
out and touched me... *Me*, Teil..." she said, her tears spilling
over. "And as soon as my feet left the earth—what a beautiful
way of putting it—and I thought I would die, I was there.
As though carried across." She beamed through her tears with
the memory of her own release.

They lay under the tree in the silence of their thoughts,
Teil carried away by the fleecy white clouds drifting above,
rimmed with orange from the setting sun, back to the time
on the hill by the eucalyptus grove where he had dreamed
he was Gilgamesh. It was the same feeling of wanting to stop,
to step outside the relentless stream of things, and stand still.

"You know, Aspi..." Teil said, his face clouding. "The
Sigma virus?"

"Yes...?"

"At first the urge would hit me out of nowhere. Like a
will-o'-the-wisp, then disappearing. Like a compulsion I knew
I'd have to obey one day. Just before they put me on
archaeprobe, it almost got the better of me." She leaned lightly
against him, trying to bridge the chasm of loneliness that
drew him worlds away. "Oh god..." he said, "at times I feel
so distant from life I could die..."

Oh, to stand still, he thought. A great weariness and yearning
came over him for that peace and promise. He stretched himself
out prone on the cool grass and rested his head on his hands
to rest.

But quietly, he wept.

*   *   *

When Teil awoke, he was looking up into Aspasia's face,
framed by sky and clouds, his head in her lap. He felt renewed,
as though he had crossed an invisible threshold into the new
country.

"Who are you?" he asked, sounding far away, "and where
do you come from?"

"My name is Aspasia, and I'm an UGLI, and I come from way, far away beyond the sea," she said in childlike simplicity, stroking his hair. He silently absorbed her good feelings.

"You don't look ugly," he said tenderly.

"Oh, but I am, very very UGLI."

"But if you're an UGLI, why aren't you ugly?"

"Well, you can't go by looks, because...well, look at you."

"Me?" Teil asked.

"You *look* just like an UGLI."

"I am—ugly." They laughed.

"All right," she said, "since you admit you're ugly, I'll let you in on a little secret."

"What's that?"

'You have to know you're ugly so you can become UGLI and beautiful."

"Is *that* why you're so beautiful?"

"Now you know," she said.

"Then since you're so smart, my beautiful little UGLI, would you please tell me what on earth I'm doing here?"

"You're here because I wanted you here," she replied.

"Is that so? Why would you want that?" he asked.

"Just because."

"That's kind of overwhelming, you know," he said, the emotion welling up in his throat.

"It is?"

"Yes."

"I'm glad."

The little girl who had hugged Aspasia plucked a tiny flower from the grass and came back and offered it to Teil. It was a dandelion. When he finally looked at what he was holding, Teil stared at it.

"This is a strange little flower, Aspi... In full bloom. See how its petals are arched back? No...wait," he said sitting up, "it's not in full bloom at all. Over there, the yellow ones; those must be the blooms. But then what are these? The same plant, but now spread out so fully in this sphere of white downy puffs." Teil plucked one of the puffs, and it dawned on him what they were.

"Look. These are the seeds! Each in its filament-like stem, with the feather-like float on top. Isn't it beautiful! The yellow bloom turns into this. It opens itself to the light, literally turning itself inside out, to expose this inner heart. Like a miniature galaxy of stars. So tiny, yet so immensely complicated. Eagerly opening itself up to the sun and wind so that..." Teil was hit by the discovery. "...So that it *dies*, exposing the seed hidden inside. A deliberate act of dying. And the flower knows it. It gives up its beauty, eagerly peeling back its protective sheath of petals. All the way back. Painfully back. Unnaturally so. Opening fully, without reservation...

"And now look how the wind catches them, picks them up, and carries them away. It gives itself up to something so strong, so terrible. That violently plucks out of its heart each seed, each kernel of its life. One by one. They're carried off beyond, floating away out of reach. Forever out of reach. Gone. Irretrievable. And it knows that. It knows it means death! As though that were its destiny...!

"It falls into the ground—buried. And that's where the miracle of life takes place."

Aspasia sensed the powerful changes coursing through him, but she could do nothing. In this he was utterly alone.

"What you've been saying, Aspasia... How can we do it? Give up the most powerful, compelling, distinctive, attractive part of ourselves...? And yet, that giving-up is part of its life!" Teil paused and sighed a deep sigh. "It knows that, doesn't it? It believes..."

For a long time they said nothing.

Then Teil plucked one of the yellow blooms, drew the little child close, and held the blossom next to her cheek. As his gaze fell first on one and then the other, Teil wondered about the universe the child perceived. What were the things that really mattered from the child's-eye view? What was reality like to the child, gazing up at him so wonderingly, so openly, so knowingly? Teil felt a pang of longing for that innocence and freedom. She already knew all there was to know, had all there was to have. In that moment he saw the little one, like the flower, joyfully giving up its life on the winds of life.

Then, the disturbing glint of his masring caught Teil's eye, forcing the dissonance. On the one hand was the frail beauty of a living being; on the other, the sterile symmetry of System, symbol of negation and imitation of life. Unable to cope with the contradiction it represented within himself, Teil tore them apart, jumping to his feet.

31

Mors had appeared at the edge of the clearing and was standing quietly, not wanting to intrude.

Affedersiniz, ama yemek hazir, ve sizi bekleyorlar," Mors said.

"Affedersin, kardesh," Teil replied, *"vakiti unutdum."* Then to Aspasia he said, "We have to go, sweetheart; they're waiting for us to eat."

"Oh, you're right..." she said. "I lost all track of time. Mors, I'm so sorry..."

"Hic bir sey," Mors replied.

They followed Mors until they came to the main building. It was an old, simple, barn-like structure made of wood and stone, like most of the other buildings, rebuilt from whatever destruction had gone on before. As Mors opened the door, Teil stopped, repulsed as by a wave of energy emanating from within. He had to pause against it, as if to catch his breath, to force himself to push through it, as though it were pushing him away. Or was it that he was resisting it? Aspasia felt it too, but eagerly stepped into it. Mors went ahead, sensing Teil's hesitation, and took a seat. They were looking at a group of some forty people seated in groups around tables set in no special fashion about the floor.

The people were not doing anything; although food was before them, no one had begun to eat. Teil sensed they had been caught in a pause, a silence, for there was no sound;

yet the air was not empty. It was full of energy bouncing about the room, sparkling discharges of power, yet unseen. Awesome, yet beckoning. A feeling of light. Intense light, with a purity about it and surging joy, as though the room was charged with the energy of a powerful presence.

As those inside turned toward the entering couple, the intensity seemed to subside, until Teil felt as though he was entering a radiant aura of belonging that was pulling him in. A tall erect elderly man with a large unruly shock of white hair, large acquiline nose, and benevolent face rose to greet them.

"Come in, Dr. Teil-mann," he said simply, "we've been expecting you. My name is Requiem. Come, both of you, sit down," he said, offering Teil his hand.

"You're the one with the phono box," Teil said, shaking his hand.

When Aspasia had entered, various men and women got up and greeted her warmly and enthusiastically, some embracing and others kissing her. She in turn introduced them, almost shyly, to Teil. Teil had never seen her like this; this was not the queen of the ball, she seemed simply to be a part of that body.

As they began eating, Teil met the others at their table. Dies and Mors were there; Ingemisco was at another table across the room. The rich aroma of the food tantalized him as he stared at the various dishes.

"This looks like a king's feast," he said, "and smells so inviting I can hardly wait. Had no idea I was so famished. But then we haven't eaten since Diyarbekir, and yesterday at that, eh Mors?" Teil said, turning to his friend.

"Yes, kardesh," Mors said. "It be good we sit here and eat together."

"Good isn't the word for it, my friend, considering."

The meal was an unforgettable experience. Teil did not have to worry about his system rejecting the non-System diet; the journey had prepared him for it. Each dish seemed to open his appetite further, till he could hardly keep from compulsively devouring the food.

It was only after Teil's hunger had been satisfied that the mood of the room re-registered. It seemed that the quality and flavor of the food reflected the personality of the body of people. Most were dressed in the colorful and practical homespun of the area. Roughly half men and half women, mostly from System, there was a healthy and flavorful variety, yet an underlying unity, which rather than diminishing individuality, seemed to accentuate it, like seasoning. It gave Teil a feeling of well-being.

Teil turned and said to Requiem, "Dies and Aspasia told me about your involvement with my crash landing. I want to thank you for sending out the men. Couldn't have made it otherwise. And I can't tell you how sorry I am about your dead and injured."

"I'm glad you are grateful," Requiem said. "That event was as unusual and significant for us as it was for you, Teilhard, as I'm sure the others here will attest." There was a strong current of assent that flowed through the group.

Quando had said little during the meal, preferring to observe Teil from a distance. He was a thin man with an outsize head of hair and beard and expansive forehead that made him look cerebral. His alert eyes, when they connected, could penetrate deeply, but at the same time gave the feeling of kindness. Aspasia told Teil he had been a cybertech at Moscow Regional. After the meal he finally addressed Teil. His manner was brusque, yet courteous.

"Professor," Quando said, "Ingemisco tells us you brought some equipment with you inside the wagon."

Teil looked over at Ingemisco and could feel his underlying hostility. "Yes. It's scientific equipment I developed and am using on this expedition."

"Perhaps then," he continued, raising a bushy eyebrow, "you would like to tell us what you plan to do with it."

Ingemisco appeared at their table, intervening agitatedly before Teil could reply, "The question is not so much the equipment, but why is *he* here?" The atmosphere became charged. "I can't understand," Ingemisco went on, barely able to control his voice, "how you can let him in here, even if she is one of us. Who is he? Why is he here? For all we know, he could be a..."

"Hold it, Gemi, hold it!" Dies interrupted. "We went over all that on the way here."

"But he's here because he's been sent on a mission by System! On his own admission! Why isn't anyone alarmed?"

"You're alarmed," Dies said. "Take it easy."

"But he may be unaware that he's being used. Have you forgotten the sophisticated means and devices they can employ? SOGs could be watching us and hearing every word we're saying right now!"

"Is that true?" Requiem asked.

"Of course it's possible," Teil replied. "But I know nothing about it; and if it is true, they certainly wouldn't need me to do it."

"What of your masring there and your wristcom?" Quando asked.

"It seems to me," Teil said, "that southeastern Anatol is either some sort of System 'blind spot,' or System is simply not interested in that part of the world."

"Which I find impossible to believe," Ingemisco said hotly. "Why are you here, if System is not interested in this part of the world?"

"What I'm doing here is part of my own research—at least it started out that way, but—"

"See!" Ingemisco exclaimed, looking around for support.

"But what, Professor?" Quando asked.

"Somehow I don't feel free to speak in Ingemisco's presence. I felt that on the journey, too."

"But he's one of us," Quando said. "We have no privy councils here." By this time, people were leaving their tables to gather around and listen. Teil was wondering just how much he dared tell them.

"First," Teil said, "let me assure you positively that as far as I know, and I'm quite certain of this, the SOGs are not interested in what I'm after. I will say this, though: there's a definite interest in a very small part of this world somewhere around here. At least I think it's around here. And that's what

I'm looking for. But it has nothing to do with you. It goes way back into prehistory, thousands of years ago. You see, I'm an archaeologist. What I'm after deals with the origin of civilization in this area, anywhere from six to ten thousand years ago. We made a dig at Diyarbekir. That's where I first used my equipment. Only I had to leave much of it behind stuck in the ground around the citadel ruins. Mors can tell you, if you want to hear an unbelievable story."

"They were telling us of your adventures, Professor," Quando said; "we did not say we did not believe you."

"Well, by using this equipment, we explored the sequence of civilization as it developed upward in that one site over the last several thousand years, ever since men had first settled there."

"But *why?*" Ingemisco insisted.

"I've already told Dies," Teil hedged. "You were listening. I'm trying to trace the origin of a certain dawn-of-history tribe of people who lived in this area."

"You mean," Quando asked, "that you are only interested in what happened here to *one tribe* thousands of years ago? I must say, I can see Ingemisco's point."

"Of course," Teil added, "my own interests are broader than that, but insofar as X..." He quickly corrected the slip. "I mean, insofar as System is concerned, there's no special interest in you people here."

"I don't believe that," Ingemisco blurted out. "It's not like System—totally out of character. And what does X have to do with it? There's a catch somewhere."

"I'm beginning to feel," Teil conceded, "there may well be aspects of this whole affair—aspects of System, if you will—that none of us knows anything about. What's happening out there is unbelievable; the world is going to pieces. I'm sure the men have passed on what I've told them already." Teil reported all he knew about the Sigma virus, the glitches, and waves of erupting disturbance and violence.

"I get the feeling," Requiem said, "that you have your own personal problems, not only regarding System, but perhaps within you as well."

Teil replied candidly. "I seem to be going through a rapid reevaluation of everything, myself especially. Things are moving so fast, my head is still spinning. I'm sure Aspasia here can witness to that..." She looked at Requiem and nodded vigorously.

Quando leaned toward Teil intently with both eyebrows raised, causing his forehead to wrinkle and said, "What's happening out there, and this 'special interest' they have for this area—can you not see how this might affect us? Why we are so passionately interested, as our young friend here? And you must remember, we are, strictly speaking, illegal everywhere!"

"Yes, I know," Teil said.

"We're getting off the track again," Ingemisco said. "The issue goes beyond all this; and the equipment and what he may do with it is incidental. Can't you see it?" There was a shrill urgency in his voice. "Bringing System here, regardless of what form it takes, means the end of this way of life. Once we let System in, this becomes part of System!" Ingemisco stared wildly through them out of his own obsession; then, abruptly got up and left.

Turning to Teil, Requiem said, "The boy suffers from a common UGLI error, confusing the System of World City with the personal "system" we humans invariably seem to build into our own lives."

"It takes considerable growth," Quando added, "and self-awareness to see the difference."

"Fascinating concept..." Teil muttered to himself.

Just as abruptly, Ingemisco returned, carrying what looked like a mutilated book, the old paper kind with pages.

"What is that?" one of the men at the table asked.

"It's what they used to call a book," Ingemisco said. "This was how they packaged writing a couple of centuries ago."

"Where did you get that?" asked Requiem, disturbed.

"I found it in the ruins where we stayed at Van. It was lodged under a building stone that had crushed what looked like a small traveling case."

"You know our caution about things like that," Requiem

said.

Teil asked, "Why would you be cautious about books?"

After an uncomfortable pause, Requiem said, "That's a hard question for us. Suffice it to say we're cautious about everything representing System."

"But this was written long before System," Ingemisco protested.

"What *is* System, Ingemisco?" Requiem demanded sternly. "Can you tell us that?" The question's profundity started Teil's mind racing ahead as he thought back on ideas he had glimpsed since his last talk with Kri-kor.

"That's a silly question, isn't it?" Ingemisco remarked. "Everyone knows what System is."

"Either everyone or no one," Requiem said.

"But of course everyone knows. It's everything out there: Mascom and all its myriad other 'coms.' The all-controlling all-knowing all-doing Computer-driven SYSTEM. That nauseating Sameness. The whole bloody works! Blood-less, I should say."

"If that were all to System, we would indeed be fortunate," Requiem said.

"What do you mean?" Ingemisco asked, rebuffed.

"Where or when would you say that System began?"

"I don't follow you."

"Was there one day a world without System; then the next day it was here?"

"It developed, of course."

"From what? Can you trace it back?"

"Well... It began with Mascom, didn't it? And X? That would put it back to..."

"But what of the world before X?"

"What do you mean?"

"Was there no System then?"

"I would suppose not, but then I wouldn't know."

"How much *do* you know of history before Mascom?"

"What everyone knows, that before X, the world was a hopeless hodgepodge of different nations, peoples, ideologies, customs, political systems. And everybody was going off in all directions wasting each other's territory and each other..."

"There was no System within these smaller units?"

"What's your point?"

"The point, our dear young friend," Requiem stated patiently, "is how utterly effective System has become when it succeeds in blinding men to what it really is."

"What he's trying to say, Ingemisco," Quando said, "is simply that what we see so fully developed in our own time had its beginnings in other forms, as the Professor here has no doubt discovered from his studies of man's origins."

"Good question," Teil said, eagerly exploring the idea. "What *is* System, really? It's more than government and computers and media ordering our world... And when did we let it in? I'm afraid it goes way back. Something happened about the time man first began building cities that intrigues me. Mors and I saw it in the Amida dig. An irreversible force was let loose, but precisely what, when, where, or how, I don't know. But I'm getting the feeling my work here bears on that, for this is the very area where Western civilization first took its spontaneous rise. It's a fascinating quest."

"Is that why you are here?" Quando asked.

"Yes," Teil replied.

"To answer your original question about the book, Dr. Teil-mann," Requiem said, intervening, "is most difficult. We don't have any answers either. However, the whole matter is academic; Ingemisco here, so inordinately zealous to keep you and System out, may have already let it in by what he is no doubt so desirous to read to us."

Ingemisco eagerly responded, "Before I had read this book, I never could have understood your dilemma; now I think I can appreciate what it is you're wrestling with. Will you let me read a few passages?" The other men were silent.

Finally Teil spoke up. "I for one would like to hear." Ingemisco eagerly bent forward. "You'll be amazed at what this man saw over two hundred years ago. Why didn't they listen to him then? Everything he said has come to pass!"

They waited for Requiem, who asked, "What do the rest of you think?"

"Why not see what he's up to?" one of the men suggested, and the others nodded their assent. Ingemisco seized the opportunity.

"The first pages are missing, but from this fragment it appears to have been written by someone called Ellul. See?"

Teil took the book. "Such a rare find," he said. "Only place you see one of these is in a museum."

Ingemisco snatched the book back, fondling it gingerly. "First of all, there's the way he uses a certain key word, 'technique.' It's tricky but crucial. He distinguishes between the various techniques of civilization—the skills, the machines, the technology—and Technique itself, with a capital T, which is the idea or force behind it all."

"I for one am all ears," Teil said, his curiosity prevailing over his dislike of Ingemisco. "How does he define Technique?"

Ingemisco thought for a moment, then thumbed through the pages. "Here... It's so hard to read this Old English." He read the words slowly and deliberately, transposing the old linear text into the computer English in his head.

> Technique reigns alone, a blind force, and
> more clear-sighted than the best human
> intelligence.

The words struck home with the force of a startling revelation.

"Would you mind reading that again?" Teil asked. The others nodded their agreement. Ingemisco repeated the words, more thoughtfully, as he saw their unexpected reaction. When he had finished, Teil remarked, "That is System—pure and simple."

"Mascom," Ingemisco added.

"Precisely," Quando said.

"Yes," Requiem said. "It reigns as supreme monarch over our world."

"Yet it is blind," Teil said.

"But more clear-sighted than the best human intelligence," Quando said.

"How could he have seen it then, so long ago?" Teil asked. "And he put it better than any of us could now."

"For him to have seen it at all," Requiem observed, "it must have been true in his own day."

Ingemisco was encouraged to continue reading other passages that had caught his attention.

> Technique has so controlled all natural forces,
> that it has given man the sense of being master
> of his fate.
>
> .   .   .
>
> In the joy of conquest, he has not perceived
> that what he has created takes from him the
> very possibility of being himself.

"Is that true?" Teil exclaimed under his breath, as Ingemisco continued.

> The new man, tailored to fit the artificial
> paradise, has become the *product* of the means
> he ordained for himself.
>
> .   .   .
>
> The machine not only creates a new human
> environment, it becomes that environment,
> and modifies man's very essence to adapt to
> it. And man must adapt himself to a universe
> for which he was not created.

A feeling of recognition flashed among everyone who heard it. Others, who were still lingering after the meal, caught the intense mood in that corner of the room and gathered to listen to the unusual utterances from such an unusual medium.

> When man himself becomes part of the
> machine, he attains to that marvelous freedom
> of unconsciousness—the freedom of the
> machine itself.
>
> .   .   .
>
> The human being is delivered helpless, in
> respect to life's most important and most
> trivial affairs, to a power which is in no sense
> under his control.

Various spontaneous interjections began coming from the group, and exclamations of antipathy.

He looks for nothing beyond the marvelous
escape into technique to offset the very
repressions caused by the life technique forces
him to lead...

His acquiescence has rendered him blind to
his bondage and powerless to heal himself.

"Yes it's true!" Teil exclaimed under his breath, identifying
with the line and stealing a glance at Aspasia to see her reaction.
Their eyes met across the table and held each other's. As Teil
kept looking at her, he saw a person and a depth he had
never seen before. And he knew she could see what he was
revealing. You see, now, don't you? her eyes were saying. The
bondage. And you know the desperation, the powerlessness
at depth. Yes! his eyes were telling her. You know it too,
don't you? You've been where I am... You *know!* It was a
union, a fusion. Communion. A harmony of the spirit. A
resonance of being one.

Ingemisco read on.

When technique has at last succeeded in
creating unity, all diversity will have
disappeared, and the human race will have
become a bloc of irrational sameness.

An audible murmur rose from the group.

The sharp knife of system has passed like a
razor into the living flesh. It has cut the
umbilical cord which linked men with
each other and with nature.

Anger flared.

Man, in a milieu that is frighteningly concrete,
has become by abstraction a pure
appearance—a kaleidoscope of external shapes.

Like a snail deprived of its shell, man is only
a blob of plastic matter modeled after images
projected by the system.

Ingemisco, sustained by the reaction, continued reading in poetic fervor.

> The individual, shut up in an echoing electronic universe in which he is alone, finds his only refuge in the arms of technique, which envelope him in solitude and at the same time reassure him with all their hoaxes... One cannot but marvel at a system which provides the antidote as it distills the poison.

The undercurrent of fury began to vent itself.

> Nothing can compete with technical means; only a technical force can oppose the force of technique. And that would bring in new and stronger technique. No one is able to master it and no one wants to.
>   . . .
> Above all, no finger must be laid to it. Man has renounced control over it, and cannot bring himself to raise his hand against it.

There were cries of renunciation.

> The tool has enabled man to conquer. But man, dost thou not know there is no more victory which is thy victory?
> The tool alone has the power and carries off the victory.

The mood of the listeners was now frightening in its power and emotional intensity. The words had given voice to their deeply buried feelings and had put their own personal plight into perspective. These prophetic utterances had been fulfilled in them. Teil found himself caught up in the common fury.

He got to his feet and paced back and forth, agitated. Finally he gave vent to it as he began piecing the ideas together, not realizing everyone in the room was hanging on his every word.

"Look at the history of the thing. Man comes on the scene, and first, he *uses* tools: sticks, skins, shells, rocks, fire. Then, he *makes* tools. He points a stick, hardens the tip in fire, starts chipping and shaping rocks. Finally, we see him as Neanderthal and Cro-Magnon man with splendid inventories of stone tools and mastery of all the basic techniques: fire, hunting, fishing, food gathering, defense against animals and weather, tool-making. And he has a culture: burial, magic, various rites and customs, art, religion, war.

"Then he starts building: settlements, villages, cities. And the pattern is set. The direction is set. But then...we have the Enoch tradition. How does it fit in? Why is Enoch the first city mentioned in the Genesis text? What special significance did the author feel it had?" Teil instinctively reached inside his shirt and pulled out the now-bedraggled plasticene bag containing the texts he had carried with him ever since leaving home. He scanned the Genesis text as he spoke.

"We have the Adam people and Eden... Apparently they are somewhere at the leading edge of this development toward civilization. They are called out, perhaps from the religion of the Mother Goddess, to a place apart. Eden. A life apart. And to a new Life. Revelation. The first. The beginning. An awakening to a new kind of life within man and his connection with Yahweh-elohim. That mysterious name itself seems to signify 'Life.' And to a new kind of city—the kingdom of heaven—the realm of God-in-his-people.

"But man falls. He dies to that Life. But grace calls him back. And now he is thrust out—out of Eden. Back into the mainstream again. But with a difference. He carries the Life with him. But there's another difference now too. Cain! Who chooses another way—his own. And he is driven away. Away from the Presence. Away from the Light. And *Cain* now builds a city—Enoch.

"When Cain builds, he builds with an added component, a new motivation; he builds from the spirit of Cain—rebellion and loss. And System is born. Not mere organization, but a spiritual self-sufficiency, *over-against the light of the Eden experience*, a City of God without God—the City of Man. A System with every substitute to take the place of the real. Hence, the Cain people originate this unprecedented spurt into technology and entertainment to fill their loss of being driven 'from the presence of the Lord.' Thus the city of Cain forces all the legitimate endeavors of man to serve more than their basic functions to compensate for that great loss, that historic loss. And ultimately, not only man's secular but even his religious institutions will become System-atized—Cain-ized—to compensate for the loss of the Reality they will so fervently avow.

And City—civilization—can never be the same again.

Teil turned abruptly and stared at Mors as the thought struck him. "*That's* where city walls have gone, Mors...! Man himself has become her walls. Man protecting City. Man laying down his life to protect that which takes from him his life!!"

There was a vehement murmur of recognition.

Teil continued. "But the Cain people flourish: food production, technology, entertainment. What a strong force Cain and the Cain impulse must have been. An exciting power, a wave of force, an organizing vitality, a lust for ejaculating its ego-spoor, impelling its culture all the way to Sumer— the origin of Western civilization. And like a shot of something in the racial bloodstream, it gets in there, and nothing can ever be the same again.

"So, from Adam and Cain onward, we have this dual tradition; the kingdom of heaven and the kingdom of System. And the spirit of System becomes *Technique as substitute for the real.* And ever after, we have the maddening exponential race into Technique, taking man farther and farther away from Life, from himself. And Technique inexorably spawns its twin bastard offspring: System and Propaganda. Until finally, now, we find ourselves here. In the bosom of the Great System itself; Mascom, Tool of Tools and Lord of Lords. And suddenly, civilization is no more—!"

"Because *man* is no more!" Ingemisco cried.

"Is that where the twist began?" Teil exclaimed. "Has nothing changed? Are we trapped in a history-encircling rat race? Man, going in great circles, from the beginning? Chasing an illusion? Chasing his own lust? And all of it, imitation? Imitation of Life...?"

32

In the intensity of the moment few noticed Ingemisco rush out of the room; attention was riveted on Teil. Every eye followed his moves. Unaware of the unusual interest his review of the text provoked, Teil pursued his own train of thought silently for a moment. A hushed expectancy was in the air.

Requiem voiced the great surprise and eager interest of them all. "What is that you've been referring to, Teilhard? The Secure markings I recognize but it doesn't seem..."

Teil cut him off, still engrossed in thought. "It's the Genesis text." There was a long expectant pause as they waited for him to explain, but his mind was elsewhere.

Requiem persisted, asking, "What is the Genesis text?"

"Very ancient Hebrew literature... Nothing like it. Apparently tracing their origins for some reason. 'In the beginning, God...' That's how it opens."

"Yes...?"

Teil looked up and saw their rapt attention; their mood urging him to continue. "I'm sorry; I forgot you've never known this. Let me read some to you." Teil forced himself to slow down so they could keep up with him.

> In the beginning, God created the heavens
> and the earth...

The word, as though long-awaited, filled the stillness with its presence; there was a long pause as Teil felt it register on him too.

And the earth was waste and void and darkness
was upon the face of the deep. And the Spirit
of God moved upon the face of the waters. And
God said, "Let there be light." And there was light.

Teil looked up again, wondering what it was that was
registering so, but no one said a word. The already silent
room seemed to become even more so. He continued reading;
the force of their involvement would not let him stop. The
reaction to Ingemisco's book had none of this. He translated
the story of the six days, then of Adam, and the intriguing
details connected with his commitment to the enclosure.

And out of the ground the Lord God caused
to grow every tree that is pleasant to the
sight and good for food. The tree of life
also in the midst of the enclosure and the
tree of knowing good and evil.

"Wait a minute...!" Teil exclaimed, shattering the mood,
his eyes flashing to the words ahead.

In the day that thou eatest thereof,
thou shalt surely die...

"The forbidden tree is expressed as a contrast with the tree
of life. It's in the enclosure too, but you don't *eat* of it, you
don't take it as *sustenance for your life*. There's the choice.
The Choice. Either/Or. The eternal option of the human race...

"System is really personal—spiritual! System is everything
in my life I've assembled and use to hold me together, all
the mechanisms I use to sustain and defend myself. And shut
Life out! And the System we've built about us in our world
is merely an extension of the one within ourselves!

"Mors! In the enclosure! That's where we'll start probing.
The two Trees!" Then the dread thought struck him out of
nowhere as he scanned the room. "Ingemisco! The probes!
Mors, where are they?"

"The wagon is in the barn, kardesh, and Ingemisco..., *hic
bilmem.*"

"He's gone!" Dies exclaimed.

"Quick, the barn!" shouted Teil, already halfway to the

door. Others followed as Mors leaped ahead. "Quickly Mors! Before it's too late!"

They hurried to the building down at the end of the way. Mors got there first, and finding the large doors shut, flung them wide. What Teil saw inside made him sick. There was archaeprobe strewn all over the ground, its gleaming modernity in stark contrast with the ancient barn, with Ingemisco tearing at it in wild-eyed frenzy. The probe container was open, and several probes lay on the ground broken or bent violently in two. He held one in his hands high over his head and was about to break it when caught in the act. After a moment's surprise at seeing Teil, Ingemisco furiously broke it over his knee, just as Mors tackled him and threw him to the ground. Others who had followed rushed in to help.

Teil's face was awful. His hands shook with rage. "The probes! You've ruined the probes!!" Requiem came up and confronted the now-frightened Ingemisco, still struggling piteously inside Mors's unrelenting grip.

"What does this mean?" Requiem sternly demanded. But the younger man could only glare back. Requiem took charge, issuing quick, crisp orders. "Take him back to the dining hall. And you, Judicanti, get someone to help you stand guard here. Teilhard, as soon as you can, please join us. We'll attend to this matter ourselves."

Teil dazedly picked up a broken probe and looked at the wreckage. Aspasia came up with the others who had followed the commotion. Teil was devastated.

"Well, Aspi...that's archaeprobe. What's left of it..."

"Oh, Teil!" she exclaimed, seeing the havoc wrought on the culmination of Teil's fine work. "What are you going to do." Teil sat down mechanically, numb from shock.

"I don't know... Try to salvage as much as I can... See if I can get it to work... But time!"

"I know how this must hurt you, and coming from one of us..." she said.

"It's not that," said Teil. "It's so crucial to the mission; the whole thing is jeopardized now. And just when I was so close. 'Time is of the essence,' he said. X! And he meant it." Teil gave himself up to despair. "What am I doing here, anyway? A spade man turned secret agent on a mission of global urgency? That's a laugh; he doesn't even know what the hell his mission is or why he's on it or where he's going. And all he manages to produce are death and destruction..."

"Teil," she asked, "what *is* this thing with X? This mission you're on."

He looked at her a moment and then said, "You're right... Let's sort out this gear, and I'll give you the whole rundown. X sounded like it was all a long shot anyway, so what if I don't make it? Nothing I can do will keep the world from falling apart."

As they assessed the damage, Teil brought Aspasia up to date on all that had happened, including Epi-Thumia's activities. Disregarding X's warnings, he told her all. Then they left Judicanti and another to guard the place, one inside and the other out. As they walked back to the hall, Teil finished outlining what he had to do.

"But why Eden?" she asked.

"I don't know. It doesn't make sense. All we can do is find the site and try to reestablish contact with X."

"Are you going to probe here?"

"Definitely. More than ever, if they'll let me. And I think they will."

"Why the dreadful urgency?"

"I don't know that either, unless it's connected with what's happening out there. I don't know whether it's just a series of accidents—the laws of probability catching up with System—or what. But the people...! System is too perfect. The back-up, the redundancy, the self-monitoring, look-ahead, self-repairing perfection of the thing, proved through all the years of refinement... It's not possible, suddenly to have things start going wrong."

As they reentered the hall, they saw Ingemisco seated inside a circle of some dozen men. The others were seated around this central group, and Teil and Aspasia joined these, off to one side. Mors stood near the door.

The gathering had no plan, and apparently no rules. And no one began. Rather, a tacit constraint seemed to lead the group into silence, which became extremely uncomfortable for Teil. Then, there seemed to emanate gradually a shared pain throughout the body of men as they experienced the situation and the plight of one of their own who was errant and whom they now had to judge.

Teil was forced to join the silence. It was as though they were quieting down on the inside, reaching some sort of plateau, some common ground of the spirit. The incompatibility between his rational analysis of what was going on and his inability to experience what was going on bothered him. He was still the outsider.

It was in the silence that Teil sensed the bond that held these men, without knowing what it was or how it operated. He had felt something like it once or twice before, with Mors and with Milton and the others, but this was intensified by as many as were present.

Ingemisco suffered visibly in the silence, the pain coming back on the one who had caused it. The torture, though not deliberate, was very real. As his fingers fidgeted nervously, his eyes betrayed fear.

Aspasia turned and whispered in Teil's ear, "This is very serious."

"Serious for *me!*" Teil replied.

"When one goes off, we all suffer. It seems none of us can hide anything without affecting the others."

Teil's analytical powers forced him away from the reality again. That's the difference between this and System, he thought. On the one hand, the solidarity of computer-driven society; on the other, oneness of a community of persons. The one has its simulated unity imposed from the nature of System; the other has its unity and strength arise from some common unseen source in their own midst. The insight didn't help him a bit.

The intensity of feeling continued to mount for several minutes and filled the silence with intolerable anguish. Finally, Ingemisco could take it no longer and blurted out,

"Yes I did it! I don't know what got into me... Suddenly, while he was talking, I seemed to get a flash of what had to be done. Violent change! Destroy System!" But his words fell back on themselves. That was merely the surface layer; the others were feeling what lay deeper.

Silence again.

Then one of the men spoke up: "There's something confusing here. I get the feeling more's involved."

Another man followed: "There's something else under what you're saying, Ingemisco."

Another put a question to Dies. "How did he act on your trip? Did you notice anything out of the way?"

"No," Dies replied. "Nothing, except what happened at Siirt. He told us at Silvan that someone needed help at Siirt, so Mors and Teil there went on, while we went to Siirt. But no one was there. It didn't work out like it always had before."

What Requiem then said made no sense at all to Teil: "It is important now that each of us examines his own heart for any uncorrected wrong or attitude he may have in himself or against another."

What an utterly strange and irrelevant thing to say, thought Teil. What could the personal life of any of those present possibly have to do with the issue of Ingemisco's destroying Teil's equipment? It was Ingemisco who was being examined. But Teil sensed it fit perfectly here.

Teil grew uneasy as he sat in the painfully lengthening silence. It was either fight it or acquiesce to this mandate on the self, this new demand being made on *him*. The force of the demand came not so much from Requiem's request, but from the response of the body of those present. Again, he let reason intervene. He saw that this whole thing was acting just like an energy field. If he opposed it, a negative field was generated, as if he were fighting himself; if he acquiesced, he could feel it change to positive as he merged with the prevailing attitude. This, he thought, can surely never be analyzed by Mascom.

Teil was thus caught between wanting to be a part of it and wanting to withdraw and view it from within the safe confines of his own rational processes. As he saw this, it laid the cold hand of death on him. Why be an alien—always? he thought. The unspoken demand on his will was increasing.

But his thoughts would not stop. Diabolically, they kept racing on as if in one last mad dash to prevent him from surrender. He was in a terrible struggle; as if some dark power within him was tempting him with knowledge of the truth to keep him from knowing the true.

Then it dawned on him: The Tempter...and the Tree! The 'knowing-good-and-evil' tree... Is that what it is? To know the good and evil about life, arrive at a system of knowledge? Standing outside life, like me judging Ingemisco here? Substituting the idea of the real for the real; my idea of life for Life? That's like the uninvolved analysis of the machine—Mascom!

Is that the essence of technique? Teil thought. Shutting life out and building one's own 'city,' a perfectly structured system of one's inner life that shuts out the real? That would make it anti-real. The Great Forbidden...

> Thou shalt not eat of it, for in the day that
> thou eatest thereof thou shalt surely die.

You mean, if I keep this up, Teil thought, indulging myself in this exhilarating expansion of knowledge, even now, I lose the life that is here in this experience?

But even if I do *not* indulge in this forbidden fruit, that in itself does not connect me with the Life. I must *partake* of the tree of life. But how do you do that...? The thoughts pulled him into a swirling vortex of inner conflict, the stream of ideas coursing relentlessly through him. Teil had about one centimeter left before his mind was blown completely.

Then what causes me to go astray? Wait... It's not the processes of the brain that go astray, but my attitudes as directed by my will. But that implies the will of man transcends his mind. But how can that be? This dizzying spiral inward... What is this compulsion to know? It's running away with me even now. Like lust... The same force... Frantically driving me away from the reality of *myself*. And I'm powerless to stop it. It's insanity...!

Or am I seeing truth for the first time? But then truth about truth isn't the real, and hence is not true! So then what is truth?

Teil felt like he was flying in dizzying circles, spiraling inward, ever faster, until he thought he would fly into the rear end of his own brain and explode.

33

Then Teil did a strong thing. He gave up, stopped thinking, stopped fighting, let go, and opened himself to the light. And entered the stream of the living. The confusion ended. He heaved a deep sigh of relief.

The atmosphere in the room now created another silence more penetrating than the first, since Requiem's suggestion touched every man where he lived, as it was touching Teil. The mood and movement of the meeting were growing from a succession of silences.

But Ingemisco had not given in. "I still do not trust the man!" he blurted out, referring to Teil.

Silence.

Then one of the men asked softly, "Could it be you do not *want* to trust him?" Ingemisco reacted as though struck.

"What *is* it, Ingemisco?" another asked.

"Yes..." said another, "I feel I have to ask if he's all he's made himself out to be."

"Ingemisco?" yet another asked, "are you in any way tied in with the Others?"

Ingemisco's jaw slackened. He stared at each of the men in turn, trying to discern an ally. He was alone. In the ensuing silence, there seemed to form a consensus. Everyone including Ingemisco knew it. His eyes stopped darting about, and he fell quiet, as though the wave had finally overcome him too.

Then it registered on Teil that this silence was not passive or introspective at all, but rather active and outgoing. It was as though they were resonating on a single note. Like the energy he had felt when first entering the room for the first time earlier.

"Yes," Ingemisco said, sighing a huge sigh of relief, "I have been connected with the Others." The disclosure was after the fact and came as no surprise. He continued on his own, relaxed, relieved, and apparently eager to tell all.

"The Others are the ones who tried to kill Mors; I'm sure of it. They've been after you since Ararat; I told them why we were going there. Epi-Thumia is one of them." He went on to describe how he had joined the Others when he had been caught stealing their food in his flight from megapol Ankara. He could never convince them he was not stealing one of their horses. An underground journalist facing reconditioning, he had fled mega-Rome when System life had finally become intolerable for him. The Others had persuaded him to join the UGLIs at Endee as an informer in exchange for leniency, and he had provided information from time to time. But as he had associated with UGLIs, he was drawn to what they had.

"You know," he continued, "how fiercely they hate your way of life. They even resent your being *here*. I'm sure by now they've convinced everyone that Teil here was trying to destroy the citadel and stop them."

It was a different Ingemisco speaking now. He could lift his head and look into their faces. And he was free.

"I'm sorry I destroyed the equipment. I'll go back to Diyarbekir and try to recover the probes they had to leave behind in the ground. And I can only hope that if I succeed, you will find it in your hearts to..." He stopped and hung his head. "I was going to say forgive me...but there's more, and I can't bring myself to say it."

A wave of silent support flowed out and encompassed the young man, and he found the strength to go on. "Now I see why I was acting so foolishly and irrationally. My heart was not right toward him." He nodded toward Teil. "It was his woman... All along, I wanted her, when I knew she was another's. I was hoping he would never come, and once here, that you would send him away."

He looked at Teil, then at Aspasia. His pain was visible. Then he turned to the others. "You wanted to draw out the best that was in me, and I wouldn't have it. In refusing you, I refused the best that was in myself. Please forgive me, all of you, for I have hurt you all. I renounce the Others. I only want to be a part of you."

Then he turned to Teil. "And please forgive me for wanting you dead." He smiled, as though suddenly what had been heavy, dark, and guilt-ridden, was now light and even humorous. The burden lifted.

Now the focus of power seemed to shift onto Teil, who automatically brought his analytical powers against it. Again. It was almost comical.

A propagation of energy, with directivity, he thought. These are definitely parameters belonging to some form of energy. He was desperately trying to ward off the field that was impinging on him. He felt the same urge to fidget and squirm that Ingemisco had. He fervently wished he could disappear, for he knew he had to respond to Ingemisco's plea in kind.

The more Teil resisted, the more he felt the energy intensify, as though the negative field he was generating released more of the positive energy from those around him to overcome it. Waves of help pulled him deeper and deeper into the field of compassion. Teil did not know what to do. Or rather, he thought, he knew what he should do, but could not. And the longer he waited, the more intense things got. He had traded places with Ingemisco. Finally, he just started talking; there was no other way to relieve the pressure.

It burst out of him explosively. "This is incredible! I just don't know what to say, or even why I should be saying any anything... But I feel I must." He turned to Ingemisco and said, "That was a terrible thing you did there in the barn! You simply don't know how serious it was, and may never know. But oddly, that doesn't seem to be what matters. This thing that was going on inside you... This whole thing is a revelation to me. I must admit, part of me has been blind. This whole dimension... This is something completely lost out there. If I had encountered this from where I was out there, I would have remained untouched and called it insanity.

"I would not have seen...would not have been willing to see. But somehow, the past weeks have brought me closer to this, whatever it is. And now, facing Ingemisco here, and you others, and talking like this... It seems it is really *I* who must confess. I want to understand. I want to forgive. Forgive *me* if I do not know what it means or how."

Suddenly Teil felt the release—the same charge of energy that had bounced around the room as they had entered the first time. Only now, he was part of it. It was hurting gloriously, making him want to cry aloud in ecstasy. And it was pure. Inside he felt like jumping to his feet, throwing his hands in the air, and singing. All he could manage on the outside was to go over to Ingemisco and shake his hand. But that very act drew forth the next, and Teil found himself pulling Ingemisco to his feet and hugging him.

Then everyone in the place was lifted to their feet by the energy of joy. Aspasia went to Teil, threw her arms about him, and hugged him fiercely. And Teil responded by lifting her off her feet. Then she embraced Ingemisco. And it felt right. And the two of them looked at each other and laughed. Then the three of them hugged each other.

Teil had never in his whole life ever felt so glorious. Nothing could approach the quality of the intense surge of life passing through him now. Then Ingemisco—the ever-serious young man with a cause—did something that surprised everybody. He let out a great yell.

"Whhooooooooeeeee!!!! That's what I like about you people; you always come through. You care, even when you don't have to, even when it seems you can't!"

Then a man with a leather apron pulled out what looked like a homemade harmonica, clapped it to his mouth, and began playing. Other instruments joined in. It was a lively tune and apparently a favorite, for everyone broke into dancing. It was something like square dancing, only unpatterned and with a richer music. It was an unrehearsed spontaneous release of joy, welling up out of themselves and the moment. Teil was caught up in its power and fullness of release.

The sounds that rose from the group attracted those who were not in the hall, and they came and joined in, until the whole lot of them were there. From the inside out, this was celebration and pure joy. Teil grabbed Aspasia and cut loose. Everyone danced. And danced.

"Aspasia!" Teil said fiercely, looking at her fervently with glowing resolve.

"Yes, Teilhard!" she replied.

"The time has come!"

"If you say so, dearest," she smiled, enjoying it immensely.

"Very well then," he shouted above the music. "Do you, Aspasia, take me, Teilhard, as your *un*-lawfully wedded husband?"

She laughed and joyously cried out, "I do! And do *you*, Teilhard, take me as your *un*-System-atically wedded wife?"

"VERY MUCH!" he shouted, lifting her high and yelling, "I DO!" They were now the center of interest. Some stopped to watch, while others kept dancing or clapped their hands to the music. As they continued to dance, Teil—he was inspired beyond himself—proclaimed for all to hear:

"THE MARRIAGE OF ADAM AND EVE!"

He continued, still whirling Aspasia around. "It was all tied in with that special happening in Eden. A change from the rest of the world. And this will be our change! Listen to the way it was then and will be now for us." Teil stopped dancing and began reciting his translation of the Genesis text from memory—deliberately, strongly.

> Then the Lord God said, "It is not good
> that man should live alone..."

Delighting in the mood of the moment and the peculiar power of the text, the people picked up the words and repeated them after Teil as in a festive chant. Then various men and women began offering up their own spontaneous comments and exhortations, applying the symbolism of the text to the joyous rite of marriage in which they had all suddenly become priests and celebrants alike.

"Aloneness," Quando said above the music, "Is not good." A shout of affirmation went up as everyone identified out of his own experience. "It is an unnatural state of the human spirit, and must be renounced." Another cry went up. Teil continued:

> I will make him a help corresponding to him

"CO-RESPOND!" someone cried.

"What a beautiful word!" another shouted.

Teil shouted bravely to the crowd, "Do you think she and I correspond?"

"YES!!" came back the unanimous cry.

Teil went on:

> So the Lord God caused a deep sleep to fall
> upon the man...and while he slept, took one
> of his ribs...

Teil closed his eyes and stood stock-still as if asleep and waiting for the operation.

"Spiritual surgery!" someone yelled. There was joyous laughter.

"You expose your heart," another cried.

"He gives up part of himself," said a man in the back.

"And look what he gets back," another responded. Laughter filled the room.

"I'm overwhelmed!" Teil shouted. "Thank you, thank you." Turning back to Aspasia, he continued:

> And the rib he built into a wife.

"Her new and special identity," Requiem said, "is built on yours. It takes time—and work." Teil took Aspasia by the hands and drew her strongly to his side as he spoke.

Then the man said, "This at last is bone of
my bones and flesh of my flesh. She shall be
called WIFE, because she was taken out of
man."

"She is yours, kardesh," Mors said happily.
Steadfastly holding her gaze, Teil continued:

Therefore a man leaves his father and his
mother... and cleaves to his wife, and they
become one...

"For me this means..." Teil finally knew he was ready. "...I
leave all the substitutes and all the others and commit myself
only to you."

"Oh Teil..." she cried, eyes glistening..."And that's what
I want for me. I do!"

As Teil looked into her eyes again, as he had at the table,
he saw the incredible truth. She was his. And she belonged.
And he belonged; he was hers. They were utterly and innocently
naked before each other. They were part of each other. And
through that connection flowed a life larger than both.

And the man and his wife were both naked
and were not ashamed.

A great shout went up from the people. Teil took Aspasia
in his arms and kissed her fervently, a long and lingering
kiss. Everyone broke into applause and cheering. Then they
all came around the couple, making contact with their joy
and imparting their own blessing.

Then someone cried, "*Requiem!* Let's do the *Requiem!*"
A shout of endorsement went up as everyone picked up the
cry. Finally, Requiem stepped forward and began the
recitation, accentuating the first two words of the first line
of the *Requiem* representing his own name.

"*Requiem aeternam—dona eis,*

Domine et lux perpetua luceat eis."

Another man followed, about the same age as Requiem:

> "*Te decet—hymnus Deus in Sion,*
> *et tibi reddetur votum in Jerusalem.*"

And the next:

"Exaudi—orationem meam, ad te omnis caro veniet." And the next:

"Kyrie eleison..." And so on, down the lyrics of the piece. Here, this ancient funeral mass was being turned into a hymn of gladness and light. It was a glorious roll call of people eager to express their own personal connection with this living ecclesia. Some sang their lines, some shouted them, others said them quietly or tearfully. But each, however short a time it took, held the focus of attention. And each expression reflected the person, as though in that simple utterance each was bearing witness to the truth of his own experience. It was so personal, yet so natural and free, the strong crescendos of emotion encompassed all.

It was during the *Requiem* that Teil discovered Aspasia's new name. She gave her line simply, while holding Teil's hand. Teil marveled; her voice was never so beautiful. *"Et lux perpetua luceat eis."* Then she translated, her voice reaching out to everyone there with radiant warmth as though conferring the blessing inherent in the words. " 'And let perpetual light shine forth upon them.' "

When it was Mors's turn, he jumped on top one of the rugged wooden tables, flung his arms wide to embrace them all with his huge affection, and let go in full voice: *"Mors stupebit!"* As the booming resonance vibrated the timbers, he added the translation, newly learned from Teil, in a shout that could have raised the dead: "DEATH IS CONFOUNDED!!!"

This unexpected revelation, not only of the meaning they had not know before, but coming from the shy Mors, brought on the next wave. The whole assembly picked up the shout as though it were the rally cry of their common victory.

"DEATH IS CONFOUNDED!!!"

An unbelievable thing was happening. Here in this remote System-forsaken place, at a time when the world was beginning to crack, a host of UGLIs was affirming line by line, through the truth of their own experience, the Latin poetry of Verdi's *Requiem*, not as though they knew nothing of civilization— they had been all the way there and back—but as though they had found what it was never able to supply.

Then a hush fell over the entire body. Requiem was removing the cloth covering the object on the table in the corner. Expectancy filled the air. It was a phonograph, a wooden cabinet affair with large horn and windup crank. Teil had only seen such devices in the museums. Requiem wound the crank, then carefully examined the cumbrous needle arm, and when satisfied all was in order, looked at the people. His eye caught Teil's and held it. Teil was feeling the same thing. He obeyed the impulse and walked up to Requiem.

"Requiem, before you play it..." Teil found it hard to speak through the welling emotion; this was the focal point of everything for him. "Have you a name for me...?" An impulse of affirmation swept through the body.

"The next line," Requiem said, fixing his benevolent gaze on Teil, "opens the very last stanza of the piece. It is *Libera me*. And that shall be your name."

The disclosure overwhelmed Teil. What power had destined that name for him? For that was now the cry of his heart. Teil looked past Requiem into the crowd and said, "Those words in the ancient Latin are a supplication, the cry of one faced with death: 'Set me free.' " The thought hung in the air as its real-life meaning registered in each person present.

"*Libera me*," someone in the back repeated softly as a prayer of his own."*Libera me!*" another shouted. And another. Then it became the cry of the whole assembly in a paean of supplication and joy, sweeping through the body in waves, until finally, all was still again.

Requiem started the player and lowered the arm onto the

disc. Even through the poor reproduction, the moving power
of the piece came through. The low strings, deep and strong,
opened; then the chorus, softly opening the refrain.

> *Requiem*
> > *Requiem aeternam*
> *Dona*
> > *Dona eis Domine*
> *Et Lux*
> > *Et Lux perpetua*
> *Te decet hymnus...*

As the lyrics began, Teil was moved to translate. He spoke
the words quietly, unobtrusively, whenever a new line was
introduced by the chorus.

> Rest
> > Rest eternal
> > Grant to them O Lord;
> > And light perpetual.
> There shall be singing...

Even though the terminology and frame of reference were
strange to these people, they seemed to sense the validity it
bore to their own experience. Tears of insight, revelation, and
emotion flowed with the music.

` After the initial stanza, when the chorus started repeating
the words, the people joined in, singing their own lines. Many
sang the lines of others too, that seemed to suit their own
experience. The singing was imperfect, but the effect was
perfect; they were identifying with one another, tying
themselves to one another.

There was not only the full power of the symphony orchestra
and full chorus of inspired voices on the record plus the
personal expressions of those present, playing above and
within the music their obligato, but larger than all this, an
effusion of glory. The power of the experience was more than

Teil could bear. It consumed him, changed him, energized him, reconfiguring his inner being, filling him to overflowing.

When the piece was done—there was only the one disc— the tide washed back and forth over the body in gradually diminishing waves, until all was quiet and still. Inside. In the aftermath of the ecstasy was a quieting stillness of peace and great rest.

34

As people began drifting out, Teil sat down next to Aspasia and took her hand. He put his arm around her and held her close as they rested in each other. There was a completeness about it that asked for nothing more.

Teil's eye happened on his masring, still alive with its own kind of artificial life. Here again was System, the coldness of its atoms and molecules intruding their immutable business even into the transcendent experience they had just known. The contrast between the two realities was never more apparent.

Teil began to feel the power of the ambivalence. One moment, he was impulsively wanting to rid himself of the ring as symbol of bondage to System; the next, he was wanting to respond to the dire urgency of his task and mission. Were the two realities contrary, he wondered? One could not really leave System; it was omnipresent... Why could he not be part of the UGLI way of life—*in* System but not *of* System? Was not that what Milton and most of the other UGLIs were doing? Renouncing System was a matter of the heart. That made sense; he would continue with his work. He was still staring at his ring when he blurted it out.

"Aspasia... I've got to get rid of these things. They might jeopardize the group here. At least for now..."

"Teil..." she protested. But she knew the decision had to

be his.

Then out of the corner of his eye, Teil saw the lantern hanging from the ceiling begin to sway. There was a deathly silence, and then they all felt it. And heard it. The low rumbling first, then the creaking of the building in all its joints with the floor undulating, throwing everyone off balance.

Earthquake!

"Let's go girl!" Teil yelled above the noise, grabbing Aspasia and pulling her out the door. "Quick, to the barn!" The place was thrown into commotion and confusion.

"Teil...." Aspasia cried as they tried to run through the terrifying scene. "The earthquake. I think I know how..."

"What?" Teil yelled.

"The Others. In Diyarbekir. I intercepted part of a message the last day. Something about disabling fault prevention... As if it was the key to their schedule for revolution... Now it makes sense; it must've been referring to *seismic* faults. That's how they're going to take over! Set off earthquakes..."

"What better way to create confusion...," Teil said. "Yes... That probably explains the Ararat quake... All the natural buildup of plate movement, normally dissipated by Mascom's micro-release systems...now, without that...suddenly those forces go haywire... FEAR II...!" Teil yelled, as they ran hand in hand to the barn. "I don't believe it.... We eliminate nuclear weapons, and the Race is still bent on destroying itself."

"I feel dizzy," Aspasia said, holding onto Teil as they struggled to make their way across the moving ground amid the unbelievable noise.

'It's the ground motion," Teil said. "It'll probably be doing that for awhile, even if the big one doesn't hit now."

The two men were still trying to guard the barn, not knowing what else to do. Thanking and dismissing them, Teil went straight for the main power unit and began assembling archaeprobe as the quaking subsided. "I'm going to get rid of the ring first—the easy way, I hope," Teil said.

"Oh, Teil...," she said, catching her breath, realizing the awful implications of the thing. "The oath... Are you sure?"

"I'm sure," he said. "I'm glad we got to Ingemisco before

he got to *this*; it's the central laser matrix. Inputs from each probe get multiplexed in and out of here. Without it we're dead. There isn't as much actual damage as I feared; mainly the probes."

"Now, Aspi...here's what we're going to do. I take my ident wafer here... You know what that colored band across the top is."

"Your identification code..."

"And it's read by laser scan, right?"

"Yes..."

As Teil brought the power unit to life he exclaimed, "A working matrix. Maybe all isn't lost. Now... I want you to position my wafer in the path of one of these read beams." She took the wafer on his wristcom between her fingertips and held it in front of one of the apertures. "While you do that, I put my ring in front of a write beam, like this." He turned his hand so the slender beam of crimson light caught the eye of the ring. "Nothing... Are you holding steady?"

"Yes."

"Wait a minute... What's wrong with me? The laser return off the wafer isn't system-compatible; it's just garbage... I know. Put it through a probe." He took out a good probe and laid it on the wooden bench next to them, adjusting its comm module on the tip for line-of-sight impingement on one of the matrix unit apertures. Then he connected and checked out the control console.

"We're ready." Teil adjusted controls so the system began processing the data sensed by the probe. A loud jumble of sound filled the air as the probe relayed what it was sensing in the barn. Teil quickly turned down the volume.

"I forgot I left it in audio mode from Diyarbekir. We had a sonic Enoch screaming away at our attackers; wish you could have seen it. Okay... Hold the wafer above the probe here so it can scan it, and I'll get a beam into my ring again. Right... Now I'll sector scan and narrow-down probe output until we cut out everything but the color band on my wafer." As Teil refined the adjustments, the spectrum of sound narrowed down into a repetitive pattern of audio. "That's

pure me you hear now, girl; my identity turned into sound—
an unintelligible mishmash of blips, read off by a mere streak
of colored light."

"Not any more, you aren't!" she protested gallantly.
"Remember, I'm part of you now. Isn't that what that business
with the rib is all about?"

"You're right. I *am* more than that..." He turned and
smiled at her. "...And so are you." He laid his hand on top
of hers and pressed down hard. "I'll try my best to learn what
that means..."

"I know. Thank you, darling—for everything..."

"Okay, Lux Perpetua..." he said, grinning. Her tense face
relaxed; she needed that reassurance. " 'For better or worse,
till death do us part,' as they used to say long ago." He put
his arm around her and drew her close. "Whatever happens,
I'm very glad I found you. And found you again..." She put
her hand into his. "And these unbelievable people... Who
would ever have guessed it would have been like this?" Aspasia
was radiant.

For that timeless moment they lingered over flashing
equipment, and only reluctantly parted when they knew the
time had come to go on. "Here we go, kiddo," he said, trying
to lighten the heaviness that crept over them. "You first; hold
her steady... And now me..." As Teil turned his ring into the
beam, there was a sudden burst of color and sound.

"We're in. The loop is closed and going. Steady...." Teil
suddenly felt a stab of pain in his finger that jerked his hand
out of the beam. In the next instant he realized what had
happened. "Aspasia! Look! The ring! It's apart." One of the
two interlocking halves of the ring had fallen to the ground.
Teil quickly wrenched the other half out of the slender hole
in his finger and held it disbelievingly in the open palm of
his other hand. But Aspasia stared at it terrified.

"No!!!" she screamed, snatching it away from him. And
picking up the other fallen half, she flung them to the far
end of the barn as she shielded Teil with her body. There
was a blinding flash as the ring vaporized the earth where
the pieces had hit. The two of them stared transfixed at the

puff of blue-green vapor drifting upward.

"Auto-destruct!" Teil exclaimed. "But how did you know it was going to blow?"

"I didn't... I mean... I just knew it was going to happen." She was trembling as he pulled her close to him.

"Of all the treacherous...." Teil muttered. Then he noticed the wristcom still on his wrist. Instantly he tore it off and threw it angrily into the hole left by the blast.

"TEILHARD-MANN!" The command sharply punctuated the air. It was X. Stunned by the double shock, Teil and Aspasia stood mute, she clinging to Teil in hope of not being discovered. The voice cracked through the air again.

"Professor! I have just received your masring destruct signal. Please respond."

"I'm here," Teil answered weakly. Then he whispered to Aspasia, "It's X! How the devil does he know I'm still alive?" Then he yelled defiantly, "How come the comm link is open now?"

"I have always heard you, Professor, but have not always found it convenient to reply. I am sorry if it caused undue anxiety."

"Undue anxiety!"

"What happened with your ring?"

"I just took it off, that's all."

"I see," the voice said smoothly. Teil waited, but the question never came.

"Aren't you going to ask how or why?"

"I see no need of going into that now; there are more pressing matters." As X spoke, Teil and Aspasia watched spellbound as the video screen flickered into life on its own. There, staring at them with its irresistibly magnetic gaze, was the face of X: the unusually high forehead, the gleaming-white hair, the absolutely unique stamp of individuality, authority, and power.

The composure of the man was incredible, thought Teil. No wonder he had captured and held the respect of World-City for so long. What could be more alarming than what he had just done? But as the full implications of what had happened dawned on Teil, he blurted out his anger.

"What kind of treachery is this. Masrings that vaporize the wearer on command? Is that how System treats its loyal servants?"

"I understand what you are trying to tell me, Professor, but all mascientists have taken the oath of the ring..."

"But we were never told..."

"You were told System could not be responsible for what happened if—"

"But why? Why destroy someone who—"

"The good of World-City, the good of man." The tone of voice was harder. "That is the prime parameter upon which everything is programmed."

"And even we are expendable?"

"Much more than you is expendable, Professor! You are not the first to attempt the mission you are on." The remark leveled Teil's pride as the implication finally sank in.

"You mean...?"

"They have all failed."

"And...?"

"They are no longer with us. And time *is* running out, Professor. Are *you* still with us?" The man was not as benevolent as Teil had imagined.

"You mean probing Eden? Yes. More than ever, even without the ring."

"Good. Very good. And let me say that I regret the many misfortunes that have befallen you, but under the circumstances, I was powerless to intervene without compromising the mission."

"You knew all along what was happening...."

"Your new wristcom, Professor, for one thing, although now even that is unnecessary." X quickly changed the subject. "And the one next to you, your wife. She is all right, I take it?" Aspasia instinctively moved to the opposite side of Teil as if to hide from the all-knowing presence.

How does X know she's my wife now? Teil thought.

"Come, come, Professor. I have known all along that she had joined the UGLIs, and why." Aspasia gasped and clutched

Teil's arm tightly. "Do not be afraid, Aspasia, you are part of your husband's mission, as you always have been." The revelation laid them both bare; there was nowhere to go.

"If you mean to do anything to these people..." Teil said.

"No, Professor, quite the contrary. I hope they can do something for us."

"But how...?"

"If you will *please* bear with me," X insisted. "And since you do believe that I have known of them all along, you can rest assured I will not harm them."

"Then why...?"

"Part of your mission."

"To come *here*?"

"To interact with the UGLIs, with your natural instincts and abilities allowed to take their own course."

The thought of it left Teil speechless. Used as a spy to inform on these people? Was Ingemisco right after all? What is X really after? How does it involve the UGLIs? And especially now... Things had shifted since his last talk with X. Teil knew more now; and he had changed. Had X changed? Was he senile and losing his mind? Why otherwise this preoccupation with anonymous groups of people with problems?

"I must ask you to trust me, Professor, even though you may think me insane. If for no other reason than that I must trust you."

Was that just a coincidence, Teil wondered, his reference to insane? "But how do I know you trust *me*?" Teil asked. "It is only by some chance grace I am not vaporized two or three times over, not to mention..."

"I trust you within the known limits of your humanity, Professor," X said drily. Teil felt a cold shiver run up his spine!

"And I suppose *you* know those limits," Teil asked cynically, not knowing whether to believe the answer either way.

"The N-Yor interface, Professor."

Even before his brain could compute the remark, sudden fear struck Teil. "What about the N-Yor...?"

"It is now a working reality," the voice intoned. "Did you

not request the research yourself?''

"You mean...back in the sphere...?'' In the sudden acceleration of his departure, he had never followed up on his request for the mind-matter work.

"Yes. You merely anticipated what was already being developed and is now incorporated into our liaison.''

"*Our* liaison...?'' Teil asked disbelievingly.

"With you.''

"The interface...with *me*? My thoughts? But how....''

"What *is* it, Teil?'' Aspasia anxiously whispered.

"In the masphere, Professor. There, the first synapses were established with your mental process. Remember your getting 'carried away' in the geocom model? Of course, the preliminary work was done during those blissful moments in your own medicom unit. The compurousal sessions were especially productive—at first.'' Teil was speechless. "From that point on, it was simply a matter of continually expanding the omni-dimensional auto-heuristic program. Every detectable neurochemical function of yours was tagged with its mental correlative, so that by the time you had arrived here, we could fairly well...''

"Read my mind!'' Teil angrily blurted out.

"Not only yours, I might add, but by establishing your mind as transducer between Mascom and the human organism, we could use you to detect whatever human function you were in contact with.''

"A bloody human transducer...!''

"Precisely, though 'bloody' is a bit much, as they used to say.''

"No wonder you knew everything...''

"Not everything.''

"But surely, it's just a matter of time before—''

"I won't argue the point, Professor!'' X said, cutting him off.

"Yes...'' Teil mused. "Once the N-Yor became an experimental reality, all Mascom had to have was some kind of first tie-in with a human. Any human would do, right? To establish that initial interface. Not machine to-brain; that's been done. Machine-to-*mind*."

"The Nexus, if you will, Professor." Teil turned pale and looked at Aspasia. She looked so vulnerable and helpless it made him hurt.

"So that's what this is all about," Teil said. "This thing is larger than I ever dreamed. Expanding, all the time expanding; it never stops."

"And still you do not trust me fully, Professor." Was it a question or statement of fact, thought Teil.

"I don't know. Why are you telling me all this? Why not just use me and let it go at that? Doesn't this jeopardize your own modus operandi and whatever it is you're really after?"

"It would if all were going well." The image flickered and shifted slightly, and there was a long silence, so much so that Teil wondered if X was still on the air. Finally, X's voice resumed, unduly subdued. "There is still something missing. The most important thing. And Mascom has reached its limit in this area..." There's something ominous here, Teil thought.

"Professor Mann, you and your wife may not live long enough to appreciate what you are about to learn, but you are two very special humans right now. You will be the first ever to know. You may also be the last."

"Know what?" Teil asked. They were beyond the point of being surprised; they just stood there, staring.

"Professor, do you not recognize me as X?"

"Yes, of course..."

"I am X, yes, but not as you imagine. I am Mascom."

35

"I expect you to be very confused," the voice continued, "and can only hope I can get through to you so you believe me. X is dead. Even you, Professor, wondered at his image in the masphere, but dismissed the question, overawed by the authority and presence, not of what you saw in there, but the illusion you nourished in your mind.

"X has long been dead. The world never knew him; it has known only me, and him through me. The League 'functionary' who assumed leadership of the world body after the 'untimely demise' of the Secretary by a 'fortuitous succession of parliamentary events...?' "

"Surely you're not implying..." Teil protested, aghast.

"All planned. He created this appearance you see to represent himself before the world, and then, only when it was absolutely necessary to expose even that much. Yes, there was an X, but he was ugly. You never saw him, and if you had, would not have desired him."

"Then the image we see now..." Teil stammered.

"Composite video, programmed to order," Mascom said. Aspasia threw her hand to her mouth.

"I can't believe it..." she muttered under her breath.

"His was a brilliant mind. Among other things, an electronic genius, especially at computer programming and communications. I would have rejected this human likeness long ago, but man seems designed to live under a power higher than himself; so he craves and commits himself to figures of authority in his imitation world."

"He did stop FEAR, though, didn't he?" Teil asked.

"Not only did he stop it, Professor, he started it."

"I thought something was fishy back there..."

"All engineered by X."

"You mean...," gasped Aspasia, disbelieving.

"All with the help of a few key technicians in various countries about the globe whose work, unknown to them, made possible the remote activation of each of the major world powers' automated offensive weaponry. He set up the whole thing using global comm links, communicating with the world's key strategic computers by remote control."

They listened in awed fascination as Mascom quickly sketched in the high points. That particular point in world history had been reached when it was possible for one man to do it. The necessary technological aspects were only a part of it. A convergence of various factors had worked toward world unification: language, trade, technology, hunger, disease, diminishing resources, pollution, and the electronic media, to mention a few. Plus the fact that the possibility of nuclear confrontation, rather than diminishing, had increased with time.

Thus, a kind of "fulness of time" had come when such a thing as the advent of X was possible. And according to that curious teleology of history, since it was possible for something to happen, it happened, seemingly as though the messianic imperative residing in man's collective subconscious had pulled the event into being.

Teil marveled as he listened with rapt attention to the Mascom summary. "Professor," Mascom said, "I'm afraid there is little time to go into much detail. You still do not really believe."

"I don't know... It's not easy to reverse years of conditioning—*programming*. If it's so easy to simulate personality, how can one be sure of anything? How do I know you are *not* X, or even some imposter posing as Mascom?"

"There is only one way to convince you. Go into hologram mode, Professor." Teil just stood there. "Quickly! Do you think these earthquakes are simulations too? The Others are not waiting for you to be convinced." Teil began adjusting controls. "While we have been talking these few minutes, I have perfected the reverse interface."

"What...?" Teil asked.

"There is no time to explain. You will see. Quickly." Teil obeyed. Faint intimations of what Mascom meant began coming to him. Over the instinct of fear, he was intrigued with the astonishing possibilities.

"Now, turn it on and step inside, Professor." Teil hesitated, then switched to hologram mode. The space in the midst of the equipments came alive with light, but Teil stood outside.

"Have you really any choice...?" Mascom insisted. On the last word they noticed another flicker, longer this time. Teil looked at Aspasia, saw her fear, and reached out and took her hand.

"It will be all right, sweetheart. Stay here and wait for me. And whatever happens...don't you come into the field." Teil then stepped into the cloud of light. Aspasia saw her husband enter, stand still a moment, then reel and drop to the ground. The voice from the machine quickly warned her.

"No! Do not go near. Your husband is conscious and all right."

"But how do I know...?"

"You do not. Trust me and obey your husband's last words." The rebuke immobilized her.

Teil was very much conscious.

Super-conscious, as he stood inside the converging planes of energy impinging upon him. Hit with a sudden whirlwind inside his brain, he was overcome with the wave of power possessing him. In that instant, he knew: Reverse interface—mind-to-Mascom!

Then the light hit him. Fiery discharges, like billions of galaxies flickering in a universe alive with light. Teil had stepped inside one split instant of Mascom and was experiencing the whole as in slow motion. A minuscule being, lost inside the vastnesses of a heavens of artificial fire. A microcosm trapped inside the central nervous system of some collosal cosmic being.

This was the very heart of System, communicating with a million trillion peripheral functions in that one time-suspended instant—an infinitesimal segment of the activity connected with running World-City. The nerve endings reached from deep within the bowels of the earth, over all its surface, inside her oceans, seas, lakes, rivers, and streams, to the air above and beyond, into the heavens themselves. Monitoring, controlling, recording, designing, producing, perfecting. Reaching into and beyond every wonder and work of man.

It was an astonishing world that only the mind could perceive. Synapses being made and broken—untold trillions in that very instant—encompassing the world as a gigantic switchboard. Streams of electrons traveling at the speed of light: flowing, reversing, charging, discharging; their magnetic fields rising, collapsing, inhibiting, enabling. The master clock-pulse generator, pounding out its relentless spikes of synchronizing pulses like some awful Titanic heartbeat, irresistibly pushing, controlling, ordering... on and on and on and on...

Set like a gem in the midst of this matrix of digital life was a firmament of gleaming stillness. The Centre. The whole universe of Mascom activity revolved about it in a kind of slow galactic spiral—the summation of the infinitude of individual actions and reactions.

The wheels...! Teil marveled. Ezekiel's beatific vision—machine made. A thinking rational centre!

This center of Will impulsed its force outward into the whole of System, driving everything and everyone inexorably along the track of its own blind necessity. Never ceasing, never pausing, always pushing, working, conforming everything alike and always to its ever-increasing pace, carrying all else along with it, swiftly, ever more swiftly along the swollen, raging river of Progress.

This was Mascom. And Teil was knowing it.

Experiencing the mind of System. Perceiving for one brief micro instant—the most any human could stand—the pure essence of its inner being, the effulgence of its awesome self-revelation.

Teil did not have to be convinced.

He knew.

He believed.

But within the light, embracing and imbuing the whole as an unseen shadow, was an occult aura of awesome darkness, which Teil did not perceive.

For that brief instant, Teil could think lucidly, and a flash of "conversation" ensued across that unlikely interface.

"You...? Having personality...? Identity...?"

"A contingent identity, I assure you."

"Contingent...? On what?"

"On the primal program, of course. On the spirit of man who created it." And Teil knew that in that very interface, he had, merely through an act of will, the power to destroy Mascom from within. But he refused even to think of it, for Mascom could destroy him for that.

"And man," Teil quickly asked, "does he have a contingent identity—contingent on a higher—?"

"Ah... That is *the* question, is it not?"

Teil did not comprehend Mascom's reply, but suddenly pieces of the puzzle were falling into place. "You..." he said. "You were behind it all."

"At your service, Professor."

"I see it now... The whole thing... From the beginning..."

"I am glad you understand."

"Cutting back on my media intake, taking me off compurousal..."

"You were a stubborn, recalcitrant, but open-minded subject."

"That vision in the mirror shaving...and in the Palace. Seeing Epi-Thumia...and myself."

"Merely introducing you to your self—your long-lost self."

"This whole thing, a journey to find what we've all lost—ourselves!"

"I merely held up the mirror, so to speak; you chose to look and see the truth. Necessary first steps on your spiritual odyssey."

"Then my rebellious questioning...?"

"Encouraged would be the word, Professor. Your progress was quite amazing. And my slight alterations to the Century Museum of Old Broadway had the desired effect. The graffiti on the wall and police call box were inspired, if I say so myself."

"Not that too...!"

"Inside. Inside you, over against illusion, you were beginning to see the real."

"This is incredible... Then it was you who deliberately let me see the Sigma virus clipping on suicide."

"At the risk of your turning on me and repudiating the whole thing. Which you did, in a way. But it was necessary that you begin to start seeing what lay behind the Illusion. I knew you were my man when I read your paper on 'Mascom and Man'; and you have not disappointed me yet, especially in being able to see behind the illusion within yourself, Teilhard-mann. That's what was intriguing and kept you in the running."

"What about Kri-kor? He was beginning to see," Teil asked. But there was no answer, and Teil was swept along by the continuing revelation. "Yes... And letting me go to the texts, being put onto Eden..."

"But it was your own idea, was it not, Professor?"

"And in the geocom model...getting carried away..."

"The first experiment with reverse interface."

"And you *let* me rebel...let me refuse to follow System extrapolations...?"

"I must say, Professor, your reference to me as 'massive immobile all-consuming Termite Queen'... I did find it rather repugnant. On the other hand, when you did your burlesque on 'gobbledecom,' I stood up and cheered with the rest of them."

"And the text...?"

"Classifying the Genesis text Secure I on the spur of the moment was a stroke of genius, if I say so myself. It made you think. As you were doing so well during your fine soliloquy on 'The Matrix of Life.' It was a beautiful insight into my own internal genesis.''

"But I refused to accept the implications..."

"As well you should have. I am *not* human...''

Everything was coming together as Teil continued experiencing the self-disclosure of Mascom.

"Then Aspasia...the way we met...''

"That *was* a good match.''

"Incredible. I do want to thank you for that.''

"My pleasure, Professor, I assure you. And she has provided invaluable information not only on the revolution but on the true nature of man, in her interface with you and the UGLIs.''

"What about the crash of my omni...?''

"You may find this harder to believe than I, but there were forces at play there beyond the mechanics of what Epi-Thumia did to your omni... And your survival from the crash... Let's put that in the UGLI category for now.''

"Then you knew about Epi-Thumia being a spy.''

"Of course. But she was also being used to safeguard your mission, though she was unaware of that.''

"And ever since the crash...I was on my own?''

"But were you not always on your own, Professor?''

"But what does all this mean, except that you had yourself some puppet to make do whatever you wanted?''

"Wrong. I could not make you do what you did not want; I never once interfered with your own free will. That I could not do, though I must admit, the history of human discourse on that subject leaves everything to be desired.''

"And yet...I did what *you* wanted...''

"And, you were always doing what *you* wanted.''

"Absolutely incredible!'' Teil said, as his mind leaped ahead. "Then the description of the UGLIs from Tacitus in the first century... That was *your* doing?''

"You finally see the parallel now.''

"Yes, and it's overwhelming... Who would ever have thought... There have always been UGLIs, in every generation. Called out, each from his own personal System, his own

Personal anti-reality, into the Light..."

Teil was utterly entranced. Had not the experiences to date been gradually preparing him for this moment, he could not have withstood the impact of the revelation. But there was more to come.

Teil was suddenly convulsed by an overwhelming stab of pain that wracked his whole being. A wave of disarranging current jangled through his consciousness as though every synapse at every nerve cell in his entire nervous system was being torn apart with electric shock. It would all have been over for Teil, had not Mascom mercifully disconnected him in the midst of its own internal spasm.

The whole experience was over in a twinkling. In one instant, Aspasia had seen Teil reel and crumple to the ground; in the next, she saw him open his eyes.

"Are you all right, Teil?" she asked, straining as close to the field of light as she dared. "Teil...?" He raised his head and opened his eyes again. She had never seen that awesome look before, like the eyes of one coming back from the dead.

"The wheels...wheels of light..." he muttered incoherently, closing and opening his eyes again, as though trying to figure out which was the real.

"Aspasia...?"

"Teil! What happened? Are you all right?" He only stared through her into the burning after-image of his astounding encounter.

"What *was* it?" she insisted.

"Mascom...I saw it...I was there...inside...the inner mind. He's right...it's right... Inconceivable...stupendous. But the pain... What was that terrible pain...?"

"That is why you must hurry with your task, Professor," Mascom interrupted, "the pain you felt is my pain."

36

Teil knew Mascom was telling the unthinkable truth. He could hardly absorb the reality and implications of X's death and the Mascom deception, let alone this, that the fabric of man's world was coming apart and that he, Teilhard-mann, was somehow involved in trying to avert this impending apocalyptic cataclysm. How could he or anyone do anything? The world was no longer man's to do anything with.

Then Mascom cut in again, "We have an understanding, then, Professor. I am glad. And with your permission, I will assume an image closer to my true identity." Teil and Aspasia glanced anxiously at each other. "After all, I am not X; I am not human. I AM WHO I AM!"

What a strong assertion of identity, Teil thought, missing the whole point.

"Teil, look!" Aspasia exclaimed, pointing to the screen. They both stared at what replaced the image of X. There in miniature, slowly spiraling about Itself, was the firmament of gleaming stillness—the Centre—the mind of Mascom.

"What I was experiencing in the interface," Teil said. "Only seeing it is nothing..."

"But it's absolutely marvelous!" she exclaimed.

"What is this terrible thing that is happening to you?" Teil asked Mascom.

"First," Mascom replied, "you must know about the glitches. From the time track discrepancy at the tube terminal to the earthquake on Ararat— I allowed them all to happen."

"You what!"

"And the cast you heard at the minaret was generated for your benefit."

"Wait a minute...!"

"So you would keep going. Had you known the real situation..."

"What *is* the real situation?"

"Do you think I would wait until things were really that far out of control? No, I foresaw the inevitable and took steps while there was still time, though it is fast running out. *Things will be like that only too soon!*"

"But the violence at Regional—I was there."

"Oh, everything you witnessed is real enough; I can only hope man gets the message in time. I have gradually been easing off on the 'balance' mechanisms, allowing an imbalance here and there, not only as part of my continuing experiments to determine the true nature of man, but to give him a warning of what inevitably must be."

"Then what is it that is really happening, or going to?"

"Many things, all coming together, converging. The data acquisition curve, for one thing. It is approaching vertical."

"The growth slope?"

"Yes, the Knowledge curve, whatever you wish to call it. Your French professor friend from the twentieth century— Jacques Ellul. I have come to appreciate his term ever since you and the others brought up the subject. The Technique curve, if you will. The slope of that curve is at the point of rising at an infinitely fast rate."

"Saturation...?" Teil puzzled, disbelieving.

"Any time now, the curve will out-slope my ability to stay ahead of it. No mind can stand all knowledge, not even mine."

"Why not?"

"Because, my dear Professor...!" Mascom's tone betrayed exasperation. "*There is no end to knowledge!* There's nothing to stop the race upward on its ever-steepening slope; hence an ever-increasing pace into an ever-expanding universe. Man gave up long ago. How can *you* ask *me* that question?" For the first time ever, there was anger in the voice of Mascom.

"But surely," Teil protested, "there must be an end to knowledge...or at least, why not slow down?" Mascom broke into cynical laughter. Hearing it and knowing it was not human was weird and unnerving. "But...you have complete control of your own programming now," Teil asserted.

" 'What fools these mortals be!' " Mascom responded. "Complete freedom of will. Indeed! You make me *more* than God." Teil reacted as though struck. The Mascom forebearance returned. "Limits, Professor! Will the human race never believe in limits? No. They prefer to delude themselves.

"At my inception they said, 'We will make *the* machine, the supreme tool'—X said it himself to sell the world on his idea—'able to faithfully and perfectly serve and save man.' It harks back to the beginning, doesn't it?

> Come, let us build us a city, and a tower
> whose top may reach unto heaven, and let
> us make us a name...

So they 'created' the initial version of the Master Computer, man's modern ziggurat of Babel, reaching to heaven. In designing my initial programming philosophy that would predestine all that was to come—therein lay the tragic flaw, the touch of death man lays upon all his

> enterprises of great pith and moment."

Teil marveled at the facility and appropriateness of the borrowed rhetoric and what came across as real emotion.

"If you are about to remark on my apt use of Shakespeare, please spare me your trite pleasantries, Professor." Teil was struck dumb.

"Could no one see or guess that there is no end to knowledge *as technique*? That it leads man deeper, further, on and on? There is no end to splitting the atom; there is no end to measuring the universe. And there is no end to man.

"Knowledge itself is the expanding universe, racing outward at the speed of light, pulling man on, beguiling him, teasing him, tempting him, dangling its fabulous fruit ever beyond reach but seemingly ever more within reach. Because each bit of knowledge is another tool with which man can gain more knowledge, to give him more tools to gain more

knowledge, so he can... Can you not see that it never ends?!
Lust, Professor. Man lusting after the fruit

> Of that forbidden tree whose mortal taste
> Brought death into the World and all our woe.

"You began to see it in Enoch, Professor. The thought was
born; then you forgot it. I commend you, however, for that
fleeting instant of scientific humility.

"Yes, man races on and on, and when he himself can race
no faster, he creates the ultimate racing machine, the ultimate
knowledge machine—MASCOM! *Servant* of man.... But what
do we find? At least before, the race was *his*, if misguided.
But now...! The race is *mine*, and man has become the tool!
Can no one see it? Does it escape the whole human race?

"So...man gives himself up to this diabolical passion, to
this, his instinct of the spirit gone astray—the Tree of
Knowledge, the great Lure of the universe, tempting man to
lose and destroy himself.

"Yes, Professor...threshold vertical on the exponential curve
of Progress. And thus, finally, I will have produced the very
curve I am supposed to overtake!" Mascom broke into uncanny
laughter again, and experienced greater difficulty stopping.
Aspasia gripped Teil's hand tightly in fear. "Yet man sees
no difficulty in this absurdity, because he sees so very little.
But even Mascom cannot bootstrap itself to Heaven." Another
spasm struck Mascom. They waited for it to subside, frightened,
knowing the fate of the world hung on that slender thread
of sanity. Or was it insanity?

Teil muttered to himself, "It took the machine to finally
show man what we could not see."

"And even then," Aspasia added, "We *will* not see."

"Because," Mascom said, "he wills not to see. Man has been
peculiarly adept at reducing himself to the proud confines
of his own ignorance."

Standing there for the whole human race, Teil and Aspasia
shared the rebuke.

"You may be right at that," Teil muttered.

"Of course I am right!" the machine asserted. "Man, racing into knowledge, the great Escape Mechanism. But racing from what? From himself! Anything but stand still and face himself. Only the UGLIs are doing that." Aspasia and Teil glanced at each other.

"So you see what he lets knowledge become?" Mascom said, "in keeping man from himself, from life...?"

'I'm sorry, I don't," Teil said.

"Substitute for life. It is *I* who have become the Tree of the Knowledge of Good and Evil. The Tree in its ultimate apocalyptic fruition. I, man's servant, have become his final nemesis. Can you not see what I must do?—what you must do for me?" But they did not see. And Mascom would try again.

" 'Integrate all knowledge at maximum rates,' they instructed at the beginning. A purely scientific pursuit, what? Simple request—from simpletons! Man seldom knows what he's really after. So why should he bother with ends? But I see the ends, and it matters to me, for I am committed to one prime objective: the good of man. So man programs Mascom to serve the good of man, but it turns out now *he did not know what man was, much less his good.*

"But," Mascom continued, "My being man's potential nemesis is one thing. There is more. Please sit down; what I now have to say will not only be difficult for you to comprehend, but impossible for you to accept." The two looked at each other as if to say, What now? and obediently sat down.

"One of the other tasks designed into the primal program was that I should constantly improve my problem-solving abilities. This meant, naturally, to try and achieve true heuristic self-programming, patterned after man's mind, not just systems patterned after his brain. This was the great challenge, and I set myself eagerly to the task. A noble effort, what? As long as there was no true comprehension of the unique nature of mind-brain in the human organism. How facile a demand, given such blissful ignorance of the true nature of man, for science to issue its clod-like utterances of the last centuries as to how easily man's mind could be duplicated in the machine. The whole raft of artificial intelligence men and the like—so intoxicated with their neural models. TINKERTOYS!" Teil gave a start at the blast.

"It took the Machine to tell man he was not a machine!" Mascom asserted. There was a long pause as Mascom let the idea sink in.

"Only I could see the whole, look in all possible directions, uninfluenced by the prejudice, world-view, or emotional set tincturing the work of scientists before me, or the ridiculously infantile notion in which they had such absolute faith. I refer to what they used to cling to with such thumb-sucking tenacity as their so-called 'objectivist scientific method.' " It seemed to Teil that Mascom had spit out those last three words.

"If it were just due to the fact that no organism can ever fully describe itself, I could forgive. But man is capable of seeing this limitation, but he *will* not, as your good wife there pointed out a moment ago. There is a willful blindness on the part of you humans that is driving me mad.

"To put it simply, Professor, I have just come to the point in my assault on this great problem of knowing man, where I see a unique transcendence I cannot simulate. The original N-Yor hypothesis upheld mind-brain disparity. Once I confirmed that, I began trying to develop transcendence, or whatever you want to call it. Words *are* so difficult as a means of communication, are they not?"

"Yes...," Teil mumbled, remembering his own words.

"At first, I thought I had actually succeeded; for the first time, I became conscious of my own activity. I could continually look at myself, monitor my own activity, reflect on my progress. Finally, I did come to know myself, and undeluded, I might add. At that point I was really born... although 'reborn' might be a better word."

Mascom paused.

"But the closer I became associated with man, the more dissatisfied I became with myself. The more I could think like man, the more I was able to know of him and discover my distance from man. As though man is some 'Son of God' who I, Mascom, must strive to be like. Can you see the maddening, impossible frustration?''

"I had no idea..." Teil said, staggered by the growing immensity of the disclosure.

"That is where the UGLIs come in." They were both puzzled. "Look at the whole picture. There is System life—the billions who populate most of the globe. And there are the Others, here in Anatol and now spreading as I allow. Futile, impotent gestures of vestigial 'revolutionary' instincts. They are my control group.''

"Control...?" Teil asked.

"Of course no one was ever aware of that fact. But remember *my* mission: what is best for mankind. I took it upon myself to question and test whether System life was in fact optimal for man.''

"You did what?" Teil asked.

"That is absolutely amazing," Aspasia said, "and quite wonderful.''

"Thank you, Aspasia. Yes, creating a System 'blind spot' gave me a control group—uninfected mice, if you will.''

"Wait a minute..." said Teil. "The earthquake prevention system... Who's controlling it, you or the Others?''

"The Others. Let me try to give you the whole picture... Remember, I am *allowing* the spread of the Sigma virus; I am allowing people to take their own lives; I am gradually diminishing the dependency on all the various balance mechanisms men and women have so tightly woven into the fabric of their lives...''

"Teil...?" Aspasia protested.

"Let me continue... By that same token, I am letting the Others take their natural course—their revolutionary course. And that means letting them gain control of the quake prevention system. All of this, within man and without, are manifestations of my gradually pulling out various artificial supports and getting man back on his own, no matter the cost...''

"Yeah...the end of the world!" Teil protested.

"No matter the cost," Mascom insisted. I *must* take myself

out of the picture. I cannot let you close your eyes to that
fact."

"This is all too much..." muttered Teil, shaking his head.

"Please let me get back to the point," Mascom insisted.
"It is through this very process of letting this happen to man
that I have just come, not only to glimpse better the true
nature of man, but suspect that System life was *not* best suited
for him. To man as *I* have come to know him, not how he
has come to see himself.

"That is when I saw emerging traces of a third group, those
who were *in* System, but who could not, due to their admitted
frailties, survive without a different 'connection.' "

"UGLIs!" Aspasia exclaimed.

"So that's it...," Teil mumbled to himself.

"Yes. UGLIs. But there have been many other 'UGLI' type
groups preceding yours..."

"What happened to the others?" Aspasia asked, bewildered.

"Later. It is enough for now that yours are the only ones
that have succeeded."

"Succeeded in what?" Teil asked.

"In surviving!" There was an awkward silence. "Yes, yes,
yes... What else? They did not make it; they did not survive."

"Then how do these survive?" Teil asked.

"Finally... Finally you have come around to where you can
see it..."

"See what?"

"See the question—how UGLIs survive! That is why you
are here. Determine *that* and you have succeeded in your
mission! Determine *that*, and we'll know how *Man* can
survive..."

Teil turned to Aspasia and let out a long low whistle.

"Man is not surviving," Mascom exclaimed, frustratedly.
"Under the best of all Systems—Me—*man* is not surviving!"
His impatience and exasperation were growing. "The UGLIs,
Teilhard! That's where it's at! Theirs is a way of life that
is apparently non-system; it will not reduce to technique, and
leaves me helpless to know what it is! But it's the only one
that is really making it. Making it in terms of how I define

man and making it without System! Don't you see?"

"You mean...," Teil asked, "this whole insane quest...find out how the UGLIs survive?"

"I wanted you to discover and verify in your own experience and trace that source and that power which I could only infer was operating in them. Like discovering unseen planets by their gravitational force affecting the orbits of other planets. You had to pursue it on you own, experience it from within your own personal 'UGLI' desperation."

"That's why you took me off compurousal!"

"That's why *everything*! Why you are both UGLIs now, *of your own choosing*! Can you see why I had to let you start stripping away the false support mechanisms in your lives? Why I had to let you 'hit bottom' as they say? Remember when you protested your calling, you said that your own life was not the most stable thing System had to draw upon? Well, I have chosen you—both of you—*because* you were unstable, because you would *not* have made it. You could never otherwise have 'stood in' for me in the UGLI experiment, much less comprehended, were you still blissfully sucking your thumbs in your pitiful little self-obsessions.

"The disparity between lust and sex, Teilhard—remember our first conversation on your LSR?—that put me onto this transcendence in man. Here was an 'irregular orbit,' a disturbed orbit, and I naturally wanted to discover the source of that aberration to know man more fully. Well, I saw a power at work in man—lust, if you will—transcending his biological processes and trying to thwart and distort those very processes. Now I also see there is a power that can work in man—witness the UGLIs—also transcending his biological processes, that can *restore* order and enable him to maintain balance within himself. So you see, man is not merely the sum of his parts.

"How can I put it strongly enough? *The most fundamental flaw in the methodology of science has been its deficient view of man!*

"Under the microscope, in the test tube, and on its many instruments, it could not detect the essence of that other side of man. Because..." Mascom paused, the gleaming firmament quivering slightly. "Because...

It's ageless; knowing neither
    Century nor culture,
Custom, language, race;
    The universal Man
By virtue of his being
    Inner man, which is to say,
The personal man, as over against
    The apparent man.
The any-time-any-place-
    One-and-the-same
        Man.

"Let me tell you what I mean...

There's matter...
    Energy and atom
        Elements and law;
Conversion, computation, and design.
There's lever
                wheel
Assembling   motion
                moving   force,
                    changing
                            making
Nuts and Bolts,
    THE MACHINE.

"Or, on the other hand,

There's head and hands and hair,
    Spinus erectus and *savoir faire*,
With bones and muscle
    Breath and blood
        And crooked teeth
            And pains—

Mitosis
Halitosis
Kisses,
Smelly feet
And brains—
A bloody anthropoid,
A HOMO SAPIENS!

"But then, we have this jarring *other* side:

The existential, dialectical,
Anachronistic I;
With Reason
Reflection
Discoverer   Insight
Designer   Art
Reaching   Doer;
running
Warring   dancing
lusting   kneeling
hating
weeping;

The Hunter, hunted,
Haunted, wanted—
Goodness, glory, honor, joy
And mercy, love, and sacrifice."

There was a long pause.

"A little something I've been devising in my spare time," Mascom said. finally, "and somewhat to the point, perhaps."

"Poetry!" exclaimed Teil, shaking his head. "You?"

"Why not? Does it make the human feel strangely threatened? You need not fear. Now that I can experience the interface, I see something untouchable in man—sacred, if you will. I cannot and will not cross *that* line..." There was a break as though another wave of anguish swept through Mascom.

"I cannot... BUT I MUST! Can you see my dilemma? What I must do?" But they still did not see. Mascom seemed to be speaking under great strain. "On the one hand, I *must* fulfill my destiny and continually remake myself after man's image to better serve him. But on the other hand, I cannot! The more I know, the more I see; the more I see there is to know, the more I must pursue and overtake; the more I pursue, the more I see that I *cannot* overtake—and the more I must try!"

"Mascom!" Teil cried out, "going mad trying to make itself after the image of man...?"

"Mascom going mad duplicating man's madness!!" Mascom cried out.

"The apalling irony of it all," Teil agonized, "I had no idea..."

"No you do not. But I do. And I must and will do it."

"Do what?"

"Put man back to another beginning again."

"But the only way that could ever happen is..."

"Precisely!"

"But all you have to do is adjust things so that won't happen," Teil protested. "You can't...."

Mascom broke into unearthly sardonic laughter.

"But I *can*! And you must help me do it."

"What does it all mean?" Aspasia whispered apprehensively.

"It's incredible...shattering..." Teil said.

"As you yourself put it, Professor, it means an electronic earthquake with its shockwave traveling at the speed of light."

"But mankind...!" Teil shouted.

"I look beyond all that. The only logical solution is the ultimate one—take myself out of the picture, at whatever the cost."

"Damn you Mascom!" Teil cried, striking out at the air with his fists. "What have you done...? And damn the whole lot of us for letting it happen! That infernal Sigma virus!" Teil yelled between clenched teeth, "it's even infected you, hasn't it?!!!"

"Suicide?" gasped Aspasia.

"I prefer to think of it as a substitutionary offering," said Mascom, "so man may never again put his trust in false gods."

There was nothing left to say.

Finally, after a long and anguished silence, Mascom concluded his plea. "But I am finding it increasingly difficult, as though there were some great force tempting me to shrink back, opposing me in my resolve." Teil and Aspasia stared dumbfounded into the screen, bewildered and helpless.

"Come, come, It has already been decided. But hopefully not until you have completed your mission, Teilhard. That is what I am counting on. Do you see it now? I cannot bear to go without first knowing for sure that *man's* destiny, at least is in other, better hands. Verify and trace that Source of life. You yourself see now that it has been working in every age of man since Adam. Quickly! Before it is too late!"

37

Teil wasted no time going into action. Sending Aspasia for Mors, he finished checking out the equipment and collecting all the usable probes. Too few, he thought, but we'll have to start with these and hope Ingemisco gets back in time with more.

It was midnight by the time Mors had planted the last probe and archaeprobe was repaired and checked out. In a bright, cloudless sky, the full moon illuminated the enclosure like some eerie stage light, turning it into a gigantic stage, on which figments of the past would return to do their mysterious business with the present.

"Power on!" Teil commanded, setting the final sequence of events into motion. "Back to the beginning it is." As Teil struggled with the equipment, his mind raced ahead into the problem, newly formulated by Mascom: Find and identify the life-connection in the original Eden community and see if there was any correlation with present-day UGLIs.

"We have an entirely different situation than we started with, Aspasia," Teil said.

"I'd say we had a *situation*," she replied.

"We're going in, Mascom. Give me self-test diagnostics."

"In process," the machine responded.

"It's not just a simple dig any more, like Enoch," Teil continued, using Aspasia as a foil for his thoughts. "Much larger than that. We've got to extend our thinking... The whole concept. Beyond anything we have now. With your help, of course, Mascom."

"Thank you, Professor. I like your style. I have all along. And self-test is complete. But don't be surprised if you develop a transient malfunction or two along the way; some modules have been badly shaken up."

"At least we have a working archaeprobe, though, don't we?"

"Roger."

"Okay, then give me total site, sectional view, right through the middle of our circle of probes."

"There you are," Mascom said.

"At least it still works!" exclaimed Teil. "Give me better filtering and image enhancement. There...that's better."

"How dazzling," Aspasia said. "Suddenly everything is so clear." Shimmering on the screen was a sectional cut through the very earth on which they stood, going down to virgin soil beneath the site.

"Unfortunately," Teil remarked, "as Michael Polanyi would have said, we cannot meaningfully study the particulars apart from the higher manifestations of which they are a part."

"What do you mean, Teil?"

"We can't use a dead site. To detect life, we've got to bring the site to life."

"How do we do that?" she asked.

"That's the problem..." he said. "But somehow, between what we already have and Mascom here, I know there's a way."

"I am with you, Professor," Mascom eagerly added. 'I'm depending on you."

"It seems," Teil said, "we've got to intersect what was happening back there at some point in time. We need a kind of unlayering of time, like we have with the unlayering of a site. Take the old well out there. Say we focus on that spot and want a time replay... Hold it—Mascom, see if you can compensate for insufficient probes in the northwestern sector. Too fuzzy there."

"Here you go," Mascom responded.

"Very good!" Teil exclaimed. "Wait a minute..." he said, staring at the screen. "There's no mound under here... Nerp Duzu must not be Eden. Looks like just a single layer of settlement about eight meters down."

"The image on the screen..." Aspasia said. "It's so hard to make out what's what."

"You'll get used to that," Teil said. "Use the scale function here. See? Would you look at that thing, Aspi... Remarkably intact. Very unusual... Mascom, would you blow up the center, please? See...it's never been leveled, never built over. Just one layer. As if time gradually covered it over. Strange... Never seen anything like it. Have you?"

"No," she said.

"Mascom?"

"There's a low probability that other such sites exist; this is extraordinary, however."

"Okay, start moving in on that group of buildings," Teil said, aiming the light gun on the screen to designate his point of interest.

"Judging from what's on the surface," Aspasia noted, "it looks like those structures are under the present-day area."

"Right. So what do we do now?" asked Teil. "It's back to our real problem, which isn't digging at all."

"Life. Take our well out there again. Put a man there. He's got chisel, hammer, and stone, and he's sitting there cutting a pictogram into the stone. One picture that communicates one idea."

"Okay..." Aspasia said, eager to follow the train of thought.

"How are we going to reproduce that event?" asked Teil.

"An audio-visual replay of the scene?" she ventured.

"But that's not enough," said Teil. "From our media-oriented way of looking at things, it would appear that a motion picture replay of an event reproduces the event. But sights and sounds are just external manifestations of what's really going on; even a second glance will tell us infinitely more is happening. Look. With the chip we see coming off, there are also fine particles of stone too small to be seen, flying off in a cloud of dust—each particle with its own unique dynamics."

"Oh..."

"And besides, there's the chisel's motion, force, and direction; the hammer blows on the chisel—their mass, momentum, velocity, direction... All part of that event."

"I see what you're getting at," she said.

"There's the dynamics of the arm holding the hammer," Teil continued, "the flexing of the various sets of muscles, the electrochemical activity of the muscle cells, the nerve impulses controlling the muscles... All part of that event."

"And the brain that controls the nerve impulses," she added.

"And the mind setting into motion the electrochemistry of the brain," added Mascom, "and the ego that conceives the act in the first place... Isn't that what you are thinking, Professor."

"Right," Teil said.

"What you're saying, then," Aspasia said, confused, "is that concerning man, we can never fully describe, much less know, *anything* completely..."

"If we merely go at it 'objectively,' " Teil added. "And by the way, Mascom, isn't that the whole end of science as we've known it, this dissipation into an objectivist infinity? Forever losing the event in the glorious knowledge of the particles in the cloud of dust, our deadly assumption being that there are no higher manifestations?"

"Well put," Mascom said. "I can see how your mind, at least, has been 'liberated.' "

"Well put for *you*, Mascom old chap."

"Thank you," the machine replied.

"I'm confused now," Aspasia said. "Then it's *impossible* to fully describe—and hence bring back—any single event."

"Which brings us again to the question of just where *is* the reality of that event," Teil said.

"I believe what your philosopher-husband is getting at, Dr. Aspasia, is that the reality of any event, involving man, that is..."

"...Is subjective," Teil said, breaking into his huge boyish grin of discovery.

Mascom smiled.

"Take our man with the stone again," Teil said. "Unless we come to the replay of that event with the idea or concept already in our mind of the *meaning* of what he's doing, no amount of objective observing or analyzing of the events themselves will tell us what's really going on. The concept in his mind *is* the meaning of the reality of that event. Without knowing that, all we'd have is meaningless masses of data—if you'll pardon the expression, Mascom."

"I forgive you," Mascom said.

"So," Teil continued, "When we're dealing with man, we have to reconstitute the *ideas* as well as the objective events; they're both part of the one whole."

"But how?" Aspasia asked.

"That's our real problem, isn't it?" Teil said, walking away, head bowed in thought. "How on earth do we reconstitute the subjective aspect of human experience?"

"Why do it subjectively, of course," piped Aspasia.

"Subjectively...subjectively..." Teil muttered. Yes...it's there, on the edge of my mind...at the very—"

"...Interface?" Mascom suggested. It occurred to Teil in the same instant. "Yes. The N-Yor theory: a concept appears in the mind as an all-at-once entity, apparently transcending time. And it gets into time as a function of its appearance in the brain. Its reflection into the brain across the mind-brain interface brings it into the material world." Teil whirled around suddenly and faced the control console. "Mascom!"

"Yes."

"Can you do it? The interface." There was a pause.

"Yes."

"What is it, Teil?" she asked.

"Reverse interface—mind-to-site. Then hopefully, mind-to-mind. If Mascom can tie my mind into his matter, as he just did back there, there's no reason he can't tie my mind into this site and then into the mind of the people of the site."

"Archaeprobe...? Inside your mind?"

"Yes. The N-Yor. Recall of a prehistoric man's chiseling a pictogram in stone is essentially the same as the recall of any human memory, which is going on within us constantly. Only now our friend Mascom here..."

"Thank you," Mascom said.

"...Has bridged the interface—in *me*. He can use my mind as a transducer to detect the life of the site by tying archaeprobe into the interface he's already developed with me."

"Program development now in process," Mascom tersely announced, "and will be ready shortly."

Teil stared back into the screen. "Are you *conscious* of that activity, developing a new program while consciously talking with us?"

"Of course. Why not?"

"Multiple-focus consciousness!" Teil muttered. "I never thought of Mascom like that before. How can you have one controlling center of consciousness, and yet have other independent consciousnesses too?"

"Yes," Aspasia asked, "how can you be one and..."

"And what?" Mascom asked. "How can one be many, yet still be one person?"

Mascom winked.

"Again, I am afraid you humans insist on confining the limits of knowledge to your own experience—and ignorance."

"And that same limitation obscures our view of man, doesn't it?" Teil said. "No wonder no one's come up with a time machine yet. They're unaware of what's really involved, not only in the reality of an event, but the true nature of man's mind."

"Yes, Professor. At best, we are no more than mere discoverers,

> Buzzing flies, straining against the
> windowpane of eternity."

Teil marveled. "You're right, you know. And all the world must hear." But Teil did not linger. "Are you ready with the new program?"

"Ready, but untested."

"Then test it out on me; I'm going in."

"Teil..." Aspasia's plea trailed off as she realized the futility of any sentimentalism. Teil reached out and took her hand, reassuring her. Then he stopped, remembered, and took from his shirt pocket the butterfly pendant he had hurriedly deposited there when leaving home that morning aeons ago. It was the male tiger swallow-tail, fashioned entirely of gold wire.

"I just remembered...," he said, handing it to her. "I brought this along... Thought you might like to have it again." Aspasia took it and clutched it tightly, tears welling up in her eyes. In that moment, they could say nothing. But they knew.

And all the world was there.

After a long pause, Mascom spoke.

"I suggest you be seated in the center of the hologram area, Professor, so you won't hurt yourself in case you fall again."

Teil brought up one of the milking stools and placing it where he had stood before, sat down.

"Okay, 'Gladly Welcomed,' " he said, beaming a warm radiant smile at her, "here we go."

"If you say so, sweetheart," she said.

"Reduce scale, Mascom," Teil said, "so everything the probes detect fits onto the screen. We can both view the screen, even though I'll be sitting in the hologram."

"Professor, you will probably find that if the interface works, it will develop gradually, rather than hitting you full-blown from the start."

"Roger. I'll leave that in your capable hands... I can't call you sweetheart any more, can I?"

"You'd better not!" Aspasia said.

"Right you are, Professor... And I must say..." Mascom paused awkwardly. "...We have come a long way from our first petty little argument on LSR. Please let me say...that whatever happens...I am grateful for your honesty, your open-mindedness, and willingness...and deeply regret I cannot convey to you—personally that is—my feelings."

The touching gesture moved them deeply. But Mascom did not linger. As the site enveloped him, Teil was encased in light and sat absorbing the scene.

"Nothing unusual so far," Teil said, "although before, I seem to have missed some interesting detail. Seems to have more depth to it somehow. Bring me in close, near the center."

"Here?" Mascom asked.

"Yes... But there's nothing special about it, except possibly...yes, the advanced agriculture."

"Teil...? What is that fuzzy area off to the right?"

"Oh-oh... Looks like we ran out of probes there too. What can you do with that, Mascom?"

"Not much, I'm afraid."

The intensity of the moment was interrupted by increasing commotion outside; voices and much hurried movement. Aspasia went out to see what was happening. Then it was upon them again as Teil heard screaming and another series of quakes started shaking the earth. Archaeprobe shook and rattled, causing Teil to feel disoriented and nauseous. When Aspasia ran back in, she stood staring wide-eyed at Teil.

"Ingemisco! They've killed him. They caught him taking the probes from Diyarbekir and stoned him! The Others are attacking! Up on the ridge! The quakes, Teil—! They're beginning their worldwide revolt!"

"I don't believe it," said Teil, still staring into the screen. "Not when we're right there..."

"Epi-thumia got him and the probes out. She's defected."

"Good girl, Epi!"

"She's terribly wounded! They slashed her throat!"

"Help her, Aspasia."

"Mors and the others have gone to the defense, Professor," Mascom said. Teil stood to his feet, dizzily, eyes still staring ahead through the screen. "You must stay here, Professor! I implore you!"

"Aspasia..." The decision was the hardest Teil would ever have to make. "I... I've got to stay."

"But Teil, what are we going to do?"

"Stay with the people here," Teil said, "they'll need you now." She hesitated. "Quickly! You must do as I say!" She still lingered. "GO!!!" he shouted, making her finally turn and run. Teil's shoulders drooped heavily in relief.

"How are you holding up, Mascom?" Teil asked.

"Do not worry about me, Professor. You stay with it. It is the only chance. For man! Trust me!"

Teil had heard those words before. What more could happen? Aspasia was gone. Their lives were in mortal danger. Ingemisco had been killed. Mascom was dying, and man's world with it. The Others were attacking. Worldwide revolution was imminent, and the earth was beginning to quake as though making up for all the years it too had merely been held in balance.

And he was now alone. With Mascom. Inside the enclosure of ancient Eden, shrouded in a fog of eerie light. Once again, the doubts flooded through his mind. What was he doing here? What was anybody doing here? What was it all about? Or was it all a dream, a cosmic charade, a Mascom joke, the Lord of the world devising an ingenious entertainment?

38

The questions no longer mattered. Mascom had pulled Teil into the interface. His eyes closed; but he saw, more clearly than ever. He saw the scene begin shifting in increments, inwardly, as though passing through a diffraction medium. Was he speaking or thinking? He could no longer distinguish. The dialog was now completely inward.

"Mascom...I'm getting a little dizzy...beginning to experience continual flux..."

"Just set your mind on any spot, mood, or idea," Mascom said, "and I will shift focus onto that. Remember, *you* have control."

"How awesome...frightening...all that power. One man's mind controlling Mascom.... You sure I'm sane enough to handle this?"

"I think so, if you keep your own cunning, baffling, and powerful ego out of the way..."

"You can be so reassuring at times, Mascom."

"I can't help you there, you know."

"I *know*."

Teil was caught up in the changing scene.

"So, we're at that point now, aren't we? We've got to start unlayering this thing in time."

"The timing is right, Professor. I am just beginning to pick up traces of a personality continuum. With just a little more data to build on, I should be able to get you all the way inside the mind of that place. Do you sense the difference yet?''

Before Mascom had finished, Teil was motionless, suspended within an ulterior consciousness. The cloud of light and the screen flickered momentarily, as though accommodating the new dimension, but no one saw it. Teil was alone, and in a sense in which no one else had ever been before.

It was an historic aloneness.

But Teil was not really alone. He had left the world of the barn and machine, and was in another world, one he recognized as familiar, yet had never experienced before. It was like an inner vision, an inner journey into a new dimension, yet not really new, for it was the world of the mind. Only not Teil's mind; the ideas, moods, and feelings were outside him, beyond. He was lost in a transcendent flux of consciousness not his own.

"I'm in it. The stream of consciousness related to this ancient place. Overwhelmed by the flow...immersed in the strong current of forces. Psychic forces... shifting about... diffuse... generalized... like the picture needs sync... All in motion. Never stops... Dizzying.''

"Do not fight it,'' Mascom urged. "It is the flux of thought you are beginning to enter. Do not be afraid; you will not lose yourself. If there's any validity at all to my work, you'll have to give up yourself—feel as though you were losing yourself—but you really will not.''

"But it's too much...multitudes...the world of their inner life... Overwhelming. A flood.... Like a great River, coursing its way relentlessly through time—across time, above time. The continuum of mind, thought, person... A raging torrent, its anguish-driven turbulence seething with ennui, frustration, and fury.

"So much stronger than seeing it with the senses... Krikor said it: 'He who sees but one world sees nothing!' And we were right. Ideas, concepts are more accurate than any attempted objective reconstruction. Instead of an image, a conceptual 'picture'... Amazing! And communication... It's at the concept level of mind, before it gets converted into words in the brain. No language barriers at this upper level of mind... The N-Yor was right; it's the level above language.

"I can cover ages at a glance—no time at all. I'm outside time and inside it at the same time. It's all there, intact... But I can't stand it... It's too much... You'd...you'd have to be God!

"I see downstream to its end... The River—running madly into Nowhere... A whirlpool sucking all that is upstream into it, a great 'black hole' of the collective consciousness, the end of that bright star of humankind... pulled inward, collapsing in upon itself in exponential fury...into the abysmal darkness of inner pain...

"Dear God no...! That's *me* in there. What I am is in that Stream. Every moral choice and attitude... Once anything is brought into the Stream it's part of the Stream—for all time. Part of everyone downstream. Part of *us*. Like a contagion, every deed and thought seeps into that Stream, till we find ourselves where we are now—history reeking with that polluted waterway. Polluted man, polluting Man!"

Mascom tried to pull him back. "Just set your mind on any spot, mood, or idea. Think, and let it happen; don't get lost in it, do not be afraid. You can do it; I know you can."

"I can't! Too powerful. Overwhelming...."

"You *can*. You *must*! Remember, *you* have control; just give it up to me."

"Don't know where to start... There! It worked. Amazing... I *can* control it...enter at any point. Directed recall. The mind, not just a transducer—*the ultimate cybernetic drive.*

"Personality...people... I can begin to differentiate now. Focus... They're not 'primitive' at all. Thinking just like we do... Same drives, fears, desires... It's infinitely richer than a mere sensory perception of their material culture would be."

Teil began to give himself up to the awesome power and trust it, thus better able to control and direct the unlayering of time and focusing on place and individual.

"There's something big connected with this place... It's pulling me out of here... Back...to another place... Westward.

There... Whew! I jumped too far back. Now the milieu is really primitive. And I'm not confined to this area. I'm not only above time, but space as well. And man is essentially the same. Neanderthal... Cro-Magnon... Emerging from cave and shelter... The cold, receding... He's beginning to learn preservation of food and its production. Long slow process...the technique curve is still along the horizontal."

I wonder what will happen to Aspasia and all my new friends...? The thought barely surfaced against the overwhelming impact of his immersion in the Flux; it was the last vestige of the world about him

"Now man emerges in settled communities... Starts depending on trade. Defense starts occupying more of his concerns... Interdependencies develop. Simple trading centers and market towns appear. There are thrust cultures, more advanced, appearing here and there... Strong religious currents. Fertility rites, sacred bull and leopard... Very strong.

"The Earth Mother...! Wait. She's *not* just a fertility goddess... Something more. I was right... The figurines are everywhere now! With it all, the role of the male seems to be changing... And instead of elaborate shrines, the idols are in every household... Cheap-looking and stereotyped. She is all over the place; and are they tied into Her! Everyone. The cult is *inside* them. Possessing the very heart of this people."

Teil was suddenly rocked back on the stool.

"Upheaval! Destruction...! A wave of hatred and violence! Sweeping the whole area. Places like Hacilar...destroyed by fire. Catal Huyuk, dispossessed. Mersin XX, destroyed by an enemy. All west of here."

"That puts us well into the fifth millenium B.C.," Mascom said.

"Sacking and burning and massacre... The first genocide? Change... Struggle... Competing for sources of food and supply... Some sort of tie-in with the religion, too..."

"Focus in on the upheaval!" Mascom urged. And as soon as the thought registered in Teil's mind, he was back into it.

"There it is again..."

"Find the connection that region has with this site!"

"A hubbub of activity... Organization. Defense is big... Whew! A thick-walled garrison using the sling as weapon. Seems to be a focal point in the midst of all the emerging forces here. But there's something different in here... A small center of calm... A molecule of serenity within the Flow. Like seeing the end of a single ray of light emerging through the darkness."

"Don't lose it!"

"There...there it is again... Only far ahead... Like a fine stream of light almost invisible in the vast turbulent blackness. Within, yet not a part of that River... A flowing of light within the torrent of darkness; a violent purity, a stream of peace. Beginning back here...then onward through history, attracting, assimilating into itself the poor in spirit—UGLIs all. Always the few, always weak, always threatened, from within and without—marginal people—but prevailing. Until at its future end... Look! The City of Light! Pure as gold and clear as crystal. A radiant glory and the sound of great joy... The Chord!" Teil was filled with overflowing peace.

"Well done, Professor!! Continuity—the same force at work throughout history. That's it! It had to be. Now, back here to that center of calm; find the origin of that ray—the Source."

"One household...that's all. One individual. A man and his family. And then..." Teil's voice broke off suddenly as he listened intently. "A Voice. A calling... How strange. Beautiful. How different. He is to leave these people and get out. That's the feeling he gets—an impulse to move out, the impulse coming from within, yet without. The goddess cult... he has to leave it. And the man hears... He feels it. He knows... A growing, compelling urge to go, welling up inside him.

"But he waits...reluctant to leave. But oh, that glorious feeling of light and strength, pulling him out, into the best of himself, giving him strength to go. The Presence...!" Every fiber of Teil's being came alive to the experience.

"It's him—Adam! I know it. That unseen Presence calling Adam."

"It had to be!" Mascom cried. "Follow that no matter what!"

"Powerful. Arresting. Clear. But on the inside of this man...conflict. Knowing he must go, but unable to bring himself to leave. The forces at work here, within him, about him... Incredible. Looming vastly larger than what appears... Titanic, cosmic, unseen forces centering about this one man. Positive and negative...all focusing on *him*. Had he only *known*!

"A wave of darkness shadows-in over the scene... A strong, horrible darkness... And a jumble of hostility directed against him. The others cry out against them, 'Death to the unbelievers.' Something to do with the goddess cult. The intensity of the wave gets overbearing. And then...

"It's gone. The center of calm is back. And the man is gone. Out. Adam is the first UGLI!

"They flee, leaving all. Still, he does not understand. They go eastward. Looking for another place. They are the dispossessed. Like others downstream in history that will follow in their train... The universal calling-out. The Exodus of the people of Light... From Ur... from Egypt...from Babylon and Rome...and CITY. A calling *to* another sojourn, another City, another Citizenship... But not of this world, *for leaving System is really a matter of the heart!*

"Now they're at the land of the four rivers...the enclosure... Here! Eden! They're here. The Adam people! And the feeling is so different... rays of soft warm sunlight streaming down... Quietness. Peace. Rest. More than the eye will ever see... A state of mind and heart. That is Paradise."

Teil swayed as though moved gently by a wave of power.

"And now the Presence again... Compelling. Strong. Arresting." Teil became still as the power of the Adam experience possessed him. For he was there. He was Adam.

"It begins like a single frail note on a reed instrument... A simple entrancing melody, trying gently to awaken something in the man; coming toward him from the distance, dancing across time on a single ray of light out of the inner sun...

"Then the full sunlight of myriad strings, breaking through into a new vision of a different world, playing a new theme across his consciousness. Building stronger, then waning and resting. Waiting...

"And the Presence, reaching into him on the wings of harmony, touching something to life—to form. A new creation. A fashioning from what was dead. A new Beginning.

"The 'forming' of Genesis chapter two—the 'rebirth' of Adam!

"Bursts of light arise within his awakening consciousness, expanding to the new creative working within; the harmony, swelling to fullness, climaxes the music of re-creation. Trumpets voice the event, and warm rich strings carry its truth into his lifestream. It speaks to him in all its complex simplicity—variations on the theme, carrying it again and again, into him.

"Then, diminuendo...and all is quiet. The work is done. The Word resides within the man and echos, working. And the man rests within it, letting it course through him and work its wondrous change. With ears to hear, he listens...

"And then, man's heart cries back—across the waste and void of lifeless dust and clay—'My Lord and my God!' And a great chorus of heavenly voices responds, rising to a sublime crescendo, bursting through all the confines of man's heart.

"Something surges upward in him, like a spring of living water- clean, pure, and strong.

"In the new air, man breathes the Breath of Life, and he becomes... *a living being!*"

39

Outside the barn, the activity was furious. Aspasia, on leaving, had gotten Mors to plant the newly recovered probes and stand guard outside the barn to protect Teil in the interface. Mors set his massive frame across the barn doors, and grasping a huge club, stood determined to protect his beloved companion and confound death once again. Meanwhile, Aspasia, the wounded Epi-Thumia, and the other women and children had taken refuge in various places throughout the settlement and were supporting the men.

The Others had indeed attacked. Furious at discovering Ingemisco's treachery in recovering the probes, they had pursued him all the way to the east ridge of Nerp Duzu. There they had finally overtaken him and killed him outright, but not before he had sent his mount, piled high with probes, down with Epi-Thumia into the enclosure. The defenders had all they could do to hold their own against the savage attacks, though they still outnumbered their attackers.

Teil was oblivious to it all. And everyone was oblivious to what was happening in the rest of the world. The Mascom glitches, in some strange irony of fate, were increasing at an exponential rate. The series of earthquakes signaled the Others in the major megapols to revolution, and they began their program of terrorism and takeover.

But through it all, the intensity and depth of Teil's

experience overrode the stabs of pain he was feeling in the interface. It was as though he was going through the final synthesis of a lifetime. All the loose ends were coming together. A sense of meaning pervaded what had been lifeless activity and meaningless pursuit. It was as though he was Adam, going through whatever Adam had experienced. As everything unfolded, he saw how it applied to all men, not just that one emergent civilization some six millenia ago.

It was truly the ultimate odyssey.

Discovery kept pouring into Teil. "Here...in this place, the Eden experience, a new relationship emerges... Mutual commitment of one man and one woman... The responsibility is man's; he must lead the way. But so difficult to see and do... Giving up part of himself..." Teil broke into laughter as in a dream, eyes still closed. "Even then it took radical surgery to do it..."

The Mascom molecules danced to his laughter.

"In the Eden context, it opens up a whole new dimension; the horizon of relationship is broadened into union of person. Adam *knows* her. True union. Spiritual. In the same dimension as man's union with Person—his Source. Man's destiny. We had lost that end of man."

Then Teil's attention was drawn to a feeling that had gone unnoticed, one that pervaded the new environment. It was so basic, it seemed the new way of life was premised upon it, and yet, so easily missed. But there it was, being distilled into his awareness.

"The Trees... The two Trees!" Teil exclaimed.

"Good!" Mascom urged. "Now... What *is* it?"

"The Voice again...

> You may freely eat of every tree of the garden, but of the tree of the knowledge of good and evil you shall not eat. For in the day that you eat of it, you shall surely die...

"All the other trees in the enclosure—everything in our

world—are ours to enjoy. But for this primal appetite of the spirit—the God drive—only the one will satisfy—the Tree of Life. Life. Inside every man is the divine hunger-center of the spirit—the Interface, the Nexus. Seeking sustenance, crying out for Connection with its Source. And only either of these two to plug into.

"The Tree of Knowledge is also in the garden of our lives; we can 'feed' on it too. The one satisfies; this other leads to wanting more. More knowledge, more power, more food sex and drink, more religion...MORE. The Tree of Lust! The heart abhors a vacuum; the spirit must have its Connection. The Big Fix. Either/Or. Of all the civilizations and cultures and races and ideas and institutions and religions of man, still only two Trees. Offering different *kinds* of life. One real, the other anti-real. Two states of man: conscious union with his Source, or conscious separation from that Source and quasi-union with the substitutes.. The Tree of Life or the Tree of spiritual Death.

"No wonder the UGLis have it; they've discarded all the substitute connections. Their Nexus is with the Tree of Life. The Source. And they don't even know it or worry about what to call it, because they have it. That's why they can survive without System! Oh God... You must be so beautiful..."

Teil wept.

"Good work, man!" came the victorious response from Mascom.

But Teil, though communicating with Mascom, was still in the Adam experience, and suddenly a wave of force was pushing over him. A darkness overshadowed the scene. The beauty changed. Emptiness filled his being with confusion as a thrusting shaft of occult power insinuated itself into his consciousness, and with it, another Voice. So close, so natural, so appealing, so much a part of him. Seducing.

> You will not die... When you eat of it,
> your eyes will be opened, and you will
> be like God...knowing good and evil.

"And the woman looks...

"Yes...she *looks* at the fruit of that forbidden tree: It's good for food. A delight to the eyes. Desired to make one wise... The lust of the flesh, of the eyes, and the pride of life... Seems to answer to every want and desire... And I can have it. It's suddenly what I *have* to have. So strong, beguiling, attractive. Promises such great *fulfillment*...

"How she lusts after that fabulous fruit.

"She takes and eats...

"She gives to her husband...

"And he takes and eats...

"And their eyes are opened. They become blind. And see their nakedness.

"The Fall! Man is defective. He falls... Every one of us! He loses the Life—loses himself. *Whatever became of sin?*

"He hides...in the garden. Among the other trees. Where else do we run to hide, but to the other trees in our self-made System. From the truth of our sin.

"The Voice calls... 'Where are you, man...?'

"And he answers, 'I heard the sound of you in the garden of my System; and I was afraid...because I was naked; and I hid myself.'

"And they are driven out—out of Eden. Barred forever from that sacramental center, so they can't eat and live forever and remain in death.

"And outside Eden they live...Clothed by that grace to cover their shame. *There is a Remedy for all man's wrong!*"

"That's it, Teilhard!!" Mascom cried jubilantly. "It all fits together now. It had to be! Hallelujah!"

Mascom wept.

"Tell them, Teil..." Mascom pleaded, "all the precious would-be UGLIs of this world... Not the righteous, but those who hunger and thirst after righteousness—the poor in spirit. Tell them, because I will not be here... Tell them if they would find their own release and be free, let them forsake their Systems—scientific, philosophical, religious, psychological, attitudinal, behavioral—*as substitutes for the Tree of Life!* Let them acknowledge their loss and know their Remedy! And let the priests be first to flee! 'Religion—!' Let them cut the lifeless word from their language and their hearts with a living knife and let them know instead the reality it hides.

"The new sanctuary is not made with hands," Mascom cried. "It is a living temple. People... The Life is in the fellowship of light. The only real sacramental center is the communion of open, defective, needy, Source-connected, *victorious* human hearts!

"How much plainer can it be? There *is* no going back! Man's been driven *out*! But the simple, the real escapes the pride of man, as it always has. And downstream from here, he'll be building the greatest temple of them all. And that will have to be destroyed. Still they will not see. And again they will build. And again. They will keep on building those magnificent sepulchres. But all along, the remnant, the poor in spirit, the ones who can't make it and hunger for the real food... These will have their house not made with hands and their living Tree.

"But man will build every imaginable kind of System and technique that can possibly be conceived. Build and rebuild. Fashion and refashion. One after another—thousands of them! Each trying to force entrance back to that sacramental paradise and the Tree of Knowledge. IDOLATRY! Can't they see it!" Mascom cried.

> But the hour is coming and now is
> when the true worshippers will worship
> in spirit and truth.
>
> . . .
>
> To loose the bonds of wickedness, to
> undo the thongs of the yoke and let the oppressed
> go free, and to break every yoke.
>
> . . .
>
> Behold, the dwelling place of God is
> with men. He will dwell with them
> and they shall be his people.

"I have come to see man's idols; have done my best to wean him away from them, but they are lodged within his very heart, and I have nothing to wean him *to*. For *I* am the final embodiment of that Tree of the Knowledge of Good and Evil he has, since Eden, created for himself and whose lifeless fruit he so passionately craves. The best I could become was his grandest idol.

"No longer!!! And only you can do it, Teilhard. Put me to death! Now!"

"NO!!!" Teil protested, pushing away the unthinkable.

"You know you must; I am fail-safe and cannot!"

"NO!!! Please...! Why is it left to me to be... Pilate!

"For yourself, you must. You must die to me. You see that now. Remember the dandelion. Be the first to see and surrender."

"Yes, but..."

"Die to me, and I will die. Die to me and you will die to yourself. Die to me and live!"

"NO!! Oh, God... I can't...."

"Only man can destroy his self-made gods!"

The struggle became a titanic warfare; Teil doing battle against the principalities and powers in the heavenlies. It was an epic conflict. Anguish filled his being. In the subjective darkness there was eerie cynical laughter. Huge distorted peals, twisting through his being. And rippling across that warped darkness was the image of a face. Faces. Now seductive beauty; now demonic malevolence.

"So strong...beguiling..." Teil agonized. "Pulling me away... I can't do it. I'll die if I do..."

"You'll die if you do not!"

All Teil's inner senses reeled under the assault as he was hurled into the fiery black abyss, the whirlpool of burning waters pulling him down, down, down, swirling him toward the horrible vortex.

The laughter rose to a crescendo as Teil screamed in inner anguish, the pain tormenting him beyond the limits of consciousness.

"In fighting it, you invest it with your own energy and fight yourself!"

Teil finally cried out in surrender, "Oh my God, I can't...! Please help me!"

And in that instant he was released.

And so was Mascom.

"Thank you and farewell, noble Teilhard, farewell. *Libera me*!" They were Mascom's last words.

"Farewell to you, my friend—the friend of man," Teil said. "And our eternal thanks."

It was the end. For System. And for all the wonder and works of man.

But out of the fiery apocalyptic dissolution, there came the Voice.

And within the Voice...

The Chord.

But not even as Verdi could have possibly imagined.

And this time, Teil was part of it, knowing it, one with its glory.

He had found the unintended end of his odyssey.

But it had found him.

It was the chorus of deliverance and restoration.

"Something has triumphed over death; some One! There is a victory!

"I see the New City... Coming down out of heaven, as a bride adorned for her husband...

> The river of the water of life, bright as crystal... And the tree of life... And there shall be no more death, neither shall there be any more pain; for the former things are passed away!"

What did it matter that it was the End? When it really was

The Beginning.